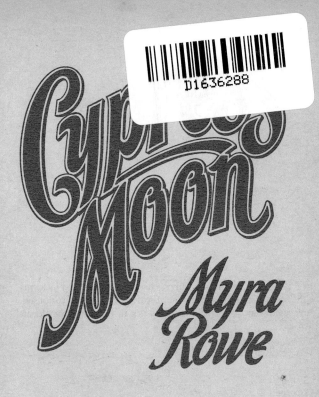

Cypress Moon

Myra Rowe

WARNER BOOKS

A Time Warner Company

In this work of fiction, the names, characters, places, and incidents
either come from the author's imagination or are used fictitiously.
Any resemblance to actual events, locales, or persons is coincidental.

WARNER BOOKS EDITION

Cover illustration by Sharon Spiak

Warner Books, Inc.
666 Fifth Avenue
New York, N.Y. 10103

 A Time Warner Company

Printed in the United States of America

First Printing: November, 1990

10 9 8 7 6 5 4 3 2 1

Fire Meets The Flame . . .

uke's lips blazed a fiery path to her breasts,
a tried protesting again, achingly aware that
dy had no use for her words. "No, Luke,
e. . . ."

Diana dropped her forehead to rest against
his, a feverish torment bedeviling her. Who would
have thought that touching and being touched
could lead to such blissful feelings of giving and
receiving pleasure? If he was not going to help her
end this flame that seemed bent on consuming
them . . . "Oh, Luke—"

With a look into her passion-filled eyes only
inches away from his own, he confided in a voice
husky and unsteady, "We must stop this right
now."

Diana sat up, jolted into reality by his words.
Openly adoring her with his gaze, Luke leaned to
help her fasten her blouse, but she brushed away
his hands.

"Was that my first lesson in kissing?" Diana
asked as he helped her to her feet. That was all it
was, she concluded. Another one of his dratted
lessons. "I assure you that I shan't need a second!"

*   *   *   *

"Myra Rowe has a special flair for writing
breathtaking descriptions and a rare talent for
creating warm, believable characters."
—*Rave Reviews*

ALSO BY MYRA ROWE

•

Cajun Rose
A Splendid Yearning
Treasure's Golden Dream

Published by
WARNER BOOKS

To my readers, especially those
who write to me.

Prologue

Mobile, Alabama, May 15, 1831

"As usual, dear brother, you are wrong," Luke Greenwood stated with authority. A biting edge honed the customary softness of his Southern drawl. "Whether or not a man wills it to happen, the right woman can turn his world upside down."

From his chair, Luke squinted through the haze of his cigar smoke, marking that while impassive expressions claimed the faces of the other two men sitting at the table, a smug look marred the even features of his older brother, Frederick. "Your problem," Luke continued, a note of irony hitching a ride on his bantering tone, "is that you've never fallen in love—likely because you have no heart."

"What is this absurd business about hearts and falling in love?" Frederick Greenwood retorted with a recognizable sneer. "At thirty, I know there's no such thing—outside ridiculous poems and romances written for women and fey men. My theory is that if you can't see it or touch it, whatever you're discussing doesn't exist."

"I hate it when you're so damned wrong and won't admit it," Luke replied, his cleanshaven face flushing and his dark eyes shooting sparks of anger at his only brother. "In this situation your two years' seniority counts for little."

Luke Greenwood leaned back in his chair and glanced at Frederick's and his dinner companions as they sipped brandy. He was uncomfortably aware that the other two men in the private room of the tavern on Mobile Bay had become quiet ever since Frederick had broached the subject of women and become dogmatic.

Perhaps after being absent for three years, Luke mused while drawing on his cigar, he had made a mistake by returning to Mobile even for his sister's wedding on the previous afternoon. Though he had paid little attention to how much Frederick had drunk during the evening, he figured it was his brother's usual portions: too damned much.

Luke flicked an ash from his cigar and reflected that if Frederick dared bring up Sylvia's name, to hell with propriety! Feeding his rising indignation were treasured memories of black hair, pouting lips, and voluptuous curves. Sylvia, his lost love; his only love, the woman who, in the end, had embittered him against all women. Yes, if his brother mentioned her name, he would smash his face and shut him up. With a start, Luke realized that he had been waiting over five years for that very opportunity.

"My two years's seniority must count for something," Frederick remarked after an awkward silence. "Plus, unlike you three, I once had the dubious pleasure of claiming a bride." Searching the polite faces of his companions, Salathiel Morgan and Nathaniel Dace, and not finding compassion, Frederick sipped more brandy. He swung his attention back to his challenger.

As if reassured from the fiery taste of brandy, Frederick licked his thin lips and continued. "I still maintain that a pretty face is nothing more than a covering for an empty head. Filling both hands with hot teats is the only way to become properly acquainted with a woman." He swirled the brandy in his goblet and watched the thick, amber liquid reflect the flames of the candles sitting on the table. "I confess I've sampled the tasty tidbits from the belles here in Mobile.

From the soft mounds of womanhood above the waist, I move down—''

"Damn it, Frederick!" Luke interrupted. "That's enough. You've had too much to drink. We're here to celebrate Salathiel's forty-fifth birthday and bid him good fortune in his future endeavors, not to listen to you brag about your success with countless women."

"Don't pretend you're any better than I am," Frederick shot back. "I've heard about your mistresses."

"I've never claimed to be a saint," Luke responded, irritated further in spite of not wishing to be. Calling up the calm facade that contributed to the notable success of Luke Greenwood, gambler, he picked up the half-empty decanter sitting on the table and splashed brandy into all four goblets. "I propose a toast to Salathiel Morgan, our former tutor and our good friend forever."

Luke's dark eyes warmed with affection as they rested on the dignified older man sitting beside him. Since the last time Luke had been in Mobile, gray had streaked Salathiel's dark hair and mustache, somehow complementing the Englishman's habitual mien of reserve. Luke pushed back his chair and stood, waiting until both Frederick and Nathaniel Dace, friend and neighbor to the Greenwood brothers since childhood, also rose and lifted their goblets.

"Salathiel," Luke said, "may your next position prove as challenging and successful as the one at Southwinds. And may the happiness of each succeeding birthday surpass the one before."

"Thank you, gentlemen," Salathiel Morgan said after the three young men had saluted him and seemed to be waiting for him to make some kind of statement. He harrumphed, surprised that he was deeply touched. Whenever possible, he avoided displays of an emotional nature. "Please be seated again."

Salathiel seemed to search for words among the flames of the candles that had dwindled during the leisurely dinner. "No assignment I can ever take could compare to the one I recently completed—the only one I ever had, to be quite truthful."

A smile softened Salathiel's rather square face as he looked around at his former students. "Now that Maurine is married and Delilah is eighteen, I can indeed look back upon the past twenty-two years as successful." His smile turned into a wry twisting of lips when he went on in his clipped, British accent, one that had resisted successfully the slower, softer speech of the Southerners. "Whether I ever achieved much with their older brothers is another matter."

Masculine laughter, good-natured and full of camaraderie, spilled out into the small back room of the popular tavern beside Mobile Bay. The earlier awkwardness pushed aside, the talk moved, as it had for most of the evening, into spirited reminiscences.

Sons of wealthy cotton planters, the three young men had spent countless hours studying under the Englishman's tutelage in the ballroom-turned-classroom at Southwinds, the plantation home of the Greenwood family near Mobile. When they reached eighteen some ten or more years ago and went away to college, Salathiel had stayed on to continue tutoring their younger sisters.

Nathaniel Dace, who along with his sister, Delilah, had traveled daily over the years from the neighboring plantation to study at Southwinds with the Greenwood brothers and their sister, Maurine, asked, "Where will you go now, Salathiel?"

"I have two interviews set up next week in New Orleans after Luke and I reach his townhouse. I gather there are girls and boys on nearby plantations in need of schooling," Salathiel replied, a serious expression settling on his even features. The passing of the unsettling moments between Luke and Frederick pleased the part of him preferring civility at all costs. One of his most difficult tasks as tutor had been to keep these brothers, who possessed similar looks but opposing temperaments, on good terms.

Frederick Greenwood had displayed a propensity for arrogance and hardheadedness, Salathiel mused, while Lucius, two years younger, had appeared to vacillate between spirited but acceptable behavior and volatility. Ever since their parents had died from grippe three years ago, the brothers had been on their own.

Lucius, or Luke as he now preferred, pursued some elusive, undeclared goal as he gambled in various cities, recently settling in New Orleans. Frederick, while making a home for Maurine until her marriage yesterday, managed the family's cotton plantation. Salathiel did not like discovering that the handsome young men—both were black haired, over six feet tall, and of lean, muscular build—even after being apart for three years, obviously still found it difficult to get along.

"Perhaps you can turn at least one of your new female pupils into the kind of woman that Lucius is certain exists," Frederick said. His indolent gaze raked across the face so much like his own. The differences setting the two faces apart were subtle: the expressions and sets of their brown eyes underneath heavy, dark eyebrows, the shapes of their mouths.

"Come on, Frederick," Nathaniel Dace chided. "Stop trying to rile Lucius. You don't have to believe in love."

"Do you agree with him?" Frederick glared at Nathaniel.

"Let's just say I don't know," Nathaniel temporized as he slid an apologetic look toward their former tutor.

"As the only one here who has ever been married, I speak the truth." Frederick poured himself a measure of brandy, making no offer to replenish the other goblets, then frowned across at Luke. "Even the fair Sylvia was passable only to the eye—and in bed, of course."

"To hell with you, Frederick! Shut up!" Luke leaned across the table threateningly, jamming the fiery end of his cigar into a sand-filled pewter bowl sitting on the table. He had lost his taste for tobacco.

"Don't tell me that after all this time—what is it? Five or six years?—you're still mooning over my dead wife, dear boy," Frederick intoned. Drunken mockery laced his words and hovered around his mouth after all sound faded, except for the persistent sputtering of the candles on the table.

"You are no gentleman to speak of Sylvia in such manner," Luke retorted.

"Who says I care to be a gentleman, if one must pay lip service to empty-headed females when they aren't even around to hear and be seduced?" Frederick fixed Luke with a cold smile.

"Sylvia died trying to give birth to your son five years ago. Have you no respect for her memory?" Luke pushed back his chair with a loud scrape against the board floor and rose, forcing his clenched fists to remain on the top of the table. How he longed to smash them against that arrogant face!

Frederick taunted; "God! You were such a fool over that woman—and after the way she used you to get to me. I've always wondered how you ever left her long enough to return to finish up at Oxford that year."

Luke sucked in a deep breath. For a moment his high cheekbones and generous mouth seemed carved from marble. "From the minute I sailed away, you set out to marry her, didn't you? Until I returned and saw firsthand what was going on, I thought it was because you loved her. Sylvia may have made a fool of me, but not nearly as much as you did. That marriage was nothing but a farce, a way to get at me, was it?"

"She was most willing to go to the highest bidder." When Frederick shrugged then and lifted his goblet to his mouth, Luke shoved his chair back farther and strode around the table. Frederick slammed down his glass and half rose. Before he made it to his feet, Luke's fist smashed against his chin. The sounds of the chair and its occupant crashing to the floor brought an attendant rushing to the curtained doorway.

"Stop it!" Nathaniel ordered, waving away the curious attendant and jumping up to push Luke back. Though predisposed toward settling misunderstandings peaceably, Nathaniel Dace was no coward, and he sent a stormy look at the still-scowling Luke. Frederick, cursing and struggling to get to his feet, slapped away Nathaniel's proffered hand.

Nathaniel righted the upturned chair. "Let the matter drop, you two. Nothing can be served by fighting over something long gone." As if soliciting support, he glanced over his shoulder at Salathiel, who had risen from his chair and was observing the scene with poorly concealed repugnance.

"Nathaniel is right," Salathiel said, his tone revealing his disapproval of unbridled emotion. "This is hardly the way to end the pleasant evening that you three planned in my honor. Please let us forget this happened.''

''No, by God, I won't forget it!'' Frederick muttered as he scrambled to his feet. With trembling hands he straightened his tail coat and skewed cravat. ''I still say that no woman is more than a good time in the bed and that I was a fool to marry.'' While settling back onto his chair, he darted baleful looks at his brother. ''Once was too much.''

''I hope you live to eat those words.'' Luke realized with surprise that since hitting Frederick, he felt better than he had in years. Damn Frederick for having married Sylvia—the only woman he had ever loved, or could ever love, Luke amended—and then resuming his philandering ways during her pregnancy. Frederick deserved more than a sock on the jaw. He could do with a few swift kicks on his behind as well. The last thought cheered Luke and brought a smile to his face. ''I hope some woman brings you to your knees, you conceited ass.''

''That won't happen.'' Frederick lifted his glass of brandy and drained it, then set it down with a loud *clank*! as if in punctuation. ''I'll wager my half of Southwinds against yours that I never meet a woman worth loving or marrying.''

Determined to make no further response, Luke felt his teeth clamp together and a muscle twitch in his cheek.

''Damn it to hell!'' Frederick exclaimed. ''And here I thought you were a gambling man, Lucius—or, Luke, as I hear you're called in the gaming houses around the country.''

''Call me whatever you like.'' Luke shrugged one broad shoulder, watching Frederick with open disdain. ''Father left the plantation to us both. If you want my half, buy me out as I invited you to do when the will was read three years ago.''

Frederick turned to Salathiel. ''Will you get me a piece of paper and a quill?'' At the older man's perplexed expression, Frederick rose sluggishly, stalked to the doorway, then hollered down the hallway for what he wanted.

Silence reigned until the young man serving their table during the evening hurried in with paper, quill, and inkpot.

"I, Layton Frederick Greenwood," Frederick intoned as he scratched each word unsteadily, "state that no woman exists who is both beautiful and intelligent and can cause me to fall in love. If I were to meet such a woman before this year, 1831, ends, I will relinquish all rights to Southwinds unto my brother, Lucius. If no such woman materializes, Lucius gives over to me any and all claims to our inheritance." He laughed into the faces of the three men sitting at the table watching him with varying degrees of disbelief and disapproval. "When you go searching, Lucius, see if you can find a blonde. I like my women fair—though not necessarily chaste."

"This is asinine," Luke announced to no one in particular, jamming his hands into his coat pockets and staring hard at his plainly inebriated brother.

"Asinine is my style." Frederick's thin lips quirked into a mirthless, one-sided smile. With that telling action, the considerable family resemblance between the brothers lessened.

"Here, Salathiel,"—Frederick was holding out the paper he had signed—"get Lucius to sign, and then you keep it until the first of January. Let's plan to accept the standing invitation from our cousins in New Orleans and meet there for the holiday season. I recall how many beauties always showed up at the parties when we used to go over, but especially at the Charity Ball before Christmas. All of you will learn in New Orleans that Lucius is dead wrong about women and this silly thing called love."

"Would you admit it if you were to meet a woman whom you deemed worthy of your love?" Salathiel asked, his wry tone revealing how little faith he had in the word of his former pupil. He did not take the paper.

"He won't have to admit it," Luke drawled. "I believe there's one woman for every man. If Frederick meets the one who can bring him to his knees, it will show."

"What drivel! Me brought to my knees?" Frederick scoffed. "Lucius, since you and Salathiel are the only ones leaving Mobile, I've an idea that should satisfy you about my honesty. Our friend, Nathaniel, was always the peacemaker, so he can keep an eye on me around here—unless he objects."

"I don't object," Nathaniel Dace said. He looked from one Greenwood brother to the other, his softer-featured face a study in consternation. "I think you're acting like a fool, Frederick, but I'll dog your steps."

"Good. Following me around might teach you a few things." Frederick dipped the honed point of the well-used feather into the inkwell and turned to his brother, proffering the quill. "Sign and make it legal. Salathiel and Nathaniel will be our witnesses, and Salathiel can safeguard our agreement. When we meet in New Orleans in December, you be ready to sign over your share of the deed to Southwinds on the first day of January."

Shaking his head with puzzlement and a tad of amusement, Luke rubbed his chin with a thumb and forefinger. "As usual, you won't listen to reason, will you?" Not expecting an answer, and not getting one, he took a full breath and expelled the air slowly. "Since you're tying the wager to the remainder of this year and it's already the middle of May, I can't go along with betting Southwinds."

"Aha! You know you're wrong, don't you?" Frederick replied, a gloating look deep in his eyes. "You're not the gambler I've been led to believe."

After a moment of thought, Luke stated in a resigned tone, "Oh, what the deuce! Make the stake a blooded horse of the winner's choice and I'll sign the damned paper."

Later, after he scrawled "Lucius Ashley Greenwood" on the revised wager and listened to Frederick's drunken laugh of imagined victory, Luke reflected that maybe he, too, had drunk too much. Or had he suffered an attack of the conscience that his mother had always lauded as a quality setting him apart from a host of young men?

Agreeing to the bet was absurd in itself, but reducing the stakes was akin to stupidity. Luke Greenwood knew himself to be a gambling man—an exceedingly successful one—and he intended to win. Somewhere there was a young woman. . . .

One

South Louisiana, June 20, 1831

Diana Hathaway yawned and stretched her slender body languidly, letting herself awaken by inches to the summer dawn. For a hazy moment she was a child again, not a young woman nearly eighteen and alone in the shack squatting on stilts beneath overlapping branches of cypress trees in Alligator Swamp—more commonly called Gator Swamp by the citizens of St. Christopher Parish, Louisiana.

To the young woman, the swamp around her possessed a private ongoing rhythm, one she sensed in the same unconscious way as her own heartbeat. Maybe, Diana mused fancifully, if she allowed herself to drift awhile longer in the nether region between sleeping and waking, she would hear her father building a fire in the ramshackle cookstove in the next room.

A soft bleat drifted from the porch surrounding the small, unpainted house, causing Diana to bury her face in her pillow and sniff at the beloved scent of verbena wafting from the pillowcase she had embroidered only last year. Except for the goat, Minerva, she was on her own. As if in contradiction, a whine of complaint joined the bleats and reached Diana's ears. She lifted her head.

And except for King Arthur, Diana added. Thinking about her huge dog that looked more like a giant wolf than a gentle protector and confidant brought a smile. Increasingly frequent bursts of bird calls from the surrounding swamp and chatters from squirrels in the trees overhead reminded her that even the wild animals served as companions. No, she was not truly alone, would never be as long as she stayed in Gator Swamp, the only place she had ever lived.

Rolling onto her back on her mattress stuffed with bunches of the curly gray moss cascading in thick falls from the trees in the swamp, Diana brushed her tousled hair from her face with both hands. A strand curled around one finger, and she held it up in the pinkish light poking through the fog outside her window. What color was it, really? she wondered, lucid now, but not ready to start the day. Was the color of her hair as rare as her father, Philip Hathaway, had always said?

Diana thought of how she once had read about albinos in one of her father's many books in the living room and learned that some people were born without normal coloring. But she knew from looking in the small mirror in her bedroom that her pale skin had a golden sheen, her eyebrows were a rich, muskrat brown, and the irises of her large, widely spaced eyes mirrored the exact color of the sky on a cloudless day. Only her hair suggested that she was different.

Though her mother had died from a fever nearly eight years ago when Diana had been almost ten, she remembered well that Drusila Hathaway's hair had been the same silvery, almost white shade as her own. *Blonde* seemed not quite the accurate term to describe it, or so Philip Hathaway always claimed. Like her mother, too, Diana chose to let her hair grow as nature intended, without an introduction to scissors. Already it fell below her waist in a curtain of shimmering waves.

Diana could almost hear again the wondering way her father would remark that such beautiful hair as his two girls had could be compared only to summer moonlight. *Blessed moonlight*, Philip would add in his deep voice that had never quite lost its Bostonian accent. How could Diana, even at an early age, not look upon moonlight as special?

Eyeing again the strand of hair around her finger, Diana remembered how once a long time ago Tabitha and Salem from Fairfield Plantation had told her that the color of her hair was the mark of a Silver Hoodoo Woman in their homeland of Jamaica. Her father had gently but firmly scolded the two visiting slaves for upsetting his young daughter, and the subject was dropped. Even so, Diana never had forgotten.

Rising then and stripping off her short nightgown, Diana slipped on a sleeveless, homespun blouse that came down barely far enough to cover her full breasts. As she stepped into the brief skirt of the same neutral-colored fabric and snugged it up over her slim hips, her thoughts ran back to the time when Philip Hathaway had explained to her about hoodoo, or voodoo, being a religion based on magic and practiced chiefly by blacks from Haiti.

Afterward, Diana had dismissed the careless words from Tabitha and Salem as having no justification. Her father's devotion to God was far too strong for her to entertain ideas about other deities. Philip Hathaway's simplistic religious beliefs became her own. Because Philip declared he did not believe in magic, so did Diana. Had she consulted her heart, she might have discovered that a belief in magic nestled there, a bit like a seed waiting for a nourishing drop of rain.

"Thank you, Minerva," Diana told the white goat after she had stripped the short, dark teats with practiced fingers and half filled her small pitcher with thick milk. "You're a good nanny, but you're drying up on me." Before she rose from the low stool, she patted the bulging belly, delighting in the silky texture of the animal's hair. "It won't be long now till you have your new kid, and then I'll have more milk than I can use, even for making cheese." In a worried tone, she added, "Now that Rastus has died, where will we find a daddy for the next one?"

Snatching her mind from serious thoughts, Diana turned toward her other pet. "Why are you prowling around, King?" Usually, the big dun-colored dog lay nearby while she milked the goat, hoping to be rewarded with a stream of warm milk that Diana sometimes directed playfully toward its mouth.

Today King seemed itchy. Was some bitch in heat on one of the sugarcane plantations nearby? "Go take Minerva to graze if you like. I'm staying here to get some cleaning done."

King, his ears alert, fixed his intelligent eyes on the face of his mistress before trotting after the goat. Diana watched her animals until she no longer could see or hear them on the boardwalk, her only link with solid land.

Two rough boards lay side by side atop log braces that Philip had driven in the mud until they rose a few feet above the shallow swamp water. After a few hundred feet of zigging and zagging underneath tree limbs bearded with thick falls of hanging moss, the walkway ended on solid ground not visible from the Hathaway home.

The fact that her home, the walkway, and the ground where it ended lay within the boundaries of the sugar plantation called Fairfield bothered Diana no more than it bothered her dog or her goat. Neither had it bothered her father or his friend, Owen Fairfield—Uncle Owen to Diana.

Before going inside to begin her chores, Diana paused and looked around. Not for the first time, she noticed that the house, built by Philip the year of her birth, had sagged during its eighteen years. She sometimes wondered how he could have been brave enough to come to St. Christopher Parish with his pregnant wife and make a home for his family in such a remote area. The only reason Philip had ever offered his only child was that Drusila and he had found life in New Orleans not to their liking and that since their needs were few, they had found the uncomplicated life in the swamp satisfying. He had insisted on privacy, asking the few that knew about the Hathaways to keep the knowledge secret.

If her home had ever been plumb, Diana reflected with her usual candor, it was no longer. Made of hand-hewn cypress boards, the small house with its banistered, encircling porch seemed a natural part of the swamp. Age had joined with the frequent rainfall and mists, weathering the unpainted boards into a soft gray tinged with brown.

Diana cocked her head and admired the way that rays from the morning sun slanted through the moss-festooned trees, highlighting the green mold edging some of the wide-grained boards. Unknown to her, her swaying, nearly white hair borrowed a golden sheen from the shafts of sunlight as she walked on bare feet across the porch and went inside.

"Miss Diana!" someone called.

Recognizing Tabitha's warm voice, just as the recently returned King did, Diana left her hook in the water and, with a leather thong, secured her fishing pole to the banister. Within a few moments she glimpsed a bright red dress down the shaded walkway. King bounded ahead as she went to meet her friend at the edge of the wide porch. As usual on her frequent visits to the Hathaway home, the plump black woman carried a large, filled basket, one of the many baskets of wide strips of peeled oak that Diana had woven.

Not until after the two women were sitting in the oak-slatted swing and sipping their cups of sassafras tea did the talk move beyond the customary amenities. It occurred to Diana that only recently had she begun to enjoy sitting in the swing again. One morning almost a year ago, she had found her father slumped over in it. Philip Hathaway, who had always appeared healthy and had not yet reached fifty, had apparently died from a seizure, instantly and without sound.

Diana wrenched her thoughts fully to the moment and turned to stare at the black woman who had been relaying current events. "Where did you hear that some gambler won Fairfield from Uncle Owen's nephew? I can't believe that Maynard Oates told such a story on himself, even to his mother."

"This ain't come from his mama at Fernwood. I don't know if the folks over there even know it yet. I don't hardly ever see none of them since Miss Frances done up an' married that sea captain last year. It 'pears to me that Mr. Maynard ain't gonna ever get over that, what with the way he was spendin' everythin' his mama had an' countin' on inheritin' Fernwood an' all. He don't care for nobody but hisself."

Tabitha rolled her eyes and sighed before continuing. "I hear tell his steppapa drawed up the purse strings an' nigh threatened to put Mr. Maynard off the place if'n he don't get hisself off whiskey an' do somethin' 'bout his gamblin' debts.

Mr. Maynard ain't no boy no more. He must be pushin' thirty.''

"You would think Maynard could be satisfied being heir to his uncle's plantation and be happy about his mother marrying after so many years of being a widow, wouldn't you?'' Diana's expression revealed her puzzlement.

Sliding a look toward Diana as if to judge her reaction to all she was hearing, Tabitha said, "It's plain as warts on a frog that you ain't never see'd him. The man gotta mean, hungry look 'bout him. I can't figure out how white folks thinks, but I does believe Mr. Maynard done lost Fairfield in a poker game. My news comes straight from New Orleans.''

"Tabitha, New Orleans is at least fifty miles from here. How you're always hearing news from there puzzles me, especially now that no whites have lived at Fairfield full time since Uncle Owen's death last year. I reckon Maynard's stopping by every once in a while to pick up something else to sell in New Orleans and gain money for gambling is the only contact any of you have with the whites now.''

Diana shook her head in amazement at the obvious effectiveness of what her father had called the slave grapevine. A breeze caught her unbound hair and blew it back from her face. She sniffed at the beloved smells of the swamp riding the gentle wind: fresh water and fish, wildflowers blooming in the shallows near the banks, lush leaves filtering the sunlight, and the remarkable freshness of cool, damp air.

"You sho' the purtiest white gal I ever seen, Miss Diana,'' Tabitha said, apparently no longer interested in the story about Fairfield's new owner. "It ain't fittin' for you to stay hid down here in this swamp, now that your daddy done died. It never seemed right for him to keep you hid from the world, but as Mr. Philip told me hisself one time, that wasn't none of my business. I speck it still ain't, but I cares 'bout you.''

"And I care about you, too.'' Diana thought about how Philip had his own ideas about most matters. For one thing, she recalled while Tabitha and she watched two raccoons cavorting atop a floating log down the way, her father had never allowed anyone to feed the wild animals, pointing out that to do so might rob them of their natural ability to fend for themselves. Even so, she felt a kinship with all living within Gator Swamp. Had not Philip, more than once, called her the loveliest of God's creatures and commended her for following her instincts about right and wrong?

After the frisky raccoons scurried up a tupelo gum tree, Tabitha returned her attention to Diana. "I knows Mr. Fairfield an' Mr. Hathaway meant to do somethin' 'bout takin' care of you 'fore they up an' died sudden-like."

Her warm voice sounding troubled, Tabitha continued. "Are you sure you oughtn't go stay with family till you marry? What 'bout Mr. Philip's folks up in Boston, or your mama's down in Jamaica? A gal like you gotta find a man an' get married so she'll have somebody takin' care of her."

Diana smiled and patted the older woman's arm. "Thanks for caring. Someday the right young man will come along— or so Father always assured me. Let me remind you that I'm no longer a 'gal' and that I can look after myself pretty darned well. I'm going to be eighteen in three days, grown up like you. Can't you stop putting 'Miss' in front of my name?" A mischievous expression danced in her eyes when she drawled in perfect imitation of her visitor, "We's frien's, ain't we?"

Tabitha giggled and hugged the teasing young woman for a moment. "We's that, all right—even when you act like you done forgot what your daddy learnt you 'bout how you ought'a talk." Her wide smile and sparkling brown eyes brought an even friendlier look to her round face. "The way you can soun' like all the swamp critters an' Salem an' me, too, makes me think sometimes you more'n jes ord'nary folks."

"I was remembering this morning how Salem and you once said my mother and I reminded you of a Silver Hoodoo Woman you heard about in Jamaica." Diana studied the black face close to hers. "Isn't that bad, to be connected to hoodoo? Do you truly think I'm like a hoodoo woman?"

Tossing back her head, Tabitha laughed and clapped her hands, as if at a well-played joke. "I tells you what I thinks, Miss Diana. I thinks you be in a high fettle this mornin'."

Diana had learned over the years that when Tabitha made up her mind to keep silent, she would do so. That her visitor had no intention of answering her question seemed plain. Besides, Tabitha's earlier news was beginning to pique her interest.

"Tell me more about what Maynard Oates has done with what his uncle left him. How could he lose the whole plantation?"

"He done run up 'gainst some big gamblin' devil from Mobile what outsmarted him at poker." Tabitha rolled her eyes and leaned closer, the few strands of gray in her short braids gleaming. "Heard tell that Mr. Maynard nigh laid down an' bawled when he see'd that man's hand done beat his."

Listening as Tabitha embroidered her tale, Diana shook her head in quandary at the strange ways of people living outside Gator Swamp. From her avid reading and from mulling over what Philip, Uncle Owen, and her black friends had told her, she had faced up to the likelihood that she might find life difficult in the world beyond the one she knew. Actually, Diana had never gone outside the giant swamp except to visit at the big house at Fairfield or, when summoned at night to minister to the ailing, in various slave quarters in the immediate vicinity.

Though Diana doubted that the healing practices learned from her Jamaican-born mother were more than the ordinary uses of herbs and ancient remedies, the slaves in St. Christopher Parish plainly set much store in Diana's ministrations. They took special care to approach her only at night, then escort her stealthily to whatever quarters awaited her assistance. All were friends, and all seemed as dedicated to keeping the existence of the Hathaways and the house in the swamp a secret as Philip always had.

Diana, while sitting with Tabitha in the swing, recalled how on moonlit nights as Philip and Uncle Owen sat talking or playing chess after supper, she had ventured across the road in front of the mansion and gazed at Selene Bayou with its borders of fat-based cypresses, water oaks, and graceful willows. The treeless, apparently deep channel out in the middle seemed far less beautiful than Gator Swamp—and yet something about the sparkling bayou's hidden depth and unknown destination had fascinated her.

At least here in the shallow swamp, Diana reflected with an encompassing look around, she understood the natural order of her private microcosm. She could determine no recognizable patterns outside her small universe and that frightened her, she who feared little belonging to nature. No, she had no actual need of anyone or anything from the outside world, Diana assured herself with the certainty of one soon to be eighteen and happy with her life as it was. She embraced the simplistic philosophy that whatever was meant to be would be.

Aware that Tabitha had grown silent, Diana asked, "What does the grapevine say will happen now? Will the new owner come here, or will he maybe gamble it away himself?"

Obviously feeling her importance as the bearer of big news from the capital city of New Orleans, Tabitha announced, "He may be a devil like I heard—his name be Lucifer, like in that story you read me one time—but he's a'comin' here to live."

"A big-city gambler is coming here to swamp country to live?" Diana found the idea preposterous, though Tabitha plainly believed that she was reporting the truth.

Diana stretched out her long legs and pretended interest in the expanse of naked skin showing between her short top and brief skirt, her gaze moving down then to her sun-kissed thighs, knees, calves, ankles, and feet of the same shade of pinkish tan. With her bare feet, the bemused young woman gave a little push against the rough plank floor, setting the swing into more rapid motion.

A *frisson* of doubt—or was it fear? Diana wondered—about something that she could not put a name on popped up in the way that a fish often broke the surface of the dark water at twilight, making its presence known, but disappearing before one could be certain of what was seen or heard. Somewhere out in her beloved swamp a dove cooed, and she waited for its mate to give its throaty reply before asking, "Are you sure the man is coming to Fairfield to live?"

"Heard it two times 'fore I come to tell you 'bout it, 'cause I tole Salem you wasn't gonna believe me."

"Drat! I'm afraid you and Salem are going to be in big trouble if the new owner learns we've kept up our bartering since Uncle Owen died. Father said few men allow slaves to handle goods on their own. The man certainly won't like me living on his property." Concern clouding her blue eyes, Diana said, "I don't want either of you to come here again to bring me things. You can leave the basket in the well shed at night, as you did those few times when Maynard came around, and I'll take yours and leave mine."

Tabitha frowned and drew up her mouth. "All this change is gonna mess us up good. Prob'ly I'm gonna have a devil of a time gettin' your egret feathers over to Verbena at Wingate. Them feathers keep bringin' more money ever' time. Heard tell women's hats is all fancied up with 'em more every year."

"That will be fine if you have to wait a spell to get the feathers on their way to market. I'll be all right."

Before then it never had occurred to Diana to wonder what she would do without Tabitha and Salem—her only steady links now to the outside world. The Cajun trappers and fishermen gliding through Gator Swamp with the seasons had long given up trying to be friendly to the Hathaways. She doubted that they had even learned of her father's death last year.

Come to think of it, Diana mused while she and her friend swung contentedly and gazed out into the swamp, she had seen no one paddling nearby for a long while. Philip had located his house in the shallow end—where the water was no more than two or three feet deep except after exceptional rains—and a good distance from the main travel route frequented by trappers and fishermen. Her father had done his trapping of muskrats in the distant reaches of the marsh. She swallowed hard.

Yes, Diana reflected during the comfortable silence on the porch, she would be all right. Not long after Philip's death, a stranger with an accent much like her father's had tied up his pirogue alongside her porch and invited himself to visit.

It was one of the times King was prowling on land. Not wanting the man to learn she lived alone, Diana pretended to be simple and affected the patois of the blacks.

Diana doubted she would ever forget how terrified she had been when the dark-bearded young man grabbed her and planted wet kisses on her mouth. About the time she bit his lip and scratched his face, she had remembered her father's explanations of how to use her knee to fight off unwelcome attentions from a man. The stranger had yelled and cursed, but he had released her to nurse his crotch.

Aware that Tabitha, apparently also in thought, now was pushing one foot against the floor and maintaining the sooth-ing motions of the swing, Diana recalled how she had rushed inside the house that day, grabbed the loaded rifle, and shot through an open window. The single bullet skimming barely a foot over the head of the unwelcome visitor had sent him on his way.

Ever since, Diana had become more vigilant. She vowed that as long as Philip's bullets held out, she would never again allow a pirogue or boat of any kind to reach her house. Several would-be visitors apparently had changed their minds after King's fierce barks and her well-placed shots over their heads convinced them to move on.

Tabitha broke the easy silence. "I been thinkin' that you prob'ly gonna be all right, but I don't like bein' cut off from visitin'. I been 'memberin' how I can't make no cheeses good as your'n, even if I had a goat or a cow left. An' I ain't never catched fish as big as your'n." Tabitha's thick lips pursed, and her plump hands met and interlaced underneath her ample bosom. "Prob'ly the new massah gonna bring his own keeper of the house an' his own cook, too. Ain't hardly 'nuff of us slaves left to keep the place goin', now that Mr. Maynard done sold off so many to get gamblin' money an' a bunch done run away. I don't wanna end up workin' in no field."

"Don't fret," Diana consoled. "Anybody with sense can tell you've done a good job with that house, considering you've had no help. I'll bring cheese when I come to pick up vegetables and eggs from you in the night. Since you've brought such a good supply today, I won't run short soon."

Diana remembered the scant amount of milk Minerva had given up that morning and added, ''Until Minerva's new kid comes, there won't be much milk for making cheese.'' She did not voice the new worry about how her pet might be bred again next year and thus continue to produce milk, now that old Rastus had died and there were no more goats at Fairfield. With something akin to anger she slapped at a mosquito droning near her face. Everything seemed to be changing so fast!

''I'm gonna have to go soon,'' Tabitha announced. ''It takes me half a' hour to walk from the end of the walkway to the big house. Do you have another bunch of feathers for me to take?''

Thinking that Tabitha's visit had passed too quickly, Diana fetched her latest collection of egret feathers. She knew that they were some of the most beautiful ones she had ever found deep in the swamp near the winter nesting places that the huge birds favored.

While Tabitha went on and on about the perfection of the egret feathers and arranged them in her basket, Diana remembered how it was that she had found the curly white feathers. She had discovered them on one of her journeys with King a few years ago in her father's pirogue. They had drifted down from nests high in the trees on the floating islands of marshland in the southernmost part of Gator Swamp. To Diana's delight Philip had explained that the feathers were valuable to hat makers in the cities and that he would send them to New Orleans along with his muskrat pelts. He insisted that the money would be hers and not be deposited to his account in the bank in New Orleans by Uncle Owen, as most of Philip's was. Once he told Diana he was saving for their passage to Boston to visit his family when she became eighteen; when she asked about it later, he had evaded her questions.

After nodding agreement with Tabitha's compliments on the feathers, Diana thought about the brass key lying inside a drawer in her desk, the key Philip had told her many times would open a private deposit box in the Planters Bank in

New Orleans. The savings in the bank and the small key comprised the only known legacy left her that reached beyond Gator Swamp. Sometimes curiosity about what lay in the deposit box intrigued Diana; at others she chose not to think about it because it always led to troublesome thoughts about the world beyond the one she knew and loved.

A frantic, splashing sound near the edge of the porch sent the two women rushing to where Diana earlier had set out her fishing pole. Exchanging pleased smiles, they eyed what Diana found on her arching cane pole when she lifted it from the dark water: A large catfish—weighing over two pounds, Diana guessed—had swallowed the bait, hook and all, and was wriggling wildly, its white belly flashing in the sunshine filtering through the tall trees. Deftly, Diana removed it from her line and inserted a forked limb of green cypress through its mouth and gills.

"Please," Diana said when Tabitha seemed reluctant to take the bewhiskered fish. Lifting the mud-colored catfish by the makeshift holder, and making sure that the single, needle-sharp fin on the top of its head was far below her hand, she offered it again. "I want you to have it so you and Salem will have a scrumptious supper. I can catch another before dark."

"That husband of mine do have a reg'lar gnawin' for fried catfish," Tabitha confessed, nodding her acceptance.

Within a few minutes Diana had the slippery rascal captured in the towel from Tabitha's basket. To the curly feathers and the now-quiet catfish already lying in the basket, she added one of her last rounds of cheese. It was time to hug her friend goodbye.

"Give my love to Salem and please don't take chances coming here if the new owner arrives. We can't pretend he doesn't, in one way or another, own the goods we exchange," Diana said. "I'll want an excuse to walk in the moonlight when the full moon comes in a few nights. If you've not shown up here, I'll come then." Before the black woman got lost among the gray festoons of moss and the deep shade created by the lush growth of leaves and needles on the soaring oaks, gums, and cypresses, Diana called, "Don't forget to leave the basket at the well shed on the first night of the full moon."

After one more flash of her white teeth and a wave of her pink-palmed hand, Tabitha soon dissolved into no more than a blur of red dress among the fronds of swaying moss. From her porch Diana watched her friend disappear as she followed the plank walkway leading to the back acres of Fairfield Plantation.

Whoever this Lucifer was who had won the plantation in a poker game in New Orleans, Diana reflected soberly, was certain to rearrange the comfortable patterns of her and her friends' lives. The next thought brought a shiver: Maybe he really was a devil!

Two

"At last we're at Fairfield Plantation, Salathiel," Luke Greenwood said after dismounting from Jasper. He stretched while waiting for his friend and former tutor to rein up beside him. "It looks as if I might have won a place to call home."

Deliberately ignoring the obvious signs of neglect, Luke drank in the sight of his newly acquired property. He considered Fairfield, with its dark, hipped roof and projecting dormers lending it a French look, typical of the two-story plantation homes in southern Louisiana. "What do you think?"

Salathiel Morgan, eyeing the red brick mansion with its Tuscan columns on the edges of the lower veranda, spoke without his usual tact. "I believe this is a most desolate area. We have seen nothing for miles but flat fields of sugar cane, winding streams, and forests suggestive of a jungle. To be perfectly frank, I find little to commend the area."

"You can't pretend you didn't enjoy stopping by Wingate Plantation and meeting our neighbors," Luke chided as he watched the older man dismount and loop his reins over the hitching rail beside his own. "The widow Winston seems both charming and beautiful. She was quite taken with you."

Salathiel harrumphed. "Only because you remarked that I am a tutor without a position, and she has need of one."

"Am I to blame that you didn't like either of the openings offered you through interviews in New Orleans?"

"Not at all, but I am not sure I care to become involved with so many young girls in this remote place."

"All four of the Winston daughters were as delightful and redheaded as their mother. Admit it."

"That may be true," Salathiel remarked cautiously in his clipped, upper-class British manner. "However, I cannot help but be leery of a woman who named her daughters after flowers and obviously thinks that by that questionable feat she has done something particularly clever."

Luke chuckled. Salathiel had been testy ever since the two of them had left Mobile during the first week of June and traveled to New Orleans. That his two interviews for new positions as tutor had fallen flat, according to Salathiel's stringent standards, had not improved his mood.

Salathiel might be feeling a bit lost now that he was so far from the only home he had known since leaving England some twenty-odd years ago, Luke mused. Southwinds was indeed a far piece away from the lowlands of southern Louisiana.

"I meant it when I invited you to spend as much time with me here as you're willing to spare. I need you to help me get the place furnished the way it should be," Luke said. "I want a well-stocked library and you're the best I know to take care of that. Also I've been particularly fond of British decor ever since my stint at Oxford. You can guide me in my selections in a thousand ways and earn the stipend I've set up for you." He slid a teasing smile toward the older man. "Besides, I have a penchant for your company."

"Why else but to assist you would I have left your comfortable townhouse in New Orleans and come to this God-forsaken place? The house appears to have been neglected for years. Ghastly thought as it is, there is no telling in what condition we will find the interior. I have given my word, so I am bloody well stuck with whatever turns up."

While they stood looking at the Fairfield mansion and waiting for the buggy laden with their possessions to catch up, Salathiel Morgan sent Luke a musing look. He was thinking, and not for the first time, that he was much fonder of Luke than of any of his other former pupils. Though Salathiel, at forty-five, had no desire to marry and have a family, he longed to see Luke happy again, happy as he had been before Frederick had stolen away the only young woman in whom Luke had shown wholesome interest. One reason Salathiel had decided to spend the summer in St. Christopher Parish was the hope that in calmer surroundings and over a period of time, he might be able to help the young man shed some of his bitterness.

Salathiel spoke then. "I cannot imagine why such a project as restoring this place appeals to you. Can it be that you are entertaining the thought of marriage someday?"

"I never have denied that one day I'll marry and rear a family. All I said was that I shall never again lose my heart to a woman."

"Luke, you should not judge all women by the one who chose to marry your brother over you. Perhaps Sylvia was not calculating at all, merely in love with a man other than you."

When Luke shot him a hard look and clamped his lips together, Salathiel went on coolly. "I cannot condone your absurd determination to find some unsuspecting young woman to dangle in front of Frederick's eyes in December. The wager that some young woman might or might not be beautiful and charming enough to win his heart was ridiculous, but it is beneath you to be stooping so low in your scheme to win. I hope now that we are away from the city, you will focus your thoughts and energies on something wholesome."

Luke squelched his irritation. He was not proud of his failed attempts in locating candidates to escort to the Charity Ball and parade before Frederick. How could he explain his visceral need to find some lovely young creature to bring his arrogant brother to his knees as Sylvia had done to him? "I assume you're setting the conditions by which you'll stay on and help me get this place in good condition."

"You might say that, yes." Smoothing his neat mustache with a forefinger, Salathiel fixed Luke with the piercing but caring look of an apt tutor. Whether or not the young man knew it, the Englishman mused, Luke Greenwood possessed an admirable conscience and sense of right. Salathiel did not doubt for a moment that those sterling qualities would reign once more if Luke only would give them freedom. Somehow the older man felt it his duty to help set Luke back on the right path.

To Salathiel's way of thinking, the handsome young man had far more to contribute to society and his own well-being than he thus far had managed in his twenty-eight years. Perhaps settling down on a plantation would prove a positive step.

In his precise, British manner, Salathiel went on, "I can always return to New Orleans next week and advertise for more interviews. I may make a holiday of the entire summer, even the remainder of the year. I can afford to be idle for a while and I can enjoy myself elsewhere if you do not care to hear my thoughts on this matter."

Luke considered Salathiel's words, then grinned. "Talk all you choose. I have no intention of letting you leave here until I have the place looking proper."

Salathiel peered around in the fading light. "Surely there are still some servants around. Do you suppose they failed to hear our arrival?"

The rhythmic sounds of carriage wheels could be heard bumping along the poorly kept dirt road running alongside Bayou Selene in front of the house, and both men turned to watch the familiar pair of matched bays turn into the driveway leading through the grove of huge trees in front of the mansion. Tied behind with a long leather line came the driver's saddle horse.

"Jed has made good time," Luke said, admiring the smart vehicle he had purchased for their trip of fifty-odd miles west of New Orleans. All at the gaming table that night in New Orleans a couple of weeks ago had insisted that Maynard Oates list the stock, slaves, and movables on the plantation before they ever consented to accept the deed to Fairfield as tender in the high-stakes poker game. After Luke had won with his four kings, he had discovered the list contained no passenger vehicles.

At first, Luke recalled while Salathiel and he waited for the carriage, he had tried to persuade Maynard not to bet the last of his inheritance. Nevertheless, as he had already learned over the past couple of years while gambling occasionally with the arrogant man, Maynard cared little for reasoning. Luke reflected that any one of the characteristics seeming to control Maynard Oates—impulse, hot temper, false pride— could lead a man into desperate actions.

Luke removed his tall-crowned hat and let the late afternoon breezes play in his hair, appreciating the delicate fragrances riding the damp wind from Bayou Selene across the deep-rutted road. Wasn't Selene the name of the Greek goddess of the moon?

Less romantic were Luke's recurring thoughts about the bayou as a viable means of alleviating the isolation of St. Christopher Parish. Was the bayou deep enough to accommodate one of the small packet steamers that he had seen plying other waterways on the journey from New Orleans? The idea had intrigued him all day. He felt as if he were awakening after a long and troublesome sleep.

What would Maynard do, Luke wondered as he soaked up the ambience of Fairfield, now that the new owner had come to establish residence? From what he had learned during their brief visit at Wingate with the gracious widow, Lallage Winston, the plantation on the other side of his was called Fernwood and belonged to Maynard's mother and her new husband, a retired sea captain. Luke had asked around before leaving New Orleans and learned that Maynard had disappeared from his usual haunts. Some had opined that he likely had returned to the home of his mother and new stepfather.

"If this place doesn't even have a carriage or a horse or cow, how does it operate?" Salathiel asked, sending appraising looks at the red brick mansion with its twin verandas stretching across the front. He held his hat in his hand and waved it imperiously against a threatening mosquito. With distaste, he eyed the peeling white paint of the wooden trim.

"It is obvious that painting will be required. The structural lines are quite pleasing, though the brick could have been molded with a better eye for right angles."

"I like the soft appearance of the fat brick," Luke replied after sending a perusing look and giving the matter some thought. "Probably slaves unaccustomed to making so many bricks started using shortcuts and didn't bother to level their molds before casting."

Luke gazed up at his new home. He saw a curved piece of metal edging the hipped roof in a continuous line and guessed that it stuck up some six or seven inches to catch rainwater and funnel it into a cistern around back. Since making his home in New Orleans a couple of years ago, he had learned that the level of ground water in southern Louisiana is so near the surface that dug wells produce water too brackish and muddy for human consumption.

Ramming both hands in the pockets of his breeches, and feeling an inordinate pride in the sight of the handsome though plainly neglected mansion, Luke found himself whistling as he sauntered underneath the moss-festooned oaks. On his way to the broad steps leading to the front veranda, he admired the several pairs of tall, French-style doors opening onto both the lower and upper verandas. Beaded panes of glass in the upper halves of the white doors served as windows, a Continental touch he appreciated.

When Luke paid closer attention to the foundation, he figured that the house was raised some eight feet on its brick piers for protection against possible flood waters. No doubt the once-white latticework underneath the structure concealed a large storage space.

By then Jed Latour, the mulatto whom Luke long ago had hired away from a gambling house to serve as his valet, had halted the carriage and jumped down from the driver's box. His lean agility and unlined, faintly brown face belied his thirty-six years. "Looks like you won yourself a mighty fine place here, boss. I like it."

"Thanks. So do I." Luke waved away a singing mosquito, crossed his arms across his chest, then leaned back a tad and squinted up at the second floor in the twilight. The slender wooden colonettes and encircling banister of the upper veranda accentuated the heavier Tuscan columns and open veranda below. He confessed that he had liked the character of the place from the moment he had first seen its four chimneys rising through the soaring oaks, gums, and cottonwoods in the late afternoon sunlight. "I get the feeling that I have found us a home, gentlemen. Indeed, I do."

Just then a black woman and man came from around the back of the house and nodded politely before introducing themselves with noticeable uneasiness. Both were barefooted and had streaks of gray in their hair.

"Well," Luke said after introducing his two companions and himself, "Tabitha and Salem, you give me hope that we've come to the right place. I had feared for a moment that all the slaves had run away and that we would have to do for ourselves until I could return to New Orleans and cross over to Algiers for the auctions."

"Naw, suh," Salem replied. "Most stayed behind in the quarters, but there be twenty-two of us still here. Lotsa the young ones run off."

"Tell all that I'll meet with them first thing in the morning," Luke said. "Tonight my friends and I want nothing as much as a bite to eat and a bed."

Salem nodded his understanding, then hurried to lead the saddle horses to the stables out back, motioning for Jed to follow him in the carriage.

"'Bout all I can offer to fix for supper is some goat cheese, scrambled eggs, and sourdough bread," Tabitha said as the three headed toward the dining room on the back side of the house. Removing her hands from where she had twisted them in her apron, she motioned toward the kitchen built some forty feet behind the main house. "I got a fire goin' an' water hot." She bowed her head and studied her bare feet not quite hidden by her long red skirt. " 'Less you brung some coffee or sto'-bought tea, I ain't got nothin' but sassafras—"

"We stopped in Calion at the general store," Luke told her, wondering why Tabitha would not let her eyes meet his. Surely she was not afraid of him.

Having grown up around slaves back at Southwinds where

his father had insisted that they be treated kindly by all, Luke Greenwood had never had any trouble getting along with black people. Was he, perhaps, letting his fatigue make his voice sharp? He disliked thinking that Salathiel might have been right about his having become hardened. He tried softening his tone. "Jed likely has already carried a box of staples and food items from the carriage to your kitchen."

Thankful for something to busy her hands, Tabitha lit some of her last hand-dipped candles against the falling darkness and placed them around before scooting across the back veranda to the kitchen. Her mind was racing. Thank the Lord one of Verbena's little boys had sneaked over from Wingate and told her that the new master was on his way or else she would have spent the afternoon at Diana's and not had the beds upstairs ready for use. She had not realized there would be two men with him to feed, and now she was going to have to go take some more eggs out of the basket she had already set on the ledge of the well shed out back for Diana to pick up later that night.

Tabitha's plump face screwed up in disappointment. Now that the new master was here, Diana was going to need the eggs tomorrow to bake her own birthday cake. Tabitha could think of no way she could make one without running the risk of the new master asking questions she had no plans to answer truthfully.

While hurrying around to prepare the meal for the men, Tabitha thought about the new master. *Your kitchen*. She had liked hearing him use those words and had really looked at him for the first time. He must be meaning to keep her as cook. Mr. Luke, as he said he wanted to be called—was that short for Lucifer?—did not act at all like a devil.

Tabitha, her thoughts still dwelling on all that was happening or promising to happen, knelt on the hearth and stirred the eggs bunching up into soft yellow mounds in the black iron spider. Reckon Mr. Luke planned to live at Fairfield and get more slaves and maybe put in some sugar cane. If he was going to stay, he would have to buy some milk cows and some more chickens. Somehow the last thought cheered Tabitha the most.

* * *

After their simple but tasty supper, Salathiel made no bones about wanting to get to bed early, but Luke had no wish yet to end his day. Feeling a bit cheated that darkness had prevented him from seeing much of the place, he wandered out the door opening from his second-floor bedroom onto the back veranda and leaned against the banister for a look at his property. It pleased him that the back of the house had upper and lower verandas identical to those in front, for he knew well how such wide open areas invited and circulated cooling breezes from the surrounding trees.

More relaxed than he could recall being in a long while, Luke gazed at the enormous full moon rising over the forest on the horizon. For some inexplicable reason, he remembered that the summer solstice was near. Midsummer's Eve, he recalled from his studies in classical mythology, must be tomorrow night, June the twenty-third.

Did fairies enchant and bemuse the citizens of St. Christopher Parish as myth suggested they did in Europe on the supposedly magical Midsummer's Eve? Luke wondered with more fancy than he had entertained in years. Then, scorning such romantic nonsense, he adopted a realistic view. Had he not learned too well that sentimentality could lead to pain so intense that it still flavored his reasoning? Yes, Luke conceded to a strident inner voice, he believed in the power of love . . . for one time. After that, a man with good sense steered clear of entanglements affecting the heart.

The persistent, loud noises of night callers—cicadas, tree frogs, owls, and other nocturnal birds—sounded both familiar and comforting to one who had spent the majority of the nights over the past five years in gambling establishments. How was it he had let himself become so alienated from nature? He had almost forgotten how much he had always enjoyed summer nights in the country when he was growing up at Southwinds.

Luke lifted his face to the dampness of the cool night air. Suddenly, a longing for more cleansing than he could gain from the pitcher of tepid, cistern water Jed had brought up to his bedroom seized him. Spotting the well shed on a decided rise between the backyard and the stables, he left the veranda and made his way toward it.

When he reached the well shed, Luke let the rope slide through the pulley, waited until he heard the wooden bucket splash, then drew it up full of water and balanced it on the brick curbing. How long since he had performed such a basic task? He sniffed the contents of the bucket and discovered the odor was not as brackish as Tabitha had warned it might be. He removed his gold watch chain from where it looped through a buttonhole in his waistcoat, then slipped his watch from its tiny pocket and looked for a safe spot to lay it.

Luke was aware that one of the gripes his older brother held against him was that, in spite of their father having left his sons equal shares of land, the elderly man had stated in his will that his gold-plated pocket knife went to his name-sake, but that his pocket watch went to Luke. The gold time-piece engraved with his father's initials claimed a special niche in Luke's heart.

Spying a basket sitting on the wide brick ledge running around the outer edges of the little open shed protecting the wide, hand-dug well, Luke dropped his watch and chain in the basket alongside a couple of wrinkled white cloths.

Within seconds Luke had shed his upper clothing and was dousing his head with the contents of the bucket. The tingling sensation of cold water streaming down his face and shoulders brought gasps of pleasure. He shook his head vigorously to get rid of the excess moisture, grinning and thinking that he was acting like a frisky puppy thrashing around in a stream.

Luke, refreshed then and feeling much more like stretching out on the smooth sheets awaiting him upstairs, grabbed up his clothing and, with his garments slung over a bare shoulder, ambled back in the increasing moonlight to his new home. He found himself feeling tall, surefooted, more invigorated than he had a right to be . . . and somehow younger than his twenty-eight years warranted.

Tomorrow, Luke promised himself, after he met with the slaves and inspected all of the outbuildings, he might wander across the back pastures where Salem had told him there lay a freshwater swamp. Perhaps it would be free enough of undergrowth for him to shed all of his clothing and immerse his entire long-legged body. After one lingering, appreciative look at the golden moon inching above the forests, he went inside and climbed the staircase. He was almost whistling aloud before he recalled that Salathiel likely was already asleep in one of the guest bedrooms.

Diana waited until the full moon climbed overhead before she started on the walkway toward Fairfield's back pasture, the basket on her arm holding four fat catfish and a round of cheese. When Tabitha had not arrived that afternoon, Diana surmised that the new master had arrived. To her dismay, thoughts of the man and his arrival had haunted her ever since Tabitha's last visit.

Determined to enjoy the first night of the summer moon, Diana lifted her head and gazed at the moonbeams brushing through the thickly leafed trees and turning the ghostly falls of gray moss into silvery festoons. With reverence for the mysterious pale light, she looked down into the black water and saw what she had expected to see, black velvet touched round with twinkling diamonds.

Though Diana had only read about these items, she felt certain that if she ever did see black velvet or diamonds, they would complement her assessment of the sights below the rough board walkway. Admittedly entranced by her surroundings, Diana reflected that the night songs from the surrounding swamp seemed to have swelled to greater heights while the silvery sphere rose in the star-studded sky, as if the nocturnal singers, too, chose to pay special homage to beauty.

King, keeping Diana company until after they reached land, took a moment to commune with Minerva when the goat roused from where she slept underneath a sheltering oak. Then, as if he could no longer restrain the impulse to act younger than his five years, King bounded around the pasture, chasing his shadow. Trained not to bark unless in warning, the dog let out only a few low-throated growls.

"That's all right, boy," Diana assured her beloved pet in a soft voice, no matter that the dog was too far away to hear. She could barely make out King's tail and for a moment, the big dog looked a bit like one of the frisky deer she sometimes surprised drinking at the edges of the swamp. "Go ahead and have yourself some fun. You probably get tired of staying with me so much."

Giving in to impulses of her own, impulses that she understood far less than those of her pet, Diana skipped barefooted on the dew-laden grass and felt the dance of her long hair against her shoulders and back. She held out the basket to add to her momentum and whirled around, loving the feeling of wide open spaces there in the pasture, the feeling of the damp night breezes tickling her bare midriff and legs, and the familiar smells of the freshwater swamp in the distance behind her. From one of the alluvial ridges far down the road, the haunting fragrance of a blossoming magnolia or sweet bay tree wafted on the night air, inviting her to lift her face to the elements and sniff with renewed reverence for being young, alive, and in harmony with nature.

When she reached the fenced lot behind the stables, Diana slowed underneath a protective live oak and scanned the place. If there were horses on the plantation now, they must be inside the stables off to her left. No, she decided after a few moments of judging the darkness of the windows in the slave cabins on the far side of the stables and of those in the mansion up ahead, there was no one awake.

In spite of her wish not to be seen, Diana stood for a moment beside the well shed, staring at the back of the beautiful mansion in the moonlight. She could not help but be curious about the new owner and a tad worried that if he were to find out she trespassed on his property, he might try punishing her by sending her away from the swamp. After all, she knew from having read her father's copies of Milton's *Paradise Lost* and Marlowe's *Doctor Faustus* that the name given the one who defied God and ruled hell was Lucifer. Tabitha had reported that the new master bore the name Lucifer.

Shivering from her terrifying thoughts and an eerie sense that she was being watched, Diana lost little time in exchanging her basket for Tabitha's and racing back in the moonlight to the back acres and the security of Gator Swamp.

* * *

The next morning soon after breakfast Luke stopped by the kitchen. He had just left the well shed where he had searched unsuccessfully for his pocket watch. After finding the basket on the ledge empty, a hazy memory of having walked half asleep on the back veranda during the night surfaced. The recalled images seemed too fanciful for credence . . . or voicing.

As he had dressed hurriedly for breakfast in only shirt and trousers, Luke had not realized until he was getting dressed for the day that he had left his pocket watch and chain in the basket the night before. Dismissing his half-remembered fantasy as a dream, he realized that as the new master, he must act with discretion and not accuse anybody of stealing. Probably Tabitha herself had drawn water to prepare breakfast and had put the watch aside in the kitchen. He asked the black woman casually, "Who has been to the well shed this morning?"

"I was out there, an' probably lots of others," Tabitha replied, surprised to find the new master standing in the doorway of the kitchen. She knew that she had been the first to the well, for she had rushed at dawn to see if Diana had come in the night and exchanged baskets with her. After adding Diana's gifts of fish and cheese to the "keeping" bucket lowered on a rope to rest a few feet above the water level and stay cool, she had left the empty basket on the ledge.

Going on with her work, Tabitha poured hot water from the iron kettle into her dishpan and motioned for her young helper, Chloe, to swish around the bar of lye soap in the water and try making suds, a nearly impossible task. Could Mr. Luke be asking such a dumb question because he had spied Diana in the night? Her heart kicking up a fuss at that possibility, she asked, "Is there somethin' wrong, Mr. Luke?"

Luke called up his self-control. While serving breakfast earlier in the dining room, Tabitha had let her eyes meet his a time or two, and he had no wish to lose any ground gained. From his former experiences with slaves, he judged that as cook and head of housekeeping, Tabitha held much power with the other blacks. He needed to win her over completely before questioning her about such a ticklish subject. The watch could not have gone far. "No. I was just wondering if the well has a goodly supply of water."

After a brief meeting with all of the slaves in front of their quarters, Luke went ahead with his plans to explore the fallow fields and some of the pastures. All day as he went about the place with Salathiel and Jed, the three of them looking around and exchanging ideas for improvements, Luke kept his eyes out for sly glances from any of the blacks.

All that Luke ever detected was shyness and apparent respect, tinged with what he suspected was a bit of fear over learning to deal with a new master. Had he known that his given name, Lucius, had somehow been transformed into Lucifer by way of the slave grapevine and was giving cause to suspicions that he might be the devil incarnate, Luke Greenwood would have thrown back his handsome head and laughed.

By midafternoon when Luke came up with no clues as to where his watch could be, he returned to look into the empty basket sitting on the ledge, even pulled up the keeping bucket from the well. All he found inside it, though, were cloth-wrapped catfish and a small round of what he guessed was goat cheese.

That evening after Salathiel had retired to read in his room, Luke sat on the veranda outside his second-floor bedroom and put away the fanciful idea that he actually had seen a scantily clad, silver-haired sprite in the night dashing around near the well shed, a shapely young woman with a deer as a companion. The corners of his full lips tilting upward at the absurdity of his thoughts, Luke leaned back in the tall-backed wooden rocker and propped his feet on the handrailing. Perhaps his having recalled that Midsummer's Eve was at hand—tonight, actually—had led him to imagine such an unlikely event taking place in his own backyard.

Despite his not learning anything about his stolen watch, Luke reflected as he drew on his cigar and watched the full moon coming up, the day had been pleasurable. The supper of golden, crusty catfish had lived up to his expectations.

Tabitha was going to work out fine as cook. Her young helper, Chloe, seemed capable, too.

Clearly, Salathiel was relishing his role as advisor, and Jed seemed eager to take on new duties. Luke and the two men had prepared a list of supplies to buy in the small town of Calion, only twelve miles away. They had begun what likely would become a much longer list to be filled on his planned trip to New Orleans.

Without willing it, Luke's thoughts about what he had or had not seen the previous night kept returning and teasing his mind. His right thumb and forefinger lightly traced the pattern of his strong chin; his dark eyes narrowed. What if—?

Three

～～

"This is terrible, King," Diana agonized aloud to her dog the morning after she exchanged baskets with Tabitha. "If I had paid more attention last night to what was in the basket, I could have returned this dratted watch before daylight. Probably it belongs to the new master but I can't imagine how it got there. I hope Tabitha doesn't get into trouble before I can return it tonight."

King, accustomed to his role of confidant, whined and cocked his head in apparent sympathy for the plight of his solemn-eyed mistress. Then Minerva, already relieved of her scant milk, bleated and began setting sharp, tapping hooves on the boardwalk leading to the back pasture of Fairfield.

"Go on with Minerva," Diana said when she realized King sat waiting for her permission to leave. She was too woebegone to remind King not to go exploring after seeing Minerva to the pasture. Later when she reflected on her laxity, she admitted that the big dog did not always heed that particular order.

By the time the sun was dipping behind the trees, Diana still had not hatched a better plan than to sneak back to the well shed that night and return the lovely watch and chain to the ledge of the well shed. The engraved initials, L.F.G., called up all kinds of imagined names to go with the one Tabitha had told her: Lucifer—the devil.

Diana found it difficult to finish her supper of baked bass topped with herbs and wild onions and impossible to swallow more than a few bites of the sad-looking birthday cake she had baked for herself. Until she stirred up the batter, she had not realized that she was low on brown-sugar crystals, the only kind of sugar Tabitha had been able to find since Maynard Oates had deserted his slaves. The nearest sugar mill was on the far side of Calion, the only town of any size in St. Christopher Parish—or so her father had always told her. Diana's nighttime ministrations to sick slaves rarely offered her a chance to view much more than ghostly, sleeping mansions and the deserted stores in Calion.

With nothing but pictures from aged books to guide her, Diana let her mind play with the idea of what a town or even a city might look like in the daylight with people milling around. *I wonder if Father ever missed his home in Boston —or the many brothers and sisters he left there?* From the few things Philip had ever told her, Boston was a real city, larger by far than New Orleans. A startling question formed. If Philip had lived, would he really have taken her to Boston to meet her kinfolk when she reached eighteen—now?

Because Diana enjoyed and felt comfortable with her uncomplicated life in Gator Swamp, she did not like dwelling on the increasingly nagging thought that she should have already made plans to travel to New Orleans and investigate what was in the deposit box at Planters Bank. She was going to have to make that trip soon, whether or not she liked thinking about it. She sighed. It *was* time to be putting away childish things. . . .

Eighteen years old and not even King to wish her a happy birthday, Diana reflected with a tad of rare self-pity. A sudden chorus of *be-deeps* from some bullfrogs out in the swamp brought a smile.

"Thanks for reminding me you're out there, you rascals," she called from the porch, more like her old cheerful self again. "I'll come looking for one of you in the pirogue later tonight and treat myself to some frog legs for breakfast."

From somewhere deeper in the swamp, an owl hooted. Calling up her talent for mimicking, Diana answered, giggling under her breath when the owl responded.

Without her usual zest for the nightly ritual, Diana shucked off her skimpy articles of clothing, knelt at the back side of the porch running around the small shack, and bathed, sniffing appreciatively at the little sliver of sweet-smelling soap that Tabitha had included in her basket as a birthday gift. Afterward, she washed her hair with the remaining soap and fanned it out with her fingers in the twilight breezes until the silvery blonde mass fell in damp clusters of loose waves and curls below her waist.

Remembering her eerie sense of being watched at the well shed the night before, Diana decided to bunch up her long hair and hide it underneath one of her father's old hats. There was no sense in taking unnecessary chances now that old Lucifer was in residence, she reflected. Not until the moon was almost overhead did she venture down the walkway.

The smells of King and Minerva on the rough planks discouraged snakes from tarrying on the walkway, and Diana padded alone and unafraid in the moonlight. King had not returned after shepherding Minerva off that morning.

The beauty of Midsummer's Eve was not lost on Diana, in spite of her disquieting thoughts. She fancied that to have been born on June twenty-third signified that she enjoyed a special kinship with the moon and the moon goddess Diana. Often she had pored over the books of Roman mythology, devouring with keen interest the tales connected with her namesake. Diana. She had learned that the name came from the root word *di*, meaning "to shine," and that it also meant "the bright one."

Once when she had spilled her thoughts to her father, he had laughed indulgently while touching her hair and pointing to her brain and told her that if what she had read were true, she fit the description in two ways. With his pride and love showing in his eyes, he indulged her by telling her that the mythological Diana had been called "Diana of the Wood" and that the cypress tree was sacred to her. Also, the goddess had favored animals, but especially the dog, the goat, and the deer. It was all right for her to entertain such childhood fancies sometimes, Philip said with his quiet smile and feverishly bright eyes, especially since she seemed happy living in the swamp.

Diana reached the shadows of the live oak near the well shed then. She wished King was along to help her determine if it might be time to take her basket holding the pocket watch and set it on the ledge. Just to be on the safe side and prove to Tabitha or whoever might be looking into her basket that she had not taken the watch knowingly, she had included four more catfish caught late that afternoon and wrapped in a cloth.

"Aha!" came a deep masculine voice from the shadowy, far side of the well shed when Diana set down her basket. Only six feet separated them. "I've caught you stealing."

Luke was already hurrying to catch the rascal before the first syllables left his mouth. Swift as a startled deer, the small, hatted figure ran toward Selene Bayou in front of the mansion.

Luke could easily see the flashing bare legs and feet in the bright moonlight, and his far longer legs had scant trouble catching up with the culprit. He dived headlong at those pale legs and rolled with the runner to the dewy grass beneath a giant cypress tree beside Selene Bayou. A fleeting glance upward through the branches showed him a moon etched with mysterious, needle-like tracings, a cypress moon. Gamely, the creature fought, kicking and slapping until he covered the wriggling, scantily clad body with his own.

"Let's see what we have here, little one," Luke said when his weight prevented his panting captive from fighting back. Only then did he have an opportunity to turn his captive over and see facial features. Eyes of such blue as to appear almost silver in the moonlight glared up at him as if he might be something evil. The oversized hat slid off when Luke shifted his arm, and he gasped. He stared with disbelief while masses of white-blonde hair came tumbling down to frame a beautiful face. "My God! You're a girl."

Diana almost lost her breath when the man's voice had sounded back at the well, and now after the mad dash and her ensuing struggle, she had none in reserve. Even had she known what to say—and she knew that she did not—she would not have had breath enough to say it. Her heartbeat had gone berserk. She gasped for air, all the while watching the handsome face so near her own in the bright moonlight and wondering if she might not be looking at the devil himself. What was he going to do?

In spite of her preoccupation with regaining normal breath and heartbeat, Diana saw that the man's eyes were huge and dark, almost as black as his hair and his eyebrows. He was not smiling, but his full lips were open, as if in surprise, and his teeth shone white with sharp, even edges that looked to her like those of her hunting knife. His body still lying half atop her own was hard and firm and gave no indication of lessening its pressure.

"What were you doing back at my well shed?" Luke demanded when the girl continued to stare at him with a silent fascination that reminded him of when he was a child and had watched a barely feathered mockingbird on the ground being held immobile by the unwavering gaze of an approaching water moccasin. Then, as now, he realized that he could break the eerie spell. A movement and call from him had sent the black snake slithering in the opposite direction and allowed the young bird to recover and flutter on shaky wings to a nearby tree.

Figuring that his pulse still raced due to the spirited chase and ensuing struggle, Luke rolled off the girl's body and sat up. He kept his hands lightly around both her slender wrists and helped her to sit facing him. It was then, during her graceful movements, when he saw the brief covering over her full breasts and the skimpy skirt reaching barely below her thighs that he realized he had been wrong a second time. This was no girl.

Before him in the moonlight, Luke reflected with mouth gone dry, sat a young woman of amazing, almost ethereal beauty, both in face and form. He never before had seen hair like hers, not even in places where women had no compunction about doctoring the color of their hair.

For a moment Luke Greenwood wondered if he might not

be caught up in the same dreaming state that had bedeviled him the night before. Nothing seemed real except his rapid pulse and the echoing beats in the unwilling dainty wrists he gripped.

"Who are you?" Luke asked. "What are you doing here?"

Panicky at the thought of what the man might to do her, Diana increased her attempt to loosen his grasp on her wrists and escape. She failed. The way the moonlight seemed captured deep within his black eyes reminded her of the stars reflecting in the dark swamp water earlier. Fascinating. Unfathomable. Like a devil, maybe? From faraway came the screech of an owl, its eerie call matching up with the goose-flesh prickling her spine.

Luke did not give up. "Tell me your name."

Diana failed that time in escaping the demands of her captor's resonant voice. Recalling how she had dissembled and fended off the young fisherman who had appeared at her house and frightened her with his questions and his kiss, she replied in a faked, lush tone, "Diana Hat'away."

"Where do you live, Diana Hathaway?"

"Up the bayou, suh."

Luke frowned. Somehow he was disappointed to learn that the beautiful young woman spoke in the same thick-tongued dialect of Tabitha and the other slaves. "What are you doing sneaking around my well house? I lost a valuable pocket watch last night, and I want it back."

"I brung it back jes' now. I didn't mean to steal it, suh. I swear I never knowed it was in the basket."

"You came last night to get the basket, didn't you?" Luke watched as Diana's tongue licked her lips, spellbound at the close-up view of her wet lips in the moonlight. They were full and formed with the same pouting, feminine symmetry he had admired in the paintings in the great art museums in London and Paris. Sitting close together on the ground as they were, he could see the infinitesimal pulse hammering in the hollow of her throat. When he sensed her rising fear, he almost relinquished his firm hold on her delicate wrists.

Luke's need to know more about his fascinating captive overcame his momentary compassion, and he retained his hold on Diana while continuing to absorb the perfection of her face and hair. It stunned him to realize that he was looking at the most beautiful creature he had ever seen. A brief downward glance told him what he thought he remembered from his first half-conscious glimpse of her on the preceding night—the same grace and loveliness also marked the rest of her body. When Diana evaded his gaze and straightened her slender shoulders, Luke went on. "Who's your cohort here at Fairfield?"

"Cohort?" Diana asked, swinging her gaze back to his and pretending not to understand. Did all young men have such full, well-shaped lips? She tried to recall those of the fisherman who bothered her that day at her house, but no image formed. "What's a cohort?"

"Friend." Luke could see no change in her expression and he wondered why she was staring at his features with such open-mouthed wonder. If the idea were not so farfetched, he might suspect she had never before been so close to a man. "A cohort could be a partner in crime." He recalled vaguely that when he had put his watch in the basket, a towel or some kind of white cloth had lain in it, but he had not looked to see if it hid anything. "Somebody could have set out the basket for you last night."

"Crime, suh? I ain't committed no crime an' I ain't got no partner." Indignation plumped up Diana's voice, helped her regain partial control of herself. "If'n you go look, you'll see the watch is in the basket I brung tonight. You can turn me loose now. I ain't kep' yo' watch or yo' basket."

"What's going on here, Diana? And quit calling me 'sir' as if I'm an ogre. I'm Lucius—Luke—Greenwood, the new owner of Fairfield. I suspect you and somebody here at the plantation are up to something. Am I right?"

"No, suh, Mr. Greenwood. I don't know nobody livin' in Fairfiel'." She consoled herself that she had not lied; the blacks did not live in the mansion. "I jes' happen to be out las' night wanderin' an' I see I done wrong to trespass on yo' property. I 'pologize."

When Luke's stern expression did not alter, Diana took a deep breath and went on. "I shouldn't a picked up yo' basket a'tall. I was some upset this mornin' when I looked inside an' found it had a gold watch an' chain in it. I felt bad 'bout takin' what didn't belong to me, so I brung the basket an' the watch back tonight." So his name was not Lucifer as reported by the slave grapevine, and he was called Luke. Still, *Lucius* was close to the name of the one denoting evil, and he was certainly acting the part. Aware that he was looking doubtful, Diana added with force, "I ain't no thief. I ain't even kep' the basket."

Luke relaxed his grip on her wrists, but not enough for her sudden movements to gain her freedom. "Stop trying to get away and I'll not have to keep such a tight hold on you."

Diana sent him a blazing look. "Why not let me go?"

"Because I don't believe your story."

"Let's go back to the well shed an' you'll see I been tellin' the truth."

"No pretty young woman like you runs around in the middle of the night just for the hell of it. What are you up to? Is there some young man waiting for you somewhere? Since you're trespassing on my land, I have the right to know." Diana's chin shot up higher and her gaze roved upward through the sparse limbs of the cypress tree. The action set her long hair into a sensuous dance around her shoulders and made Luke think of perfumed, silken moonlight. "I can always hold you and turn you over to the sheriff tomorrow and let him find out who it is around here you're working with." Luke felt her stiffen. "Are you mixed up with the slaves in stealing from their masters and then selling the goods to somebody?"

"No, suh, Mr. Greenwood. I tole you I don't know nobody livin' in Fairfiel'. Nobody a'tall. I ain't no thief, else I never would'a brung back yo' watch an' basket."

"Very well. We'll go to the well shed and get my watch. Then I'll take you home to your parents."

"They's dead. I ain't got nobody." To Diana the high-pitched song of a tree frog from a nearby tree seemed a plaintive echo of her inner turmoil. From down the bayou she heard bullfrogs bellowing in a lazy, monotonous bass. She wondered if she was trying to hang onto things she understood. There was nothing about the man confronting her that she understood—not his penetrating looks and questions, least of all her inner quaking. The entire business was downright scary.

"You don't even have a beau? Do you mean there's nobody waiting for you somewhere?"

"Nobody!"

"All right. I'll hold you overnight and take you to the sheriff in Calion tomorrow. Perhaps he knows better than I how to get you to tell who you're working with and why. If there's a ring of thieves around here, I want it stopped."

After Luke pulled Diana to her feet and handed her Philip's old hat, he held her free hand and they began walking away from where he had captured her on the banks of Selene Bayou and toward the well shed behind Fairfield.

With each step Diana agonized over her predicament. From what her father had told her and from her vast reading in his books, she knew that traipsing around alone at night was bizarre behavior for a well-bred young woman. She also knew that the sheriff had no idea who she was—she had complete faith in the slaves' sworn promises never to tell anything about the Hathaways—and that he likely would stir up a small tempest if he got curious about where she lived and what she was doing at Fairfield in the middle of the night.

Diana's disturbing thoughts ran on as Luke Greenwood led her back down the walkway to the tree-screened mansion, around its side, and on past the staved cistern towering up beside the second gallery. She welcomed the shadows underneath the moss-laden trees, for they gave her opportunities to send sidelong looks at the tall man as she tried to determine his mood.

True, he was mad as the devil, Diana reflected uneasily, but he had made no move to molest her. She could not help but be encouraged from that observation. When he had been lying on top of her back there and she felt his breath on her face and smelled an alien fragrance hinting at masculinity, she had felt more confused and helpless than ever before in her eighteen years. A new thought jarred her, adding to the dizzying pace of her blood: She had never before felt more excited either.

It occurred to Diana that a man as handsome as Luke likely did not have to stoop to forcing his attentions on women, even if—as Tabitha had said and she herself suspected from his lying in wait for her—he did happen to be in cahoots with the devil. Probably, women encouraged him to be affectionate whenever it pleased him.

Using her free hand to brush back her hair from her face with Philip's crushed hat, then plop it on her head, Diana faced up to the realization that she had no inkling about such intimate matters as might go on between a woman and a man. Animals she knew about, but not humans.

Diana had always figured—and hoped—there was much romance in the mating of humans, romance such as she had read about in Philip's volumes of literature. Upon questioning from his precocious young daughter, Philip had told her that she would know when romance entered her life and would also know how to act when it did, that nature governed humans, too. It seemed no answer at all.

While Diana's thoughts scudded like birds trying to escape a hurricane and her bare feet glided with almost no noise on the dew-kissed grass, she kept hearing Luke's shoes making small whispering sounds. Judging by what she could surmise from his profile and his tense grip on her wrist, Luke Greenwood was in deep thought himself. She figured the continuing wild tempo of her pulse was caused by her still being so frightened at all that had happened over the past several minutes. How would she explain to him her having a house on his property in Gator Bayou? And a goat grazing on his back pasture?

Worse than Diana's fear for herself, though, was her fear that Tabitha, Salem, and the other blacks might get into trouble. What if they were accused of aiding and abetting someone trespassing on their master's land? If the long-legged man leading her to the well shed in back of Fairfield ever found out about the bartering going on between Tabitha and her. . . .

Diana felt less sure of herself and more fluttery inside with each step. Since Luke's first accusations, the thick knot that had formed in the back in her throat seemed to be growing. Swallowing offered her no relief from its pain. Where had her former confidence in the goodness and beauty of moonlight gone?

"Here we are," Luke said when they reached the well shed. After lifting his watch from the basket and slipping it into his pocket, he smiled down at the lovely but woebegone face lifted to his and led the reluctant Diana back into full moonlight. "My watch is here, just as you said."

Surely, Luke reasoned, when Diana saw that he was not going to harm her she would offer a believable explanation. On the way to the well shed his mind had dipped and delved into all kinds of absurd thoughts. The young woman was an innocent caught up in a gang of thieves. She was an innocent who did not know enough to respect private property. He should help her since she had no family, should teach her to read and write as well as to act properly. Diana Hathaway was too exquisite to set free, for he might not ever see her. . . .

Luke discarded his last thought as soon as it formed. "Now, do you tell me all about what is going on between you and some of my slaves and let me handle it, or do I have to take you to the sheriff tomorrow and report your strange behavior?"

Wincing, Diana visualized her black friends being punished in some of the cruel ways she had heard some masters employed. "Why can't you jes' turn me loose now that you got all yo' property back, Mr. Greenwood?"

Even in the moonlight, Luke saw Diana's inner pain and fear mar her lovely eyes. What secrets lay within those shining depths? His mind labored to find a way of preventing the beautiful blonde from racing away into the night. He did not know why it seemed so important that he keep her there, only that it did. Swooping from some dark well in his mind, an idea rose that appeared to be a solution to more than one problem. "Perhaps there's a way you can makg it right without having to tell who your cohorts are and without my having to take you to the sheriff."

With her eyes narrowed and her countenance a study in suspicion, Diana cocked her head to one side. "What'cha mean?"

"You can promise not to skulk around in the night anymore and move in here at Fairfield and get some tutoring from my house guest, Salathiel Morgan. If you did that, I wouldn't be interested in learning about your cohorts and your thievery."

Luke did not let the remainder of his startling idea form into words. With the beauty before him molded as he saw fit, he would have no trouble in dazzling his brother, Frederick, with her at the Charity Ball in December. It seemed as plain as the full moon overhead that Diana Hathaway in the trappings of cultured speech, elegant clothing, and socially acceptable manners could knock Frederick senseless. Another plus was Frederick's stated preference for blondes. With rising excitement—secretly fueled by exultation that he had come up with a plan to prevent Diana from dashing into oblivion—Luke thought of how fortunate that Salathiel was going to be around over the next few months. He could win the bet, hands down.

Diana, mindful of the way Philip had always encouraged her to express her feelings, saying it was a way of purging one's soul and remaining in contact with nature, jerked to free her hand. When Luke still held her firmly and watched her as if she might be no more than an untamed creature caught in a trap, she blurted what first came to mind. "You soun' like a lunatic!"

Chuckling and looking up at the moon before replying, Luke said, "I may be at that. It's a good night for such. Doesn't my plan sound better than jail?"

"Maybe, but how can I know you'll not keep pesterin' me 'bout why I was here?" Something kept nudging at her mind, something to do with her feeling keenly female, and she gave it voice. "What'cha got in mind doin' with me if I agree?"

"Not nearly as much as I could do to your friends here if you don't."

"How did you come up with such a crazy idea?"

Afraid Diana might be able to read his mind, Luke glanced

across the back yard. "Let's say that I like helping those who are young and beautiful and in need of help."

Diana swallowed hard. Beautiful? His last words reminded her of her father. *But nothing else does*, she told the inane part of her that was dithering over the man's compliment. *This Luke Greenwood is up to no good. Best you go along with him now to save your friends and figure out how to escape later*. "An' you promise you won't be lookin' for nobody to beat if I stay?"

Luke frowned. Did she think all owners beat their slaves? He figured it was no time to explain his stand against physical punishment, not when she seemed to be giving in. "I promise."

"How long I gotta stay?"

"Until I tell you it's time to leave."

"I'm not that dumb, Mr. Greenwood," Diana said with a newly angled chin. She despised her feeling of helplessness. Where in the devil was King when she needed him? The big dog's presence might have enabled her to escape before being captured. "If you's got plans to 'buse me or—"

"You'll have no worries on that score, Diana. My only motive is to improve your mind and manners." It bothered Luke a little that neither his mind nor his body was going along with his words as readily as he would have expected. The way the scantily clad Diana stood—with her long legs slightly apart, her shoulders thrown back and her breast thrust upward daringly as she assessed him—reminded Luke of some primitive goddess.

Goddess? Luke found himself remembering how once while in Paris, he had slipped off from his cronies to the Louvre one afternoon and become lost in admiration for the statuary. Now he almost caught his breath when the memory of Houdon's life-size, undraped bronze figure of the Greek goddess Diana with bow in left hand and arrow in right matched up with the sight of the Diana before him . . . and with the graceful feminine figure he had glimpsed the preceding night as he walked on his back veranda in a half-wakened state.

Not willing to stretch his sanity to the breaking point by

connecting any of his absurd thoughts with the fact that it was Midsummer's Eve and that he possessed the fiery passion of the average young man, Luke shook his head and raked his free hand over his face and eyes. His fingers were trembling. He was feeling flustered all over. Perhaps he should draw up a bucket of water and splash it on his face. *And*, his thoughts mocked him, *pour some down lower, as well*.

"Why would you keep me an' teach me things?" Diana asked after pondering the situation and almost forgetting to adopt the patois of the blacks. The earlier spate of gooseflesh was returning. Maybe what was creating havoc with her emotions was a combination of fear and dislike of the domineering Luke Greenwood. Did he always impose his will on others?

"I have private reasons, but I assure you I have nothing in mind that will bring you harm."

"You has to tell me 'fore I'm gonna make up my mind." Her direct gaze warned him she was taking nothing he said lightly. "An' we has to shake han's on your promise not to be lookin' for ways to bother other folks 'sides me."

Her audacity shocked Luke. How could she make such a demand when he so plainly held her captive? It seemed apparent now that Diana did, indeed, have connections with his slaves and that she placed their well-being beyond her own.

What with Luke needing to work smoothly with the blacks as their new owner and with him keeping a close watch on Diana to prevent further collusion with whoever she thought of so highly, he saw no reason not to offer her the handshake. Would she honor it? How much dared he tell her about why he wished to transform her?

"I'll confess," Luke said, "that I want to have a beautiful young woman to escort to a fancy ball in New Orleans in December, one who can speak and act the part of a genteel young lady."

New Orleans? Diana echoed mentally. She needed to get to the capital, but. . . .

Diana stared and cocked her old hat back farther on her head so as to get a better view of him. She wondered why a man as handsome as Luke Greenwood would be searching for a woman to escort anywhere. Was it because he was a kind of devil who ordered women around? If most women disliked his bullying ways as much as she was finding out she did, she figured that must be his shortcoming. The longer she stayed with him, the more she was noticing that in the moonlight, Luke had no visible imperfections of face or form.

"I never heard'a such. I ain't never been outside St. Christopher Parish, an' I ain't goin' to N'Orleans with no man."

"I'll release you and shake your hand to show my promise to forget tonight is made in good faith. We won't ever have to discuss it again. We'll make a pact . . . of friendship."

Feeling Luke's fingers lessen their pressure on her wrist, Diana assessed her situation quickly. His eyes seemed to be sending out messages inviting her trust, but she was determined not to let outward appearances gull her. Enemies could take on all kinds of forms and shapes, or so her father had always told her. She doubted she could outrun Luke and escape; she had been unable to earlier. If her dog had been along, maybe things would have gone better, but King had not shown up yet.

Anyway, Diana's thoughts ran on, where would she go? She was not about to head in the direction of the swamp and allow Luke to see where she might seek refuge. "Do you promise that we'll have us a workin' relationship an' that you won't never try to turn me over to no sheriff or be askin' nosy questions 'bout why I showed up here?"

"I give you my word as a gentleman. Let's shake hands."

As a gentleman? Diana hooted to herself. Had his earlier actions hinted that he was a gentleman? She figured she was going to be black and blue on the morrow from where he had thrown her to the ground and fallen on top of her, not to mention the cruel capture of her wrists. The term more aptly describing him, she decided, was *enemy*.

Even as Diana narrowed her eyes in thought, she felt Luke's strong fingers free her hand. Should she go on instinct, the instinct telling her she could trust him to keep his word? Or should she listen to the secretive voice that kept whispering Luke Greenwood was in league with the devil and up to no good? What about the one hinting that the reason she was feeling so unlike herself was his presence?

Not sure what to believe, Diana reflected that she did not have much choice. Whatever decision she made now would affect her future enormously and perhaps the future well-being of her dear friends at Fairfield as well. Had it been only a few days earlier when she had faced up to the fact that everything seemed to be changing too fast?

Looking down at her bare feet and thinking how the moonlight bathing them seemed to have lost its silvery benevolence, Diana sighed under her breath, then looked up at Luke Greenwood. She held out her hand. "I'se s'pectin' you's a man with no heart, Mr. Greenwood, but I can't see no way outta 'greein' to the pact. I don't see how you can call it one of frien'ship 'cause I ain't feelin' frien'ly towards you a'tall an' I ain't likely to. If nobody at Fairfiel' so much as gets questioned, you an' yo' frien' can try turnin' me into what you think a lady ought'a be. I doubts it's gonna work, though."

"I dote on challenges. I assure you my plan will work."

Then, with a huge smile dancing around his mouth and setting up new sparkles in his dark eyes, Luke took Diana's small hand in his much larger one and sealed the pact. His heart rejoiced and he chose to believe it was because now the odds were in his favor that he would win the bet with Frederick. He gave no thought to Diana's assertion that the pact was not one of friendship.

Four

"I refuse to go along with such a preposterous idea and I am mortified that you dared think I would," Salathiel exclaimed the next morning after hearing Luke's gleeful plan for turning Diana into a choice morsel to tempt Frederick. "How can you entertain such a monstrous plan for meddling in this poor unfortunate young woman's life? It is a dastardly plot."

Luke drained his coffee cup and leaned back against his chair at the head of the dining-room table. "It's not like you to have such a closed mind. You haven't even met her yet."

"Small wonder, what with your having locked her into one of the bedrooms. Had I awakened I would have insisted you set her free last night. How could you do such a vile deed?"

Salathiel did not care that his tone revealed sharp edges. He was more disgusted with Luke than he could ever remember. Damn Frederick for getting Luke riled and egging him into agreeing to such utter nonsense! Both had acted more like schoolboys than when they had been just that over a score of years ago. "Do you plan on starving her into submission?"

"I've sent Tabitha up with a key and a cup of coffee. After

she got over her obvious shock, Tabitha promised to stay with Diana while she gets dressed and then escort her down here. I got the feeling that I may have lost any ground gained with Tabitha. When I told her about how I caught Diana prowling around the well shed in the night, those sharp eyes of hers displayed more emotion than I've seen in them about anything.''

"How old is the girl?''

"She's no longer a girl. She told me yesterday was her eighteenth birthday. It's strange that she seemed to know what I was talking about when I commented that she was born on Midsummer's Eve. I reckon myths get told and retold all over the world. Maybe her parents told her about such things while they were still alive.''

Remembering the titillating feel of Diana's slender body underneath his when he threw her to the ground and then the sight of her scarcely concealed breasts and thighs, Luke ran the fingers of one hand over the bottom of his chin. He glanced out the window in the direction of the well shed, his lips pursed. "I wonder if Tabitha might not be the one Diana is protecting.''

"You said you promised the poor young woman not to inquire into her reasons for being at Fairfield.'' Salathiel sent Luke a hard look. "Perhaps you need to reexamine your code of honor.''

"I'm not going to change my mind. You may think I'm depraved for pursuing this matter, but I haven't sacrificed principles and I don't intend to.'' Smiling at his obviously irate friend and former tutor, Luke sent him a beseeching look. "Come now, Salathiel. I know how you abhor heated talk, but you're the only one getting upset. Don't turn your back on me before you even meet Diana Hathaway.''

"Diana Hathaway,'' Salathiel mused aloud after patting his mustache with his napkin and acknowledging the truth of Luke's statement about him being the only one getting upset. He disliked that his penchant for calm demeanors and exchanges had become so apparent to the younger man. Was he, perhaps, becoming a bit senile . . . at forty-five? The idea frightened him. "A fine old English name. Wonder how she came to be here in this Godforsaken place without kith or kin?"

Luke rose and fetched the coffeepot sitting on the sideboard, refilling both of their cups before replying. "She wouldn't tell me anything last night, even after I brought her inside and showed her to a guest room. All I know is that she is breathtaking—until she opens her mouth."

Before the two men had finished their second cups of coffee, Diana and Tabitha came to the doorway. Both looked as if they shared black secrets that would never see daylight, but they wore docile expressions. Salathiel barely repressed his shock upon seeing the brevity of Diana's clothing and her bare feet. His eyes kept returning to her startlingly blonde hair. Unfettered, it formed a cloud around her face and shoulders and reached down to her tiny waist.

Despite Luke's comments, Salathiel Morgan was unprepared for the sight of Diana Hathaway. Not only was she fair in face and form, she appeared the epitome of innocent young womanhood that rare canvases sometimes depicted. Within her wide-spaced blue eyes, noteworthy in their own right as objects of beauty, an innate intelligence gleamed. It occurred to Salathiel, who was seldom given to fantasy, that Diana herself was a work of art.

Smiling to himself at the noticeable impression Diana was making on the older man, Luke made introductions and pulled out a chair for her. Still inordinately pleased with himself, he then asked Tabitha to bring something for their guest to eat.

"You's kind to be askin' 'bout my folks," Diana said to Salathiel when in his tactful manner he attempted to learn about her background, "but ever since they died, I been lookin' out for myself. I ain't gonna back outta my part'a the bargain with Mr. Greenwood, even if I *was* bamboozled."

Diana lifted her chin and shot a baleful look toward Luke before she took a sip of the coffee he had served her. Her pale hair trembled in the morning light, as if giving form to her inner distress. Luke's eyes were as dark—she thought of them as being black, like a devil's—and as unreadable as she had recalled, she thought with a pang of renewed fear. "Ain't no need for you to be lockin' me in that room like I might be gonna run off. I give my word an' shook hands on it, didn't I? I ain't no liar."

"You're right," Luke answered after a noticeable pause. He had gotten lost in thinking of how Diana's beauty was as pronounced in the morning sunlight as it had been in the moonlight. The blue of her eyes was a much deeper hue than he had suspected. He had had no inkling that her eyebrows and lashes were of a rich brown. He wondered why she still looked at him with such open fear and dislike. After she agreed to his proposal, he had neither touched her again nor raised his voice. It was hard for him to imagine what went on in the mind of an illiterate, he reassured himself. Or in the mind of a woman, either.

Though at first Luke had assumed Diana was going to drink her coffee in a civilized manner, he changed his mind after she lifted the cup and poured some of the coffee into her saucer and began slurping it from the saucer with great smacking noises. Sure, he had dined with cultured people who preferred the old-fashioned manner of drinking coffee and tea from saucers, but none had made bestial, repugnant noises during the process of sipping. "Stop sounding like a greedy pig at a trough. Good table manners mark a lady. Yours are atrocious."

Diana blinked and ordered herself to slump in her chair instead of rising and slapping the arrogant sounding Luke. "I tole you I was hopeless."

"Not yet, you aren't. I'll stop locking you in your room . . . if you show good faith and cooperate with Salathiel and me."

"What would you be doing today if you had not been captured last evening, Miss Hathaway?" Salathiel asked kindly.

Salathiel reflected that Luke had been accurate. Until she opened her mouth, Diana was perfection. The part of his conscience governed by Salathiel Morgan, tutor, ached to remedy her obvious shortcomings. The segment belonging to Salathiel Morgan, gentleman, rebelled at what Luke had in mind for the lovely young woman.

Diana shrugged a shoulder and let out a noisy sigh. "Fishin', maybe. I likes bein' called Diana."

"I gather you live a life without many rules," Salathiel remarked after a moment of thought. "Does it bother you that what Luke has in mind will change everything about your obviously carefree life?"

"Bloody balls of fire! Do you think I'm crazy? Sho', it bothers me." Diana had heard the colorful exclamatory phrase from some blacks when she was very young but had used it seldom, and never within the presence of anyone else. She felt Luke's startled gaze sweeping over her face. Recalling other terms used sometimes by the blacks, she went on in a sorrowful tone. "Lawd hep my sinful soul! I ain't gotta choice but to do what Mr. Greenwood tells me or he gonna take me to the sheriff an' get me locked up."

Diana, sensing that Salathiel was sympathizing with her, sent him a pleading look. Though his accent was not exactly like her father's—she knew enough history to recognize the kinship between Bostonians and Englishmen—it was close enough to remind her of Philip and his clipped way of speaking. "I'd jes as soon be dead as be locked up. I'se run free all my life an' I ain't likely to take to no other kind of livin'. Prob'ly it'd take years to brush the ign'rance outta me, if it can be done a'tall."

Touched by the look of entreaty in her eyes, Salathiel opened his mouth to reply to Diana but thought better of it and turned to Luke. "I'll be in the library cataloguing."

Rising then, Salathiel glared at Luke, who had placed his elbows on the table and, with his chin resting on interlaced fingers, was studying the beautiful young woman as if she were a specimen in a laboratory. To Diana, who was ignoring Luke and eyeing the plate of food that Tabitha's helper, Chloe, was setting before her, Salathiel made a courteous farewell.

"You must be very hungry," Luke remarked, his role still that of wide-eyed, critical observer. Diana was stuffing huge portions of scrambled eggs into her mouth with a spoon and, with the back of her hand, slapping away particles clinging to her lips. She had already devoured a biscuit in three monstrous bites and was gripping another in her free hand. Luke leaned and picked up the napkin lying beside her plate. "If you would use your napkin, you wouldn't be making such a mess."

When Diana saw Luke's hand heading toward her, she ducked out of his reach.

"I wasn't going to strike you!" Luke's faced flushed at the thought. "I was merely going to show you how to use your napkin."

"I'll wipe my own mouth, suh."

"Start calling me Luke." He dropped her napkin on the table beside her plate and looked at her meaningfully.

Diana felt her face reddening from Luke's open disapproval. Had she overdone her attempts to appear uncouth? She swiped the linen across her mouth and sent him a haughty look before scooping up another spoonful of egg and cramming it in her mouth, remembering to chew with her mouth slightly open and make little smacking sounds. With her free hand, filthy from where she had pushed egg onto her spoon, she shoved her unbound hair back from her face.

"Don't you know how to use a fork?"

"A spoon and fingers do fine."

"A fork does better."

She tilted her head and sent him a scorching look from behind half-lowered lashes. "I can't learn everythin' all at once—an' likely not by December, neither. You might as well let me go, now that you's seen what kind' a gal I am. You ain't never gonna be pleased wit' me."

"We made a pact, remember?"

"You's 'bout the meanest man I ever seen." She purposely left a few scraps of egg sticking to her upper lip and bit into her third biscuit. "Or heard 'bout either."

"I don't care what you think of me personally." Luke picked up his coffee cup and drank, no matter that the liquid was thick and cold now. Her heated words and gaze were more upsetting than he cared to admit. He had been called a lot of things during his twenty-eight years, but *mean* was not one of them. "Use your napkin."

When Diana grabbed it as if it might be a weapon, he snatched it from her hand and dabbed at her lips lightly. "And use it for what it is, not as if it's a wash cloth. Don't take such large bites. Try eating your grits with a fork; you may use your knife in your other hand to help get the food on it until you master using a fork."

Diana glared at Luke as she threw her spoon down on her plate with a clatter. "I hate grits, an' I won't eat nothin' when you's 'round to tell me how."

"Yes, you will, and you'll eat with good manners or I'll—"

"Or you'll what?" she broke in angrily. She had been right last night. Luke *was* a bully. She wished she had the nerve to tell him exactly what she was thinking. Her soul was becoming overburdened.

"I'll make you sorry. Maybe I won't let you have anything but grits until you learn to behave."

A momentary staring contest ensued, won by neither.

"If you're going to be so childish that you won't eat unless you can do it your way, I'll stop trying to be nice."

Diana elevated her nose and gave in to her need to spout her thoughts. "When was you nice? I must'a missed it."

Luke squelched her with a cutting visit from his dark gaze. "Practice using the fork"—he leaned and lifted a portion of egg on her fork—"like this and using your napkin the way I showed you." He rammed the end of her fork in her resisting hand. God! but she was stubborn. "At noon I'll be expecting you to use both fork and napkin like a civilized young woman—or you'll be served nothing but grits."

"I won't eat 'em."

"You will," he grated, "or else I'll feed them to you." Luke had not meant for his tone to sound quite so dictatorial but when it did, he let it stand. The way Diana's eyes widened with fear, as they had when he was gripping her tightly last evening in the moonlight, tore at his conscience, but it riled him, too.

With her hand clenched into a tight fist, Diana watched

Luke stalk away from the dining table toward the central hallway. Her plan to repulse him with terrible table manners had fallen flat, she reflected with keen disappointment. While lying awake most of the night, she had come up with the idea that her only chance for freedom was to convince him that his plan for transforming her would never work.

Diana was still watching Luke with both fear and cunning when he wheeled around and commanded in what sounded to her like the voice of doom, "After you've practiced on your manners, come to the library where Salathiel and I will be."

As soon as Luke entered the library, Salathiel began his prepared speech opposing the transformation of Diana Hathaway into a cultured young woman. Luke listened, or seemed to, while standing and looking out the upper, glassed-in portion of the closed French doors facing Selene Bayou. A part of him was drawn by the tranquil sights out front and he swung the tall doors open.

Hoping the fresh air and the clearer view might soothe his jangled nerves, Luke noted how the gray moss dripped from the huge trees, each tapering mass looking to him as if it were the frizzled hair from an old, unkempt woman. A pair of green-headed hummingbirds flitted among some lush vines hugging the trunk of a nearby oak. A closer look showed him that small orange flowers shaped like miniature trumpets served as targets for the needlelike bills of the tiny birds.

When the Englishman ended his spirited oration, Luke asked over his shoulder, "Do you suppose you should begin with the alphabet?"

"Were you not listening?" Salathiel demanded, hurrying to stand beside Luke. He rammed his hands down in the pockets of his broadcloth coat, the black one he always wore in the daytime, no matter the temperature. "I am not, I repeat *not*, going to go along with this farce. You set that lovely young woman free or I'm leaving here today."

"Where will you go?"

Salathiel sputtered for a moment, then lifted a hand to the tall ceiling and made a fist. "Anywhere but here!" Realizing what he had done, he returned his hand to his pocket and attempted a more normal tone. "I cannot assist you in stirring up another person's life for no good reason. It borders on being a sin, my boy. If I am no longer around, you will have no choice but to set her free. You are no tutor."

"You might be surprised." Noticing the pink staining Salathiel's face, Luke added, "You're breaking your rule about becoming upset. Go ahead and let it out. Sometimes a good yelling at the top of your voice can work wonders for clearing the air, not to mention how satisfied you can feel after getting something off your chest and realizing it wasn't nearly as burdensome as you had thought."

Salathiel swallowed with a gulp so loud that it shocked him. "It is my theory—and that of my former professors at Oxford—that only animals and the untutored allow their feelings to reign. Refined, educated people handle their emotions with restraint."

"I believe you're the one searching for restraint right now." Luke sent him an affectionate, teasing smile.

Harrumphing and vowing silently not to respond again to Luke's apparent needling, Salathiel returned to his topic. "It is plain that Diana does not like you, Luke, and with just cause. She would not cooperate with you if you were to attempt teaching her, not that I blame her. You have shown the tact of an elephant in forcing her to stay here even one night against her will."

When Luke made no reply, showed no sign of remorse, Salathiel continued. "She brought your watch back. What possible charges could you file against her if you took her to the sheriff? I am mortified that you have frightened one so lovely and innocent. After I learned of your generous support of that orphanage in New Orleans, I hoped you were letting some of your better qualities guide you now. Obviously I was wrong. I am quite disappointed in you."

Turning from the window, Luke went behind the desk across the room and sat down. After leaning back in the chair and propping his feet on the mahogany surface of the desk, he said, "You've disappointed me in that you're going back on your word to help me refurbish the house and stock the library. I thought I had offered you a goodly sum for your expertise. I was planning on paying you considerably more money to take on the tutoring of Diana.''

"You know that recompense does not count that heavily with me. It is the moral issue, a truth I have been trying to point out for the past several moments. As for my promise to stay on for the summer and assist you, I meant it, was even looking forward to it.''

Luke pursed his lips and tried to look contemplative. "You can always go down the road to Wingate and accept the position Mrs. Winston offered you. She's a young and pretty widow, and her four daughters seemed bright and—''

"Do not be absurd. I have no interest in taking that position. I prefer staying here at Fairfield awhile, but you are making that nigh impossible. You can forget our earlier plans until you admit you are wrong to impose your will over that of an innocent young woman. Can it be that you are not the young man of good conscience that I remember?''

As if Salathiel's words had washed over him as gently and pleasantly as the morning breeze that was straying inside the open French doors, Luke said, "Simmer down, will you? I can tutor her myself. It won't be cane-planting time until this fall, and I'll not be terribly involved with plantation matters until then. Jed has already agreed to serve as overseer. I'll have the time.'' Pretending he did not notice Salathiel's expression growing more horrified at each word, he added, "Actually I might find the task enjoyable.''

Salathiel sputtered, sawing the air with one hand. "Why, the poor girl is scared to death of you. You know nothing about teaching. You cannot possibly be serious!''

Luke fixed the older man with an unfathomable look. "I've never been more serious in my life. Diana Hathaway is going to the Charity Ball with me in December and she's going to be the most charming, cultured woman there—even if I have to teach her everything myself.''

A knock on the door intruded then, and when Luke called out, Diana entered the library. She looked from Salathiel to Luke, then back again. Whatever had been causing the raised voices she had heard from the hallway had something to do with her, she was almost certain of it. She had done her best to eavesdrop but the thickness of the door and walls had thwarted her. With as much spunk as she could muster in the presence of the two men, she said, "I done practiced usin' a fork, Mr. Greenwood. What'cha want me to do now?"

Luke had risen when Diana entered and now stood with his arms folded across his chest. In an uncharacteristically gruff voice, he ordered, "Don't call me that again. You may have many undesirable traits, but I didn't take you for a numbskull. I told you to call me Luke. Come have a seat so we can talk about where we need to start your lessons. I suppose it would be too much to expect you to know the alphabet."

Salathiel sucked in a deep breath and shot Luke a murderous look before turning to Diana and tendering a smile. "Please forgive him, Diana. He knows nothing about the rudiments of teaching and at the moment he seems to have forgotten his manners. Perhaps it would be wise for the two of us to become better acquainted before we begin trying to muddle through this matter of teaching you to read and write and speak properly. Would you like that?"

During Salathiel's overture to Diana, Luke became interested in checking the condition of his fingernails so that he could fight down the smile of victory threatening to surface. He had counted on his forced gruffness and pretended indifference to bring the tenderhearted Salathiel around.

When Diana made no reply, Luke, in a tone suggesting that he did not care one way or the other, remarked, "That sounds like a workable idea, Salathiel. I'll leave the two of you alone until time for the noon meal." He half turned at the doorway and said over his shoulder, "I hope you'll be able to come up with something to cover up her nakedness."

Sidestepping so as to remain a goodly distance away from Luke as he strode out the door in what she deemed an arrogant manner, Diana eyed the Englishman. Was he as gentlemanly as she had suspected from their first meeting? If so, why was he in the company of one as irascible as Luke Greenwood?

"Why's he so dratted mulish?" Diana asked after Salathiel pulled out a chair for her beside the desk and took a seat on one next to it. "He 'minds me of a cantankerous billy goat I once knew."

Stifling a smile, Salathiel harrumphed and looked down at his hands where they rested on the arms of the chair. "We have not begun lessons yet, but I must point out mistakes when they appear. *Dratted* is a euphemism for *damned*; young ladies do not use such expressions. Neither do they compare humans to animals."

Diana giggled under her breath as Salathiel went on to explain in detail about such breaches of good manners and proper speech, an explanation that she had never heard before, since Philip had not been concerned with the finer details of etiquette. She sent the older man an appraising look. Even Philip could not have reprimanded her more gently or effectively.

Then Diana and Salathiel began to get acquainted. Leaning toward him and gesturing with her pretty hands at times, she told her version of what had happened on the evening before, sometimes almost forgetting to talk in an unlearned manner. She liked the way he pursed his lips and toyed with his mustache, as if he were giving comprehensive thought to her story.

When it came Salathiel's turn to reply, he made a few excuses for Luke's bizarre behavior but never revealed what he believed spurred him on—not only the stupid bet with Frederick but also his general distrust of beautiful young women. A few adroit questions from Salathiel and Diana was telling about her goat and her dog and how she worried that they were waiting for her. Privately, she had fretted that Minerva needed milking. She was quick to hint that she lived down Bayou Selene on one of its small tributaries. By the time Tabitha came to announce it was time for the noon meal, the two were talking like friends.

"Do not fret over your dog or your goat," Salathiel said to Diana when they reached the double doors leading into the dining room. Both saw Luke enter the front door and start down the wide foyer stretching straight from front to back veranda. "If King does not come looking for you by dark, we will ask Salem or somebody to go with you down the bayou where you say your home is and find him. As for Minerva, it should be simple to have someone fetch her. With her kid due soon, I can see why you are concerned."

Luke reached them then and they went into the dining room together. Diana sneaked a glance at Luke, figuring he had overheard Salathiel.

"I been wonderin' where that ole nanny goat come from what showed up at the well shed this mornin'," Tabitha said from where she had paused in the doorway. She addressed no one in particular but sent a sidewise glance toward Diana. "It must' a done picked up Miss Diana's smell an' come lookin' for her."

"Oh, my, I'se happy to hear Minerva's not lost," Diana said, her eyes round and fixed on the smiling black woman. "I'se been worried about her. Did anyone milk her?"

"Chloe an' I tried, but we didn't get much milk," Tabitha replied. "She commenced to grazin' out back so we jes let 'er be."

"Have you seen a big tan dog?" Diana asked.

"What do you have following you around, a zoo?" Luke asked, following the exchange between the two women with a puzzled look on his lean features. A goat? What in tarnation was Diana doing with a goat? "I never did like goats."

"Ain't seen hide nor hair of no dog," Tabitha said before she left to fetch the soup that she assured them was going to be scrumptious.

Salathiel steered the conversation to safe channels until Tabitha and Chloe served the soup.

"This is intolerable!" Luke roared after the third noisy slurp from Diana. She quickly dabbed at her mouth with her napkin as he had shown her and turned to him with a wounded air. "Sip the soup from the side of your spoon."

When both Diana and Salathiel glared at him, Luke countered by softening his voice and demonstrating how she should eat her soup. That she never quite managed to sip without a crude, sucking sound annoyed him. He chose not to pursue the matter.

If he had not known better, Luke reflected once when he

glanced at Diana and found her sneaking a look at him while taking soup into her mouth with an unladylike noise, he would have suspected she was making a nuisance of herself on purpose. There was something about the expression in her eyes, something mischievous. . . .

Luke discarded the notion as ridiculous and began telling about his morning. "While riding beside the bayou to get to one of the back fields, Jed and I ran into Julius Waskom from Fernwood, the plantation north of us. Waskom is the former sea captain who married Maynard Oates's mother last year."

"I hope he was courteous," Salathiel said. "Is that foolish young man living back at Fernwood? When you introduced him to me in New Orleans, I got the impression that behind the facade of Southern amiability, Maynard is sly, not a man to be trusted. Something about the set of his eyes, you know."

Luke smiled at Salathiel's way of sizing up people upon first meeting them and, as often as not, being correct. "Maynard came home right after he lost Fairfield to me, just as I heard in New Orleans. Julius was cool but not downright antagonistic. He made disparaging remarks about poker games with high stakes, but he never out-and-out accused me of cheating his stepson out of his inheritance."

When Salathiel appeared troubled and Diana stopped eating to listen, Luke added with a note of acceptance, "Julius said he and his family will come calling on us. I asked him to give us some time to get the place in order. I doubt there'll be further mention about the possibility that I cheated Maynard. We had some pretty straight talk, with Jed and Captain Waskom's own man as witnesses."

"Forgive our personal exchanges, Diana," Salathiel said before returning to the discussion with Luke. "What an abomination! Maynard Oates should have had better sense than to get in a poker game with stakes beyond his means. And Julius Waskom should think twice before making any kind of slurring reference to an incident about which he knows nothing, especially when it involves his stepson. Not that I approve of gambling as more than a means of amusing oneself, still I dislike anyone insinuating that you might stoop to cheating."

Puzzled over the obvious closeness of the men, Diana sat between them at the long dining table and watched as their exchange continued. Though it made no sense, not when she had learned that morning from Salathiel that the two were not kin, she got the impression that the relationship bordered on that of father and son. How could the kindly, gentlemanly Englishman put up with the arrogant, domineering Luke Greenwood?

"Diana and I had a productive morning also," Salathiel remarked when Luke's story of the events of his morning ended. He sent her a gentle smile. "I have learned that Diana might as well be freed to return to her home. Since she has had no teaching at all, there is no possibility of having her pose as an educated young woman by December. That is scarcely six months away."

Diana shot Luke a smug look, but when he frowned and stared back at her, she diverted her attention to her empty soup bowl. Each time he studied her so intently, she experienced uncanny sensations. What else could they be but signs of fear?

"You don't even know the alphabet?" Luke thundered as he glared at Diana. All morning he had imagined several kinds of delightful surprises that Salathiel might be able to pry from Diana, such as that she could read no higher than on an elementary level but could actually read. He did not bother asking himself why the news was hateful to his ears. He had had such high hopes. . . . "Weren't your parents educated?"

Recognizing that Salathiel had helped her stifle her initial fear of Luke but that now the black-haired man had brought it back with piercing looks and two rude questions, Diana replied in a quavering but defiant voice, "No. My folks never had no learnin'. I speck I ain't gonna be able to learn a'tall."

"You will stay here and you will learn," Luke said with steel underlying each word, "even if I have to spend every day making sure of it."

Bang! Crash! came from the back veranda, followed almost immediately by feminine wails.

"Lawd hep my sinful soul!" Chloe exclaimed, her words

carrying clearly through the open doors and windows. "I done dropped the whole tray full'a blackberry cobbler." She began wailing again.

"What the devil is going on?" Luke demanded after he hurried to the door to see if the black woman was injured. Behind him came Diana and Salathiel.

"Stay 'way from her!" Diana yelled when Luke took a step toward the distraught slave. With her eyes blazing blue fire, she threw herself against Luke's chest, beating against it with her fists. "Don't you dare bully her!"

"What is this," Luke asked as he grabbed Diana's arms and held them down by her sides, "a crazy house? I'm merely trying to find out if the woman is hurt. You've been here less than twenty-four hours and you're turning the place into bedlam."

Tears of frustration formed in Diana's eyes. Drat the tall raven-haired man staring down at her! Why did he have to come to Fairfield and throw everything into turmoil? It smarted to admit that she should have already made herself go to New Orleans, use the key to her father's deposit box, and make some kind of decision about her future.

Diana suspected that she knew what had caused Chloe to become unnaturally clumsy, and she suffered a twinge of guilt for having told such whopping lies about her parents and herself and forgetting that she could be overheard on the veranda. How else, though, could she protect her black friends from the wrath of the fiery-eyed devil, Luke Greenwood?

Five

The next day at dawn, Diana paused at the head of the staircase that ran straight against the foyer wall. Eyeing the outside banister with its highly polished handrail, she let a pleasurable childhood memory surface. Dared she give in to impulse?

Smiling mischievously at the thought of what the sober-faced Luke Greenwood might say or do if he were to catch her in the act, Diana hopped up on the handrailing. She gave one last cautious look around in the dim light, then balanced her dainty rump and went sliding down the smooth railing.

Within seconds, Diana, her heart lifted from her act of defiance, was rushing barefooted across the dew-dampened grass toward the barnyard. Tabitha had told her last night that she could find Minerva there. She had also passed along other good news: King had shown up before dark. Not to be stayed by anyone, or so Tabitha reported, the dog had dashed toward Alligator Swamp, apparently in search of its mistress.

Diana was hoping to see King this morning, but he was nowhere around. She recalled Luke stating he disliked goats, but he had given no hint of his feelings about dogs. Her mouth drawn up in disapproval, she wondered if maybe Luke was the kind of man who did not care for domesticated animals. What if he refused to let either of her pets remain at Fairfield?

Though Luke had been noticeably absent from dinner last night, Diana reflected as she detoured by the empty kitchen and picked up a small tin pitcher, she had not mentioned his name. Neither had Salathiel. Both had been so involved, as they had nearly all afternoon, with the alphabet and the soundings of syllables that Diana had been relieved not to have to share the meal with the one she thought of as her tormentor.

"Minerva, you're a darling," Diana called lowly when the goat bleated and rushed over to the fence where her mistress stood. "I missed seeing you yesterday. I couldn't get away."

Within moments the nimble, scantily clad Diana had climbed over the board fence and was on her knees embracing her softly bleating pet. A joyful bark sounded then and Diana turned to welcome King, a King looking properly soulful when she hugged him, then looking apologetic when she scolded him for being gone so long. In between dramatic looks, whines, and tail wags, the big dog licked her face and hands and seemed to revel in the loving pats and words Diana gave him.

It took Diana only moments to strip the small amount of milk from the nanny's dark teats. She patted the goat's engorged belly and laid her ear against the silky fur, all the while murmuring to Minerva, "You're going to be a mama again right away." Recalling another Hathaway nanny of several years back that had died during a difficult birthing, she leaned and planted a kiss between the bright eyes of her pet. "I'll be here to help you, like always. 'Bye for now."

"What on earth are you doing?" a deep voice demanded from behind Diana. "Talking to a goat?"

"Are you spyin' on me?" Diana countered when she wheeled around and faced Luke Greenwood. Had her words to Minerva been low enough to keep him from hearing the pattern of her speech? The fact that the big dog dashed over to lick at the tall man's hands without having uttered a sound to announce a stranger's approach rang in Diana's mind like a distant, warning bell—but warning of what?

"I hardly look upon anything I do on my own plantation as spying," Luke replied with a lazy smile. "I expect you would feel the same way." Did Diana have any idea of the charming picture she presented in the first rays of sunshine as she held the small, gracefully shaped pitcher close to her body and looked up at him? A host of sassy birds in the nearby trees must know, Luke decided irrationally, for even as he stood there, their songs seemed to take on happier, lovelier notes.

While Diana combed her fingers through her flyaway hair and appeared to be searching for something to say, Luke's thoughts about her took over his mind, much as the morning sunshine was taking over his fecund patch of the world in southern Louisiana. He watched infinitesimal fragments of soft, pink light play in Diana's whitish hair and lend the long mass of waves and curls a delicate rosy hue. Her eyes appeared bluer and brighter than the western sky serving as a backdrop, for the rays from the sun rising behind Luke were young and had yet to bathe the horizon.

The sight of the brief top and skirt on Diana's slender body left so little to Luke's lively imagination that he doubted she would look more enticing completely naked, especially when the exposed midriff and thighs revealed the smooth feminine firmness of her pale flesh as readily as they did. Too well he remembered how silky her skin had felt two nights ago when he captured her.

Luke's thoughts raced onward while he and Diana stared at each other. What a tiny waist she had above her slender but flaring hips! Her pretty little bare feet and her legs, so long and perfectly contoured in outward curves at the calves, so delicately tapered at the ankles, kept capturing his admiring gaze. If the mesmerizing sight of Diana in moonlight had scorched his senses, Luke realized with a shock, the glorious sight of Diana in the light of a pink dawn was blistering them anew.

"I reckon you be right. I'd not figure I was spyin' if I owned Fairfiel'," Diana replied after a long spell of searching for words to reply to the one watching her with black-eyed intensity. Gooseflesh prickled at the base of her skull, then marched down her spine.

She noted that Luke wore no cravat or waistcoat, only a white shirt and nankeen trousers. Held tightly in place on his long legs by straps looping underneath his low-cut shoes, the yellowish brown trousers clung to his lean hips. She marked how smoothly the fabric stretched over his heavily muscled thighs and calves, manly calves that tapered abruptly before becoming ankles encased in creamy silk stockings. Was Luke Greenwood the kind of man her father had referred to once with admiration as a fine figure of a man?

Taking advantage of Luke's preoccupation with her dog, Diana continued her perusal of her captor. Through the deep V of his white shirt, which appeared to be buttoned only in its lower section, she could see clusters of black curls on his broad chest. Then she was looking at the hollow at the base of his throat, which somehow seemed to mark him as more human, even vulnerable. A dark shadow on Luke's high-cheeked face told her he had not yet shaved. His hair seemed a casually controlled mass of silky black, its loose waves apparently having been brushed back from his face and across the top of his curly side whiskers and ears before ending at the base of his head in a somewhat ragged style.

What, Diana wondered when she realized Luke was watching her again, made his dark eyes dance? A hint of a smile hovered around his mouth. Tiny crescent-shaped lines near its corners indicated that his lips often tipped upward like that.

"I see your dog found you." Luke's fingers ruffled King's thickly furred neck, then lingered around the floppy ears of the plainly adoring animal. "I've always liked a dog big enough to touch without having to stoop all the way down. You know," Luke confided as he darted Diana an almost shy look and a true, open-mouthed smile, complete with a flash of even, white teeth, "I can't remember how long it's been since I've petted a dog. Your King is a fine specimen."

Diana could not figure out what seemed different about the handsome man right now, but she found herself tempted to step closer. She wanted to tell him all about King and how when her father had brought him to her five years ago, he was no more than a golden ball of fur with a wet black nose and pink tongue.

She squelched the notion. The less she told about her life and herself, the less Luke could use against her if he found out she was a squatter in his section of Gator Swamp. For a moment there, she had forgotten that Luke Greenwood might have more than a speaking acquaintance with the devil. She blinked. The man was her enemy.

"I'm gonna go wash up at the well shed an' take this spot of goat's milk to the kitchen," Diana announced over her shoulder as she circled around where Luke was kneeling on the grass, stroking King's back and talking in a low, kind voice. Why had he never used that tone with her?

Diana chided herself for feeling hurt when King stayed behind with Luke. Likely the bossy man was restraining him.

When Diana reached the house, Salathiel greeted her at the foot of the stairs. "In your room you'll find some clothing that Luke brought last evening. It may not fit properly, but perhaps it will suffice until the seamstress that Luke arranged for arrives."

Diana could not hide her surprise. "Where'bouts did he find clothin' for me?"

"He went into Calion yesterday afternoon after stopping for a visit with Mrs. Winston at Wingate. He concocted some tale about my niece having arrived from Mobile without her trunk and she offered some gowns she was no longer wearing. Then in Calion he purchased some, er, various other items Mrs. Winston was kind enough to list for him on paper."

Salathiel took a step toward the back veranda, then turned again to the visibly stunned Diana. "My dear, there is one more thing. Luke bought a small dinner bell so that Tabitha will be able to ring it ten minutes before she is ready to serve our meals. He likes people being on time. It is likely there was one here originally and Maynard Oates sold it along with almost all of the other movables of value."

After Salathiel left her with the assurance that he would

see her soon at the breakfast table, Diana's mind reeled. Luke Greenwood was wasting no time in taking over every aspect of her life! Her dog, too. Too well she recalled his adamant declaration yesterday that she would remain at Fairfield and that she would learn, even if he had to work with her every day. Stars above! How important could it be to have a new woman on his arm at some party in New Orleans?

Whatever kind of insanity had led her to think Luke might not be as cold and calculating as she had first believed no longer claimed one iota of space in Diana's alerted brain. During the past few years she had heard the saying that one could successfully fight fire with fire. Could one also fight ice with ice?

"You look charming, absolutely charming, my dear," Salathiel said when Diana came down for breakfast.

Diana murmured, "Thank you," then slid Salathiel a look laced with gratitude for his kind words and with guilt for having slid down the handrailing earlier that morning. She realized that though she might have enjoyed annoying Luke with her coltish actions, she would not have liked finding censure on the face of the older man.

Salathiel's dark eyes warmed as they raced over Diana's slender form in a morning gown of blue chintz with barely scooped neckline and puffed sleeves. The fit had much to be desired, but the effect was pleasing. "Don't you agree that Diana looks charming this morning, Luke?"

From where he stood near the sideboard pouring coffee, Luke replied, "At least she gives a more reasonable *appearance* of a cultured young lady." Something within moaned that no longer could he see the pure lines of her graceful body. When his gaze wandered down from Diana's chastely covered breasts and midriff to the full skirt concealing her slender hips and legs, the secret voice of disapproval pointed out another loss—the sight of her dainty bare feet.

"Well," Diana said with a toss of her hair, still unbound but brushed into a tamed state, "I ain't no cultured young lady an' I ain't figurin' I'll ever be one." She had found several lengths of satin ribbon in the packages but had ignored them.

While sending a testing look toward Luke, Diana tried wriggling her toes in the confining slippers, dismayed upon learning that there was scant room to do so. Only during the few truly cold weeks in winter had she ever put on her single pair of shoes. Even then she despised wearing them.

The unlearned sound of Diana's thick words gouged at Luke's perfect mental image of the properly dressed young woman standing before him. He was a man who had never expected things to happen overnight, still. . . . With undisguised impatience, he retorted, "Yes, you *will* become a well-mannered young lady. Open your mouth when you speak, Diana. Let the words form before we have to listen to them."

"How can you tell me how I gotta sound?" Diana shot back. The soles of her feet were burning inside her new shoes and she thought of how much she would like to yank them off and throw them at her captor. Did he have to look so smug? "I figured you was int'rested only in what I says."

"Now you know I'm not, so I'll expect Salathiel to begin work on proper enunciation right away." He poured her a cup of coffee and offered it to her with a mocking little bow. "Try not to swill your coffee this morning."

"You drawl yo'self." Diana took the coffee and poured some into the saucer. Then, her gaze fixed on his stern face the whole time, she slurped it greedily.

"True, but I don't swallow my words and forget to put endings on them." There was little doubt left in Luke's mind now that sometimes—if not at all times—Diana deliberately made a mess of eating and drinking just to spite him. He decided to ignore her horrid manners. "You'll be much prouder of yourself when you begin sounding like a cultured young woman."

When Diana and Luke continued to glare at each other, Salathiel stepped in quickly and explained to her how a gentleman escorts a lady to the table and helps seat her. Then he settled her on her chair as if she were royalty. Diana sent the Englishman a grateful smile after he sat at the end of the long table opposite Luke. Sitting down relieved the pinch of her shoes and she almost let out a sigh of relief.

Only because Luke chose to overlook Diana's table manners did the three manage to have the most pleasant meal they had shared, though it had much to be desired. Diana tried every trick she knew to upset Luke. She finally disgusted herself when she decided to douse a biscuit with honey and eat it with her hands. No matter how much she smacked or how often she wiped her sticky fingers on the tablecloth, Luke remained as imperturbable as Salathiel.

Never before had Diana been one to employ the word *drat* frequently, either aloud or silently, but now she found herself saying it over and over to herself as she struggled with the god-awful mess of biscuit and dripping honey. Drat! What kind of predicament had Luke pushed her into? she fretted, conveniently blind to her own part in the matter.

Diana's fingers became stuck together and she licked them noisily, miserable when she could not clean off enough of the thick liquid to keep her fingers separated. She sensed that while Salathiel sympathized with her plight, Luke was gaining a kind of perverse pleasure from her misery.

Drat Luke!

"I don't want to hear any more arguments about letting Diana go," Luke said to Salathiel a few nights later as Diana entered the darkened hallway on bare feet. "I'm willing to bet there's deliberate deception on her part, the bit about not being able to learn as well as acting like a dimwit at the table. If you look into her eyes, you'll see more than average intelligence there. Diana Hathaway is no numbskull."

Diana, her torturous new shoes in her hand, was on her way to her bedroom after having checked on Minerva. When she realized the two men were in the living room and heard her name mentioned, she had paused.

Diana thought of the time when she had overheard Philip and Uncle Owen conversing—from almost the same spot, she realized. Later she had asked her father about something she had overheard and Philip had reprimanded her for eavesdropping, explaining that it was unacceptable behavior. He had also pointed out that oftentimes eavesdroppers overhear things hurtful to them.

Nevertheless, Diana stayed in the darkened hallway and listened to Luke and Salathiel. Since they were clearly discussing her, she figured she had more to gain than to lose by listening. What could Luke say to make her life more miserable than it was?

"I have no reason to be suspicious of Diana, and I have given up petitioning you again for her release," Salathiel said. "I am reporting her remarkable progress in mastering the alphabet and reading simple words. I am still opposed to your meddling in her life. However, since you seem determined to follow through with this, I intend to do all I can to make Diana's life more pleasant. She does not laugh enough, Luke."

"Doesn't laugh enough, you say?" Luke parroted, a note of amusement in his voice.

From the shadowed hallway Diana rolled her eyes and silently mimicked her jailer. Drat the man!

"You might not have given it much thought, but I have spent most of my life working with young people. They normally laugh a great deal and enjoy just being alive and looking forward to what life offers. Diana's eyes reflect an inner sadness. She refuses to talk about her past or her future. There is something wrong about this entire business. I cannot believe you do not sense it, too."

"What's wrong is Diana's stubbornness and refusal to adjust to a new situation."

Out in the shadows, Diana noted an increased smell of cigar smoke and figured Luke must be pausing to puff on one before continuing.

Then Luke's deep voice started up again. "I have already sent papers to my attorney in New Orleans settling a sum on her after the first of the year if she completes satisfactorily her part of our bargain. I am only trying to make her achieve what she's obviously capable of achieving."

"I could repeat my earlier observations on that distasteful

subject, but I choose to direct my attention to the actualities. For one, you have been a monster during meals.''

Luke laughed lowly. ''Diana is the monster with her abominable manners. If you ask me, she does a lot of those disgusting things with food and drink just to spite me. Sometimes I'm tempted to turn her over my knees and give her a spanking.''

Out in the hallway Diana made a face and stuck out her tongue. He wouldn't dare lay a hand on her! He might suspect she was hoodwinking, but he couldn't prove it.

''I would never believe Diana has a devious nature. The poor girl simply does not know better. You should exhibit far more kindness and tolerance.''

Feeling like a culprit, Diana swallowed the lump of guilt rising in her throat. Salathiel was truly her friend and she was repaying him with trickery.

Luke's voice took on a different tone then, one that his unseen listener could not interpret. ''I have no wish to intimidate Diana. There's something about her that confuses me, makes me angry and frustrated, all at the same time. It's as if she's deliberately hiding the real Diana and secretly laughing at me over her success.''

Diana blinked twice. What was making him suspicious?

''Do you think you'll ever discover what there is about her that intrigues you if you continue to attack her verbally each time she makes a mistake?'' Salathiel asked.

''I never said she intrigues me!''

Sounds of footsteps on the wood floor in the living room sent Diana scurrying to the staircase, but not before she heard Luke say in that earlier, thoughtful tone, ''You know me too well, Salathiel, to think I have anything in mind for Diana that can bring her harm.''

''Yes, I do know you that well. I know you are a gentleman with a heart and a conscience,'' the Englishman replied before Diana was out of earshot. ''I think that is why I find your blind tenacity in this matter incomprehensible.'' After a moment of silence, he added, ''How about our dropping the subject? I know you find dominoes a way of relaxing, but if you will indulge me, I prefer chess this evening.''

Even after Diana crept inside the mosquito netting hanging from the tester over her bed, she pondered what she had overheard. She put much store in her belief that Salathiel Morgan was a man to be trusted. His assertion that Luke was a man of heart and conscience must contain some truth. After all, he had known Luke almost all of his life.

Still, Diana's thoughts skipped on in harmony with the song of a tree frog outside her window, the handsome black-haired man had never displayed such sterling qualities toward her. She sniffed with indignation. Toward her dog, maybe, but not toward her. Luke had roughed her up and bullied her into becoming his prisoner, hadn't he? In her point of view, the reason he had given for keeping her there suggested that he was vain, arrogant, and heartless.

"I am delighted that you are doing so much studying on your own," Salathiel told Diana soon after her first week at Fairfield. They had just finished the morning's reading and he was feeling pleased with both his pupil and himself. Her progress was remarkable, as he had told Luke the preceding afternoon. "I gather Minerva is enjoying your trying out your first readers and improved diction on her."

"Yes," Diana answered quickly. She felt guilty enough for having deceived the kindly Englishman from the start about her level of literacy without prolonging the farce. "I find my goat an' my dog make good companions on my afternoon walks in the back pasture. They's like family."

"How is Minerva these days?" He chose not to correct her.

"Gettin'—getting slower." Diana sighed. "I know she's old to be having a kid, but I'm hoping they'll both make it."

Diana's devotion to both her dog and goat touched Salathiel. Sometimes he sat on the back veranda in the late afternoons and watched her romp with King while Minerva looked on, chewing her cud with little enthusiasm.

It was Salathiel's guess, though he had not shared it with Luke, who was home less and less in the evenings as he made friends among the businessmen in Calion, that Diana was at heart a lonely young woman. She was radiantly alive at times, but at others she seemed removed from reality. Sometimes in the afternoons while he sipped his brandy and watched Diana at play with her pets, Salathiel saw her gaze with apparent sadness toward the forest and the distant freshwater swamp. He confessed that she already had won a permanent niche in his affections.

Sometimes Salathiel could barely suppress his curiosity about how Diana came to be living alone in an evidently out-of-the-way shack near Selene Bayou. At other times he questioned the sanity of the young swains around the countryside for not having swarmed Diana's home and stolen her away for a wife. A big part of the Englishman suspected that Diana would have been better off if such a fate had claimed her before Luke Greenwood set eyes on her. The questionable wisdom of what both Luke and he were doing to the innocent young woman troubled him more each day.

"We are to have guests this week," Salathiel told Diana late on a Monday afternoon. At her startled look, he added with compassion, "Please do not become upset, my dear. Mrs. Lallage Winston, the gracious widow from Wingate who kindly sent you the gowns, and her four young daughters will be coming for tea on Wednesday afternoon. I believe you will like her. She seems a vivacious woman with admirable tact and genteel manners. I am quite sure that if you commit some social error, she will understand as easily as . . . as I do."

Salathiel had almost added Luke's name, then realized he would be speaking a falsehood. Luke still balked at accepting Diana for what she apparently was. He was glad that Luke had told him that morning that he would be staying in Calion for dinner with a banker. There were letters he needed to write.

That evening when Diana retired to her bedroom earlier than usual and left Salathiel to his letter writing, he watched her climb the stairs with her candle in her hand. She had seemed so preoccupied during dinner that he had almost asked her what was troubling her. Figuring her thoughts dwelled on the pregnant Minerva, he had avoided any talk of a serious nature. He had counted it ample reward when her laughter spilled out into the large dining room during and after his rambling anecdotes about his early years as a student in England.

"Wake up, Miss Diana," Tabitha whispered late that night. When Diana's eyes popped open, the black woman leaned closer and added, "Two darkies done come from Fernwood to get you to come see 'bout Florina. She done got cut up bad. They said nobody over there knows how to sew up the way you does."

Diana lifted the mosquito netting and stepped down from her bed. Reaching inside the armoire for her homespun outfit, she whispered, "What about my satchel holding my supplies?"

"Salem done fetched it from yo' house."

Within a short time the two had crept down the staircase and met up with Salem and the two slaves from the plantation bordering Fairfield on the north. Diana remembered both Second and Tobe from previous visits and wasted no time before hurrying with them up the road beside Bayou Selene. King, a blur in the darkness, bounded along on the three-mile trip.

"What'cha gonna have to do to me, Miss Diana?" Florina asked after Diana and her escorts reached Fernwood's slave quarters and she had examined the young woman's cut face and neck.

"Now that I've cleaned the cuts," Diana said soothingly, "I'll rub some herbal ointment on them. Then I'll have to stitch up the deepest places." She accepted the clean cloth that Florina's mother, Annie, handed her, then pressed lightly on the bleeding wound curving down one side of the smooth black cheek. She had already tied a cloth over the cut on the young woman's neck and was pleased to note that the bleeding appeared to have slowed. Florina could have been killed. "Who did this?"

Florina wept, turning her head from side to side on her pillow. "He say he gonna kill me nex' time if I tells anybody. He's the meanes' man in the world."

Diana started. She had called Luke Greenwood the meanest

man in the world, but she knew with certainty that he would never stoop to such cruelty. "Whoever he is, he should be punished."

Not until Diana leaned closer did Florina hush crying enough to whisper, "Mr. Maynard Oates done it."

Diana frowned. Who in St. Christopher Parish could or would punish a white man for mistreating his slave? No wonder Florina was upset. "I'm sorry. I believe God won't let him go unpunished."

Forina went on, half sobbing under her breath. "He been makin' me meet him down by the swamp ever since he come back from N'Orleans. I don't like couplin' with no white man. Tonight I tole him I was wantin' to get married to Second an' he went crazy-like an' knifed me up. What I gonna do?"

"Right now you're going to lie back and let me put some of this numbing salve on your cuts. Then I can sew up the places where they'll heal neatly and quickly."

"I'se gonna be ugly, ain't I?"

"Shh-h," Diana whispered, already at work smoothing on the salve with steady, sure movements of her fingers, movements learned from her mother. "You'll never be ugly, Florina. My father always told me that nobody can be ugly unless he lets himself become ugly inside."

Soon Florina was succumbing to the magic of Diana's soft voice and comforting words as well as to the numbing effect of the salve. With her needle of black silk thread flashing silver in the light of the candle, Diana pursued the task before her, pleased that her patient seemed barely aware of what was taking place.

Throughout her ministrations Diana talked softly of beautiful thoughts, some of them learned from those times when she had lain against her mother in the porch swing and listened to Drusila lulling her little girl into peaceful sleep. Florina was a beautiful young woman, known for her cheerful willingness to help others. As she heard herself crooning one of Drusila's favorite sayings, Diana thought of the evil creating Florina's pain and wondered just how much truth lay in her mother's words: "Goodness begets goodness."

"You's gotta be kin to the Silver Hoodoo Woman, even if you ain't her," Annie told Diana when she gave her a jar of salve and instructions about how to apply it to Florina's wounds. "You's come over an' helped lotsa us slaves, but I ain't never see'd no magic like you worked on my pore little gal tonight. The Lawd gonna bless you, Miss Diana."

"Annie," Diana said while watching the sleeping Florina, "I've never known what the Silver Hoodoo Woman is supposed to be, but from what I've heard through the years, I gather she must have done much good in the world." Diana returned her supplies to her satchel as she continued. "I claim no magical powers and neither did my mother. If I've been able to help others, it's because of her teachings and my love of being needed and useful."

Taking Diana's hand and kissing it even as tears ran down her black cheeks, Annie said, "Go 'fore somebody misses you. We's been powerful sorry to learn how you bein' made to stay at Fairfiel' by that devil man."

Diana was almost at the door of the shack then and she stopped. *Devil man?* Letting bits and pieces of deliberately hidden truth float to mind, Diana tried making sense of them. No matter that Luke's words and actions incensed her or that she, in fits of pique, often thought of him as being in cahoots with the devil, could she in honesty view him as an instrument of Satan?

During the years Diana had learned that the black people viewed good and evil in far more concrete terms than she did. She realized that she had been fooling herself by continuing to link Luke with the devil. Had she been trying to absolve herself of any wrongdoing by placing on him all of the blame for her predicament? If she had faced up to the fact that she was now alone and grown and had gone to New Orleans to seek counsel from the officer at Planters Bank, she likely could have reached a mature judgment about her future.

Diana recognized that her fear of strange places and people and her greater fear of leaving St. Christopher Parish, maybe forever, had crippled her, leading her to stoop to deceit. Her belief that what was meant to be, would be, had not helped matters.

Childish. She had been childish.

Determined to set the record straight, Diana turned to Annie, who was hovering over her sleeping daughter. "The talk about Luke Greenwood is not true. His given name is Lucius, not Lucifer. Though I might rather be living in the swamp and have my old life back, I can't go along with people whispering that he's a devil."

When Annie appeared doubtful, Diana added, "From what I've learned, he didn't cheat Maynard out of the plantation during their poker game, but won it fairly. He has no more connection with Satan than I do with the Silver Hoodoo Woman. In a way I invited my misfortune by being on his property when I had no right to be there. I should have left Fairfield soon after my father died and done something about my future. I could have hunted up members of his or my mother's family, but I didn't. Please tell your people not to judge him too harshly."

"If you wants it," Tobe said from where Second and he had come to stand in the doorway and listen, "it's your'n, Miss Diana. Tabitha done sent word things lookin' up over at Fairfiel'. We'se glad to learn the new master ain't treatin' you bad an' we'll strow the word 'round."

Before Diana left with the two men to make the long walk back to Fairfield, Annie added her assurances that she, too, would stop talking about Luke Greenwood being a kind of devil.

By the time Diana crept back up the staircase in the silent mansion and fell into her bed, she had a heart and mind brimming over with new, weighty questions. If, as she had believed until that evening, fear and anger from his having taken over her life were the only emotions Luke called up in her, why had she cared what others might think or say about him? Why was it that even when she tried casting thoughts of him aside, they hung around and intermingled with all of her others?

Sleep did not come to Diana until the cocks at Fairfield began crowing.

Six

Awakened the next morning by footsteps on the stairs, Diana bolted out of bed and began her toilette in something akin to panic. What time was it? she wondered as she hurried to her wash stand and poured water from the porcelain pitcher into the matching wash basin, then splashed its coolness on her face with her hands. Before coming to Fairfield, she had never had to be concerned with a clock. She abhorred the idea of racing with something mechanical.

In spite of the bleak light in the large, square bedroom, Diana could tell by the sounds outside that morning was well underway. Birds were chirping in great numbers, their high-pitched notes coming through both the tall, open windows.

While she dashed around getting dressed, Diana heard King letting out playful barks, as if someone might be tossing a stick for him to retrieve. Was it Luke? Somebody was drawing water at the well, for she could hear the pulley screaking in protest. Any moment she expected to hear the tinkle of Tabitha's new silver bell signaling breakfast would soon be served. What would the sober-faced Luke do if she were to arrive in the dining room late?

Not wishing to find out, Diana moaned at the time required to don the undergarments he had brought. Despite her beribboned petticoat being as pretty to her as any of the three gowns sent by the widow Winston, Diana chose to leave the filmy garment hanging on the hook inside the door of the wardrobe and get on with more telling items. A white dimity dress seemed the easiest to get into, despite its enormously full skirt.

Would she ever learn to pull on her silk stockings in a hurry? Diana agonized with her bottom lip caught between her teeth and half-formed phrases zipping across her mind, many including "Drat Luke!" She was struggling with the cross straps on her low-heeled slippers—she breathed her thanks that they no longer pinched—when the bell rang. She had time to give her hair no more than a brush and a promise before she dashed out of her bedroom, holding her long skirt high.

After sending a quick glance below and seeing an empty foyer, Diana settled her dimity-clad rump on the handrailing and went sailing down its gleaming length. She never doubted she would have made her normal, safe two-footed landing if Luke had not at that moment decided to leave the library and start for the dining room.

"What the deuce—!" Luke was mouthing when Diana screamed a warning and landed squarely in his stomach. God-awful sounds of lost breath and of bodies colliding, falling rang out. He sprawled backward on the wooden floor, unable to breathe or do anything but attempt freeing his head and face of the yards of white dimity that threatened to smother him. His hands slapped at the clinging fabric. His belly felt like a deflated balloon.

Diana's rump had sunk into Luke's belly while her elbows landed on the floor off to his side. Her exposed knees jutted upward on his other side. Despite her frantic efforts she was too shaken to rise alone and she floundered helplessly on top of him, a bit like a beached fish.

Luke was no help to Diana and not a lot to himself. He directed his efforts totally toward freeing his face from the multiple folds of her skirt and regaining his wind.

When Diana at last managed to roll off him to a crouching position on all fours, she looked into his face and saw the baffled expression there. "Luke, I'm so sor—" The apology got lost in a storm of giggles. He looked so ruffled and indignant, he who usually wore such brooding, austere airs. She sat up and tried squelching her rising giggles with her hands, but failed.

By then, Luke had recaptured his breath and was jack-knifing into a sitting position. After realizing that neither of them was hurt, he found Diana's fit of merriment contagious. Soon his bass chuckles were serving as counterpoint to her half-smothered giggles. He noted the heightened color of her face and the disarray of her thick hair, thinking that both were attributes of her natural beauty.

"What in thunder is going on?" Salathiel called as he dashed from the back veranda in search of the surprising sounds coming from within the mansion. "I was outside playing with King and—"

"I was sliding down the banister," Diana explained in between her spasmodic giggles. "I hadn't realized my full skirt was going to make me go so fast I couldn't stop, and—"

"And I was unlucky enough to get in the way," Luke finished for her, his dark eyes sparkling.

Salathiel, for one of the few times in his life, searched unsuccessfully for words. His rather square face took on a pleasant roundness as he chuckled. Dared he hope that from now on the two would get along more harmoniously? From somewhere deep within, another hope also glimmered.

Unable to meet Luke's gaze without laughing, Diana looked down at her full skirt and used its bottom edge to blot the tears balling up in the corners of her bright eyes. "I'm truly sorry, Luke. I'll not be playin' that unladylike trick again."

"May I consider your word as part of our pact?" Luke asked after rising and seeing that Salathiel had already helped Diana to her feet and was fussing over her. He rearranged his clothing into a semblance of order and with a careless hand brushed back his tousled hair.

"Why not?" Diana countered while smoothing her hair and skirt with her eyes downcast. How ridiculous that she was feeling a tad hurt that Luke plainly viewed her only as a living, breathing part of an absurd pact. Had he not made it clear from the start that he had no consideration for her as a person? She figured she was lucky that her little indiscretion had not incurred his wrath. Drat the man, anyway.

Luke seemed withdrawn throughout breakfast, though he spent as much time as usual watching his captive with forbidding countenance, or so it seemed to Diana. The incident at the foot of the staircase might never have taken place. She picked at her food but discovered that she had no appetite. Salathiel was unusually cheery, despite the light rain that began falling before they left the dining room.

"You are making remarkable progress," Salathiel told Diana at the end of the morning's long recitations. "I am extremely pleased about your improved grammar and diction."

"Thank you."

"You seem distracted this morning. I hope you suffered no major injuries from your fall."

"No. I'll be fine."

"Is there anything wrong that you care to discuss?"

From where she sat across the rectangular library table from her tutor, Diana looked down at her full white skirt and smoothed the dimity with her hands. She hated it when Salathiel asked her that question, as was his wont at least once each day during her lessons, for how could she be honest and tell him that *everything* was wrong?

Honesty, a trait her father had maintained was vital for happiness and self-respect, seemed one she had forsaken, Diana reflected with a heavy heart. Everything she had done since the night Luke had caught her was based on her first lie about where she came from and what she was doing at the well shed on Fairfield. Maybe it was because she had slept little or because she could not put away completely what had happened to Florina, or maybe it was because she had been unable to check on Minerva that morning, but Diana felt miserable. And achingly alone with her burdens. She sighed.

Was she imagining it, Diana wondered in a kind of panic as her hands moved across her lap, or could she see the lace on the bottoms of her drawers through the thin fabric? Feeling like a guilty child caught in some mischief, she sent Salathiel a sideways look. He was busy writing on a slate and seemed unaware that she had taken so long to reply.

"No, Mr. Salathiel," she said, "they ain't nothin'"—Salathiel corrected her and, as he had been doing since their first day together in the library, waited for her to stop and substitute proper English—"there isn't anything really wrong. I did oversleep, though, an' ain't—haven't—been to visit Minerva this mornin'—morning."

"Good. You're learning to catch and correct your own mistakes. Listening to others speak, particularly if they speak properly, is as much a part of learning as reading," Salathiel said firmly but tactfully, looking up from his writing. "It will be a while before noon. I shall finish jotting down your reading assignments while you go out to see your goat. I suspect King is waiting for you also."

"Not if Luke went somewhere," Diana said when she rose and headed for the door. She glanced down at her lower body and decided she had been wrong to think anyone could tell she wore no petticoat, especially since the skies were cloudy and the light was poor. "King seems to think he's something grand."

Diana found Minerva lying on a pile of straw in the little stall Salem had fixed up for her in the stables. Down the way she could hear the whinnies of horses and wondered if, perhaps, Luke and Jed had skipped riding because of the showers. She gained a kind of perverse pleasure thinking how much Luke had to learn about living in St. Christopher Parish where rain showers were apt to appear daily, sometimes even twice daily in the summer.

While rubbing Minerva's head with one hand, Diana felt of the goat's taut belly with the other. "I vow I believe you may be starting a contraction, Minerva."

The goat bleated, as if in agreement, and dropped her head to rest again on her forefeet. Concerned for her pet's welfare during labor, Diana stayed until she heard Tabitha's bell ringing from somewhere behind the mansion. "They're looking for me, girl. I'll be back soon to see about you. Maybe another pain won't come until I return.''

At the noon meal Luke and Salathiel appeared barely aware of the distracted Diana. Their plans for painting and repairing the neglected mansion formed nearly all of their conversation.

Within a short time Diana was back in the stall with her pet. She looked up when Salem appeared.

''Minerva havin' big troubles, Miss Diana,'' the big black man said. ''I brung her some water an' she ain't paid it no 'tention.''

''Thank you, Salem. If folks begin looking for me, please tell them I'll be here until the kid arrives.''

''I'll be back to see 'bout 'cha both,'' Salem assured her before he returned to his chores.

Diana lost track of time after the goat's contractions sped up and it became obvious that the kid was trying to emerge with all four feet first. Salem came and tried to turn the unborn kid, but even his big hands could not manage the feat. Tears trickled down Diana's face as Minerva writhed on the straw, bleating piteously and kicking her hind legs.

Salem stood by, as sad-faced and helpless as Diana. The protruding forefeet and legs of the unborn kid had lain motionless for some time. She resigned herself to having lost the kid and began wondering if Salem and she could remove the dead animal without killing the mother. While the crooning Diana was shaking drops of water from her fingertips into Minerva's opened mouth, the nanny gave one last kick with her hind legs and lay still.

With a high-pitched moan of anguish, Diana fell forward against the beloved furry neck and shoulders and wept. Life was cruel, unfair! Tears gushed forth from long hidden, seemingly inexhaustible sources: Her heart. Her soul.

''What's going on out here?'' Luke called as he approached the corner stall and heard weeping. Tabitha had told him that he would find Diana with Minerva but he had not expected to find such a dramatic scene. When he saw Diana hugging the motionless goat and realized the animal was dead, he sent a questioning look toward Salem.

Luke reflected that if he had ever before been around a young woman who cared deeply for animals of any kind, he had not known it. Yet here lay Diana, grieving over a goat!

Back when Luke's younger sister, Maurine, had cried during her growing-up years at Southwinds, he had found sympathizing with her made her cry harder. He had concluded that remaining detached was an effective way to deal with weeping females. In the past it had worked with his several mistresses. Calling up a casual tone to mask his deeply stirred sympathy, he asked Diana, "Whatever is causing such caterwauling?"

Unaware that her hands were filthy and that her white gown was smeared with both blood and excrement, Diana jerked her head up and glared through her tears at Luke. His features seemed as impassive as the tone of his voice when she hungered to see and hear compassion. "Minerva . . . her kid—"

Diana gulped and wiped at the tears wetting her cheeks, leaving a streak of muck everywhere she touched. She must have been mistaken to defend Luke last night to Annie. He *was* a devil! A new flood of scalding tears streamed forth, tears for Minerva, tears for all that had gone wrong since she had met Luke. "They're both dead . . . and it's . . . all your fault!"

"*My* fault?" Luke repeated defensively. After motioning for Salem to leave, he walked over and dropped down on one knee near the distraught young woman. He noted she was sitting cross-legged with her full skirt bunched up haphazardly across her lap, as if she might still be wearing her old abbreviated top and bottom.

Though Luke could see the lower edges of Diana's drawers above her satin garters and could tell that she wore no petticoat, he was enjoying the view of her silk-encased legs too much to consider mentioning the fact that she was not clothed like a proper young lady. She must have been a sight to behold lying across him at the foot of the staircase. He picked up a piece of straw and toyed with it. Her obvious pain tugged at his determination to remain detached. In a less aggrieved tone, he asked, "Why do you call this my fault?"

"If you hadn't made us come here to live," Diana explained between gasps and shuddering sobs, "Minerva wouldn't have died. She could tell you don't like goats."

"How could she tell that?" Luke struggled to keep his voice calm. Diana's tears were needling him without mercy. "I never cared much for goats, but I never said an unkind word to her." Should he tell her about the old billy goat that had butted him into a rail fence when he was a youngster and ripped his thigh with its horns? "When Salem told me she was with kid, I even asked him to put new straw here in her stall."

"Minerva could tell," Diana insisted, her gaze raking over him hotly and her mind refusing to register his earlier thoughtfulness. "I know she could." She hiccupped then and thought about how she was speaking. Maybe because of her teary voice Luke was unable to tell much about what she was saying, much less how she was saying it. Lies. So many lies had led to that moment, and there was no undoing them. "She could tell jes' the same way"—a fresh shower of tears streamed down her face—"I can tell you don't like me."

"I do like you, Diana," Luke assured, so shocked at her impassioned words that he snapped the blade of straw he was holding and dropped the broken pieces. "Don't cry anymore."

Whatever methods had worked with other weeping females were not working with Diana Hathaway, Luke reasoned. Allowing his compassion to deepen his voice and soften his words, he asked, "Why else would I want you to stay here and be groomed for going with me to New Orleans?" Luke's conscience poked up its head but he refused to acknowledge his duplicity. "Why, if I didn't like you, I would have just let you run off into the night after I got my father's watch back."

Not to be put off easily, Diana straightened up and looked at Luke. A partial view of her exposed legs registered somewhere in her mind and she yanked down her skirt. The action seemed to have put a stopper on her tears. "You're jes" sayin' that to make me stop cryin'. My fath—my pa allers tried everythin' he knew of to get me to stop cryin'."

"I can see why, too. When you cry, you spoil an incredibly lovely face." Luke dropped to both knees then and pulled out his handkerchief. After wiping Diana's eyes and cheeks, he folded the soiled linen to find a clean spot and held it to her reddened nose. "Blow your nose now." When she did, noisily and quickly like a child, he returned his damp handkerchief to his pocket. "I'm not just saying words to end your tears. Did your father tell lies to stop your crying?"

"No." She shook her head so hard that sections of her unbound hair swung over her shoulders. Curls almost as white as the unsoiled areas of her gown slid down across the swells of her still-heaving breasts.

Diana sniffed, bravely she thought. Pathetically, he thought.

"Philip Hathaway never lied," she said. "He always said honesty is 'bout the most important thing a person ought'a live with." A new batch of tears threatened to form but she held them back. She was stuck with her falsehoods, and no amount of feeling sorry for herself was going to change that troublesome fact.

"Your father must have been a wise man. Believe me when I say you're wrong about my not liking you. Let's go to the house now and leave everything out here to Salem." Luke took her hand and urged her to her feet. Thinking it might be wise for her to dwell not on the death of her pet but its life, he put his arm around her and guided her outside. "On the way to the house, why don't you tell all about how you and Minerva became such good friends?"

Diana shot him a wary, sidewise look from her tear-swollen eyes. Even as she tried to figure out if his seeming kindness was genuine, she welcomed his strong arm reaching across her shoulders and his hand touching her waist as he guided her away from the stables. This was a new Luke, one she had never before met. She took a deep breath and willed her runaway pulse to slow.

Though his legs were much longer than hers, Diana noticed that Luke had slowed his pace so that they walked in harmony. He appeared unaware of her untidiness and her fierce, barnyard smell. She had not realized how weary she was until she relaxed against him and began answering his questions about her long friendship with Minerva.

Strange and disturbing, Diana reflected as they slowly walked and talked underneath the clearing afternoon sky, how the solidity and warmth of Luke's body seemed comforting and exhilarating at the same time. Something about his deep, resonant replies seemed to reach lower than her ears and soothe her roiling insides. She scoffed at the ridiculous idea that such a thing was taking place, but she permitted herself to imagine he was cosseting her as if she might be an adored little girl.

"I had no idea that the goat meant so much to you," Luke said after they reached the back veranda. "I'm sorry for your grief." During her candid revelations about her goat, there were times when he had found himself wondering if he might not have missed out on something special in life by not having known and loved animals as well as Diana obviously did. "Minerva was fortunate to have you as her mistress."

Diana slid him a shy look. "You're bein' kind."

"I'll ask Tabitha and Chloe to help get you cleaned up for a nice rest in your bedroom." Before she went inside, Luke added, "I'm thinking that when I go to New Orleans, I'll find a regular ladies' maid for you."

That evening and the first part of the next day, the Wednesday that Diana had dreaded, passed in a merciful blur. Tabitha and Salem had gone with her secretly to the plantation cemetery where he had placed Minerva's body inside a bricked mound. She put away her grief for her pet when the time came for her to get dressed for tea.

Diana, who was sucking in a last fortifying breath before stepping to the open door leading into the living room, heard a husky, feminine voice as soon as she came downstairs.

". . . and I sent for Sheriff Bonnet right away," the pleasant voice went on. "There's no limit to what poachers think they can take from us landowners, Luke. I resented those men setting out traps in the portion of Alligator Swamp plainly marked by my late husband as belonging to Wingate. My slaves love trapping and fishing there and they have no way of doing those things anywhere else. Do you think I'm a terrible person for having those rascals arrested?''

Diana waited to hear Luke's reply. She was a poacher of a sort, she reflected guiltily, though Uncle Owen never had put up boundary markers on the trees in his section of Gator Swamp, probably because when he arrived with the deed to his new plantation, Philip Hathaway and his family were at home there already.

''No, I don't think you're terrible, Lallage,'' Luke replied. ''I expect I would have done the same thing. Your husband left you the plantation and you have the right to do with it as you see fit. Wise management of private property is necessary for both citizens and government.''

Diana almost gasped at what she overheard. While getting dressed, she had entertained the farfetched idea of confessing all to Luke after the guests left and begging his mercy. Since he seemed to set such store on having her appear with him at a party in New Orleans, she would offer to go with him as a kind of payment for trespassing on his land. Her earlier reasoning had pointed out that Luke had seemed kind and understanding when she knocked him down accidentally, and again during her upset over Minerva. How wrong could she be?

Feeling her stomach tighten from renewed fear and from her truer view of her relationship with Luke, Diana looked back up the stairway with longing. She could never be honest with Luke Greenwood. He would call her a poacher, or worse, and send for the law—or take her to the sheriff himself.

''How happy I am to meet you, Diana,'' Lallage Winston said after Diana entered the living room on shaky legs and Luke made the introductions. While the visitor's plump but daintily formed hands clasped Diana's limp ones, her smile seemed to reach out and embrace the younger woman. ''I hope you're enjoying your visit at Fairfield and that we'll become friends.''

Shyness nigh robbed Diana of speech as well as breath, but she managed to return the beautiful red-haired widow's smile and acknowledge her kind remarks in barely uttered words. Lallage possessed the most voluptuous face and form Diana had ever seen.

Though the older woman's huge brown eyes and ingratiating smile seemed to invite instant friendship, Diana's need to dissemble in front of Luke and Salathiel permitted her to accomplish little outside stammering and feeling like a simpleton. The introductions to Lallage's four daughters came then and Diana relaxed a bit.

"I'm Japonica, and I'm thirteen," the tallest one said after her mother nodded her approval. Red-haired and pretty, as all four were in different ways, Japonica lowered her head and upper body while bending a knee and sliding one foot behind her gracefully. After straightening, she indicated the girl standing beside her. "This is Camelia, who is only ten."

After curtsying to Diana, Camelia shot a heated look at her older sister, then turned to the other two girls who were sending admiring looks at Diana. "Daisy is next at eight" —she waited for a solemn-faced Daisy to curtsy and regain her balance afterward—"and then there's Hyacinth."

"I'm four, going on five," the youngest Winston daughter said after her jerky but charming bow. As soon as she straightened, her big brown eyes sought, and received, approval from Luke and Salathiel who were standing in front of the fireplace while the feminine exchanges went on.

As talk flowed there in the large living room, Diana tried hiding her surprise upon learning that the four girls bore the names of flowers. She wondered if the long-neglected gardens at Fairfield, back when Uncle Owen's wife was alive and overseeing such matters, might not have contained the varied specimens named. Diana remembered that Tabitha's slave friend on neighboring Wingate was named Verbena.

Diana looked at Lallage Winston with new admiration. The woman not only exuded feminine beauty and love of life, but she also seemed to possess the imagination and the courage to enjoy those assets to the utmost. And she wanted to be her friend!

"May we go outside and play with your dog? Mr. Luke told us his name is King," Camelia said to Diana. "We have a dog called Pooch, but Mama wouldn't let us bring him 'cause he isn't friendly to men. King met our carriage before we even got here. He seems ever so nice.''

"You're welcome to play with my dog," Diana replied. "I hope I get to meet Pooch one day." She felt the gazes of everyone in the room and wished she were somewhere else. Never before had she been around so many white people. Would they prove as easy to talk with as her black friends?

"Lily," Lallage Winston called softly, taking a step toward the hall. A young slave appeared in the wide doorway as if she had been waiting, listening for her name. "Will you please take the girls out back? I believe they have drained me of patience for now."

"Perhaps you would prefer that the girls take their tea on the back veranda, Mrs. Winston," Salathiel said after the high-pitched voices and squeals of laughter faded down the hallway.

"What an astute gentleman you are," Lallage replied with a throaty laugh as she sent Salathiel a long look from behind dark eyelashes, a look she had aimed his way more than once since her arrival. "As I explained to you and Luke the first afternoon you came to St. Christopher Parish"—her gaze slipped lower than the last button of Salathiel's coat for just a moment before climbing sensuously back up his neat, manly body to his dark eyes—"neighboring planters stand on little formality here in bayou country. Please call me Lallage. I shall be absolutely devastated if you don't.''

Stunned at the sensation emanating from his groin after Lallage's gaze dipped to the spot even for that instant, Salathiel Morgan could barely keep one eyebrow from jumping upward into a visible sign of the shock racing through his body. He was certain it was shock. It had to be shock, he amended. He had dallied with more than a few tavern wenches in his younger days, but it had been a long while since he had entertained thoughts of impassioned feminine bodies entwined with his. He blinked hard, and his head twitched once.

Surely, the beautiful widow was unaware of the blatantly flirtatious looks she was sending him, Salathiel reminded himself when she closed her lusciously ripe lips over her pretty teeth and seemed to be awaiting his reply. He harrumphed and said in a curiously stilted voice, "I shall be honored to address you as Lallage. Please call me Salathiel." Lallage. Truly an exotic and unique name, he decided as he stroked his mustache with two fingers.

"Lallage, I was hoping you might pour for us this afternoon," Luke said when Tabitha appeared at the open doorway with the tea tray and set it on the low table before the sofa where Lallage and Diana sat.

If Lallage thought it unusual that she, the temporary visitor, should be so favored for the honor over Luke's house guest, she made no show of it and consented graciously. Talking gaily throughout the little ritual of pouring tea into the delicate cups and passing them around to Diana and the two men, she then sipped from her own cup and balanced it on her saucer while she leaned back against the sofa with innate grace. Her lush figure, draped closely by her gown of green silk, seemed to have been formed for such feminine activities as being hostess for tea . . . and flirting. She looked magnificent.

"Tell me, Diana," Lallage said in her open manner. "Do you enjoy visiting in southern Louisiana?"

Diana felt blood rushing to her face. She dreaded opening her mouth. The way Luke had seemed to keep his gaze on her ever since the guests had arrived bothered her far more than she would have him know. She liked Lallage and wanted her to like her back, but the idea seemed improbable. The obviously cultured woman would feel nothing but pity once she engaged her in conversation and heard her atrocious language. "Yes."

Lallage was off then, relating amusing accounts of happenings around her plantation and in the small town of Calion. Luke and Salathiel joined in, asking questions and adding their own observations while Diana sat back and tried to absorb every movement Lallage made. The woman exuded warmth and charm with every word and gesture, and Diana wondered how she accomplished it.

During a lull in the animated talk, Lallage turned to the reticent young woman beside her and said, "As Luke requested, I'm sending my seamstress, Lily, and her daughter, Fern, over tomorrow to get started on a wardrobe for you, Diana.''

Luke and then Salathiel rose, as if by cue, and Luke said, "I think Salathiel and I will go out back and check on the girls. We'll leave you two ladies to your talk of clothing."

"There's no need to leave," Lallage said, her sparkling eyes fixed flirtatiously on Salathiel. A note of laughter pealed from her pretty mouth before she continued in a teasing tone. "We're not going to be discussing anything but outer garments."

"I look upon your helping Diana as a personal favor," Luke said. "A pair of bachelors know little about how to plan a young woman's wardrobe."

"Ah, yes," Lallage replied with an arch smile winged toward Luke but settling on Salathiel. One of her prettily tapered fingers played for an instant at the side of her generous lips. "Such expertise as you two handsome rakes would have about milady's wardrobe likely runs counter to putting one together, does it not?"

When Luke chuckled and Salathiel stared in surprise at her bold innuendo, Lallage tossed back her red curls and laughed low in her throat. A tiny frown of apparent disappointment marred her smooth forehead as the men made their way to the door, and she said, "I shall be crushed if you gentlemen stay gone very long, as I'm sure Diana will be also."

After making assurances that they would return soon, Luke and Salathiel escaped.

Lallage turned back to Diana with such happiness that Diana wondered if she had imagined Lallage's earlier expression of disappointment. "The other day when Luke stopped by to visit, he asked me to choose some yard goods from the General Store for you. I told him I wouldn't dream of making selections until I met you and heard your preferences."

"You were mighty kind to send me some of yo' clothes," Diana said, despising herself with each faked syllable. She glanced down at the blue cotton gown she was wearing and smoothed the full skirt. "I thanks you."

"You're welcome, dear. When I outgrew them, I kept

them around to remind me that I shouldn't overly indulge myself at the table." Looking down at her generous bosom and hips, she laughed a kind of secret laugh and shrugged her shoulders. "My late husband seemed to like me more with each added pound."

"I can see why. I never met a woman so purty."

Lallage murmured, "Thank you, Diana. Coming from such a beauty as you are and knowing that I'll never see thirty again, I treasure that compliment. I understand your parents are dead, and I'm sorry. They must have been wonderfully lovely people to have such a daughter."

Making no comment on the sudden brightness of Diana's eyes, Lallage cocked her head and narrowed her large brown eyes as if sizing up the younger woman. After a moment she smiled, plainly pleased at her deductions. "With your marvelous blonde hair—I've never seen any like it; it's divine! —and your coloring, I'm wondering if white and varied shades of blue and pink might not be perfect. What do you think?"

"I never give clothes much thought."

"Why ever not?" Lallage reached to pat Diana's hand. "You're much too beautiful not to deck yourself out in gorgeous clothing and attract as many beaux as possible. How else can you find the one to make your dreams come true?"

Diana hid her thoughts behind her eyelashes and felt the warmth of a blush tingling on her face. "I never give dreams much thought neither, Mrs. Winston."

"No more of that nonsense. Call me Lallage and start thinking about clothes and dreams and young men." She waggled a shapely finger toward Diana and sent her a warm-eyed look. "Life is too much fun for you to miss one moment of it. Now let's talk about the latest styles and come up with some plans for this wardrobe Luke says you're going to need for the winter season in New Orleans." When Diana continued to look downcast, Lallage asked, "Do I detect a romance going on between you and Luke, one having a troubled time right now?"

"No! There ain't nothin' between us an' never will be!"

For an instant Lallage raised a dark eyebrow and seemed

about to spout some additional feminine wisdom. However, she changed the subject back to clothing.

Later, after the men returned and Tabitha followed behind with a fresh pot of tea, Luke sized up the obviously good rapport between the two women and decided to solicit Lallage's help in more ways than with Diana's wardrobe. The more he told her about transforming Diana into a young woman of fashion and culture, the more animated Lallage became. Quickly, he offered a plausible reason for his actions, one barely akin to the truth. "I want to surprise my friends in New Orleans by presenting a new beauty."

"This sounds like a lark," Lallage exclaimed as she set down her cup and saucer and included Diana in her magnanimous smile. "What do you think of all this, Diana? Aren't you excited about it, too?"

Drat Luke! Diana was thinking for the umpteenth time since he had returned. Why did he have to involve somebody else? The more who knew about it and cooperated with him, the less likely she was ever to convince him that she was not going to turn out as he wished. She twisted her hands together to keep from slapping his face. It was fear of him that had brought about her first lie; now he was adding his own falsehoods to hers and creating a more gigantic mess. "I goes 'long with it . . . 'cause I don't have no choice."

"What fun we'll have taking a beautiful young woman who has grown up in the backwoods near Mobile and teaching her all she has missed out on," Lallage said. "I'm so glad you've shared this with me." She turned to Salathiel who had sat stern faced and silent throughout Luke's recital. "Salathiel, you rascal, how could you have neglected checking on your poor dear niece until she was eighteen?" When Salathiel shot an indignant look toward Luke, she added, "Of course I realize you were terribly involved with your tutoring and thought your sister would have sent for you had she needed you. No matter, now that at last you and Diana are reunited."

Lallage rattled on in her gesticulating manner, blind to the wounded looks on the faces of both Diana and Salathiel. "I can just see you at the Charity Ball, Diana, looking like a dream and breaking the hearts of every young man there.'' She slid a measuring look toward Luke. ''Diana assured me there's no romance going on between the two of you, so I'm assuming Salathiel and you will be hoping Diana attracts some wealthy suitors.''

''Yes,'' Luke replied quickly, rubbing his chin with the fingers of one hand and avoiding the stony eyes of both Diana and Salathiel.

Because Luke had not planned beyond winning his wager, the thought of suitors for Diana was alien to him. He realized that he should have already considered the possibility that she might not accept his brother's attentions and likely proposal. To get Diana married off seemed the simplest way to ensure her future. After all, he would owe her more than her wardrobe and a sum of money. ''You're right. Both Salathiel and I would like to see her find a suitable husband. The timing would be good.''

''We'll teach you the latest dances, Diana,'' Lallage assured the wan-faced young woman. ''I promise to provide you with the choicest gossip to titter over. We'll make sure that you possess social graces that will exceed those of any other belle from the plantations in Louisiana.''

Diana slumped against the back of the sofa and tried to drown out the sounds of plans being bandied back and forth between Lallage and Luke. She was grateful that Salathiel chimed in only when asked direct questions, as if he, too, might have misgivings about the transformation of Diana Hathaway.

Seven

That July of 1831, hot and humid from daily showers floating in from the Gulf of Mexico scant miles to the south, marked the beginning of drastic changes at Fairfield Plantation in St. Christopher Parish.

Much to Tabitha's delight, which she shared in a stolen moment with Diana, Luke bought five milk cows and a young bull from Lallage Winston's large herd at Wingate. The contented black woman's culinary skills increased in direct proportion to the numbers of pails of foaming milk brought to her kitchen. Busy now with her welcome, increased duties, she felt important again and barely noticed that Diana's life was swerving in a direction away from her own.

Chloe and another young black, Zelia, pitched in to help Tabitha make golden molds of butter aplenty for her flaky biscuits and tangy cheese for making sauces and slicing thick. Now there was lumpy buttermilk for turning out hot cornbread sticks, clotted cream for drizzling atop warm fruit pies. For drinking, sweet milk cooled in the keeping bucket in the well.

One day Luke instructed Jed Latour to measure the slaves for clothing and shoes, then announced that he would leave the overseer in charge while he went on a buying trip in New Orleans. Since Luke figured to be gone until late August or early September, he asked Salathiel to supervise the workmen and slaves already starting the renovations at the long-neglected mansion.

At Luke's prodding Salathiel provided names of books to be purchased along with Luke's favorite titles. Lallage responded to Luke's request to prepare a list of feminine apparel and yard goods necessary to provide Diana with the kind of costumes and accessories that a wealthy young woman would need for a winter season in the state's capital.

Without so much as a private moment of farewell with Diana, Luke galloped off astride the high-stepping Jasper one misty dawn.

During that entire day, Diana did not once mentally precede Luke's name with *drat*. Instead she breathed a silent *Good riddance, Luke*! She found it maddening that throughout his absence, his handsome image intruded upon her dreams. As if it had a claim there.

Weeks before Luke's return, wagons piled high with materials from New Orleans for the renovation of the mansion began bumping over the single-track road snaking alongside Bayou Selene. Under Jed's watchful eye the hired workmen from Calion and the slaves unpacked each load and set about incorporating the materials into the renovations.

One of the shipments of furniture, art works, and books included numerous parcels of yard goods and feminine apparel, ranging from silk parasols and enormous bonnets nestling in their own satin-lined boxes to small, embroidered and beaded silk bags of varied hues, and dainty leather gloves, some white, some colored. As Luke had requested, Lallage took charge of the luxurious items, dispensing material and ideas to the seamstresses. Despite Diana's vow not to become caught up in the pretty widow's enthusiasm, she did.

Now that Diana's critical jailer appeared only in her dreams, where he played the role of handsome, enigmatic observer, she began easing into acceptable speech. The sight of the elegant apparel and accessories forced her to think about the countless strangers who in December would be attending the social outings in New Orleans and watching her entry into their circles. Such thoughts played havoc with her former complacency about who she was, about what lay ahead.

Plainly overwhelmed at his pupil's progress, Salathiel relegated some of the more tedious duties as supervisor of the workmen to Jed and stepped up her recitations.

Wide-eyed with awe when she was not studying, Diana went around sniffing at the enticing, unfamiliar scents of paint, lacquer, new furnishings, and clothing. Unbeknownst to her, she was learning to like some of the heady smells that lavishly spent money can create.

Lallage Winston became a regular visitor. She appeared almost daily in her handsome open-sided carriage with her pretty young daughters and their amiable attendant, Iris, their driver, and their spoiled pet dog, Pooch.

After having loaned two of her slaves to help Chloe sew for Diana, the vivacious widow exclaimed to Diana, and any others interested in listening, "I can't afford to be absent from here overly long. Who else can make certain that the new gowns fit properly and that you learn to pour tea with grace? I promised Luke. After all,"—she paused to flip back the red sausage curls from her shoulder and lift her plump chin higher so as to displace the fullness underneath—"I grew up on a river plantation south of Baton Rouge and seem to have a knack for such things."

Salathiel and Jed often consulted with Lallage about the decorative touches that the long-neglected mansion needed. With her brown eyes returning often to Salathiel's face—and sometimes dipping lower for a moment and causing the Englishman to become flustered and feel uncommonly male and powerful—she proffered the views of a wealthy woman accustomed to living and entertaining in splendid homes. She was in her element and was utterly charming to all. Especially to Salathiel.

In truth, Lallage recognized in July that her initial attraction to the so-proper Salathiel Morgan was growing. She promptly lost interest in her several suitors, even in two wealthy widowers from enormous cotton plantations near the one on which she had grown up. Her lovely face and big brown eyes wore a perpetual air of excitement. When she was at Fairfield, her rich laughter—more and more often joined by the delicate, less enthusiastic tones of Diana's—rang out and seemed to add as much beauty to the mansion as the renovations and redecorating. Or so it seemed to Salathiel.

"Do I have to learn to ride a horse, Lallage?" Diana asked one morning near the end of August when Lallage followed her up to her bedroom where Fern waited with a newly completed garment. Within a short time the seamstress had helped Diana into her new riding costume and voiced her approval.

Turning from the full length, free-standing mirror, which had arrived in a recent shipment from Luke and been set up in Diana's bedroom at his written orders, Diana sent Lallage a troubled look. Without her realizing it, she had come to study the fascinating widow far more carefully than she had ever studied books. A graceful, feminine gesture here, the lift of an eyebrow there, though decidedly Diana's, seemed second cousins to the more dramatic ones belonging to Lallage.

"Of course you must learn to ride," Lallage replied with a fond smile. At times she felt as motherly toward Diana as toward her own daughters. "Why else would you need that stylish riding outfit? My Lily and my Fern have done a wonderful job on it, haven't they? All properly brought-up young ladies in Louisiana are equestriennes of note." She cocked her head and studied the length of the riding gown Diana was modeling. "Perfection, Fern."

Fern replied with a smile lighting her brown face, "Miss Diana easy to sew for. She always looks purty in what Mama, Chloe, an' me make."

"Thank you, Fern," Diana replied. Sometimes, as now, it was hard for her to recognize the image in the mirror as belonging to the Diana Hathaway who existed before that fateful Midsummer's Eve. "Is Chloe helping a lot?"

"She doin' so good she ain't gonna need us 'round teachin' her nothin' else 'bout fancy sewin' by the time we goes back to Wingate and gets busy on clothes for Miss Lallage an' the girls."

Lallage said in a musing voice, a forefinger pressed against her round cheek, "Diana, one of those hats Luke sent will be perfect with your riding outfit, the one with the flat crown and dyed egret feathers.''

"How do you know such things?'' Recently, during one of Diana's brief visits with Tabitha, they had wondered aloud if any of the egret feathers decorating her new headgear might have come from those she had gathered for Verbena to send on the sly to the New Orleans markets.

"From having grown up in love with the idea of being a female, darling, the type virile men can't bear to be away from,'' Lallage responded with one of her delightful little laughs that displayed her perfect teeth to advantage. "You're going to love being adored by handsome young men! I'm having the deuce of a time holding everyone off from visiting Fairfield until Luke returns. People are dying of curiosity about all of those wagonloads of goods coming from New Orleans. They'll find the wait well worth it.''

Diana shrugged one shoulder delicately, one of the little mannerisms she had picked up unconsciously from Lallage. "You're kind to spend so much time here helping out.''

"I was so sunk in despair over the loss of my husband— darling, he was the most passionate lover and devoted husband in all of Louisiana!—that I can hardly believe how glorious life has become lately. I had decided I might have to take a lover if something didn't come along to pique my interest.''

Diana eyed her friend askance for mentioning taking a lover, as well as for referring to her late husband as a passionate lover. She wanted to ask Lallage exactly what she meant. Tabitha had hinted one time that passion and marriage were not usually partners among the wealthy members of plantation society.

Thinking that Lallage Winston was the most cheerful woman she had ever met, and the most outspoken, Diana said, "I'm glad you're happier now. It becomes your pretty face. Maybe it's good that somebody is enjoying this farce.''

Lallage pouched her lips into a becoming *moue*. "Sometimes I get the impression you're frightened at what you might find when Salathiel and I lead you to reveal the real Diana. You're talking now with such ease that I'm learning more about you each time we visit. I suspect that underneath your beautiful facade, there's an awful lot of hidden passion."

Not comfortable with the direction of the conversation, Diana returned to an earlier topic. "I've never been around horses. They frighten me, looking so tall and powerful."

Twirling before the mirror at Fern's request, Diana admired her fitted white cambric jacket, worn more as a blouse with the ultra-full skirt of navy-blue broadcloth. With the tops of its leg-of-mutton sleeves stiffened with horsehair, the close-fitting jacket gave the slender image in the mirror a sophisticated look, a look Diana had never seen until she met Lallage. She lifted her skirt enough to see the tops of her closely fitting black boots with their little decorative silver spurs. How had Luke known her size for all of the things he had sent? "Who's going to teach me to ride?"

"Luke will. Salathiel tells me he's a natural horseman and from what I've seen when he has stopped by at Wingate on that black stallion of his, he truly is. People in Calion learned who Luke Greenwood was right off from noticing the way he handles Jasper, as well as from the way he handles that magnificent physique of his. Didn't you know he's bringing you a horse that has been trained for women to ride?"

"No. Salathiel and I never discuss Luke and I never hear from him." So someone other than she categorized Luke's tall, lean body as magnificent? He still plagued her dreams. She slipped into the morning gown Fern held for her and waited until the slave had fastened it and left the room before going on. "Have you heard when he's coming home?"

From where Lallage sat on a chair between the two windows and watched Diana go to her dresser and tidy her hair, she smiled to herself. Was Diana referring to Fairfield as home for herself as well as for Luke? Interesting. Of course the beautiful blonde *had* been at Fairfield over two months now and she seemed to be more content each day. The troubled, sad look still lurked within her blue eyes, though, and pricked Lallage's tender heart.

Unless she was mistaken, Lallage mused, there was more to the relationship between Diana and Luke than either suspected. They were striking together, what with one being so fair and the other so dark. She figured Luke might be several years younger than her own thirty-seven and she knew Diana was eighteen; to her way of thinking, they were perfectly matched. Before Luke left, Lallage had concluded each was achingly aware of the other—much as she was aware of Salathiel Morgan.

Admitting that she likely was the world's most avid romanticist, Lallage almost clapped her hands in anticipation of what would happen when Diana and Luke stopped their dueling and let their hearts take over. She also had visions of what was going to take place when she finally wore down the Englishman's reserve. Her generous mouth spread into a happier smile.

Always, Lallage had favored men with lithe build who were only slightly taller than she, somehow liking the way her full breasts and hips seemed to encompass them while they danced or embraced. Thoughts of Salathiel's arms holding her naked curves against his wiry body set her pulse into a tizzy and brought a tingling flash to the secret spot that had been aching with need since her beloved husband's death two years ago.

"Luke will be coming home soon, according to a letter Salathiel received," Lallage said after crossing her legs and forcing herself back to reality. "He's bringing you a personal maid to serve as attendant and hairdresser. I gather he has purchased a number of other slaves across the river from New Orleans in Algiers."

Frowning, Diana continued taming her mussed hair. "I don't need a personal attendant. Luke is taking this matter too far. In four months it will all be over."

"Maybe not. If you don't meet a suitor in New Orleans who seems right for you, what will you do?"

"I haven't given the matter much thought." Luke's admission to Lallage about expecting Diana to attract a suitor in the city had shocked her, though not any more than the lies he had told about her being kin to Salathiel and growing up in the backwoods near Mobile.

If Luke wanted her to find a husband, Diana thought, why was he so eager to escort her to the Charity Ball? She confessed knowing too little about such matters to judge, but it seemed to her that the appearance of a handsome man at a young woman's side would put off other bachelors. Sometimes at night she could not go to sleep for thinking of the numerous lies that both Luke and she had spewed out. The pact might be over in four months, but could the lies ever end?

Lallage inspected her thumbnail before going on. "I suppose you can always come back here to St. Christopher Parish and stay with Luke and your Uncle Salathiel until the right man comes along. Or you can move in at Wingate with the girls and me until you can make plans for your future. There's always the possibility that Luke might decide to marry and then you might not feel comfortable here."

When Diana made no comment, Lallage continued. "It's only fair to tell you that when Salathiel's duties here end, I'll ask him to come to Wingate and tutor my daughters. Your uncle has done wonders for you, hasn't he?"

Diana felt her cheeks grow warm. "Yes. He's a wonderful teacher and gentleman."

"Don't you just love his voice? I vow I could listen to him talk in that marvelous, manly voice for hours about God knows what—fishing or hunting or any of those boring things men like to go on and on about. His brown eyes have a way of igniting just before he laughs and then lighting up all the way when he starts letting out sounds. Have you noticed?"

"No, I haven't." Turning from the new dressing table with its oval mirror and small drawers with hand-painted china pulls, Diana wondered how Luke had managed to find a piece of furniture made of the same shiny mahogany as the original tester bed and tall armoire. She settled on the chaise longue upholstered in dark-blue velvet, another new item. "I'm aware that Salathiel has a marvelous voice, but I haven't noticed the change in his eyes."

Diana listened to her red-haired friend as she related more seemingly obscure details about Salathiel Morgan. Though Diana had trouble labeling the exact shade of Salathiel's eyes, she knew they were kind and intelligent. Wasn't it strange that their color or their reaction to his laughter had never registered with her, yet had made a lasting impression on Lallage?

Even before Lallage had finished speaking, Diana realized with a start that she was remembering some of Luke's characteristics and quirks. She recalled the way his fingers stroked his chin when he seemed to be mulling over something important. Nobody would ever have to remind her that his dark eyes bordered on being black. Also they were sparkling, unfathomable, and quick to race over her and settle in a disconcerting manner on her face and hair. They did that in her dreams, too.

"You like Salathiel a great deal, don't you?" Diana asked. Thinking about Luke had scattered her thoughts.

"Oh, my, yes!" Lallage giggled as if she were even younger than Diana. "I'm going to make him like me as much as I like him, too, even if I have to throw myself all over him."

"But that might not be—" Diana caught herself. She had no wish to offend the one who had become her first and only white friend.

"Ladylike?" Lallage finished for her. Sending Diana a broad wink, she went on. "Ladies are expected to flirt, darling. How else can we let the gentlemen we favor know we truly prefer them? I find men are quite self-centered by nature, what with almost the whole world of business and government revolving around them and their actions. Sometimes a woman has to exert whatever charms she possesses to shake them into eyeing her in a romantic way. I think the world would be terribly dull if there was no flirting."

A brief silence reigned in the second-floor bedroom until Lallage continued. "Men are generally not very good at initiating it, but they dote on flirting when a pretty woman makes the first move." When Diana's earlier shocked expression turned pensive, Lallage added with a compassionate smile, "I can see there's much I need to teach you other than how to pour tea."

Up the winding Selene Bayou at Fernwood, the plantation bordering Fairfield on the north, action of a far different kind was taking place during those final hot months of the summer of 1831.

Maynard Oates found himself pitted against his stepfather at almost every turn and losing each time. It was more than enough to turn an already volatile young man into a desperate one.

Julius Waskom might have been a respected sea captain for most of his fifty-five years, Maynard fretted during that steamy July, and his widowed mother might have thought she was acting wisely to have married him the year before, only weeks after the two met in New Orleans. Even so, he could find no redeeming features in the man.

Maynard's mother, Frances Oates Waskom—accompanied by her daughter, Doreen, and her younger sons, Clayton and Alexander—was spending her customary two weeks in July with her sister who lived up Selene Bayou. Alone in the mansion now, Maynard and Julius had full opportunity to lay their mutual animosity on the table and examine its rotten core.

"I spoke with Simmons about the progress of the girl, Florina. Her cuts have healed nicely and she can now go about her kitchen duties," Julius remarked one night after the two had settled in the library for brandy. When Maynard made no sign he had even heard, Julius's normally ruddy face turned redder. "From what I can learn—and your mother knows nothing of this from me—Florina had been seen meeting you more than once near Gator Swamp. Do you have any knowledge about how she came to be carved up?"

"Your question is an insult," Maynard replied. He refused to meet his stepfather's gaze.

"Insult or not, I need an answer."

"By what right do you question me? I notice you've waited for the others to go away for a visit before bringing up this distasteful matter. You may have Mama fooled into thinking you have her best interests at heart, but I've pegged you from the beginning. You're no more than a fortune hunter."

"Has it ever occurred to you that I might love your mother and have no need of her wealth?"

Maynard sneered, "Never."

Julius Waskom sipped his brandy, aware that his heart was feeling unusually heavy in his chest. One reason he had given up his last ship was that whenever unusual pressures of his command plagued him, his heart began threatening to burst out of his chest and suffocate him in the process. Sometimes at sea a painful throbbing had attacked deep inside his left arm and sent him seeking his bunk for relief. Always before, he had been a rugged man able to withstand pain, but the new onslaughts became humbling.

After putting into New Orleans last year and talking with doctors, Julius had decided to enjoy his remaining years by living a more sedate life, one he could well afford since he had never done much with his generous salary and commissions but deposit them in banks. His wife had long been dead. Julius had no reason to return to Virginia, even before he met Frances Oates at a party in New Orleans and fell in love with her. He still found it hard to believe his good fortune in having the pretty widow return his love so warmly.

"Your mother loves you very much, Maynard. She asked me to use this time while she and the children are away to try getting to know you and work out our differences. For her sake, can't you meet me at least halfway?"

Maynard poured more brandy into his snifter before deigning to answer. "What's in it for me?"

Reminding himself to stay calm, Julius answered, "Money. Is there anything else you care about?"

"Not really." He drank deeply, as if the brandy were no more than water. "How much and how do I get it? I want to get away from this foul place, go back to New Orleans. All you have to do is give me—"

"Your mother doesn't wish you to return to New Orleans for awhile. You know how much she wants you to stay here and learn to operate the plantation. She tells me that since your father died, you have done little but show up here a couple of times each year before running back to New Orleans to the whiskey and cards. Ever since you lost your legacy from her brother—"

"Shut up! I don't need you reminding me that Luke Greenwood robbed me of Fairfield."

"From what I've learned, each man at that table had far more in the pot than Fairfield would have brought on the market in its deteriorated condition. The way you robbed the place of its assets was an insult to your Uncle Owen. I ran into Luke Greenwood soon after he arrived to take possession. He answered my rather pointed questions with what I considered manly truthfulness. Had he not been a gentleman and one with a clear conscience, I suspect he might have struck me or, perhaps, challenged me."

Julius studied his stepson in the candlelight. Doreen and her younger brothers seemed to have accepted him as their stepfather; what would it take to win over Maynard? Of course, Julius reminded himself, Doreen was a comely young woman of nineteen and only recently returned from school in Natchez, whereas Maynard was thirty and apparently had been something of a wealthy philanderer before Julius ever met Frances. At ages sixteen and twelve, Alexander and Clayton seemed content to have a man around the mansion during their holidays from school in New Orleans.

Even if he had not come on the scene last year, Julius reflected, and pointed out to Frances that Maynard had squandered the greatest portion of what her late husband had bequeathed his family, she would have had to face up to the matter by now. Fernwood was already in unsound condition financially and would continue to spiral downward if someone did not take positive steps soon. Julius loved Frances too much to deny her fervent request for him to try changing Maynard's style of thinking and living.

Breaking the uneasy silence, Maynard asked in a scathing tone, "What if Luke had responded differently? Would you have called him out for taking advantage of your wayward stepson?"

"Yes. I would have dueled with anyone smearing or taking advantage of a member of my family."

Maynard chuckled drunkenly then sobered and scowled. "*Your* family? Bull! I can just see you and Luke Greenwood facing up underneath a tree at dawn. I watched him duel in New Orleans a couple of years back. He would have sliced you to ribbons or else shot a hole through your heart—if you had one.''

''Unfortunately, I am very aware that I do have a heart, one that sometimes acts up.'' Blind to the suddenly alert look on Maynard's face, Julius unconsciously rubbed his left forearm and went on. ''You can put away that fantasy. I believed the man as well as the other accounts I've had of the way you gambled and caroused in New Orleans.''

Maynard's countenance suggested boredom, disinterest.

Julius continued anyway. ''Now that your allowance has been cut considerably and your mother has assigned you duties here as field manager, you should be helping set the plantation back on its feet. Work closely with Simmons. The man has obviously been a good overseer since you were naught but a boy. You need to understand about planting and harvesting.''

Though Maynard continued to drink and appear aloof, Julius added, ''As the eldest son, you're likely to be in command here someday. You need to prepare for that time. Your heavy withdrawals ever since your father's death years back have put the whole place in jeopardy. I want to be your friend.''

''Then give me your position as business manager.''

''Not unless your mother asks it of me.''

''You've turned Mama against me, and the others, too.''

''You did that on your own without any help from me.''

''What did you mean when you said this talk might produce some money for me?''

''I'll match the monthly allowance your mother gives you if you take positive steps to do as she wishes. You must agree that Frances shall never hear of this and that future discussions about your progress, or lack of it, will take place without her knowledge.''

Maynard watched his stepfather, his narrowed eyes showing their first glimmer of interest in the conversation. ''Go on.''

''There won't be enough money for you to return to New Orleans and live in your former style. However, there would be enough for you to take seasonal trips down and pursue your varied pleasures for a few weeks at a time.''

"What are these 'positive steps'?"

"No more bickering with me in front of Frances or the slaves or anyone else."

"Is there more?" He fixed his gaze on the ceiling.

"Spend some time with Simmons and some with me. Try thinking like a businessman, with responsibilities beyond your animal needs."

"So we're back to talking about the high yaller with the cuts on her face and neck." He sent Julius a heated look.

"Perhaps your last drunken binge has kept you from learning that I have already sold Florina and her new husband, Second, to another planter." When Maynard's beady eyes grew even smaller and his lips formed hard, thin lines across his bared teeth, Julius said, "You're not to discuss this matter with anyone. You're lucky I didn't send for the sheriff."

Maynard threw back his head and laughed with open derision. "You're out of your mind, Captain. Fernwood is no ship at sea where you make all the decisions, like God."

"But neither can you play God, Maynard. Furthermore, if you expect to get a copper out of me, you won't be sneaking off with slave girls again. Is that clear?"

Maynard jumped up, almost staggering as he went to the open window and stared out into the night. The slimy bastard! How dared he marry Florina off, then sell her! It was not Julius's place to be telling him what he, the oldest son at Fernwood, needed to be doing.

Why, Maynard's angry thoughts plunged on, it was beneath him to follow behind the overseer and supervise workers. Julius Waskom was stupid, knew nothing of planters and their ways. Money. His lips worked soundlessly. Damn! but he needed money to get out of this hellish hole. He had hated St. Christopher Parish and everything in it ever since he first went away to school in Virginia. Once he had discovered there were cities with diverse people and countless ways to satisfy his personal whims, no matter how perverse, his life had taken a new direction.

Until Julius had shown up, Maynard thought under the fog of drunkenness, he had been able to wheedle funds from his mother without more than a teary scene from her, scenes that he promptly forgot once money lined his pockets again. Now she refused to deal with him without the presence of her new husband, who seemed to take immense delight in looking pleasant while he refused Maynard's demands for money.

With a twisted smile, Maynard recalled Julius's words about his heart. He remembered having noticed several times during past heated exchanges that the older man had rubbed his left arm in a peculiar, almost caressing way. Was Julius, perhaps, unable to withstand the pressures of conflict?

Maynard called up an amicable demeanor and turned then to face his stepfather. "What you're saying is clear, Julius, might even make a bit of sense. I'll do my best to keep peace between us. After all, I need the money. I'll start riding around the fields with Simmons and talking with the bastard, though I still think such stooping is unnecessary for the eldest son of the man who founded Fernwood."

"I'm pleased you've thought the matter over and agreed to help turn the six of us into a family. I've been sitting here thinking how you and I could use this time while the others are gone to do some things together, like fishing."

"Oh, so you like to fish?"

"Yes, I spent a lot of time out on the bayou in the spring before you came home. Clayton and Alexander have gone with me several times in the mornings since they returned from school."

"Have you ever fished in Gator Swamp behind the back fields? The fish are more easily found in the shallow water, plus there's shade almost everywhere."

Encouraged by Maynard's seeming willingness to let bygones be bygones, Julius shook his head and chuckled in self-derision. "The only time I rode back that way, I saw some of the biggest water moccasins I'd ever seen. Since I don't like having to deal with snakes, I do my fishing in the bayou out front where there aren't so many of the rascals."

Julius read Maynard's lack of response as a sign that he was sympathetic, and he explained further. "Besides, I figured the swamp must have gotten its name from a reptile far more dangerous than a snake, and I wasn't eager to meet up with any of those monster alligators that people talk about. I didn't grow up in swamp country as you did."

"Don't tell me the fearless captain is not as fearless as he would have folks believe."

Julius heard the taunt in Maynard's voice but refused to pick up the challenge. He figured it only natural that the selfish young man would harbor some resentment toward him. "Perhaps we should do some fishing back there. You can teach me about Alligator Swamp. I understand it covers a big part of the parish."

"That's right. As a boy, I learned this end of it quite well. Any time you decide to try your luck, all we'll have to do is take our poles and bait. We've always kept a few pirogues at the swamp pier."

"That sounds good." Julius rose and started toward the door, then turned back to say, "Why don't we go fishing tomorrow?"

"Fine with me."

Had Julius Waskom turned around again before he left the room, he would have seen the fierce, calculating look within his drunken stepson's eyes.

Eight

Late one afternoon during the second week of September, Luke Greenwood returned from New Orleans to Fairfield. King, letting out giant-sized barks when sounds of travelers could be heard, raced out to the road.

Diana, who had just come in from one of her secretive forays to her home in Gator Swamp, hurried to the upper front veranda to see what was creating such a commotion. Through the heavily leafed oaks she glimpsed Luke, sitting tall and in command with a white hat cocked back on his black hair, riding Jasper up the dirt driveway.

His white hat fascinated Diana. Luke had never appeared as handsome or dashing. To her surprise, her heartbeat faltered then took off running. She felt giddy, flushed. She felt an unexpected urge to lean over the banister and call out to him and invite his black eyes to look up at her, his lips to smile, his deep voice to say her name. She squelched the impulse. Why would he welcome her greeting? He had not bothered to tell her goodbye.

To Diana, Luke looked as mysteriously aloof and masterful as when he had silently strolled through her dreams in the guise of observer. Uncanny, the way that even while absent, he had hovered around in her life, right along with his orders to transform her into his idea of a cultured young woman.

Noting that Luke seemed aware of being watched and was sending his gaze toward the veranda, Diana glided into shadows. She gained a view of a horse with flowing mane and tail following Luke's Jasper on a long lead line. When she saw the whites of the horse's eyes flashing as it pranced about nervously, she laid her hand on her runaway heart and gulped. Was that the *monster* that she was expected to ride?

After Luke and the horses disappeared behind the mansion, Diana saw and heard two mule-drawn wagons with tall side planks coming up the driveway. From her partial view through the towering trees, she could see that the obviously new vehicles carried chattering blacks, stacks of boxes, and containers of goods. Two mules guided by long ropes trailed behind each vehicle, including the third one which hauled a pen of restless, squealing hogs, as well as what appeared to Diana to be farming implements, like plows, hoes, and shovels.

Stars above! Diana thought with consternation. Luke Greenwood was stepping masterfully into his new role as planter. During his long absence she had allowed herself to hope he might find he preferred New Orleans over Fairfield. She threw that hope to the September dusk. Drat! He must be planning to stay forever. To the best of her memory, Uncle Owen at one time had owned at least that many slaves and vehicles, that much livestock and equipment.

Out back, while the pensive Diana moved from the upper front veranda to the back to watch what was happening, Jed, Salem, and Tabitha—smiles wreathing their faces—rushed to stand near Luke and return his hearty greetings. Unaware that her lips drooped, Diana chided herself for feeling left out. His voice sounded exactly as she remembered it.

To the three awaiting his orders with apparent eagerness, Luke, his white hat in his hand and his face showing perspiration and weariness, said, "In those boxes and containers you'll find supplies for your kitchen, Tabitha. Jed, I've brought shoes and winter clothing for all of the blacks, including the new ones. Salem, I'm counting on you to get the hogs to the pens beside the barn."

What had threatened to become chaos turned into order,

right before Diana's wondering eyes. Luke secured help quickly—"Look lively!" he urged the slaves appearing from varied outbuildings in answer to his call—and watched his orders being carried out.

From her shaded spot on the upper back veranda, Diana noted that a few of the older resident slaves had moseyed up to greet their master and were plainly enjoying whatever Luke was saying. Somebody was leading the new horse and mules away and activities outside had calmed considerably by the time Diana went to her room for her bath. But her innards weren't calm.

"We finished the outside of the overseer's house while you were away," Jed told Luke when he returned from his assigned activities and found his employer gazing toward the upper back veranda. After seeing nobody there, Jed went on, "We did as you said and snaked some cypress trees out of the swamp for making boards. We fixed up the old kiln and the men have fired enough bricks for us to start on the fireplace. I've already moved in, since I'd like to do some of the finishing up inside myself. I appreciate the furniture you sent. It fits fine."

"Glad to hear it. You're a deserving man, Jed Latour. Salathiel's letters were complimentary."

Luke took a deep breath there in his backyard and looked around, his gaze and thoughts getting caught on the well shed. Diana Hathaway. Diana in the moonlight. For a moment his heart felt even fuller than when a short time ago he had sighted Fairfield's chimneys poking above the trees. His relief at being home and his sudden realization of his weariness were making him feel lightheaded. Or was it lighthearted? He shook his head to clear it. "As I said that first day, this feels like home."

"I believe you're right, boss. There's one more thing," Jed said, his face revealing a trace of self-consciousness. "I've been calling on a pretty young woman close to Calion named Fonza. She and her momma take in washing from some of the townfolk. Fonza says if you give your blessing, she'll talk about marrying up with me before long."

"You both have my blessing," Luke assured his overseer

as the two shook hands. Now that he had arranged to buy seedling cane stalks for putting in a big crop, Luke welcomed the news that Jed seemed enthusiastic about remaining at Fairfield. "I look forward to meeting your Fonza. Does this mean you'll stay on here?"

"You bet."

Jed left then, but not until the last bit of the frenzied activity taking place out back of the mansion had calmed did Luke enter his home. There, an impatient Salathiel Morgan awaited his turn with the forceful young master of Fairfield.

Upstairs in her bedroom, Diana went ahead and bathed, then fretted about what to wear. She was in a dither, no doubt about it. She assured herself that her unsettling reaction to seeing Luke again came from her renewed fears about what he might do to her and her friends if he learned of her deception. That, coupled with her guilty conscience for having deceived Salathiel and him even further over the past several weeks, contributed to her nervousness at meeting him face to face.

She thought about how during Luke's absence Salathiel had relaxed his vigilance when her recitations ended. He had often spent his time pursuing matters other than watching her play with her frisky dog. At such times when Salathiel was preoccupied and Lallage was not around, which was not often, Diana would visit with Tabitha in her kitchen, where she learned what was going on at Fairfield as well as at neighboring plantations.

Diana remembered how happy and relieved she was when Tabitha told her that Florina from Fernwood was mending. Then came the good news that she had married Second and that both now belonged to a planter far up Selene Bayou.

After her visits with Tabitha, who seemed so busy nowadays with the garden and the kitchen that she seldom had time to stop and talk, Diana would make certain that Salathiel was occupied and slip away with King to visit her home in the swamp.

A slight detour would lead Diana by the plantation's fenced cemetery. There she always laid wildflowers on the rough, curved tops of the long brick boxes holding the deceased that were dear to her: Drusila and Philip Hathaway, Mona and Owen Fairfield. Off to one side of the individual mounds holding the caskets above ground—a precaution necessary in swamp country to prevent the underground water close to the surface from sucking the caskets into its sandy currents and depositing them elsewhere—lay small piles of broken bricks rounded over the tarp-wrapped corpses of her first dog and Minerva. For them she always saved a few blossoms.

Each time Diana followed the shadowed plank walkway to her home, the increased deterioration that she found there appalled her. It seemed to her that in a kind of cruel, perverse way, as Fairfield regained its former splendor, even surpassed it in some ways, the Hathaway house was losing whatever beauty and purpose it once had claimed. Once during a pensive moment she found herself wondering if the abandoned house, where she had found nourishment from infancy to the moment Luke Greenwood had snatched her up, might not represent her former life.

The sight of a new patch of green mold or black mildew on a board, chair, or book was enough to pinch Diana's tender heart and send her scurrying for soap and water. Often she spent her entire visit cleaning and scrubbing and wiping off the leather bindings of her father's precious books.

Upon her return to the mansion after her secretive visits, Diana always felt her conscience prickle. Not only did she worry about lying when answering Salathiel's kindly questions about her afternoon—it bothered her that her lies came out more easily each succeeding time—but also she cringed on the inside just thinking that if Luke Greenwood ever found out. . . .

Sometimes when Diana would awake at night and remember that Luke had again been watching her in her dreams, she wondered if he might be haunting them just to find out what she was up to. Such an absurd action did not seem beyond him. Her growing cognizance of the fact that she possessed a mishmash of turbulent emotions about her handsome jailer and understood almost none of them led her to avoid thinking about him.

* * *

Suddenly, or so it seemed to Diana, she was dressed and standing before Luke, her tongue glued to the top of her mouth, her pulse skipping around madly. She did not know what she said, but it must have sufficed. Neither Salathiel nor he had laughed or evidenced disapproval. Even so, she sensed she might not be at her best. What if she got the hiccups?

"I believe you've had some success with Diana, Salathiel," Luke said after greeting the unusually pale-faced blonde. With undisguised admiration, he had watched her descend the stairs amidst a provocative flurry of rustling petticoats and full white skirt. Her blue eyes seemed fixed on him.

Luke found it hard to believe that the stylishly dressed young woman before him was the same half-naked Diana he had captured that night near the bayou. He felt eerily alerted all over, as if jerked from a trance. After his tedious three days and nights on the road, fatigue had claimed him until now. He felt buoyed up and devilishly lighthearted. *And lightheaded, too*, an inner voice added. He couldn't deny it. Didn't even want to.

How was it possible that Diana had become more beautiful? Luke wondered as the three of them entered the dining room. The candlelight from the candelabra in the center of the table delineated for him the exquisite angles and curves of her face with its sculpted cheekbones, perfect little nose, and full, rosy lips. With a young, virile man's appreciation for beauty, Luke noted that Diana's hair, held back from her face with a blue ribbon matching the one threading through the ruffle at the demure neck of her white gown, fell across her shoulders and down her back in waves of lustrous, silvery blonde. A strange urge to touch her hair, her cheek rushed over him.

Having no idea what Diana or Salathiel had been discussing, Luke diverted his wayward thoughts and said, "Salathiel, you've made commendable progress with Diana."

"She deserves far more credit for her success than I," Salathiel responded to Luke's casual remark in a peevish tone.

"As well as Lallage." Why was Luke acting dense? Could he not see and hear the wonders wrought in Diana during his absence?

Earlier during their brief exchange, Salathiel had deliberately held back talk of his pupil's progress so that Luke would be surprised and perhaps reward her with praise. Was it weariness that was causing the young man to stand looking as if he were existing in another world? Salathiel expounded on his earlier statement. "Luke, I assure you that Diana has been a most diligent and cooperative young woman. She deserves commendation."

"I was merely living up to my part of the pact," Diana said, encouraged by the Englishman's proud smile in her direction. "Lallage should get some praise, too." What would it take to stir Luke from his trancelike state? Had fatigue overtaken him? Since she was expecting him at least to mention her improved speech, she had taken pains to pronounce the ending to each word. He seemed oblivious. She had heard Luke bestow more words—happy, kind ones at that—on King in the back yard that afternoon than he was giving her now.

Not that Luke looked fatigued, Diana reflected. Far from it. Perhaps it was the contrast of his creamy-colored waistcoat and coat with his black hair and eyes that was leading her into thinking he was more devilishly handsome than ever. She had not forgotten the white hat and its rakish angle.

While the men finished their glasses of wine and Salathiel commented at length on the weather, Diana pondered whether or not she should thank Luke for the beautiful feminine apparel he had provided. She decided that since he obviously bought them only to enhance her appearance in New Orleans, she owed him no special thanks.

After all, Diana reminded herself, she would be leaving behind the stylish trappings when the Charity Ball ended and she once more took charge of her life. If Luke was self-centered enough to believe he would benefit by turning her into a facsimile of a cultured young woman, then so be it.

Precisely what Luke wanted to gain still eluded Diana and sometimes led her into toying with her original suspicions that he might be in league with the devil. Now that she had learned more about Luke and the world outside Gator Swamp, the earlier thought struck her as childishly illogical. Was it more irrational than Luke's plan for her transformation?

Then, as had become their custom, Salathiel held out Diana's chair for her at the long dining table and took his seat at the end opposite the one claimed by Luke. New wax myrtle tapers burned brightly, leaning and sighing every once in a while when a night breeze would wander through the open French doors leading onto the back veranda.

"How was the capital city?" Salathiel prodded, still trying to engage Luke in conversation about his time away from Fairfield. Throughout the meal Luke's comments had centered on the plantation and the mansion's remarkable renovations. "I trust you found things in good condition at your townhouse. Did you enjoy seeing all of your old friends? Did you manage a visit to the children in the orphanage? I hope you got in a good visit with your cousins. Tell us all."

When Luke seemed not to hear, Salathiel glanced at Diana, noticing that her usually animated face had lain in a kind of guarded repose all evening. Was she still afraid of Luke, as he had suspected back when she had first come? "Diana and I have not set foot off this place since you left. Lallage has held off would-be visitors by telling them that you were gone to the city and that there was no one here but workmen. Give us some news of the outside world."

"It was hotter there than here and twice as humid," Luke replied with an apologetic look on his face. He could hear the Englishman's tone of mild reproof for neglecting his manners. What would Salathiel say if he told him that the sight of Diana had knocked him somewhat senseless? "Almost everyone I know, including my cousins, had gone to the Gulf, either along the coast in Mississippi or Louisiana. I gather it's becoming quite fashionable now to seek the Gulf breezes in August and escape the stench and heat in New Orleans."

Even as he chatted with Diana and Salathiel about New Orleans, Luke thought of events that he had no intention of relating. Like when he reached his townhouse and found a note from his former mistress, Sidonie. She had invited him to join her at the beach house of a mutual friend, adding that while she had accepted their breakup, she would always welcome him to her arms.

Longing for a woman to assuage his needs in the artful ways that the beautiful Sidonie had mastered long ago, Luke had ridden Jasper over to the Mississippi coast. Once there, he lost himself in the raven-haired Sidonie's charms. To Luke's surprise, the former thrill of driving his throbbing shaft deep inside the moaning, writhing Sidonie seemed diminished, as if a fire long dead were trying to become a roaring blaze again without adequate fuel and thus could not advance beyond a few noticeable but unspectacular flickers.

After a few days Luke had found himself itchy to leave Sidonie and her party-minded friends to the sand and the sea. Thoughts of making plans and purchases for his new life at Fairfield quite took over his mind.

Salathiel's next remark brought Luke back to the moment.

"I assume," Salathiel said, "that you spent most of your time attending to business and did not see many of your friends."

"Something like that," Luke agreed. "I found the townhouse and its attendants in fine shape," he continued after Chloe set down soup bowls and left. He tasted the creamy liquid. "This turtle soup is the best I've eaten. I must let Tabitha know."

"Tabitha cannot take all the credit," Salathiel replied with a fond look toward Diana, who was wearing her happiest expression since coming downstairs. "She says Diana came to the kitchen one afternoon soon after you left and stayed until the soup was seasoned to her liking. Since then Tabitha has been following Diana's recipe."

"You obviously had talent before Salathiel took you in tow, Diana. I'm impressed and I'm grateful you shared your recipe with Tabitha."

"I'm good at making cheeses, too. Now that we have milk cows, I've taught Tabitha and Chloe how to make both hard and soft kinds." Diana lifted her chin and sent him a haughty look. Did he think she had lived at the bottom of a well before he grabbed her that night? She had almost forgotten how she always felt balled up inside every time she was around Luke, as if he were a giant, invisible fist enveloping her.

Chloe had removed the fish plates, each almost empty of the servings of baked bass seasoned with herbed butter and wild onions, and replaced them with smaller plates holding fluted pastry filled with golden custard dusted with cinnamon and nutmeg before Luke said to Diana, "I nearly forgot. I brought a ladies' maid for you. She has been trained to serve ladies and dress their hair in the latest fashions."

"Do you mean she's here now?" Salathiel asked.

"Yes. She went to the quarters to meet everyone. Jed promised to show her to his old bedroom off the back veranda. Her name is Odille."

"I don't need a ladies' maid and I don't want anybody doing anything to my hair," Diana announced. All at once she was finding words bubbling forth. His first evening home and already he was reverting to his old bossy self. "What's wrong with my hair the way it is? Lallage showed me how to pull it back with ribbons and I like it this way."

Luke did not need to be reminded that insofar as he was concerned, her hair was perfection the way it was. However, his discerning brother, Frederick, might not be impressed if Diana did not present the perfect picture of a pampered, wealthy young woman. Elaborate hairstyles seemed a necessity. "It doesn't matter what you like. What counts is the way I want you to look. I would have you appear fashionable and sophisticated in New Orleans."

Diana glared at her jailer who, from her viewpoint, was fast turning into an arrogant emperor. True, she found it less taxing when he seemed unwilling to address her directly. Somehow, though, she felt more alive when he did, even when his words stirred her temper. "Well, Napoleon, I'm not your Josephine. Neither am I a Madame Pompadour."

Luke chuckled then and noted that she no longer appeared too pale. Admiring the way her incredibly blue eyes were blazing, he said, "My, but you have been a studious young woman since I've been gone, haven't you?"

Not sure she was supposed even to know about the famous people she had named, Diana rushed to the heart of her complaint. "I believe I ought to have something to say about the way I look, even if you are determined to gain attention with the one you escort to the Charity Ball. The closer December comes, the more absurd the whole matter seems."

Salathiel shot Luke a look that spoke his sound agreement with their riled dinner companion.

"I see," Luke replied. In the candlelight, Diana's long hair seemed the same pristine white as her gown. Had her smooth skin always had that golden, almost translucent look?

While Salathiel gave his opinion about hairstyles, Luke got lost in thinking about how Diana Hathaway possessed an elusive quality that seemed palpably alive. Naturalness? Goodness? That was it. She was just plain good.

Then Luke was recalling that late one evening before he returned to New Orleans, Sidonie and he and their friends had strolled on the beach. One young woman chased a scurrying baby crab to stomp it with her shoe, her long blonde hair—not nearly as pale and silvery as Diana's—shimmering in the moonlight and digging up the unbidden memory of Diana on Midsummer's Eve.

The unwarranted cruelty of the young woman as she laughed brittlely and, with her foot, crushed out the life of the hapless little crab had brought Luke other memories of Diana. Diana looking frightened and submitting to his demanding pact because—Luke had little doubt that he knew what had compelled her—she feared for the well-being of her black friends at Fairfield. Diana weeping, heartbroken over the loss of her pet goat. Other heart-tugging memories. An unsmiling Diana watching him covertly, sadness lurking within her lovely blue eyes.

Luke forced his attention back to the conversation at his dining table and said, "Perhaps we can find a halfway measure in some matters, Diana, such as the way you wear you hair except during the season in New Orleans, but—"

"Season?" Diana asked with her dark eyebrows arching up in question and her pink lips forming their own query. Indignation underlined her words. "You said I had to go to only the one party or ball or whatever it's called. That's all

I agreed to, Luke Greenwood. Lallage has told me all about what 'season' involves.''

"We'll see," was all Luke could manage.

When Luke pushed his dessert aside and concentrated on sipping his coffee, Diana affirmed in a voice still testy, "I don't need or want a personal servant." How could his dark eyes be fixed on her and yet seem to be looking at something within, something that he apparently was not eager to see? She had seen that expression before—in her dreams. "Chloe or Tabitha always help me fasten the backs of my gowns. What else do I need a servant for?"

"All genteel young women have personal servants," Luke explained. He switched his gaze from Diana. She was studying him in a way that made him feel exposed. "It won't do for you to show up in New Orleans without someone to make sure your hair and clothing are always presentable. That can prove quite a task for a socially active young woman without able assistance."

Diana wondered how Luke could sound so knowledgeable about such things, but she buried the thought and persisted. "I don't see why having this Odille around is so important. Lallage can help me if I need help."

"Lallage will be staying in her own townhouse which is two blocks away from mine. Besides, she will be busy with her children and getting herself ready for the various parties and entertainments. You might be unaware, but Lallage is a very wealthy widow. Now that she's out of mourning, there likely will be many suitors waiting to escort her around New Orleans when she arrives."

Luke let his gaze return to Diana's face then. He deduced that the pensive look molding her beautiful features revealed she was, indeed, hearing something new. "This will be Lallage's first season since her husband's death," he added. "I know you'd not want to infringe upon her time."

Salathiel leaned back against his chair. As he smoothed his mustache with two fingers, he let Luke's words about Lallage Winston sink in. By Jove, Luke was right. Once the group arrived in the capital, the beautiful, curvaceous redhead would have a busy schedule—one that did not include him. He knew that before he slept that night, he wanted to delve into the reasons that the realization disturbed him. For an unguarded moment the memory of Lallage's delicious laughter teased his ears and stirred his blood. Down low.

Before Diana left the two men in the hallway to go have their brandy in the living room, she swept Luke with a measuring look. Tabitha had told her earlier that Callie, a slave at Wingate who was big with her fourth child and had always had difficult deliveries, was expecting her baby before daylight. Callie wanted Diana to come whenever she could sneak away.

During Luke's absence Diana had been sent for only twice, but she had begun keeping the satchel in her room. She liked knowing that it now lay underneath her bed and that as soon as the mansion became dark. . . .

"Good evening, miss," a tall, older woman with coloring suggestive of *café au lait* said when Diana stepped inside her bedroom. In a straightforward but respectful way she went on. "I hope you don't mind that Tabitha showed me up here. She assured me it would be all right for me to wait for you."

Diana recovered from her surprise. "I don't mind, but I wasn't expecting you to be here." In the faint light from the candle sitting on her dresser she eyed the woman, taking in the pleasing sight of her trim form. A snowy white apron covered most of her dress. Tied in two widely spaced knots with ends standing up perkily on the top of her head, a blue kerchief the same color as her dress covered her hair. Large golden earrings dangled from her earlobes. "You must be Odille."

"Yes, and you are Miss Diana Hathaway, guest at Fairfield."

"Yes." *Guest*? an inner voice hooted. More like *prisoner*.

"Though Mr. Luke owns my papers, I gather I'm to serve you as long as you find my services satisfactory. I've been shown my room downstairs, off the back veranda."

"That man seems bent on forcing someone on me to serve as my personal servant." Diana heard the irritation in her voice and shrugged with resignation. "Forgive me. I meant no disrespect."

"If you refuse to accept me, Mr. Luke might send me back to the auction blocks or, maybe worse, send me to work in the fields. I was trained to be a ladies' maid or house servant."

"I wouldn't want to cause you to end up in a worse situation. I'm sure you're very good at what you do. It's just that. . . ." How much should she say? It seemed unfair to let Odille think she might have found a permanent place. She seemed nice, worthy of honesty. After December—

Odille said, "I served the Creole family of Madame Genette Frontage in New Orleans until her recent death. Her heirs and their friends already had satisfactory personal servants, but her family held me off the market until a kindly person let it be known my services might be needed."

Diana sighed. What could she do but go along? The woman had a lovely manner and already she liked her. "I'll make no further fuss and let you assist me as you like. I've grown up in a simple way and I have few needs."

Odille smiled. "I suspect we'll get along fine. I've learned you're much loved by the slaves at Fairfield and that you received the gift of healing hands from your departed mother."

"I'm not gifted," Diana denied. "I learned a lot about healing from my mother, and I like helping sick people whenever possible."

"May I unfasten your gown and help you get ready for bed?"

"Yes, thank you."

If, as the domineering Luke insisted, someone should assist her, Diana mused after the efficient servant left, she doubted he could have come up with a servant more likable and pleasant than Odille. Maybe it would not be all bad to have someone around to talk with while she dressed and undressed in her stylish new clothing. Everyone else always seemed too hurried to do more than handle the back fastenings of her gowns before dashing off to other tasks. Now that Luke was home, the pace likely would increase.

While waiting for the house to become still so that she could go help Callie bring her fourth baby into the world, Diana stared through the open window into the night. She did not hear anything but a question whirling inside her mind. Had Luke ever thought about her while he was away?

Nine

One mild afternoon not long after his homecoming, Luke returned earlier than usual from his rounds over the plantation astride Jasper. As had become his custom, King trotted along nearby.

Luke thought about how his feeling harmonious with his surroundings seemed to increase daily. Fewer of the workers now eyed him with apprehension when he talked with them. Already he could call all by their names.

Leaving the stables behind after pausing at the well shed to wash up, Luke, with a young man's candid pride, surveyed the newly painted outbuildings sitting here and there on the spacious grounds behind the soaring red brick mansion. Why, Luke thought while watching a yellow butterfly wing its way lazily in the sweet-smelling sunshine, a man could lose himself in such a splendid haven as he had found in St. Christopher Parish.

As Luke made his way toward the back veranda, he greeted the exuberant youngsters playing blindman's buff in the backyard, a game the frisky King was now joining. The four Winston girls and three of the black children on the place seemed to be too engrossed to do more than return his greeting with smiles and waves.

Remembering having taken part in such games with his

sister, brother, and Delilah and Nathaniel Dace from the plantation next to Southwinds, Luke smiled. He knew why nobody dared make a sound, else the "blindman"—Lallage's ten-year-old Camelia with a handkerchief over her eyes—would follow the voices, perhaps be able to touch and identify their owners, then designate the new "it." Somehow, returning to find the children at play in his yard served as a particularly fine note for welcoming him home.

For no reason that he could ascertain, Luke found himself wondering if Diana Hathaway had ever played such childhood games. From the little information that either Salathiel or he had been able to extract, Luke rather doubted it. Evidently, she had spent her earlier years in the company of no one but her parents. Could that be why she so seldom laughed, the fact that she had never indulged in childish play with other youngsters and knew little about the joy of laughter?

Since his return, Luke mused, he never had heard Diana laugh, really laugh in the way she had done after scooting down the handrailing and knocking him down. Though Salathiel told him the other night as they sat sipping brandy in the living room that Diana laughed often in his presence now, actually smiled a great deal, Luke found it hard to believe. To Salathiel's cryptic remark about one reaping what one sows, Luke had raised an eyebrow and taken himself off to the library to make entries in his ledgers.

In spite of Diana's frequent apprehensive looks at him from underneath partially lowered eyelashes, and in spite of both the veiled and open barbs from Salathiel, Luke refused to view himself as her jailer—in the cold light of day, anyway. After all, she was eighteen and had agreed to go along with his plans. Besides, she must have had no life at all on that obscure finger of Bayou Selene where she said her house lay.

Surely, Luke' thoughts reassured him, Diana must be enjoying learning from Salathiel, else she could not have made such remarkable progress in a brief time. He was planning to reward her with a sum of money as well as with the extensive wardrobe he had provided. What better place than among New Orleans social circles for a young woman to meet prospective suitors? He realized that he should be feeling good about having made plans for Diana's future. He was not.

Luke, lost in his thoughts, strode down the hallway toward the inviting sounds floating from the library: adult laughter, excited voices, and an odd thumping noise. When he reached the open door, he asked jovially, "What's going on here?"

Unaware that they had gained a new audience, Diana was resting her left hand on Salathiel's shoulder while his right hand touched the back of her waist. They were moving their feet in rhythm—or trying to—and making a wobbly circle in the center of the library, laughing each time their feet collided. With Diana's right hand clasped lightly in his left, Salathiel extended their arms at stiff angles and pumped up and down as he chanted in exaggerated waltz time: "Step; slide; step. Do not look . . . at your feet. Step; slide; step."

From where Lallage sat on a chair near the library table, she was half singing and half humming her version of a Strauss waltz, all the while clapping her hands and tapping her foot on the floor in three-four time. Pooch, her small white dog whose eyes never wavered from the moving couple, huddled in a far corner until something compelled him to take part in the merriment. Suddenly propping up on his hind legs, Pooch threw back his head and let forth a high-pitched note.

"Hello, Luke," Lallage said when she realized he had spoken and was standing in the doorway with his mouth slightly ajar. She sent him a huge smile. "We've begun Diana's introduction to dancing."

"So I see," Luke replied drolly with a smile of his own. "Is Pooch applauding or protesting?" As if the little dog might be overcome with fatigue from its impromptu song, it flopped down on the floor and rested its head on its paws, not quite relaxing its ears. It kept its black eyes fixed on Salathiel. Luke leaned against the door and crossed his arms over his chest. "I came to see what was happening but I didn't come to interrupt."

Having stopped and released his hold on Diana as soon as

he heard Luke's voice, Salathiel said, "You came in the nick of time to save the afternoon, dear boy. I am far too rusty to be much of an instructor for our fair Diana."

"He isn't rusty at all," Lallage denied with a playful but doting look at the pink-faced Englishman. "At first he hummed a tune and danced around the room with me"—Luke's black eyebrows shot up in amusement at the mental picture and his teeth flashed white—"to give Diana an idea of what dancing is all about. He's a divine dancer when he doesn't have to instruct."

Recalling that Salathiel had always taken part in the balls held at Southwinds as well as in many at other plantations near Mobile, Luke nodded. "He has always given the ladies back in Alabama a whirl in grand manner. I also recall he insisted that his pupils receive training from a dance master, not from him."

Lallage dismissed Luke's wry comments with a flip of her pretty hand. "We've been having great fun, though I fear playing the part of an orchestra is not my best talent. Salathiel has a strong, marvelous singing voice,"—when Salathiel appeared flustered and shook his head in denial, she sent him a warm smile—"but when he does the music, I can't manage to dance the gentleman's part and show Diana the steps at the same time. I suspect I'm too accustomed to having a masterful man lead." She followed her last comment with a coquettish look toward the Englishman.

"Maybe my longtime friend has even more talent than I ever suspected," Luke replied dryly. He had not missed the coy look the vivacious widow sent Salathiel. Apparently, his suspicions since his return were true: Lallage Winston was flirting with Salathiel and Salathiel was not blind to her game, was maybe even relishing it. Salathiel's recent remarks to him about the irritating habit of her pet growling at him without justification led Luke into wondering if Pooch might not also be suspecting the Englishman was edging into the affections of his mistress.

Feeling keyed up by the almost tangible excitement charging the air in the library, Luke reflected that the tangy, pre-autumn smells of the mellow afternoon he had sensed outside were drifting through the open French doors. He had noticed before, with keen appreciation for Salathiel's aid in redecorating, that the tall-ceilinged room appeared inviting. Letting his gaze rove, he admired the walnut bookshelves reaching to the corners on both sides of the black-veined marble fireplace and the newly painted yellow plaster forming the other walls. The canvases of English hunting scenes he had discovered in a gallery in the French Quarter seemed perfect. He liked the way the huge oaks beyond the front veranda nearly always kept the library, as well as the living room directly across the foyer, in cool, green-tinged shadow.

Only half listening to Lallage's observations about waltzing, Luke confessed that he also liked the way the radiant Diana Hathaway appeared in her white cotton gown. He recalled it was the one she had been wearing on his first evening back, the gown with the blue ribbon trim that matched the ribbon holding back her strikingly blonde hair. In truth, at that moment Luke Greenwood liked everything in the world.

"Luke, you have always been a fine dancer," Salathiel remarked. He took Diana's hand and led her to where Luke still leaned against the door with a devilish grin on his handsome face. He suspected that his young friend was close to bending double with laughter at the picture that Lallage had described.

Salathiel freed Diana's hand, then jerked down his waistcoat and patted the top of his hair, not surprised that his earlier exertion had ruffled it. "Luke, would you please take Diana and show her what we have been talking about all afternoon? That way perhaps I can sing along with Lallage and at least offer a stronger beat."

Diana felt her face, already flushed from her previous efforts, grow hotter when Luke continued to watch her and remain silent. A tad piqued at his seeming indifference to Salathiel's request, she brought her hands to her hips and taunted, "Yes, why don't you, Luke? After all, you're the one who will be dancing with me at the ball. It takes two to make a pact work."

Luke never had given much thought to the fact that dancing lessons were to be a vital part of getting Diana ready to go to New Orleans. Without warning he felt clumsy and heavy footed, he who had always found dancing a lark and as easy as walking. Though Diana's eyes, as usual, had seemed clouded deep inside their blue depths, they were lifted now to his with as much clarity as he had ever seen. He shrugged with good-natured carelessness and grinned. "I'm fresh from riding the fields and don't have on even a waistcoat, but why not?"

Luke took Diana's hand and walked with her to the center of the floor, thinking that her hand seemed uncommonly small and feminine as it rested in his. The same alien feeling that had made his feet become leaden moments earlier was now disrupting his pulse. Perhaps, he consoled himself, he was overly eager to appear at ease before the watchful Lallage and Salathiel. His voice a bit ragged, he said, "Promise you'll not slap me if I step on your toes. I may not be much good as an instructor."

Oh? Diana's eyes questioned as her heartbeat fluttered from his overwhelming nearness and reminded her that she obviously had not overcome her fear of him. She could think of no other explanation for her inner upheaval. When had the tall, handsome Luke Greenwood, who was seemingly oozing confidence as he stood before her in form-fitting trousers and a barely buttoned white shirt blousing above his trim waist, ever before even *hinted* that he might not be master of all things?

For some reason, Diana found Luke less intimidating now that he had admitted to the possibility of being vulnerable in one area. Though he had prefaced his *not* with *may*, she wondered if she might not be liking him a little better since his confession.

Luke, his lean face serious, said, "Lay your left hand on my shoulder as you were doing to Salathiel's"—she did, looking up at him as obediently as a meek schoolgirl—"and I'll place mine at your waist." He did, clearing his throat of an annoying itch and thinking that the beautiful young woman in his arms smelled like freshness itself—soap and water and some delicate fragrance that seemed to be wafting from her bewitching hair and whispering femininity. The wide blue satin ribbon serving as a sash around her tiny waist felt smooth and enticingly warm to the underside of his hand.

"And then what?" Diana asked. She forgot all about anybody but the two of them being in the room, for she was having to concentrate on breathing. *I wonder why the warmth of his shoulder through the fine fabric of his white shirt feels different from Salathiel's? Maybe it's because Salathiel is wearing a coat.*

Each time Luke made the slightest movement, Diana could feel the flexing of his muscles underneath her fingertips. She decided she had best keep her gaze on his face, for it kept threatening to get lost in the black chest curls peeking through the V of his shirt. Up close, Luke smelled like man, horse, and leather. Chiefly man. Virile man.

At first, Diana had labeled the combination scent overpowering and frightening. Now she was conceding that she found it not at all offensive. In fact, she confessed in the next moment as she adjusted to the heady feeling of his warm hand engulfing hers, she liked it.

"I assume Salathiel was teaching the waltz." When Diana nodded, Luke continued. "Take a step backward on your left foot as I take one forward on my right,"—she moved as instructed, her wide-eyed gaze on his face as he also stepped—"then slide your foot and take another step."

"Like this?" *Amazing*, Diana thought while, however awkwardly, her feet made the motions Luke prescribed. She was following him without having to look down as she had felt compelled to do with Salathiel as instructor. More amazing was how Luke's resonant voice had dropped to a pitch lower than normal. It sounded almost intimate, as if designed only for her ears. She had heard him speak that way before, but never to her. Gooseflesh feathered her spine and brought a little shiver. She adored it.

"Like that, yes."

As they tried a few steps, Luke heard the bold sounds of his boots and the whisper of Diana's slippers on the polished wooden floor meshing with the murmurings coming from her long white skirt and petticoats brushing against his boots and trousers. The conjoined sounds brought to his mind intriguing contrasts: hard and soft, dark and fair, likes and opposites. Man and woman.

Maybe dancing did not require music to provide pleasure, Luke reflected as he thought of how fragile Diana's slender body felt in his arms. He smiled to himself when he saw she was concentrating so hard that she was sucking in a side of her bottom lip and holding its upper edges between her teeth—pretty teeth, he amended, white and even. He realized then that from the first moment he had seen her up close that night in the moonlight, he had admired Diana's spirit.

"Diana, I'm pleased," Luke said. "You're remembering what Salathiel has already taught you and doing a good job. With some practice you'll be the finest dancer in New Orleans." Luke was feeling too heady and right with the world to note the stricken look that his mention of New Orleans brought to Diana's eyes. "Now pay attention to the pressure of my hand on your waist and learn to follow the direction I'm moving in. Keep up the steps."

From where Lallage and Salathiel sat watching the couple's stilted progress, Salathiel called, "Let us know when you're ready for us to give you some rhythm to follow."

After Luke nodded his agreement, Diana made two fairly decent turns with him at his low instructions, then stopped and frowned up at him. "Why does the man always get to dance forward?"

Luke laughed. He never before had thought of how difficult it might be for a woman to adapt all of her movements to those of her partner. For a moment she had seemed about to join in his laughter. He wished she had, though her smile was bright and nice to see. Her mouth was exquisite, much too tempting. Had she ever been kissed? "I won't always move forward. You'll see."

Within a short time Luke gave the signal to Lallage and Salathiel and they became an amateurish orchestra sending out the three-four rhythm of a Viennese waltz in far more acceptable manner than they gave out melody. Pooch trotted over to stand beside Lallage and stare at Salathiel, baring his teeth every time the man gave a direct look at his mistress.

When Lallage shook her finger at her pet, he promptly dropped onto the part of her skirt lying on the floor and pouted.

"You're improving," Luke told Diana after a brief time, "but if you'd move your hand up behind my neck, you could swing with my turns easier."

Diana did as he asked, not surprised that what he said was true and that she was able to follow his long legs with far more ease. She was not sure if the new placement of her hand was all that contributed to her increased skill, of if his having pulled her body closer to his ranked as an even higher factor.

Then Diana found she had no sense of falling when Luke whirled her around, though her head still felt too light. Beneath her fingertips the feel of his neck through the thin fabric of his shirt transmitted even more vibrancy than had that of his shoulder. Where his hand pressed on the back of her waist might as well have been a burning brand. It seemed to her that the few inches separating their bodies were turning into a space of intensity akin to that she had often suspected lay in low, overhanging rain clouds. One spark of lightning, and a storm might break loose.

"Hang on," Luke said. "We're off!" When he added his soft bass humming to the sounds coming from the couple across the room, Diana felt her feet become airborne.

"Have you ever heard anyone play a violin?" Luke asked after they made several satisfactory whirls. She seemed far more relaxed in his arms by then and he no longer felt the need to hum the beat or count aloud.

Diana shook her head, the action sending her long hair into a dance of its own as he twirled them around and took backward steps, smiling at her mischievously to let her know he was remembering to let her take forward steps at frequent intervals. She answered with a smile of appreciation.

"A violin sings sweetly," he said. "You'll love hearing an orchestra play."

"Will I?"

"I'm sure of it." How long since he had had such a good time?

"Will there be a viola?"

"Most likely." He peered down into her face with new interest. "Have you heard a viola played?"

"No, but my father—" Diana caught herself. Dared she reveal that Philip had told of playing the viola when he was a youngster back in Boston? "My father told me about it."

Luke tried piecing together what Diana had told earlier about her parents and her upbringing. How would an illiterate trapper in southern Louisiana know about a viola? "Did your father grow up in Louisiana?"

"No."

"Do you know where he grew up?"

"I can't talk and dance at the same time."

"You must learn to. Most of your dancing partners will expect a little small talk, maybe a hint of flirtation."

Diana's face again took on a withdrawn look, one Luke noticed that time. "I thought I would be dancing only with you."

"No. I'll be your escort, and I'll dance with you, but you'll dance with many other men, too."

"I'm ready to stop," Diana announced as she dropped her arm from around Luke's neck and disengaged their hands.

Before Lallage and Salathiel got out more than a few words of praise for the dancers, a god-awful noise came from somewhere out back. Pooch hurried to the door to investigate the high-pitched sounds. Though the others appeared puzzled, Lallage started toward the door. She never made it that far.

"Mama!" called Japonica, her usual attempts to act and sound older than her thirteen years vanishing as she dashed into her mother's waiting arms. Tears streamed down her face while Diana, Luke, and Salathiel moved to stand closer together and watch in concerned surprise. "I tripped and fell down and King tore off my sash and chewed holes in it. And, Mama, everybody laughed when I tried to catch him and get it away from him. I fell down again and—"

"Mama!" chorused the other three redheaded girls when they stormed into the library. All were crying at the tops of their shrill voices by the time they reached their mother.

Pooch marched out of the room, his head high and his tail waving sedately from side to side, as if signaling surrender.

"Japonica yanked my pigtails," Camelia reported, "and it hurt something dreadful." Tears rolled from her brown eyes as Lallage murmured sweet sympathetic sounds. With an agility born of experience, she eased Japonica to one side and took in her second oldest daughter with her other arm.

"But, Mama," Hyacinth, the youngest little girl, protested in between great wails and torrents of tears, "I'm the one with the most to cry about. A bumblebee stung me on my arm."

When Diana rushed to the four-year-old, Hyacinth glared at her as if earlier that day Diana and she had not been sitting on the ground in the back yard laughing and making daisy chains out of clover blossoms. Lallage's youngest attached her arms to her mother's backside, the only available spot since Daisy had leaned across her front.

"It wasn't a bumblebee, only a honeybee. She was chasing it, and I told her to stop," Daisy volunteered with loud sobs and snubby looks punctuating her words now that Lallage seemed to be more concerned over Hyacinth than anyone else. "It's her fault that I stubbed my toe on the edging of the herb garden and fell down." Her soiled face streaking with new tears when Lallage managed to free an arm and pat the eight-year-old's head, Daisy held out her long skirt. "And now my favorite dress is torn!"

Iris rushed in then, out of breath and with an apologetic look on her face. "Miss Lallage, I was in the kitchen with Tabitha seein' 'bout 'freshments for the girls an' I thought I was keepin' a good eye on 'em—"

"Never mind, Iris," Lallage reassured in an understanding tone. "Please wait outside until I get this matter settled."

Lallage turned her attention back to her four weeping daughters who had her literally surrounded and were turning her cotton gown into a damp rag. "Now what am I going to do with my darlings? I'm heartbroken that you're all so unhappy, but I believe you should stop crying now, don't you?" Increased weeping was her reward. "Please, girls, you're causing an awful commotion in our host's library." She might as well have been the wind blowing. "Please—" Almost in tears herself by then, Lallage sent a piteous look toward Salathiel.

"Stop that infernal caterwauling!" the Englishman ordered in the firmest, loudest voice he could muster and not consider it yelling. Instant silence. Four pairs of wet brown eyes swung toward him and glared, their expressions showing no more surprise than Salathiel's. "You're driving your mother insane."

Hyacinth hiccupped and stuck her thumb in her mouth, the side of her head still resting against her mother's buttocks. The other three girls seemed hypnotized.

As if he were reciting a formula tried and true, Salathiel intoned in his elegant British manner, "If you must cry all at once, you may step away from your mother, form a line, and start at the count of three. Ready? One. T—"

Gales of giggles stopped Salathiel from counting further. The four girls leaned against their mother and each other and giggled until they almost lost their breaths.

By then Lallage was laughing and Diana was giggling along with the girls. The entire situation was so absurd that Luke found himself chuckling, even as his eyes and ears focused on the delightfully animated Diana. Still in a state of shock that he had lost control of himself for even that brief space of time, Salathiel was the last to join in.

Iris stuck her head around the door, her puzzled gaze darting from one laughing face to another and settling on that of her mistress. "Miss Lallage, Tabitha an' me fixed up some milk an' cake for the girls out on the veranda an'—"

"Wonderful," Lallage said, hugging each daughter before they scampered from the room. She called after them, "When you've finished your refreshments, we'll be going home."

"But, Mama," Hyacinth paused in the door to say in her charming four-year-old manner, "I'd rather stay here with Mr. Salathiel a while longer."

"Get along with you," Lallage replied. With her pretty face flushing, she patted her red curls and sent a provocative look toward the Englishman. She sighed at the mystery of it all. When had he ever appeared more masterful? "You seem to have a winning way with women of all ages, Salathiel Morgan."

Over the next two weeks Luke returned only once to the library during Diana's dance lessons. When Salathiel accused him in private of being a coward, Luke had not defended himself. In truth, he himself wondered if he might not be running from facing up to something baffling. Her name was Diana.

As for Diana, she daily stepped, glided, and whirled with Salathiel to the somewhat shaky "te-*dum*, te-*dum*, te-*dum*, *dum-dum*!" coming from the ebullient Lallage. Often she thought of how much more exciting it had been to be held by the handsome, dark-haired Luke than by the Englishman. At other times she ignored such inane thoughts—they had to be inane, she reasoned; Luke had paid her scant attention since that afternoon, none of which was exciting—and went about the prescribed business of learning the varied dance steps.

After Lallage taught Diana how to hold up the hem of her long skirt in her right hand as she waltzed and to manage bits of polite conversation while dancing, Diana was liking far more than she had believed possible the idea of dancing to the strains of an orchestra among a room full of people. With Luke as her partner, she always added. She found herself imagining how surprised and pleased Luke would be when he danced with her at the upcoming Charity Ball. The only praise he had ever given her for her many accomplishments was that proffered the afternoon he had waltzed with her.

One afternoon a spate of hand clapping sounded in the doorway right after Diana had curtsied to the bowing Salathiel, the courtly ritual ending their minuet. When Diana, Lallage, and Salathiel turned and acknowledged Luke's applause and presence with pleased smiles, Luke said, "Nice dancing. The time has come for Diana to begin riding lessons."

Diana brushed back a lock of hair that had fallen forward over her shoulder. Luke's lean face wore the reserved expression she had never liked. Her heartbeat was stepping up its pace. ''Now?'' She heard the tremor in her voice but hoped that he had not.

''Now. I asked Odille to go to your room to help you get dressed properly. I'll wait for you out back.''

Determined not to let Luke know how much she feared horses, Diana bade farewell to Lallage and Salathiel. With her chin lifted to a haughty angle, she swept out of the library to follow his instructions. Luke was back in the role of jailer. He had said he ''asked'' Odille to assist her in changing her clothing, but he had *told* her what he wanted of her.

While hurrying up the stairs to her bedroom, Diana recalled her first view of the beautiful white horse, Duchess, when Luke had returned from New Orleans. She also recalled the aura of power and authority exuding from Luke that afternoon as he dealt ably with his overseer, his slaves, and his newly acquired livestock. Even when she tried, she could not forget that he exercised similar control over her.

''Have you ever ridden before?'' Odille asked in her warm, rich voice.

''No, and I don't see why everyone thinks that's peculiar.'' Diana's temper flared a whit when she recalled that Luke seemed to think everything about her upbringing was unorthodox. Just because it differed greatly from his own did not mean her former life was the one out of kilter, or so it seemed to her.

''Only in bayou country does it seem odd, missy,'' Odille assured as she adjusted the fullness of Diana's blue riding skirt. ''Don't be afraid. You're brave and you can manage riding a horse.''

''I know, but thanks for reminding me.'' Diana angled her chin higher in emphasis.

Uncle Owen had owned a few horses back when she was a child, Diana recalled as she dutifully sat and allowed Odille to brush her hair, back when Aunt Mona was alive and he kept the plantation in good shape. Since his wife had never been keen on riding, he obviously had assumed that few women really cared for the sport. He never offered to put Diana up on a horse. Uncle Owen had seemed fonder of teasing and talking with Diana than sharing the activities with her that Philip did, such as hunting or fishing, exploring in the swamp, and playing chase along the banks in the cool of the evenings.

Later, Diana reflected, after Aunt Mona died and Uncle Owen was alone, he had seemed to lose interest in the considerable aspects of being a prosperous planter and had allowed all of his horses, with the exception of the one he rode, to become mere work animals. On her frequent visits to the mansion with her father, which usually took place late in the afternoons or after dark so that none of the occasional passersby might discover them, Diana seldom saw a horse even from a distance.

"I'll hunt some lotion so I can rub your backside when you return," Odille said. She lay down the brush and eyed Diana's hair with apparent satisfaction.

"You're kind, but I won't be needing it." Diana had learned that her personal servant was as quick to offer advice about sundry matters as she was to give assistance in helping her dress and arrange her hair.

Despite Tabitha's assurances that she believed Odille trustworthy, Diana had found it awkward at first to have the quadroon closely involved in her private life. Maybe if she had not been without a mother since she was ten, she would already have become accustomed to having an older woman present in her bedroom as she dressed and undressed, one who always seemed keenly interested in every aspect of her being. Daily, the young woman was finding it less alien to confide somewhat in Odille and to listen to her soft-voiced comments about matters other than grooming.

Odille smiled and adjusted the ever-present, immaculate blue scarf hiding her hair, the little action setting her gold earrings to swaying. "You might be glad if I have some lotion ready. We'll see."

Piqued that everyone seemed to know more about everything than she did, Diana moved restlessly. "Why do you suppose he's gruff so often?"

Odille did not ask her to identify the "he." "Perhaps the master carries a burden inside almost too heavy to bear."

"My father always said that almost everyone does. He certainly did after my mother died. He wasn't sharp tempered and hard to please, though." Diana sighed. If only Luke would like her and show that he did . . . a little.

Odille slid her hands into the pockets of her white apron and moved toward the door. "I promised Tabitha I would help her roll out the pastry for some meat pies."

Diana recognized that she was deliberately stalling. With a sigh of resignation she rose. "Shall we walk downstairs together?"

Ten

Holding Duchess's reins in one hand, Luke stood beside the saddled horse in the fenced lot behind the stables. When Diana neared, he said, "You look the part of an equestrienne."

"Let's hope looks play a major role," she replied.

Luke's appreciative gaze swept from her fashionable blue costume, which was comprised of a voluminous skirt and brief, sleeveless jacket over a white blouse, down to her black boots with their decorative little silver spurs. He well remembered when he had spied the boots in the window of a fashionable bootery in the French Quarter and known instantly they would be perfect for her pretty little feet. She should be wearing gloves and a hat, he mused, but he liked seeing her long hair bound back simply by a blue ribbon. Maybe Diana had her own sense of style.

Diana's gaze met his unflinchingly, Luke noted, as if a will too strong to resist forced it. *His* will? He had not forgotten Salathiel's unwelcome statement back in the summer that Diana was afraid of him. "Are you afraid?"

"Yes." *Of you, the horse, what is happening to me.*

"I wouldn't have believed you had you said no. I like people who are honest."

"So do I."

Before Luke helped Diana mount and settle on the side-saddle, he insisted she look the beautiful white horse in the eyes and pat her nose, talk to her.

"What does one say to a horse?" She could think of no reason to confide that earlier she had visited Duchess in her stall where she had learned to stroke her handsome white nose with its slight dish shape and flaring dark nostrils.

"Maybe what one says to a dog."

Diana slid him a devilish look. "Or to a goat?"

He chuckled, glad to see she could now speak of Minerva in a light tone. "Why not? Try it and see. Horses are smart. They know what we say."

"I'm surprised that you realize animals understand people."

"Why? I'm not that much different from others."

Diana sent Luke a doubting look, then murmured a greeting to Duchess. She felt a bit of a fool until the horse flicked her ears and tentatively nuzzled her shoulder. When Luke pulled a handful of brown-sugar crystals from his pocket, placed some in her hand, then made her open her palm and let Duchess's black muzzle quiver against it while she took the sugar, Diana flinched. Her tension did not lessen its grip until she realized that the horse's huge, velvety lips had brushed her palm with no more than the same kind of tickling, moist pressure as had Minerva's smaller ones when she had hand-fed the goat tender leaf buds.

Luke then told Diana the names of the varied parts of the harness on Duchess, explaining their purposes in his deep, resonant voice. She grimaced upon seeing the metal bit inserted in the horse's mouth but felt reassured when he showed that the reins were attached to both ends, thus providing the rider control of the animal.

"A rider must never forget he holds the reins in his hand," Luke cautioned. "If you hold them too tightly, you hurt the horse's tender mouth. He's likely to rear up in search of relief and maybe unseat his rider. On the other hand you can't afford to hold them too lightly, for the horse can tell when the reins are loose. He could seize control and run away."

Diana shuddered at both possibilities. "How could anyone forget he's holding the reins?"

"He might become distracted by something or—"

"Don't worry about that happening to me," she interrupted with conviction. "I'll never become distracted by anything while I'm high up on that"—she almost said *monster*, then recalled about horses being able to understand human talk—"that tall horse." At his amused smile, she asked, "Have you ever become distracted while riding?"

"No, and I'm not planning to, especially not on my feisty Jasper." Both glanced over to the far side of the lot where Luke's black stallion, still saddled from an earlier ride, stood with his reins looped around one of the posts supporting the board fence. "Probably Jasper would like nothing better than a chance to dump me and prove he's the real master."

Diana shuddered. "Do you prefer riding such a horse?"

"Yes. I enjoy the challenge."

Was she, Diana wondered, perhaps no more than another kind of challenge to the seemingly cocksure gambling man? Her pulse seemed set on echoing her fear; it showed no signs of slowing. She flipped back her hair with both hands and sent him a penetrating gaze. "Lallage and Salathiel have told me that you're an excellent horseman. Do you suppose Duchess will know I'm a beginner and try to unseat me?"

"I doubt it. She's been trained to be ridden by women and respond to a light touch on the reins. I've taken her out a time or two and she seems easy to manage. There'll be times you will have to show her you're in control."

From where they stood close together on the right, mounting side of Duchess, Luke introduced Diana to the sidesaddle with its low cantle extending around the far side to the almost nonexistent pommel in front that together formed a defined seat. She sniffed at the smell of new leather and well-groomed horse, finding it surprisingly invigorating. With appreciation, Luke watched the thoughtful pursing of Diana's full lips and the momentary little wrinkling of her pretty nose. The way her thick, dark eyelashes hid her eyes and fanned in semi-circles against her creamy skin spurred him into wishing she would lift her blue eyes and tell him what she was thinking.

"How did a saddle just for women come into being?" Diana asked, looking up at Luke then and sensing that he was trying to read her mind. Her innate curiosity was helping squelch her fears, but Luke's nearness and eagerness to interest her in horses and riding contributed their part to the changed direction of her thoughts.

The sweet sunshine of the autumn afternoon kept bathing Luke's handsome face and highlighting his dark eyes and hair. It came to Diana that this tall man in the dazzling white shirt was a sight to enjoy. As when he had waltzed with her, he was not acting in the least like her jailer. Was Luke, perhaps, becoming her friend? The idea appealed to her.

He replied to her question, "I gather the sidesaddle came from an ancient contraption with a board suspended on one side so the rider could sit sideways and have a place to rest her feet." He placed his hand on the upright pommel set a few inches below the flat pommel centered over the animal's withers. "Here's where your right knee hooks, and here," —he touched a lower pommel not protruding to such a great degree—"is what your left leg can push upward against when you need a more substantial grip than the single stirrup offers."

Diana pursed her lips throughout Luke's explanations, liking the way he seemed to care that she learn more than how to hang on to a horse while perched on a sidesaddle. She looked over to where Jasper was now pawing at the black dirt with one of his front hooves.

Except for the two projecting side pommels and extended cantle, the saddle on Jasper resembled the one on Duchess. It, too, had a leather skirt sticking out from underneath the saddletree in order, according to Luke, to protect the rider from the perspiration of his mount. Though the single stirrup of silvery metal on Duchess's saddle seemed about the same size as Luke's, but on a much shorter strip of leather, Diana saw an identical stirrup hanging on the opposite side of his horse.

"Women never ride astride as men do, I gather," Diana remarked, thinking aloud without realizing it.

"Not that I've ever seen." When she swept him with a

searching gaze, he added with a wry twitching of his generous mouth, ''Something to do with the delicacy of a woman's body, I believe.''

Diana felt a wave of heat flooding her face. Without warning, the soft flesh between her legs felt achingly alive, as if alerted. What was there about the way his eyes were sweeping over her that reminded her more than his words that she was woman, he was man? Was he, perhaps, thinking the same thing she was? Her last thought did nothing to reduce the flush on her neck and face. Or the wild pace of her pulse.

Luke reminded himself that he should proceed as planned and pay no attention to the erratic patterns of his heartbeat. Would not any virile man find it difficult to ignore the nearness of the beautiful blonde? With his lean face solemn and his eyes businesslike, he showed Diana how to slip her left foot in the stirrup and was soon boosting her up to sit on the saddle.

''Are you comfortable?'' he asked, his hand still resting on the small of her back. He tried not to notice the way her long hair brushed across his hand and tempted it to explore her shining curls. ''Have you hooked your right leg over the pommel?''

Diana nodded. ''Yes.'' When she leaned with a cascade of blonde hair tumbling around her face and shoulders and rearranged the folds of her blue skirt, he removed his hand. She became painfully aware of how high she was from the ground and how her heart was thumping.

''Hold the reins loosely in whichever hand feels better.'' Luke brought them up over the horse's head and showed her how.

The moment she took the reins, Diana felt his warmth on the narrow strips of leather. Neither looked at the other when their hands met and seemed to want to linger and become better acquainted. At Luke's low-voiced direction, Diana tested the tautness of the reins, aware that while he talked, he stood almost leaning against her legs. Once when she looked down fully into his uplifted face, she thought she glimpsed something warm and provocative in his probing dark eyes.

Luke then left Diana on her own in the saddle and, with his fingers tucked underneath Duchess's chin strap, led the horse at a slow pace around the outer edges of the fenced lot. The only sounds Diana could hear at first were the beats from her thundering heart and the squeaks from the saddle. To keep from crying out, she sucked part of her lower lip inside her mouth and held it with her teeth.

By the third trip around the lot, Diana was adjusting to the feel of the powerful animal underneath her. She shed a degree of fear at each succeeding step that the horse and the long-legged man directing their path made. Her teeth gradually unclenched and released their grip on her lower lip.

Now Diana could hear the clops of Duchess's hooves upon the black, hard-packed soil and the cries of a disturbed field lark from somewhere close by. No longer did the nickers coming at intervals from the watching Jasper send quivers up her spine and remind her of the tiny river of perspiration forming between her breasts. The reins felt alien in her wet hand. Odille had been right. She should have worn gloves.

"You're doing great," Luke called from where he was standing in the center of the lot, watching Diana maneuver the white horse around the edges on her own. Her eyes still occasionally shot him blue daggers, Luke reflected with admiration for her game spirit, especially when Duchess would vary her walking gait and jostle her tense rider. It had been a while, though, since his pupil had released her bottom lip from between her teeth. He slipped his hands in his trouser pockets. Pride in Diana lifted his heart and brought a wrenching tightness to his throat.

Luke noticed the sun was sinking toward the tops of the trees in the distance, its slanting rays lending a golden sheen to the white of the horse and the white of Diana's hair. The way she held her slender body erect and her head at an elegant angle pleased him, made him think of paintings he had seen of royal ladies posing atop their mounts. "Once more around, Diana, and we'll have your first lesson behind us."

After that first afternoon, Diana and Luke made great strides toward turning her into a woman at ease on a horse.

She lost her unreasoning fear of horses and this tempered what she earlier had felt toward Luke.

The easiness and the unexplained headiness marking the time of that first lesson seemed to accompany each succeeding one, as if their relationship outside the mansion might be one entirely different from the one inside its handsome walls. Diana wondered why it was that during the few meals they shared, Luke still maintained an almost aloof attitude toward her. She liked the carefree, exciting times of riding with him too much to brood overly long about the matter. She dared not confide her baffling thoughts to Tabitha or Lallage or Odille. They might think her daft. Sometimes she thought so herself.

Soon Diana was riding alongside Luke over the back pastures almost every afternoon, gradually able to think of something other than the reins in her hand and the powerful animal she controlled with such thin strips of leather. To Diana's delight Duchess's best traveling gait was what Luke called a three-beat canter, a gait that offered a pleasant, bumpless ride.

Diana began looking forward to the challenge of the daily afternoon rides with Luke, rides postponed or moved to a different time only by the frequent seasonal rains. She also looked forward to the challenge of learning more about the man who, at least while they rode their horses, was acting less and less like her jailer. Had anyone thought to ask her if she was having a good time, she would have replied with an unequivocal *yes*.

"You're turning into quite a conversationalist about almost any topic," Luke told Diana one early autumn afternoon as Duchess and Jasper cantered side by side in the far pasture bordering Fernwood. She had pleased him with her eloquent comments about English art and architecture. "Salathiel must have ordered you to study every book in the library, now that you're reading on such a high level."

"Salathiel is my friend and he never *orders* me to do anything."

"Unlike me," he said. He threw back his head and laughed. "Is that what you're implying?"

She shrugged one shoulder and slid him a provocative look.

With relish he said, "You wouldn't be having such a good time riding Duchess if I hadn't ordered you to learn how."

She pursed her lips before admitting, "Maybe."

"It's true and you know it."

Miffed, Diana showed him her profile, then angled it a degree higher against the sky, a canvas of deep blue feathered on the edges by puffs of white clouds soaring into filmy mushroom shapes. "You always have to win."

"Not always." Luke's conscience tweaked him by stirring up a fleeting thought of his bet with Frederick.

They cantered in silence until they reached three live oak trees that had been left as shelter for livestock near the rail fence separating Fairfield from Fernwood. Luke reined up underneath the low-lying limbs draped with moss, and after she did likewise, he said, "I thought it might be good to rest the horses for a moment before starting back."

"By Jove, dear boy," Diana quipped without thinking, imitating Salathiel's accent with open fondness for the Englishman, "I do believe you have come up with an absolutely smashing suggestion."

Luke chuckled. "You'll have to do that bit for Salathiel. He'll love it. You have a flair for mimicking."

Diana started and avoided his gaze. How asinine of her to allow herself to feel so relaxed around Luke that she let her love of—and talent for—mimicry show! "I can't imagine what got into me. I had no idea that I might sound at all like Salathiel. Don't tell him, please. He might be offended."

After Luke helped Diana dismount and tethered their horses in a grassy spot of shade, he sauntered to where she sat on a grassy little knoll underneath one of the thick-branched oaks, gazing toward the Fernwood herd of cows on the far side of the fence. Standing but relaxed, Luke rested his back against the trunk of the tree opposite Diana. Then he folded up one leg and propped the sole of one black boot against the broad trunk. He slid his hands into the pockets of his trousers and promptly dismissed the bucolic scenery.

Luke looked down at the beguiling sight before him. Diana

Hathaway. More and more he was discovering that, as Salathiel had been pointing out from the first, she proved a delightful companion with an exceedingly quick mind. "Since you said you never knew any of the planters, I gather you never met the owners of Fernwood."

"No, I never met any of the Oates family." What would he say if she told him she knew the slaves at Fernwood and had ministered to many of them? Suddenly, she felt as if a string long wrapped around her heart without her knowledge was tightening. He thought he knew much about her, when he actually knew next to nothing. So much deception!

"Julius Waskom married the widowed Mrs. Oates last year. Her eldest son, Maynard, is the man who wagered Fairfield against the high stakes in the poker game we were playing in New Orleans. His mother's brother, Owen Fairfield, died without children and had named his eldest nephew as his heir."

"Yes, I recall hearing about that." When he seemed about to question her, she added, "From Salathiel or you, maybe." Another tug on the string.

Luke slid his backside down the tree trunk, settling on the ground at its base while continuing to lean back against it. He snapped off a long blade of grass, then rolled it idly between his fingers. "I'm surprised that Maynard or any of his family has not called at Fairfield."

"For one thing, Lallage spread the word back in the summer that you were gone to New Orleans to market and that she was going to have a party when you returned so that all could meet you." Straightening up from her relaxed position, Diana brought her knees up underneath her full skirt and encircled them with her arms. She could hear the horses lipping at a patch of grass on the other side of the trees as their tails swished occasionally at gnats and buzzing horseflies. The fragrance of crushed grass, sweet and redolent of nature, teased her nostrils. "On the other hand, why would anyone from Fernwood call? You took away Maynard's inheritance."

Feeling his temper stirred, Luke jabbed toward her with

the blade of grass in his hand. "Are you suggesting there's something wrong with the way I became the owner of the place?"

Diana shrugged, not liking the hard look he was aiming her way but unwilling to back down on voicing what she had thought about more than once since first learning that Maynard had lost Fairfield . . . to a devil, she added now that she was recalling Tabitha's exact words that day. The thought about Luke Greenwood maybe being a devil had not surfaced in a long while. Somehow she could not bring herself to meet his gaze. She pretended interest in brushing particles of debris from her blue riding skirt. "It does sound a bit shoddy, taking advantage of a man in a card game."

"Who says I took advantage?" Luke crushed the blade of grass between his fingers and tossed it aside. Suddenly it seemed of utmost importance to convince Diana that he was a man of honor, at the gaming table as well as in other matters. If his conscience was chiding him about the role he was forcing Diana to play in order to help him increase his chances of winning his wager with Frederick, he chose to ignore it. "The stakes were high, higher than the actual value of Fairfield, if you want to know the truth. Maynard should have left the game when he ran out of money. All of us at the table discouraged him from betting his plantation, but he wouldn't listen. You don't know anything about gambling or wagering or—"

"No, I don't" she interrupted hotly, her gaze raking over him. She listened to one of the horses blow out a blubbery breath and stamp a hoof before going on. "Or about little else that rates very high with you. I don't care to learn about gambling. It seems that somebody always ends up losing and getting hurt, though I doubt you rarely do."

"What are you implying?"

"I'm implying nothing." It shocked her to realize that they were quarreling.

"Say what you have stuck in your throat. I can tell when you're not being honest. I prefer the straight truth."

Diana swept him with a doubting look, deciding it was good that he was not as perceptive as he believed. "I'm thinking that you run over everybody and everything that gets in your way without regard for the wishes of anybody else.''

His countenance thoughtful in the silence broken only by the continuous movements of the grazing horses, Luke unbuttoned a cuff of his white shirt and folded it upward twice, then repeated the action on the other. ''You don't like me very much, do you?''

''Name a reason I should.'' *Being devilishly handsome is no reason at all*, she assured a tiny inner voice brave enough to suggest one. She firmly believed her father's teachings that outward appearances counted for little when it came to judging the true worth of people, oneself included.

''Can you honestly say I've mistreated you by bringing you into my home and offering you a better way of life?''

''Maybe not mistreated,'' Diana hedged. She had to be honest; it was her way, insofar as she could be honest with him and not jeopardize the well-being of her black friends. ''But you kept me here through threats. Your way of life might not seem a better way to me.''

''Come now, Diana.'' Luke tried for a light tone. He did not relish the look of condemnation claiming her lovely eyes and face. Her criticism of him had wounded far more than he would have her know. The deep shade and the few feet between them prevented his seeing more than a cool blue coming from behind her dark eyelashes. ''Tell me you don't like knowing how to read and learning about new things and getting to know Lallage and her daughters. Tell me you don't enjoy wearing pretty clothes.''

Diana sat still, silent. Luke cleared his throat and crossed his arms across his chest before continuing. ''Tell me you don't like having mastered the art of riding a horse.''

Turning her head so as to see Duchess where she still nibbled grass, Diana smiled happily. ''Yes, I do love riding Duchess.'' As if the horse heard her name, she lifted her head, looked directly at Diana, and nickered. ''She's a darling.''

''I knew you could do it!'' Luke exclaimed with a burst of laughter and a slap on his thigh with his hand.

Startled by the masculine sounds, Diana whipped her head

back around to face Luke. She had to catch her hair with her hands and push it away from her face and mouth before she could speak. "Do what?"

"I knew you could smile."

"Whatever are you talking about?" His dark eyes were twinkling and his smile was so huge that she wondered if it might not be contagious, for she was smiling almost as widely. As it often did in his company, her pulse was thumping rapidly.

"You never have smiled like that around me before."

"You're being absurd." For the life of her, she could not seem to stop returning his smile.

"No, I'm being truthful. You've never really smiled around me before, not when it's just the two of us."

"What about when I knocked you down and we both laughed and laughed?" The memory brought a blush and a giggle. She peeked at him from behind half-lowered lashes when he began chuckling.

"That's not the same. I'm talking about smiling for no reason other than because you're happy." Had he not known better, he would have suspected she was flirting with him. Teasingly he asked, "Or was that why you were laughing that morning—because you were happy to have knocked me down?"

"You know that was an accident. You're making me feel foolish." She tried ordering her lips into a semblance of sobriety. Her pulse was ignoring even more completely her commands to slow down. Had she lost control?

Luke wondered why the beautiful sight of Diana smiling across at him was upgrading his heartbeat as well as his spirits. If shadows still lurked within her eyes, he did not want to know. "You should smile more often. It makes you look ravishingly beautiful."

"And more attractive as the woman you're escorting to the Charity Ball, no doubt."

Luke's face sobered. Unfolding his tall, lean frame in one liquid movement, he stood and covered the brief distance between them. "Here," he said, sticking out his hands. "Let me help you up. It's time for us to start back."

Diana lifted her hands to his and rose, wondering about a new gleam that was sparking his dark eyes. She paid no attention to the way the touch of his hands always made her feel slightly giddy, having already decided the feeling came because of her fear of him. Though the fear sometimes seemed to have disappeared, she had no reason to assume it was not still lurking within. "On our way back could we take a turn through the woods beside the swamp? That was such fun yesterday."

Luke appeared not to have heard Diana until after he helped her mount. "So you liked that trail down near the swamp, did you?" When she nodded and tendered him a partial smile, he went on with a decidedly devilish note in his deep voice. "Maybe it's time I taught you a little about the pleasures of betting."

Diana watched Luke tighten Jasper's cinch belt, then step up into the stirrup and settle on his saddle in an amazingly swift, coordinated movement. How did he manage looking both masculine and graceful at the same time? "What does betting have to do with taking a ride through the trees?"

"I'll race you to the big gum where the lane to the barn begins, and we'll make a wager on which of us will win."

Feeling invigorated and decidedly challenged, Diana grasped her reins in one gloved hand while smoothing the fingers of her other glove.

"Don't get careless with those reins," Luke admonished.

Diana lifted her chin and sent him a crushing stare. "I'm not a numbskull or a dimwit."

Not liking to recall how he had heaped such demeaning terms on her during those first weeks, Luke looked properly chastised. "What about making a little bet?"

"I have no money for betting."

"We'll bet something else," Luke said as they cantered off toward the trees and the shaded path they had followed the previous afternoon. Jasper tossed his black head as if looking forward to a spirited race.

"Like what?"

"If I win, you'll give me a kiss."

Attempting to conceal her shock at his bold suggestion, she countered, "What if I win?"

"Then I'll give you a kiss."

Suddenly, Diana became alive in a way totally new to her, a way that she took not a second to decipher. The sensation was sheer delight and far too heady for a young woman who never before had indulged in flirting with a handsome man to question its source. Laughing and sending her tall, raven-haired companion a measuring look from behind thick lashes, she said, "That's no honorable bet, Luke Greenwood. I'll have to beat you without winning a prize."

And Diana was off, Duchess's dark hooves thundering toward the trees in the distance. Luke and Jasper tore out after them.

Relieved, as at former outings, that Luke had never once suggested riding near the lower section of Gator Swamp where her house sat, Diana turned to look back. He was gaining on her! Just as she reined Duchess into the tree-shaded patch of hard dirt forming the bank of the upper section of the cypress swamp, Luke let out a yell of what she guessed was imagined victory, and she tossed him a sassy look before turning back to the business of staying in front.

Mindful of the large tree roots snaking across the packed black earth, Diana wrenched her attention to guiding Duchess past the treacherous obstacles without losing speed. The smack of the noticeably moist swamp air on her face added to her mood of exhilaration and she sniffed at the familiar scents wafting to her nose. Never had she suspected that she could savor fully the sights and smells of her beloved swamp from any vantage point other than her little house set on stilts above the still water. But now she was doing so while riding the racing white horse through the dense shade on its banks. Up ahead birds flitted. Squirrels scurried out of her way, as did a fat rabbit and a shiny black snake.

Luke let out another yell, from much closer this time, but Diana did not waste time looking back. With desire for victory goading her like a thirst for water might do on a muggy day, she found herself leaning forward, close to the straining horse's neck to avoid low-hanging limbs and falls of curly moss. The increasingly rapid rhythm of Duchess's hooves drumming on the hard soil fascinated her, made her think about flying, maybe like one of the enormous blue ibises that she had often watched lift gracefully from feeding in the alligator grass deep in the swamp and take to the air.

Though Diana already had suspected that she enjoyed riding because she felt one with the powerful animal, she now knew it with certainty. A fairly clear path showed up ahead and, remembering it from the afternoon before, Diana took a moment to glance back at Luke. He was nowhere in sight.

"Whoa!" Diana called, pulling back on the reins until the horse slowed. She wheeled Duchess around and shouted, "Luke! Where are you?"

When she heard no reply, no hoofbeats, Diana urged Duchess back down the path as rapidly as she had encouraged her moments before to dash up it. This time she paid little heed to the hanging moss and when one thick fall contained a small limb that tore at her blouse, loosening her top bottons, she was unaware. Another limb a few yards ahead stole her hair ribbon with the deftness of a practiced thief. "Luke? Answer me!"

Diana glimpsed Jasper up ahead. The horse stood still, reins trailing on the ground, saddle empty. She felt her heart plunge, then buck high as if to punish her by filling her throat with scalding pain. Nearing the black horse then, she saw the gleam of a white shirt beside a tree with giant roots splaying out from its bottom. With trepidation she realized that the man wearing it lay motionless, sprawled face down on his stomach.

Dropping her reins and landing on the ground at almost the moment the leather strips touched down, Diana raced to the prone figure, discarding her gloves on the way. After dropping to her knees and grabbing his shoulders, she attempted to turn him over. With tears and a maelstrom of emotions threatening to rob her of voice she crooned, "Oh, Luke, you've been hurt."

Luke flipped over from his stomach, his teeth flashing white in the deep shade as he chuckled and reached for her. "Nothing a kiss from you won't cure, Diana."

With her knees weak from fear and her lips parted in surprise that he had been playing possum, Diana could not move fast enough to avoid Luke's imprisoning arms. His mouth captured hers. Maybe she had no real wish to escape, she thought once his warm lips settled on hers and tempted them to conform to the sweet shape of his. His arms held her against his broad chest with a strength that robbed her of breath and normal pulse. His fierce embrace crushed her breasts against his chest, coercing her feverish brain into thinking about things like hard and soft. Man and woman.

Luke kissed Diana long and he kissed her hard, doing a meritorious job of initiating her into the mysteries and endless delights of yearning mouth meeting yearning mouth. He kissed her then with gentleness and wonder and with a kind of awe at the honeyed taste of her soft lips. He could feel her heart beating wildly against his and thought about things like how could one woman taste so deliciously female and be responding with both passion and innocence at the same time. Later, while they moaned and struggled for breath, his moist lips pressured hers for even more tumultous response. She answered with a fervor that surprised, thrilled.

Swept into a haze of rushing heartbeat, Diana never knew when her arms slid up to Luke's shoulders or when her hands got lost in his thick hair, not that she gave the matter the courtesy of a thought. She delighted in the feel of his skin underneath her fingertips. Warm, stimulating. When his hand moved to cup her head closer to his during their kisses, she wondered if she might not have discovered a divine secret about communication between a woman and a man. Had serendipity, without her conscious knowledge, belonged to her all along?

Suddenly, Diana wanted to touch Luke everywhere, ached for him to return her touch. How could one man create such a fierce burning throughout her body by doing no more than setting his lips on hers and sending his hands to caress her face, neck? It seemed plain that the intimate way he held her against him served as a part of the exhilaration.

Luke, who still lay on his back with Diana half sprawled across him, began pulling her body closer. She acquiesced, her mind observing from where it seemed to be hovering overhead that even had it entertained the notion to protest, languor now drugged her body and blocked out sensibility.

It was while Luke was gathering Diana closer and lining her body up with his that he felt the warmth of her bare skin on his chest, a warmth feeding what was threatening to become a roaring blaze in his loins. A minute bit of exploring with one hand told him that his shirt front had become unbuttoned during his fall after a snarling wildcat leapt from a tree up ahead and bounded across the path, frightening Jasper into rearing up suddenly and unseating him.

Luke's little foray also relayed the message that the top buttons on Diana's blouse had slipped from their slits. Without his brain willing his hand to move—well, if the truth could be known, it might have sent a tiny message—Luke's fingers inched down the firm curves of her full breasts. They sought and found a nesting place in her wonderfully tight, silken cleavage. By then his blood was blazing with desire.

Diana felt the searing pulsations from Luke's fingers on her hardening nipples and moaned back in her throat. Her blood was aflame, driving her into partial frenzy. What must he be thinking of her, the way she was clinging to him and kissing him like some mindless creature?

Diana sensed that at any time since the initial kiss she could have freed herself. She could have huffed and slapped Luke and called him all kinds of names, likely could have received the apology she should have demanded. Why hadn't she done any of those things? she was asking herself when his tongue began tracing the inner edges of her lips and started a whole new series of fiery, shivery sensations.

New ripples of tingling thrills tore throughout Diana as Luke's tongue teased the outer edges of her lips and mouth. The ripples then trebled and quadrupled into an encompassing wave of excitement when his tongue plunged into the inner recesses and nigh stole away her crippled breath and reasoning with one tormenting, marvelous foray that seduced her own tongue into joining his in tender duel. A part of her noted the uncanny way the mating of their mouths matched up with the wondrous feel of his fingers stroking her breasts. A magical warmth claimed her everywhere, even in places never before having proclaimed existence.

As if she knew what would ease the fierce tightening of her nipples, Diana shifted to allow space enough for Luke's caressing fingers to reach and tenderly abrade the tight nubs. The burst of electricity throughout her being was so powerful, so threatening, that she trembled anew. She freed her mouth and whispered brokenly, ''Please stop. Please.''

Bringing her to sit up with him then, one arm lingering around her shoulders, Luke tipped up Diana's face. ''You're incredibly sweet. Did you know that?'' His lips brushed against her unbound hair, her ear, ending up on her jaw and lingering a moment before easing down to nibble tenderly on her satiny neck. She tasted and smelled like sweet, pulsating woman. He felt her tremors and recognized them as echoes of those attacking him from within. ''And so beautiful.''

Already his gaze had lighted on the tantalizing sight of her partially bared breasts. He was not surprised to see through the thin fabric that they were as his hands had already told him: full, firm, richly tipped with rosy, budded nipples. Perfection. A massive constriction claimed his throat.

As Luke's lips blazed a fiery new path to her throbbing breasts, Diana tried protesting again, achingly aware that her body had no use for her words. ''No, Luke, please. . . .''

Diana dropped her forehead to rest against his, a feverish torment bedeviling her. Her fingers fondled his ears, his neck. Who would have thought that touching and being touched could lead to such blissful feelings of giving and receiving pleasure? If he was not going to help her end this flame that seemed bent on consuming them. . . . ''Oh, Luke—''

He murmured something guttural back in his throat that on one level might have been agreement to her earlier request that he stop. His hand reached out and gently freed one breast from her barely confining garment. He watched it thrust upward and fill his waiting palm. Then, while laving her throbbing nipple with his tongue, he felt her tremble anew and collapse against him. He lifted his head.

With a look into her passion-filled eyes only inches away from his own, he confided in a voice husky and unsteady,

"We must stop this right now or I shan't be able to end it. We don't want anything like that to happen, do we?"

Diana sat up, jolted into reality by his words and from the awareness that not far away their horses were stamping their feet and making blubbery snorts. The afternoon air there in the deep shade beside the swamp felt cold and cruel to her abandoned, kiss-dampened breasts.

Why was Luke acting as if he was the one calling a halt to their wild kissing and caressing? Diana wondered irritably. Just then she heard some squirrels in a nearby tree jump to a new perch and almost fall, judging by the thudding sounds coming from trembling, overhead limbs and the whisper of dislodged leaves tumbling downward.

As the leaves settled onto the ground close by, Diana's mind was completing its journey to clarity. Had Luke failed to hear her ask him to stop earlier? Did he have to be master of every situation in which he was involved? Drat the arrogant man!

Openly adoring the still-faced Diana with his gaze, Luke leaned to help her fasten her blouse, disappointed that she brushed away his hands and fumbled with the buttons herself. What an armful of passionate young woman! What spirit and grace she possessed, he added when the first epithet seemed too meager.

Diana had appeared to like kissing him, he mused during a feeble attempt to quench the fire in his groin by being dispassionate about what had happened. Was he the first to kiss her pretty mouth and—?

Then Luke was thinking how no other woman had so stirred him in years. He disliked the nagging suspicion that he might have been near to losing control, maybe close to examining something long buried in his heart. If he had not had his thoughts and attention on the fleeing Diana and lost mastery of the reins when Jasper reared up from the near attack of the snarling wildcat, would he ever have kissed her?

Flexing the muscles of first one shoulder and then the other, Luke decided, as he had when he first hit the ground, that nothing was broken. There *was*, however, a decided pain in his lower back.

Ignoring the signals from his back and his groin, Luke smiled at Diana when she fastened the last button on her blouse and met his gaze once more. He had halfway expected to see hesitation or shyness within her eyes. He was surprised.

"Was that my first lesson in kissing?" Diana asked as Luke took her hand and helped her to her feet. Dropping his hand and stepping back, she leaned over and brushed debris from her skirts in an attempt to camouflage the ghastly wound to her pride. That was all it was, she had concluded. Another one of his dratted lessons! "I assure you that I shan't need a second!"

Their ride back to the stables was one without conversation.

Eleven

"Did you two have a pleasant ride this afternoon?" Salathiel asked during dinner that evening. He looked from Diana to Luke and back again.

Surely, Salathiel mused, one or the other would have to reply and go through the motions of making conversation. He might have to give Diana a private talk tomorrow on the duties of cultured people sharing a meal. Strange that one who had mastered astronomical amounts of knowledge in both erudition and etiquette should be so careless this evening about her deportment.

Salathiel recalled that even before Chloe set the fish course on the table, the meal had dragged. He eyed the flaky white meat on his gold-rimmed china plate and stared at the fish in the silence. It seemed to return his baffled gaze.

Salathiel doubted he ever would have heard about Luke's fall had he not glimpsed his torn trousers and soiled shirt when he came in from the stables right before dark. As Luke was wont to do when it came to talking about his private life, he had been downright reticent, almost to the point of being rude, Salathiel recalled with his adamant dislike of emotional displays. Luke had muttered something crude in a distasteful tone, something like, "Damnation! I'll never understand horses or females. Leave me the hell alone!"

More than once during the evening meal, the normally observant Salathiel had caught Diana sending murderous glances toward Luke when she thought no one was looking.

After patting his neat mustache with his napkin, the Englishman plunged ahead. "The afternoon seemed a perfect one for a gentle autumn in this idyllic spot." He was unaware that since the afternoon of their arrival some four months ago, his term for the area had taken a drastic turn for the better. "Lallage and I took our tea on the back veranda and watched the children play with the dogs. I hope you had a pleasant outing, before Luke's horse spooked and then spilled him, that is."

Diana, her expression speculative and suspicious, sent Luke a disdainful look. She had just speared a piece of fish and was wondering if she could manage to swallow it if she placed it in her mouth. How dare Luke pretend to Salathiel that Jasper had truly thrown him? Abandoning the fish, she drank some wine and awaited Luke's reply.

Caught up in the mystery of the flames of the tapers burning in the silver candelabra on the long dining table, Diana entertained the ridiculous notion that Luke truly had been thrown. She smiled to herself at the image of the arrogant man flying through the air and landing with a splat on his backside. No, she corrected as she recalled the earthy talk of the blacks, landing on his *butt*.

"The afternoon was quite nice," Luke said noncommittally. Before dressing and coming downstairs, he had sent for Jed to give him a rubdown. He had not been surprised at Jed's report that huge bruises were showing on his thighs and butt from his ignominious landing atop the jutting tree roots.

When the solicitous Jed had chided his employer for doing without proper care from a manservant now that he, himself, was involved with his duties as overseer, Luke had agreed to look for a man on his next trip to New Orleans. Merely walking down the stairs had caused his entire backside to ache. Though a light padding of cotton underneath embroidered tapestry covered the wooden bottom of the dining-room chair, he found that sitting was causing him excruciating pain.

"Obviously," Luke went on, "Jasper was no more expecting to find a wildcat screaming and jumping down from the tree in front of him than I was.'' More than once Luke had berated himself for having been lost like a fool in gazing up ahead at Diana and relaxing his hold on Jasper's reins. ''We were both fortunate that the cat had no thought but to get away.''

Diana rolled her eyes, then looked down at the fish on her plate. The pale meat seemed as lifeless and unimaginative as Luke's lie. In her eighteen years she never had seen or heard any wildcats near Gator Swamp. Somebody had mentioned once in her presence that wildcats lived in St. Christopher Parish, as well as brown bears, but. . . .

No doubt, Diana surmised, Luke Greenwood would go to strained lengths in his laughable attempt to lend credulity to what appeared to her as no more than a crude hoax to trick her into falling into his arms. Like a harlot, she added with her self-styled penchant for honesty. Her breasts tingled from just thinking about. . . .

''How fortunate that Diana was riding ahead of you on the path and missed the meeting with the wildcat,'' Salathiel intoned, wishing he knew what in the bloody blazes had happened between Diana and Luke to cause them to act so alienated. They never had communicated easily, and seldom politely. But never before had they both at the same time appeared quite as loaded with inner turmoil plainly created by the other. When neither saw fit to make a comment, Salathiel continued in his placatory manner. ''But also how fortunate that she realized you might be hurt and returned to find you.''

''Yes,'' Luke replied. He sent a testing gaze toward the unusually pale-faced Diana. Her beautifully sculpted features might have been carved from finest alabaster. Had he imagined her warm smile, her eager responses to his kisses?

Casting aside his punishing thoughts, Luke forbade himself to give in to his urge to stand and finish his meal that way. A shift of his rear end against his chair offered no relief; in fact, it almost caused him to grimace. ''Diana proved to be exceptional help when she came back and found me. Just what I needed.''

"How kind and gentlemanly you are," Diana said sweetly, her glittering eyes sending a contrary message. She noted that ever since they had ended their embraces in the woods, Luke's face had worn that brooding look she had come to detest, the one suggesting to her that he bravely bore an inner agony that would crush ordinary people. A smug look. "I never would have forgiven myself had I not hurried back to discover what happened to you. Winning a race was not half as important as ministering to your needs."

Salathiel swallowed the last bit of fish on his plate and sat up straighter. The edges of Diana's sugary tone were razor sharp. Disbelief honed his English accent as he exclaimed, "Ye Gads! Were you two racing?"

"Yes," Diana answered, "and I was leading before—"

"Only because I allowed it," Luke interrupted hotly. He had not meant to let her know he was deliberately holding Jasper back, but her arrogant manner and blazing looks were setting his teeth on edge.

God! Luke thought, if only he could rub his aching behind. Another thought followed that brought a near smile: If only he could swat Diana's derriere and set it to aching as well. He suspected only something as drastic was going to alter her maddeningly haughty manner. Why was she still acting as withdrawn and disdainful as she had ever since he ended their passionate embraces? For the life of him, he had thought she was enjoying their intimacy.

"Oh, yes," Diana said as if overcome with contrition, "I was forgetting that you allow things to happen only as you see fit. Always the man in control of everything." He was lying, just as he had been about seeing a wildcat. She had been winning on her own.

Tossing her hair over her shoulder, Diana smoothed the wide lace collar edging the demure neck of her blue gown to hide the fact that her hands were trembling. When she noticed Luke's dark gaze following each movement of her fingers, she despised the flush staining her cheeks and grabbed her wine glass. Why was he staring at her so intently?

Diana managed no more than a sip before returning her glass to its place on the white tablecloth. The wine reflected the candlelight in such a way as to suggest that a liquid flame dwelt within the crystal glass. "I beg your most humble pardon for daring to forget you're the master."

Salathiel drank a slug of wine that almost choked him, his eyes darting all the while from one incensed face to the other. What had happened between Diana and Luke? They might as well have had swords in hand, so viciously were they dueling with their cutting words and glances. Since those first volatile days back in June, he had witnessed countless sparring matches between them but nothing like the one taking place.

Salathiel sensed that whatever spurred the couple on sparked the air. It never occurred to him that for someone who had repeatedly declared that he had no use for emotionally charged scenes, he was gaining a dose of excitement from the one unfolding.

"That's perfectly all right, my dear. I forgive you," Luke replied after draining his wine glass and thinking suspicious thoughts about Diana Hathaway. Was it merely by chance that she toyed with her collar and drew his gaze to the swells of her breasts, reminding him of the way he had caressed her that afternoon? He doubted the hell out of it.

It seemed plain to Luke that he had been wrong in entertaining thoughts that perhaps Diana was different from other young beauties he had known, no matter that she apparently had grown up as naturally and unaffected as one of the numerous wildflowers on the place. A creature of nature? Bah! He squirmed against his chair. "I didn't really expect anything more than that from you. After all, you're still a beginner in a number of things."

"Don't forget I'm a fast learner." Diana blinked her eyelashes rapidly while torching Luke with a fervid look. She had no desire for him to suspect tears were threatening to form and dissolve her brittle composure. Dissembling around the perceptive, inquisitive Odille while getting dressed for dinner had been difficult; dissembling around the object of her wrath was proving far more distressing. Drat Luke Greenwood for toying with her, for taking over her life!

Maybe it truly was innate with beautiful women, Luke

reflected with what seemed to him perfect logic, to be deceptive and flirtatious. Why, just look at the way Diana was batting her eyelashes and openly flirting with him after she had turned away from him that afternoon as coolly as if he had been doing no more than kissing her cheek!

Thank the saints, Luke's mind ran on while both Diana and Salathiel sipped their wine and awaited his reply, he was not subject to getting caught in her snare as he had been entrapped by Sylvia back when he was too young and vulnerable to know better. Sure, he consoled himself with little comfort, he had loved Sylvia, but once burned. . . . His brother Frederick was a man deserving Diana, and Diana deserved—

Luke allowed no further words to form, for his bruised rear end, as well as some other muscles he had not realized were battered, was throbbing like thunder. Besides, he had no relish for completing the unexpected thought. "Why, Diana, how could I forget what an apt pupil you are, when I'm one of your most valuable instructors?"

Salathiel, fearing something explosive might come up next, could stay out of it no longer. "I hope you are not contemplating racing with Diana again, Luke. I cannot conceive of her being accomplished enough as an equestrienne to race with a man so long acquainted with horses as you."

"I'm good enough to race," Diana said, "but I'm not interested in racing Luke again." She turned fully to Salathiel then and flipped one hand prettily in seeming dismissal of whatever reward had been offered that afternoon. "You see, he has no prize to offer that tempts me."

Stung from her barb, and vividly aware, as if he had uttered it only that moment, of his teasing talk about a kiss being the winner's reward, Luke flushed and retorted, "Why don' you name a prize you consider worthy?"

Turning to face Luke so rapidly that her pale hair tumbled around her face, Diana settled a measuring look on his grim countenance. "My freedom."

"Your freedom?" Luke parroted. He despised the way his gaze, as now, kept getting lost in her hair, as it had all evening. Each time she moved, the candlelight bathed its lustrous whiteness with an amazingly lovely glow. Blue always set off her large eyes, he thought with distaste for his lightning reflections, all of them centering on Diana. "I don't see any chains binding you here."

"They're there, though, and you know it." To her surprise, Diana found herself thinking of how different Luke's eyes had looked that afternoon up close, all soft and dreamy, a bit like her beloved swamp water at night when stars reflected from the heavens. Now his orbs might as well have been wet, black stones holding secretive fires deep within.

"You and I made a pact. If you choose to break it—"

"You know I'll never give you freedom to mistreat your slaves to find out what—"

"Do you truly think I might mistreat them?" Luke's harsh tone lashed toward Diana like a whip.

"Why wouldn't I think so?" Diana's impassioned voice raced back with matching intent to wound. "You mistreat me!"

"That's your privilege to think about me as you choose. If you two will excuse me," Luke said as he rose shakily to his feet and hoped his legs would carry him and his paining muscles and self-image out of the room, "I think I'll go find something soothing to read—like Dante's *Inferno*."

Late the next afternoon, Diana, having completed her assigned reading for the day, welcomed the happy sounds drifting from the front door, down the hallway, and into the library. Since her arrival, Odille had become the unofficial greeter in the mansion. Diana could hear her gracious, slightly accented words to the callers.

Across the spacious library, Salathiel was ensconced behind the desk with a notebook in which he kept copious notes about what needed to be purchased during the upcoming trip to New Orleans. As soon as he heard the lyrical notes of laughter, he privately confessed that he had been awaiting that particular music. Lallage Winston, her four daughters, their attendant, and the belligerent family pet, Pooch, had arrived amidst the curiously fetching commotion that accompanied them wherever they were.

Sweet greetings, hugs, and little personal revelations for Diana and Salathiel gushed from Japonica, Camelia, Daisy, and Hyacinth, lasting until Lallage called a doting-voiced halt and sent them on their way out back with Lily. Upon arrival, Pooch came over to Diana with the usual docile mien and wagging tail reserved for her, then waited for the girls to leave before straightening his tail, twitching his ears, and sending his staccato barks of disapproval toward Salathiel.

"Why does the infernal dog dislike me so?" Salathiel asked Lallage after she sent Pooch to play with her daughters. Patting his brow with his handkerchief, he leaned back against the sofa and let out a sigh of confusion. "I never before have had any trouble getting along with dogs. I kept thinking that over these past few months—after all, it's November now —the animal would give up on trying to intimidate me. Is this a plague that comes along with one's forty-fifth year?"

"Darling," Lallage said in the flirtatious tone she used frequently with the man with whom she had fallen madly in love, "don't you recognize jealousy when you see it?" She sent Diana a smile and a wink across the library. "As for your age, I suspect a man is only beginning his prime at forty-five."

"Jealousy?" Salathiel asked, almost sputtering in his surprise at the unexpected thought, as well as at Lallage's remark about his age. *Beginning* his prime? A part of him wondered more and more lately if the beautiful young widow meant any of the suggestive looks and double-entendres she freely winged his way.

Salathiel dragged his thoughts to the moment. Why were Lallage and Diana exchanging such knowing looks? Come to think of it, he reflected uneasily as he ran a forefinger inside his neckcloth and cleared his throat, they had been doing a lot of that lately. He despised it when people sent each other knowing looks in the presence of those who did not know whatever was being implied. Especially when *he* was the one left in ignorance. "Why would the blasted dog be jealous?"

Lallage threw back her pretty head and laughed low in her throat in that titillating way Salathiel had come to adore. She sobered and asked, "Can't you tell that I pay you much more attention than I pay my only other current male companion?"

Salathiel harrumphed and felt his face redden. Diana giggled first, then Lallage. He confessed that both sounds had come to mean a great deal to him, he who had scolded his two female pupils back in Alabama numerous times for creating the piquant noises. What in blazes was happening to him?

"You are teasing, of course," Salathiel managed to say after giving in to a bit of nervous coughing and clearing of his throat. He smiled to show that he, too, possessed a sense of humor, the kind that obviously had plunged the two women into fits of merriment.

"Perhaps I am," the widow replied coquettishly, "but again, perhaps I'm not. Anyway, Pooch does no more than bark and carry on. He never even attacks your trouser legs anymore, so obviously your charm is winning him over."

As usual, Salathiel did not know how to interpret the remarks coming from the pretty redheaded widow and he decided he had better introduce another topic. "Have you had any replies to the invitations to your party?"

"Indeed I have. Almost everyone from St. Christopher Parish will be there. I'm delighted that some of my family will be coming from near Baton Rouge, as well as a few gentlemen friends who began calling on me early in the summer." Lallage watched Salathiel's face closely throughout her little recital, but especially during her last words. She liked seeing a decided spark flare deep within his dark eyes. She also liked the way he cocked his well-shaped head to the side just a tad and tendered her lush figure a look bordering on being proprietary.

"What party?" Diana asked.

"My dear," Lallage explained, tearing her attention from Salathiel, "you're so often gone horseback riding with Luke lately that you must not have realized Salathiel and I feel the time has come to introduce all of you from Fairfield to society. I'm having a huge house party this coming weekend. I've invited everyone from all around to come this Saturday afternoon at three for refreshments and to meet my new neighbors. Afterward there'll be dancing and a midnight supper. I've already spoken with Odille about which of your gowns—''

"Please. I'm not ready for this," Diana broke in to say. She jumped up from her chair and went to stand by one of the open French doors leading to the veranda. "Can't we wait a little longer? It's only the first week in November. We won't be going to New Orleans for several weeks."

"You are as ready as you will ever be to get this first social gathering behind you," Salathiel assured Diana. He went to where she stood gazing out toward Bayou Selene. "Actually, my dear, we'll be leaving in a couple of weeks. The Charity Ball is being held the first Saturday night in December and we have much to do after we get to the city. I'll not leave your side at Wingate, and I assure you that you will not feel nearly so nervous as you suspect."

Lallage said as she joined them, "You'll be far more at ease when we reach New Orleans. It's good to have a few affairs behind you." She laughed at her unconscious play on words and slid a knowing look toward Salathiel. Her hand itched to touch his and let him know she shared his apparent amusement. Their gazes got tangled for a moment. "Diana, please don't be upset. I'll stay beside you, even after I introduce you in the receiving line, the way we practiced."

"No," Diana said with what she hoped was dignity, "I don't want to be in a receiving line. I prefer not having everyone look at me as if I'm on display."

"But, darling, you three must be beside me in the line, else how can I let all know you're my new neighbors and honored guests?" Lallage frowned, but prettily, and glanced at Salathiel for support. He shrugged and looked puzzled.

"I don't want anyone hovering over me after you've received all the guests, either," Diana said. "If I'm going to make a fool of myself, I much prefer doing it without either of you witnessing it. You've both been wonderfully kind and I appreciate all you've done for me, but—" She sighed and looked down at her tightly clasped hands, noticing that her knuckles had no color.

"Luke will be around, too, and—"

With a sudden lift of her chin and a gleam in her eyes, Diana cut off Lallage's statement. "I certainly don't want Luke around. You've already told me I'll have to go to more functions than the Charity Ball or else I'll not know how to act there. How can I feel confident about attending any social affair in New Orleans if I don't try on my own this first time I'm with so many strangers?"

"You might well have a point there, my dear," Salathiel remarked after a little silence.

"Very well, then," Lallage said, winking conspiratorily at Salathiel, "we'll make no fuss over you. We'll treat you as any other guest and let you wander around on your own."

"I have no doubt you will captivate everyone at the party," Salathiel said as he put an arm around Diana's shoulders and guided her back to her chair. Hoping for a smile, even a small one, he said teasingly, "You are beautiful now even when you open your mouth."

"Thank you, Salathiel," Diana replied softly, comfortable only recently about acquiescing to his request that she call him by his first name.

"My dear Diana, you deserve more praise than I can express," Salathiel replied. Genuine fondness coupled with pride in his pupil enriched his diction. He allowed himself a glance at Lallage, pleased that her doting look at Diana reflected his own. Together, he thought, Lallage and he made a jolly fine team.

A flood of guilt washed over Diana. How could she call Salathiel and Lallage her dear friends when she had lied to them about her background and could think of no way to rectify matters until after the dreaded trip to New Orleans ended? It was true that both had added a wealth of knowledge to that which she already possessed. Still, the falsehoods she had strowed here and there to stave off Luke's finding out about her house sitting on his property plagued her tender conscience. Since his cruel trick to get her in his arms, she had resorted to her old way of thinking about Luke Greenwood. He was a hard man who had no heart. She asked, "Will everyone wonder why I'm at Fairfield?"

"Not after you're introduced as my niece," Salathiel replied, relieved that Diana seemed to be getting a firm hold on her emotions. For a moment he had feared she might burst into tears. He needed no extra tug at a conscience already heavily burdened from his having taken part in Luke's madcap scheme to best Frederick, no matter that Luke had coerced him into cooperating.

Salathiel almost pitied Frederick Greenwood, for he had little doubt that the stunning blonde was indeed going to force him to his knees. How was it that Luke had managed to escape her charms? "Diana, you and I will be presented as Luke's house guests from Alabama."

From where she once more sat on the sofa beside Salathiel, Lallage said musingly, "It's rather strange to me, Salathiel, that though the talk has gotten around about you being here as Luke's former tutor and dear friend, nobody—not even Calion's queen of gossip, Linda Lee Bergerone—seems to have the slightest inkling that Diana is here also. I would have thought the slave grapevine was too alive for such a fact to be overlooked."

Diana looked down at her skirt and smoothed an imaginary wrinkle. Though guilt for deceiving her friends washed over her, at the same time she felt gratitude for the slaves' silence during the years about the Hathaway family in Gator Swamp. Only three nights ago she had hurried to the quarters on Lallage's plantation to apply a poultice on the foot of a child bitten by a water moccasin. Tabitha had reported yesterday that the little boy was hobbling about, back at play. Diana liked thinking about how Luke did not control every aspect of her life, even toyed with the idea of taunting him with the knowledge when she finally became free.

After a brief pause, Lallage continued. "I realize that the blacks keep their secrets, but I would think the news that a beautiful young woman suddenly appeared at Fairfield would have their tongues wagging at both ends. The entire matter seems peculiar."

When neither Diana nor Salathiel commented, Lallage fluffed her hair and said, "During the past two weeks, Linda Lee Bergerone has been trying to overrule my admonition to everyone not to call at Fairfield until all of the alterations have been made.''

Enjoying the sight of the pretty redhead's feminine movements, Salathiel replied in a soothing tone, ''Luke and I are appreciative of your keeping people away until we made headway with Diana as well as with getting the house back into decent shape. We needed the time.''

''Where is Luke?'' Lallage asked. ''It seems I've not run into him for days.'' She turned to Diana. ''Why aren't you out riding with him? It may have been cloudy and threatening earlier, but it was fairing up during the thirty minutes it took us to drive here.''

''He hasn't been around all day,'' Diana replied. ''Since Odille has come, she insists on bringing a tray to my bedroom when I wake up''—she watched Lallage smile and nod hearty approval—''so I no longer see him at breakfast.''

''Actually,'' Salathiel said after both women turned to him for clarification, ''I suspect Luke is not feeling chipper and has chosen solitude.'' When Lallage looked concerned and Diana, skeptical, he added, ''He took a rather beastly fall yesterday from that monster of a stallion he insists on riding.''

With her brown eyes sparkling and the tapered ends of her pretty fingers meeting, Lallage was a picture of anticipation as she begged to know all about the events of the preceding afternoon. Diana could do little but oblige, insofar as she chose to, that is.

Odille, unnoticed by anyone but Diana, appeared at the open doorway. With a few gestures she signaled questions about bringing a tea tray to the library and learned from Diana's nods that she approved. Diana tried not to look disdainful when Salathiel added what he knew, or thought he knew, about the wildcat spooking Jasper and unseating Luke.

''That handsome man had better take better care of himself than that,'' Lallage said afterward. She watched Odille set down a pewter tea tray on a low table before Diana, then silently withdraw from the library. ''There are too many young women interested in doing more than catching glimpses of him charging around Calion on that black horse. Why, the man has dined at least once with all of the leading families in town. I believe he has charmed everyone.''

Lallage waited until Diana had poured tea in the graceful manner she had taught her and all three had cups in hand before she revealed more. ''Would you believe Linda Lee Bergerone has gone so far as to tell me outright that if I didn't have everyone over to Wingate soon to meet Luke, she was going to invite him to spend a Sunday afternoon with her family and ask people over, no matter what he might think of her being so bold? 'Just to be polite?' I asked her. She doesn't give one hoot in Hades about showing hospitality to that black-haired charmer, I told her. She just wants him to be around her two unmarried daughters again.''

Salathiel chuckled, delighting as always in Lallage's effusive accounts about her friends and neighbors.

Diana smiled to herself, knowing that neither Lallage nor Salathiel was paying her much attention. Now that she had come to know and love Lallage and her children as much as she loved Salathiel, Diana liked thinking that there might be something serious going on between the older couple, something more than a casual flirtation. Lallage need not have shared nearly so many secrets with Diana for the naive young woman to figure out what was creating the extra sparkles in the eyes of Lallage Winston and Salathiel Morgan. Both were smitten.

What about the unmarried daughters of Lallage's friend, Linda Lee? Diana wondered while Lallage continued her versions of the rumors being circulated about Luke Greenwood. Though Luke had often been gone in the evenings—making valuable business contacts, according to Salathiel—he had not spent an evening away from Fairfield in nearly a week. Were the Bergerone daughters beautiful and elegant enough to interest her arrogant jailer? Though she assured herself she did not care if Luke danced with them or maybe stole kisses—just the fleeting memory of his mouth on hers sent her tongue tracing the underside of her lips—she had no wish to meet the sisters.

Diana recalled the nights after her father's death when she had lain awake thinking how nice it might be to have a young

woman as a friend. Not that she discounted her lifelong friendships with the blacks, but she realized an invisible barrier,
which seemed to increase with her every birthday, separated
them and her. She counted Lallage as a friend and confidante,
but obviously the older woman no longer entertained the
doubts that plagued maidens—such as the romantic aspects
of courtship, marriage. Diana chided herself for not looking
forward to meeting the Bergerone sisters and becoming
friendly, then assured herself that their reported interest in
Luke had no bearing on her apathy about the matter. None
at all.

Salathiel's clipped syllablgs edged into Diana's musings
and she offered more refreshments.

"Darling," Lallage said to Diana after settling back against
the sofa with her second cup of tea, "Salathiel has agreed to
come early on Saturday and help me oversee the placement
of furniture so as to make more room for the large gathering."
She shifted her legs and peeked to see if Salathiel heard the
rustle of her silk petticoats. His quick, surreptitious look into
his cup reassured her that he had. "We were just saying how
it will be perfect for Luke and you to ride over in his carriage."

Diana made no outright protest. "Or we could ride our
horses."

"You would have to change when you arrived, though that
wouldn't be a particular problem, not if you brought Odille
along to assist you and neaten your hair. She could pack your
petticoats and gown in a portmanteau. Several of the women
I know choose to travel that way, insisting that they like being
able to rinse away the dust of the trip and don fresh clothing."

"You can work out details later," Salathiel assured the
women. He supposed that by now he should be more accustomed to the way Lallage ducked no topic to discuss in front
of him, but at times she still shocked him. Only last week
Lallage, with him in the same room, had shown Diana how
to flirt with her dance partner and how to take deep breaths
to make her bustline appear more enticing. "I expect all to
have a ripping good time at your party, Lallage. You seem
to have everything planned minutely. Your orderly way of

organizing impresses me. Not many young women I have known could do half as well.''

"Thank you, darling, but as you well know, I'm no green girl just entering womanhood,'' Lallage replied with an enigmatic smile toward the even-featured man sitting beside her and favoring her with praise and looks of open admiration.

By the saints! Lallage confessed to herself, how she loved Salathiel Morgan. She loved his cultured voice, his quick mind, his masterful influence with her daughters. Loved his neat, manly body, too. At the moment she desired nothing more than to reach over and lay her hand on the inside of one of his thighs, thighs that she sensed from having sneaked looks at them ever since first meeting him would be leanly muscled and a pathway to—

Instead, Lallage touched her stylishly coiffed red hair with one hand and sent a testing finger to make certain the loose curls still lay in feathery disarray in front of her ears. She also checked her dangling pearl earrings. After she realized Salathiel's dark eyes followed each movement her hands made, she leaned toward him slightly and fluffed up the lace ruffle edging the scooped neck of her yellow dimity gown.

Not wanting to tear his gaze from feasting on the partial view of Lallage's full breasts and the intriguing dark shadow between them, Salathiel found himself wondering how it was that the redheaded widow, who was the epitome of all that he had previously abhorred in women, had captivated him so completely. When in his bedroom at night, he would upbraid himself over his growing attraction to Lallage Winston. He sometimes confessed that, quite frankly, she was rather loud, plump, outspoken—yet overpowered by her daughters. She was too emotional about everything.

At times, Salathiel's thoughts whirled on, Lallage seemed boldly, naughtily sensuous, both in manner and speech. And, being in her mid-thirties as he figured she must be to have a daughter thirteen, Lallage likely put something on her hair to keep it so richly red. He tried not to be appalled that a seemingly respectable woman would dye her hair, but he failed.

Salathiel's ruminations skipped on while Lallage talked to

Diana about the gown she should wear to the upcoming party. Despite his attempts to sift through the facts, he found Lallage beautiful, bright, open, generous and friendly to all—especially to Diana who desperately needed a woman friend. The ultimate in alluring femininity, she was a joy to behold around her pretty, energetic daughters who were much like her. As for the widow's plumpness, to Salathiel she was rounded only in the right places. She had a small waist that he fantasized his arms were fashioned to encircle.

Encircling was not what came to mind when Salathiel let himself imagine how it would feel for his hands and mouth to become acquainted with Lallage's generously curved breasts and hips and let his fingers slip between. . . . During the past month such thoughts had strayed into his mind with increasing frequency and, as now, always played bloody hell with the long-curbed fires in his loins. He harrumphed and shifted against the sofa.

A burst of Lallage's rich laughter led to a startling moment of truth. Salathiel recognized Lallage as a charmingly fashioned package of feminine emotions, a beautiful package whose contents would ever prove surprising, perhaps unsettling at times, yet a constant delight to the man fortunate enough to win her heart and her hand in marriage.

For the life of him, Salathiel could not believe that at forty-five he might be falling in love for the first time with any woman, least of all with the vivacious, sensual Lallage Winston. The reality of his predicament scared the living hell out of him.

Twelve

"Luke sent his apologies, my dear," Salathiel told Diana that evening when she came down in answer to Tabitha's silver bell and found him alone. "He has always been too blasted stubborn to heed advice. Both Jed and I warned him his muscles needed some rest from that pesky fall yesterday, but today he insisted on riding about the place as usual."

Diana did not say much, but several disturbing thoughts tumbled through her mind. Had there truly been a wildcat? Had Jasper thrown Luke? How could such a thing have happened, even had there been an unexpected scare, when Luke supposedly was a master horseman? Memories of his numerous admonitions to her about keeping a good grip on the reins surfaced, puzzling her even further.

By the time the meal ended, Diana was entertaining the thought that there really might have been a wildcat leaping in front of Jasper and spooking him. Even if there had been such a distraction, it was hard for her to imagine Luke not having control of his reins. After all, he always seemed to control everything around him—including her.

When Diana recalled how shabbily she had treated Luke last evening at dinner, her conscience twitted her. True, the man had no heart and showed no mercy in his dealings with her, but he must have been aching and feeling terrible.

"No, Diana," Salathiel responded to her question as they left the dining room, "your wish to visit Luke for a moment in his bedroom is not at all unseemly. In fact, I deem it exemplary of your usual thoughtfulness and charm. He said he would like to play a restful game of dominoes. I am quite sure he will be happy you chose to accompany me."

Doubting Salathiel's cheerful reassurance and thinking his compliment was unmerited, Diana lifted her skirt of rose-colored percaline and preceded Salathiel up the staircase. She blamed her sudden spate of unruly heartbeats on the brisk climb as she waited for Salathiel to knock on the door to Luke's bedroom.

"What a delightful surprise to have two visitors," Luke said from where he lay propped high against pillows on his bed. He waved a hand toward the tray sitting on a nearby table. "Tabitha said she would return to take away the supper tray and bring some brandy." Did Diana's apparent uneasiness spring from her being in a man's bedroom, or from being in his presence? "Sit, both of you, and stay a while."

"Diana was eager to see how you are feeling this evening and asked to come along," Salathiel said as he made certain Diana was seated on one of the upholstered chairs beside the fireplace before he settled on the other, the one nearer the bed where Luke lay. When he had tried guiding her toward that chair, she had demurred and claimed the one farther away. Whatever had Diana and Luke at odds the evening before apparently still lingered. Salathiel harrumphed before asking, "Did Jed's back rub help?"

"Yes," Luke replied with a devilish grin, "it helped so much that I was sorry I hadn't dressed to join you downstairs. I feel more comfortable now. Having both of you come to visit makes me feel even better." He guessed it had taken quite a bit of spunk for Diana to come see him when she had been mad enough at him last evening to snap off his head. All day he had upbraided himself for having lashed out at her. Though he had figured he would dismiss all thoughts about their passionate embraces, the memory of them still seared his soul. "Salathiel, I hate it when you're right. I shouldn't have ridden today."

Even as Diana made polite comments when need be and watched Luke talk and smile with his old friend, she thought about how the large high-ceilinged room smelled and looked as if it could belong to no one but a man of good taste and considerable wealth. Recent renovations and additions had changed its appearance since she had been in it visiting Uncle Owen during one of his illnesses, but the basic furniture of gleaming mahogany appeared the same.

A waft of something spicy and manly had met Diana's nostrils as soon as she entered. Still aware of the fragrance —hadn't she smelled it while he kissed her?—she realized for the first time that the elegant furnishings were of massive proportions, unlike the more daintily fashioned ones in the guest room she used. Strange how she never before had noticed such details. Even the several silver candelabra sitting around the large room had noticeably bold-lined bases and arms. She guessed they might be new since Tabitha had told of Maynard selling nearly all of the valuable movables.

Diana admired the new velvety rug before the marble-faced fireplace, marking the way its earth colors complemented the polished wood floors. Heavy drapes of forest green silk hung at the single window on one side and at the two tall French doors leading onto the upper veranda. Guarding against the chill of the autumn night, the floor-to-ceiling drapes were closed. A small fire burned in the fireplace, giving off the pleasant, homey fragrance of wood smoke.

Curious about Luke's apparently genuine welcome toward her, when they had parted last evening with open hostility, Diana stole a glance at her dark-haired jailer. She thought of how handsome he looked in his silky, maroon dressing robe with piping of black silk edging and emphasizing its tailored lines. Apparently, Luke wore nothing underneath his robe that showed above or below its casually lapped and belted front, a fact that intrigued Diana in a way she did not care to examine. The sleeves of the garment were rather full and reached no more than halfway down his heavily muscled arms. Those arms had hugged her close and—

Diana switched her attention to Luke's patch of curly black chest hair that proclaimed as boldly as the deep voice relating an event of his day that she was looking at a devilishly virile man. His complete ease with himself fascinated her. Plainly, he was not recalling their kisses.

While Luke gestured and told his visitors of his amusing encounter with a fisherman on the bayou, Diana allowed herself a closer look at the way his robe reached no lower than his calves and revealed his long legs lying crossed at the thickly muscled calves. His black slippers, made of what looked like heavy satin, rested on the white sheet as if they belonged there. Even while lying abed, Luke emanated that latent aura of power she had sensed from the first night she had seen him bearing down on her in the moonlight.

Suddenly, Diana was wrenched into the present, for Salathiel was looking at her and saying, "I hope you have no objections to taking my place as an opponent for Luke tonight, Diana. I had planned on working up translations of some Greek poems for you to read tomorrow. If you do not already know how to play dominoes, I am quite certain Luke will be happy to teach you. He positively dotes on the game."

Diana pursed her lips. Would it seem logical that the daughter of a simple trapper might have knowledge of the game? Keeping him company for a while might soothe her conscience. "I know how to play dominoes. If Luke has no objections to playing with a woman, I'll stay."

"I can think of nothing I'd enjoy more," Luke replied, swinging his long legs over the side of the bed and standing gingerly. An inner voice would have suggested another activity involving her, but he quelled it. "I find the game relaxing."

A soft knock on the door came, followed by a smiling Tabitha carrying a small tray with a decanter and several small glasses. "Did you finish up all your supper, Master Luke?" She slid a soft look toward Diana as she set down the tray. Her full attention back on her master then, Tabitha said, "It seems nice to have folks callin' on you when you's feelin' porely, don't it now?"

"It does," Luke replied with a smile for the black woman. "Before you take away the supper tray, will you please move the game table over in front of the fireplace?"

"Sho' will," Tabitha replied with a flash of white teeth while bustling over to the game table in the corner. "Guess you gonna be playin' somethin' with Mr. Salathiel an' get your mind off your pore, tore-up backside. Jed done tole us 'bout it last night."

"No," Luke corrected her. "He has other plans for the evening. I'm going to play dominoes with Diana."

Tabitha's eyes rounded noticeably and her plump face broke out in a huge smile. "Now ain't that nice?" After Salathiel rose and helped her slide the small square table in front of the fireplace, Tabitha said with a knowing look toward Diana, "I speck if'n you ain't careful, Miss Diana gonna beat your stockin's off playin' dominoes."

"I'm not that good," Diana denied, dying to signal Tabitha not to tell too much. She had noted over the past several weeks that Tabitha was becoming increasingly enamored with Luke Greenwood, as was Salem. As was everybody, now that she was thinking about the matter. Except her, of course.

Sometimes, as now, Diana feared the good-hearted Tabitha was going to forget what Luke might do to her and the rest of the original slaves at Fairfield if she let it be known that all listened attentively to Luke's occasional talks about the ways he expected his slaves to show their loyalty and receive benefits, then conspired daily to keep secret that someone poached on his property. Worse, far worse to Diana's way of thinking, was the fact that the poacher lived in Luke's home in blatant deception. It was *his* fault, but. . . .

Within moments Tabitha had poured Luke some brandy, thrown a stick of wood in the fireplace, retrieved Luke's supper tray, and followed behind Salathiel. Diana and Luke sat alone before the fireplace. Both were acutely aware that there was more between them than the game table with twenty-eight ivory dominoes lying face down on its surface of inlaid wood.

"You don't have to keep looking at me as if you expect me to grab you," Luke said. He met her measuring gaze with honesty as he sipped his brandy. "I asked that the door be left open. Go ahead and draw a bone for lead."

Diana despised the flush she could feel creeping up her

neck into her cheeks. "I wasn't looking any special way, and I'm not concerned about what you might do. With your injuries I assume you'll be forced to behave properly." No more interested than Luke apparently was in continuing their bickering, Diana turned over a domino, or bone as Luke had called it, smiling when she showed him its twelve black dots. "It appears that I win the shuffle and the lead."

Luke grunted, wriggling around on his chair to find a more comfortable position. At least she had rewarded him with a smile. "Seems that way. Are you sure you wouldn't care for a brandy?"

"I'm sure." Deftly, Diana returned the ivory rectangle to the others and shuffled the twenty-eight bones, faces down, around on the smooth surface of the game table. After drawing seven of the dominoes and lining them up in front of her, she watched Luke draw his lot and make ready for play. She cleared her throat. "I'm sorry you fell yesterday."

"Is this something new you've learned from Lallage—to wait a certain length of time before offering sympathy?"

"No, it's nothing like that. I never believed you had really fallen until this evening." Diana played her six-four bone out in the center of the table.

"You must think I'm rotten through and through." Shoving a piece of paper and a slender spear of waxed charcoal toward her, he said, "Here. You keep score." He played a four-five and leaned back against his tall-backed wing chair, his sore behind and thighs appreciative of its thickly padded upholstery.

"I would like keeping score much better if you had asked me instead of ordering." She played a domino, then sent him a testing look that hinted she was finding him lacking in a quality she deemed important.

After brushing back a lock of hair falling down across his forehead, Luke smiled and nodded his head toward her mockingly. "It seems that *I* am in need of instruction this evening." He set his empty glass down firmly. For a bruising moment the memory of their fervent kisses teetered in the air between them. To her surprise he said in a genuinely polite tone, "Will you please keep score for us this evening, Diana?"

"I'll be happy to." Diana heard the relief riding her voice. There was something infinitely appealing about the handsome man sitting across from her, the one obviously intent on being mannerly. Was he, perhaps, going to show her more of the amiable side of him that he had begun revealing recently during their horseback rides—until yesterday? "I enjoy being around a courteous gentleman."

"Oh?" Luke questioned. Her implication smarted. "Is the way to your heart through fancy manners and talk?"

"No. I don't give a fig for such outward trappings, but I've never become accustomed to being ordered around. I don't intend to try liking it."

"Your father must have given you a free hand in making decisions." Luke never had thought about the possibility of such a relationship between parent and child. Back at Southwinds his father had ordered his wife and children around almost as frequently as he did his slaves, but he was never cruel and he provided generously for the needs of all dependent upon him. What kind of man had this Philip Hathaway been? He apparently had provided no decent life or formal education for his beautiful daughter and yet he had instilled in her a remarkable resolve about her personal dignity and rights.

"He did. He was a prince of a father and a gentleman." The remembrance of how Philip had taught her to trust her own judgment about matters ever since she was very young brought a smile to Diana's face that lighted up her eyes in a way Luke never had seen before. He tried not to stare, but failed. The sight was breathtaking.

Diana went on, for once not noticing Luke's intent perusal of her features. "I can see I was wrong about what happened yesterday. I'm sorry about how you came to be lying on the ground and got hurt and . . ."

Diana's low voice trailed off as she watched Luke match up his domino with hers out in the center of the table. *Click!* Two had become one. Suddenly, she could think of nothing but the way she had permitted him to kiss her and fondle her with those same strong hands now engaged in rearranging his dominoes. What but devilry could have enticed her into responding with matching ardor and desiring to become one with Luke?

The fire in the fireplace blazed up and crackled, snapping Diana back to sanity. She swallowed and licked her lips before asking, "Was there really a wildcat?"

"Do you think I lied about that, too?" His eyes blazed with black indignation and he sat up straighter. Here he was, forcing himself to pretend nothing had happened between them and she was still needling him. Did she think he could forget her derision of his kisses after he freed her—and again last evening at the table? "God, but you paint me as a monster every chance you get!"

Diana felt and looked miserable. "Don't you know how to let somebody who makes a mistake apologize for it? Maybe *forgiveness* is a word not in your vocabulary."

They played in silence for a spell, first one and then the other gaining points in multiples of five. Luke thought about how he had ridden hard over Diana ever since he first chased her down that night and came up with the idea to keep her around and transform her into a cultured creature to dangle before Frederick.

In spite of his not liking the direction of his thoughts, Luke thought about how he might have made a mistake and how Salathiel likely was right when he warned him that he had no right to meddle in the life of another person. Luke figured it took somebody with a powerful spirit and innate pride still to insist that she receive fairer treatment when, insofar as she knew, she actually had little choice but to submit to his wishes. The fact that after he recovered his pocket watch he never intended to pursue the reason why Diana was at the well shed reared up in his mind as the basest of trickery.

So what if the slaves, after the death of Owen Fairfield and during the prolonged absences of their new master, had indulged in a bit of bartering with goods from the plantation? Luke reflected while the game went on. It was obvious that Maynard Oates had done little but show up occasionally during the past year. The blacks had had to find a way to look out for themselves until someone came to provide for them.

Well, Luke consoled himself, he was here now and he had

seen no more evidence that anything unusual was going on. He felt it his duty to keep a close eye on the happenings around the place. Jed and the slaves knew his policies, actually seemed to respect him for them.

Even when Luke returned from Calion after spending an evening with his growing number of acquaintances in the small town, he always took a turn around the stables and outhouses and checked for signs that anything might be out of kilter. He prided himself on his belief that nothing went on around Fairfield without his knowledge.

The time came for another shuffle and when both had drawn new hands, Luke asked, "Why don't we start over tonight?"

"Start what over?" Diana tossed back her hair and sent him a speculative look. His eyes were beautiful. Suddenly, she was recalling that up close while they kissed, fascinating specks of light had danced within their black depths.

"Our relationship." They needed to put away memories of their kissing episode. Or at least he did. It apparently had affected her very little, he concluded as he sent her a direct gaze. Damn, but Diana had a way of searching his face and eyes that reminded him of a hunter stalking his prey. Did she still expect to wangle her freedom? "Let's forgive and forget the past mistakes we've both made and start over fresh."

"Can we forget about our pact?"

Luke let out a sharp laugh. He had been right. She was still trying to get out of going with him to New Orleans. "Nothing changes the pact, but we don't have to be fighting every minute. We might find we can have a good time together, both here and in New Orleans. Can we call a truce and try to become friends?"

"I'd like that, Luke." Her smile reinforced her simple statement.

"Get set then, because I'm going to knock out your eyeballs with this next play of mine. It might take a true friend to accept such phenomenal skill." Sending her a mischievous grin, he played a bone and proudly pointed out the twenty points gained. With boyish enthusiasm he leaned to watch her mark his score. "By Jove!" he said teasingly. "I'm probably the best player in St. Christopher Parish."

"How can you say that when I won the first game?"

"Maybe I let you win."

"Don't try to feed me fish bait!"

Luke grinned. Here he was, playing one of his favorite games with the most beautiful young woman he had ever seen. And truth to tell, Diana Hathaway was an able opponent. Maybe his having become distracted by the sight of her riding up ahead and loosening his grip on Jasper's reins had not been a disaster after all. He put down forbidden thoughts about how the accident brought on their sizzling kisses.

Had he not been laid up with his battered backside, Luke reasoned, his getting to know more about Diana might not ever have taken place. Except when they were away from the house riding, he never had been able to talk with her without antagonizing her. Had he, perhaps, been too intent upon turning her into his idealized version of a cultured young woman to allow his natural liking of her just as she was to show through? Maybe Salathiel was right; maybe his often solemn mien did project a deceptive image.

"Are you looking forward to the party this weekend at Wingate?" Luke asked after the end of their third game. He had won only the second one, but since they had agreed to play five, he figured he would trounce her during the final two rounds. Ever since their agreement to start anew, their talk had continued in a light vein. He had not realized how much time had passed. He had already thrown the last piece of firewood on the smoldering fire, sending Diana a dazzling smile of nonchalance when she had protested that he might strain his back.

"Do you prefer honesty or politeness?" Diana countered.

"Honesty."

"No, I'm not looking forward to the party. Are you?"

"Yes, and I'm sorry you aren't. If you're frightened about being among so many strangers, I think it's perfectly natural."

"You have a different perspective." Diana played a bone that gave her ten points, then sent him an arch look.

"True, but I'm trying to understand yours. I'll do all I can to make the affair easier for you if you'll give me some hints how to do that. Salathiel or Lallage or I will stay by your side every minute if you'd like.''

''That won't help at all.'' Diana shuddered mentally at the thought and evaded his piercing gaze. ''I prefer being left on my own. If I stay around you three who know me, I'll not learn much about conversing with strangers, will I?''

''I guess not.'' He wished Diana was not looking down at the lines of dominoes and hiding her thoughts behind her dark lashes. He had no inkling of what was going on within her blue eyes. But, he confessed, when had he ever, except right after he first kissed her and . . . ?

''After all,'' Diana said in a conciliatory tone, ''Lallage's party isn't the same as the Charity Ball. I thought that was the one where it's so important that I do everything right.''

''That's true.'' Luke played his domino after seeing no way to gain more than five points.

Somehow Diana's lack of enthusiasm for Lallage's party diminished Luke's own. He had not realized how much he had been looking forward to showing her off to everyone he had met in St. Christopher Parish. The occasion was merely a way to mix with his fellow citizens and a kind of rehearsal with Diana for attending the Charity Ball next month. Still, he had relished the idea of being at her side during her first social affair. ''Salathiel dotes on making plans so I figure he has already decided exactly how we'll be traveling to Wingate.''

''Yes, Lallage and Salathiel talked with me this afternoon. He plans to go that morning and assist Lallage in making preparations.'' Remembering the way Luke seemed to pay scarce attention to Salathiel's sometimes protracted explanations about such matters, Diana plunged ahead. ''Later Salem will drive Odille and me in the carriage. You can ride Jasper over nearer to three o'clock when the party begins.''

''Good. That way I can see to things around the place without having to hurry. The crews are cutting firewood in the forest and when I can, I like to help Jed keep the wagons moving.''

''You really should rest tomorrow and let your muscles heal.'' All evening Diana had noticed that Luke frequently shifted his weight around on his chair and she felt sympathy for his plight. Also she had noticed the way his maroon robe fell from his broad shoulders and how the loosely wrapped front sometimes gapped open enough to reveal almost all of his furred chest before he realized it and lapped it closed again. At those times she also felt an inner reaction. She was not sure what it was, but she knew it had no relationship to sympathy for it kept her keyed up and achingly aware of some facts she kept trying to forget. He was man and she was woman and they sat alone late at night in a bedroom.

Trying not to visualize what lay underneath Luke's silk robe, Diana asked, "Does Jed know how to give a rubdown with herbal ointment?"

"He used something but I don't know what it is. When I complained about the smell, he said Tabitha gave it to him and swore by its powers."

Diana nodded, pleased that Tabitha had apparently passed on one of her jars of soothing ointment made with crushed maypop seeds, fennel, and snakeroot. Because the odor was not offensive to her and because her source was at hand when Philip was alive trapping, she nearly always used the fat scraped from muskrat hides to hold her concoctions together. She promised herself she would try sneaking off to her house and getting one of the few remaining jars with mint leaves added to counteract the animal smell. Tabitha could give it to Luke. "You should be feeling fit before Saturday."

"Good. I plan to dance you around and around, bruises or not." Luke liked the way Diana had begun looking at him with more frankness during the evening, as if maybe she was losing her fear of him, or what Salathiel had said was fear.

"Lallage is afraid the group from New Orleans that she engaged to play might not arrive in time for her party, what with the roads and ferries between here and there being so unpredictable."

Luke shrugged his shoulders in good-natured defeat as he watched Diana play her last domino and win the game, her third out of four. There was no need to play the fifth round. She had him skunked.

Winning at dominoes no longer seemed important to Luke,

not when he considered all he had won that evening. "If no musicians show up, I'll hum a tune like this and dance with you anyway." He hummed a few bars of a Strauss waltz, purposefully off key, then grinned across at her.

Diana laughed at his clowning. "You wouldn't dare."

"I might." His countenance serious then, Luke said, "Speaking of travel to St. Christopher Parish, what do you think about having some small steamboats running on Selene Bayou? That way people would have only a few miles to travel on land to the Mississippi and be able to reach New Orleans in almost half the time it takes now. There are some canals being cut this side of New Orleans that could be lengthened and used in conjunction with the Selene."

"That sounds fascinating." Diana's eyes widened with interest. Only since she had gotten to know Lallage and Salathiel had she been able to supplement her news from the slave grapevine and find out more about what was going on in the world beyond Gator Swamp. What surprised her was that her appetite for reports of all that was new seemed insatiable. Several times she had pondered the reversal of her thoughts about many things since coming to Fairfield. No longer did she decry change simply because it was change; she looked forward to embracing certain aspects of it.

But not yet, Diana reminded herself when the thought of Lallage's party surfaced and terrified her. Not until she was ready. "Has there been talk about steamboats on the Selene?"

"I've been thinking about it ever since I came here in June and realized how hard it is to get back and forth to the capital." Who would have thought a young woman might find such a topic interesting? Luke could not remember when he had seen her lovely face as animated. Or when he had spent such a delightful evening. "I've done a little investigating, both here and when I was in New Orleans. Nearly all of the businessmen in Calion like the idea. They say they would like shipping and receiving by steamboat and that they and their families would prefer traveling that way, too."

"You're a very intelligent man, Luke Greenwood." She cocked her head and sized him up as if for the first time.

From where he sat watching her, Luke got the impression

that at least for once, Diana was not finding him lacking. He felt amazingly right with the world. "Since civilization has always made use of waterways whenever possible, I can't claim the idea is original."

Diana eyed Luke with new respect. Apparently, he was not always puffed up with false pride. She had been seeing different sides of him all evening. He seemed far more complex than she had believed. Were his thoughts about bringing steamboat transportation to the area what kept him gone so many evenings to Calion? She had not forgotten Lallage's comments about how the town's single women and their mothers paid him a great deal of attention. Judging from Luke's behavior all evening, it was easy to see why. And she had never denied that he was handsome to look upon. "I think the idea likely will be welcomed by everyone. Are the boats huge?" In her eagerness she leaned forward. "Tell me about them."

"The riverboats on the Mississippi and other major rivers are large with two and three decks, but there are also compact ones traveling the smaller streams all across the country. They displace no more than a couple of feet of water and if they're made low and short enough, they can maneuver the sharp curves of the Selene without difficulty. We planters could get our cane to the mills faster. Then we could send our harvests and our sugar to market easier and with less cost."

A voracious flame attacked the remainder of the last log in the fireplace and splintered it into a popping burst of red coals that showered the black, dying ones. Both Diana and Luke turned to watch the showy display, attuned in ways neither would have thought possible earlier that evening.

"I think it's time I left now," Diana said, glancing down at the forgotten dominoes on the game table. "It's late."

Despising the stiffness of his muscles, Luke rose as Diana stood amidst a provocative rustling of long skirts and pushed back her chair. The candles had burned low. He noted that the reflections of dancing light were turning her pale hair into a puffy white cloud tinged with ethereal gold. Her pretty lips—parted slightly as if she was lost in contemplation— might have been the essence of an inspired artist's brush strokes: soft, pink, sensuous. What would she do if he hurried around the table and kissed her, just once?

With a slow smile that bordered on acceptance of something unpleasant, he rammed his hands into the pockets of his robe. "I wish the clock had stood still." Luke recognized that though he had used the words lightly in the past, he meant them literally right then. Aware that she was moving away from him, he glanced ruefully at the handsome timepiece sitting on the marble mantel.

In the doorway, Diana paused and turned for one more look at the raven-haired man gazing at her with open bemusement claiming his handsome features. A lock of his usually controlled hair dipped across his forehead and gave him a boyish look. She watched the fingers of his right hand move up and lightly stroke the bottom of his chin. "Maybe the clock didn't stand still, but I'm not so sure that time didn't slow down a bit. Good night, Luke."

Thirteen

On the day of Lallage's party, Diana's plans went so well that she wondered if she might not have slipped up somewhere in her thinking.

Salathiel, claiming the mild fall weather had him feeling chipper, rode off toward Wingate soon after breakfast. Along with comb, brush, and curling iron, Odille packed Diana's rose-colored silk gown, slippers, and other essentials in a portmanteau shortly after the noon meal. Diana walked with her to the front yard where Salem waited beside the carriage.

"When you and Master Luke get there on your horses," Odille said after watching Salem set the portmanteau on the leather seat, "I'll have a spot picked out for us to use. Tabitha promised to help you into your riding costume since you say it's too early to get dressed." Her tone revealed a rare testiness.

Odille gathered up the edges of her long blue skirt in one hand and set her foot on the mounting step, then turned back to face Diana. The quadroon's gold ear hoops gleamed as they swung from underneath her ever-present blue tignon with its perky ties sticking up at the top. "You've been acting skittish all morning. Are you sure you don't want to go now?"

"I'm sure. Don't worry. I'll be fine." Diana averted her eyes and watched a butterfly dip its black-edged wings and glide through the warm air. Odille, her lips pursed and her eyes narrowed, was sending speculative looks toward her. "You and Salem have a nice drive."

Tabitha, the only one in whom Diana had confided, frowned at the ecstatic young woman when she dashed into the kitchen and reported the carriage had left. With her hands balled into fists and propped on her generous hips, Tabitha scolded, "You gonna get into trouble for this, sho' as the worl', Miss Diana. You done give Master Luke your word an' I never thought I'd live to see the day when you ain't backin' up your word."

"I gave my word only about going with him to a party in New Orleans," Diana hastened to say. She leaned to peer out of the kitchen door toward the stables. "Thank goodness he hasn't come back to eat yet." Her lips twisted into a momentary pout of jealousy. "No doubt King is following him as usual."

"I seen the dog leave with him early this mornin'. You oughten be actin' jealous 'cause King runs with the master most'a the time now. When do you have time for him anymore?"

Tabitha watched Diana duck her eyes and fidget with the sash on her blue morning gown. "He say he ain't comin' in till it's time to get cleaned up for Miss Lallage's party."

"I'm not asking you to lie, Tabitha. All you have to do is say everybody has already gone. Just don't say where we've gone. That way you'll not be truly lying."

"Humph! I don't like it some a'tall. You gonna get that man so mad—"

"Don't fret. I intend to live up to my agreement with him, but I'm not ready to go to Wingate and meet the people from St. Christopher Parish. I would much rather be facing total strangers in New Orleans than people I've heard about most of my life. Oh, Tabitha,"—she swallowed but the fullness remained in her throat—"can't you understand my feeling that I might not fit in anywhere but the swamp?"

Sympathy and devotion oozing from her dark eyes, Tabitha patted Diana's tense shoulder. "I'll fix it good if'n I can. Scoot on now 'fore Master Luke an' King get back."

Diana threw her arms around the black woman's neck, murmured her thanks, and turned to go. Tabitha said, "Wait up. I fixed you a little somethin' to eat. You get on back 'fore too late, you hear?"

Smiling and accepting the amply stuffed napkin, Diana replied, "I will and thanks for the food. I'll count on you to tell Salem no more than you have to."

"He ain't gonna like it no better'n me. He ain't gonna see no better'n me why you gotta act this way when Master Luke ain't done much more than fix you up like the proper folks you is. More good than bad gonna come outta all this, if you'd jes wait an' see an' don't mess up things. If yo' papa ain't seemed to care more for what he wanted for hisself than what his chile might be needin', ain't none of this would'a happened."

Tabitha finished her grumbling to an empty kitchen. Before the second sentence rolled from the black woman's mouth, Diana had raced away toward Gator Swamp.

After detouring to gather some blossoms from a late-blooming catchfly-gentian and decorate the brick crypts in the cemetery, Diana hurried to the familiar board walkway snaking through the trunks of fat-bottomed cypress trees in the swamp. Through the deep shade she saw her home still perching at a slight angle on its stilts, reminding her of an aged, gray bird nesting above the shallow water.

The sounds of her slippers shuffling on the rough boards and of her long skirts being caught by the trees' low limbs and rough bark seemed alien to Diana in the peacefulness of the warm November afternoon. Only the lazy, echoing calls of birds and the occasional plops of turtles slipping from floating logs back into the black water seemed as she remembered.

Diana winced at the way the front door of her home sagged on one side and scraped heavily against the floor when she opened it and went inside. The numerous fall rains had taken more than their usual toll, she reasoned after she noted other signs of deterioration. Dark circles on the ceiling and on the wooden floor told her that the shakes on the roof needed repairing.

In a shadowed corner beside the bookshelves, a spider had woven a monstrous web that equaled in size any Diana had ever seen. Always before, spider webs had fascinated her, had even seemed to invite her to lean close and examine the intricacies of each variegated yet similar pattern. Such a receptive attitude had ruled, she concluded with a sigh, only when the cobwebs appeared outside. The web inside the Hathaway home served as a reminder that it now sat deserted, little more than a hull of its former self.

Diana despised the sudden thought that her home might be akin to the hollow, brittle shells of insects she often had found clinging to tree bark after the larva inside each had developed its wings and then burst free from its dull chamber as a beautiful airborne moth. As if trying to outwit nature, she flung open the wooden shutters to let in fresh air and afternoon sunlight.

Sloughing off her maudlin thoughts, Diana shed her shoes and clothing and slipped into one of her old homespun tops and brief skirts. She set about cleaning the four small rooms, lingering overly long in the kitchen where last spring's collection of herbs and roots lay drying here and there on small shelves, on upended boxes, and on strings of braided moss hanging from the ceiling.

She fretted over having missed out on gathering many plants during the summer. Even if she managed to sneak away long enough to make new potions, there were not enough ingredients. She rolled her eyes in annoyance. Though she viewed Luke in a kinder light ever since she had played dominoes with him two nights ago, Diana now redirected her anger toward the man plucking her up from her life and forcing it into new directions not of her choosing.

Drat Luke Greenwood! Diana's thoughts ran on as she padded around barefoot performing tasks that had been hers since she was very young. The slanting rays of the afternoon sun began filtering through the lofty tree branches, adding their bit to the rejuvenation of the house before she felt at all satisfied with her efforts. By then, the smell of the place upon her arrival, an odor redolent of mildew, rot, and decay had returned to the clean one she remembered and sought.

While Diana was sweeping off the last leaf and cypress boll from the porch, she let the sight of her father's old pirogue floating near the back corner register in her troubled mind. She had not been out in it since she had gone to Fairfield that fateful night in June.

A nostalgic smile lighted the young woman's face as she knelt in the pirogue and cleared away the collection of dead leaves and other debris on the bottom of the hollowed-out tree trunk. Her paddle and pole still lay along the dark bottom that Philip Hathaway, when Diana was small, had carved out through controlled burning of the cypress log and then scraping long hours with a short-handled adze.

If King were here, Diana thought with fondness for her dog, she might take him down to the place where the egrets nested and let him romp on some of the floating islands along the way. But, no, Luke Greenwood had usurped her pet's affections. Her pretty mouth drooped. He had turned her life upside down. Could she ever again be the same?

Why not make a visit to what she had always called her *secret bower*? Diana reflected with determination to enjoy her stolen afternoon of freedom. The thought of once more climbing the huge cypress tree and sitting up high where the fallen tupelo gum trees leaned against the cypress and formed a kind of sunken room pleased her.

Within minutes, Diana had grabbed a volume of Shakespeare's sonnets, the napkin full of food that Tabitha had given her, and was poling through the still water toward the main channel. Once she reached deeper water she made good use of her paddle.

Not long after Diana had hidden her pirogue in the thick alligator grass growing at the edges of the soaring cypress and settled into her secret bower, she heard thumping sounds and water rippling rhythmically from the lower end of the well-traveled main channel. A boat or pirogue was coming! She detected the echoing slap of wood on wood. Not many, Diana included, could propel a vessel rapidly without occasionally bumping it with their paddles or, when in shallow water pushing against the muddy bottom, their poles.

Lifting her head enough to see over the felled tree trunks

lying crisscrossed against the upper limbs of the cypress, she spotted a man below, dressed in a white shirt, dark tailored coat and trousers, rapidly propelling a pirogue. On a rope stretched behind, he pulled another pirogue that at first appeared empty. As he neared where Diana watched warily from her lofty perch, she saw something large and covered with a tarpaulin lying in the bottom of the towed vessel and weighting it down low in the water.

Strange, Diana reflected as she peeked again and watched the two pirogues pass some twenty feet below, that a man would be so well dressed in the swamp. Even stranger was the man's hair.

From her distant, overhead angle Diana could not see the stranger's face. His hair looked to be a kind of pinkish gold—which in itself was new to her—but the most remarkable aspect was that it grew from two large whorls at the back of his head, and the whorls, or crowns, grew in opposite directions. The centers of each appeared bare of hair and as wide as the tip of her little finger.

Diana recalled that one of the black children at Fairfield had a noticeable, reversed swirl at the front of his hair and that Tabitha had called it a cowlick. Perhaps the man in the pirogue had twin cowlicks at the back of his head. She had not been around many white people and did not pretend to know much about how their hair grew, but she sensed that what she was seeing was extraordinary.

Later, when she heard a pirogue coming down Gator Swamp, Diana could not judge how much time had passed since her arrival. Lost in reverie from her recent reading of sonnets and close to being asleep, she realized the sun would soon be sinking. The shade had deepened considerably and she was feeling chilled in her scanty clothing. It was past time to leave.

Cautiously, Diana peeked from her overhead perch and saw the same man with the odd double crowns in his pinkish hair. This time she gained a partial view of a large red nose. He no longer wore his coat, and he no longer towed a pirogue.

Still paddling briskly and making good time as he went back in the direction from which he had come earlier, the man seemed to sense someone might be watching, for he kept moving his head around and looking over his shoulder. Diana sank back down. When she looked again, the man was gone.

Diana scrambled down from her secret bower. Dark likely was going to fall before she reached her home, she realized, and she dipped her paddle quickly, first on one side and then the other. If her calculations were right, a full moon would rise that night and lend her enough light to find her way if she did not reach the cabin before sunset. The party at Lallage's home would not be over for a long while.

All afternoon Diana's thoughts had annoyed her by straying to Luke and wondering what he might do when he arrived at Lallage's party and discovered she was not there. If all went as she hoped, nobody would miss her right away, not when she had insisted on being left on her own.

From the beginning when Diana decided she was not ready to attend a social gathering, she had counted on the understanding of both Lallage and Salathiel afterward when she explained her consuming fear of mingling with the citizens of St. Christopher Parish. She hated that she could not plan on being completely honest with her dear friends; still, she figured she could elicit their compassion and win their forgiveness. Somehow she knew both held the same deep friendship for her that she felt for them.

It was Luke Greenwood over whom Diana fretted. What did he mean to her? Her feelings seemed to vacillate from fear to admiration to complete quandary before starting all over again. Always, the memory of being in his arms loomed as an unidentifiable factor. She felt her lips tingle from just thinking about how they had felt beneath his. She was lost in mulling over her mysterious relationship to the handsome, black-haired man when she nosed her pirogue into its resting spot near the back side of her porch.

Child of nature that she was, Diana could tell the full moon was on the verge of rising because here and there a magical, silvery haze was fingering the tops of the whispering dark trees with their long beards of swaying moss. Not for the first time, she imagined her small home nestled in the edge of one of nature's vast cathedrals. Often, she had pretended that the tops of the soaring trees served as a kind of Gothic roof. She viewed the dim recesses, sweetened by the incense emanating from lush vines and their blossoms, as aisles leading to deep chambers for private worship and meditation. Fitting music came from the wind and the innumerable creatures inhabiting the secluded freshwater swamp.

The thought that the moon soon would reveal its luminous face above her imaginary cathedral lifted Diana's heart in the way the appearance of a full moon always had. Feeling gloriously alive, she sighed in anticipation.

"Where in hell have you been?" came an angry masculine voice from the shadows. "I've been waiting here an hour."

Having just stepped from the pirogue to the back side of the porch, Diana froze. Had the voice come from a stranger, she would have been helpless because her rifle lay inside her house. Deciding she was not a lot better off to have Luke waiting for her, Diana felt her mouth go dry.

Not once had Diana considered that Luke might get back from the party in time to search her out before she returned to the mansion. Had Tabitha been forced to tell on her? If Luke had mistreated her or tricked her—

Diana lifted her chin and put her hands on her hips, a picture of defiance, anger, and a host of other tumbling emotions. "What right do you have to come spying on me, Luke Greenwood?"

"Every right. This house sits on my property."

Diana felt herself grow rigid with fear. Coatless and with his white shirt only partially buttoned, Luke was walking toward her and looking as fierce as when she had first seen him that night in June. Again he appeared tall and threatening, a man seething with the unspoken need to conquer whatever riled him. The faint light from the moon rising deep in the swamp should have softened the strained lean features below the mussed black hair falling across his forehead, but it did not.

All of the emotions bottled up inside over the past months warred with each other and attacked Diana like a swarm of angry honeybees forced from familiar quarters and now seeking a new place to live. The fluttery, inward battle robbed her of normal breath and heartbeat. While pushing back her unfettered hair from her face with hands that trembled, she took a step backward and stood as tall as her five feet and seven inches allowed.

"If you come any closer, you devil," Diana threatened with unmistakable hostility, "I'll make you sorry. I may look small but I'm strong and I'll not take any more of your bossing."

"I want to know what in hell you've been trying to do since you came to Fairfield! Why lie about where you live and the kind of life you've led? I ought to—" Despite his overweening anger, Luke realized he had no idea how to finish his statement. Gratitude upon finding Diana was battling with his earlier anger at being duped. Damn! Had he been duped!

"Ought to take me to the sheriff?" Diana asked, supplying words for the man scowling down at her. "Go ahead. I don't care. Tell him how my father built his house the year I was born on what was then unclaimed land in a swamp nobody seemed to care about. I confess I'm a poacher."

Luke's dark head slipped to one side a few degrees, as if digesting with surprise what he was hearing. Somewhere far away in the swamp a bull alligator bellowed, the primeval call echoing rapidly in eerie relays to the couple on the porch of the Hathaway house. Tree frogs teamed up and screeched in syncopation from nearby trees. Something heavy, like a turtle or a frisky bass, splashed the shallow water surrounding the porch. Mosquitos circled, dipping near enough to warn their intended victims with high-pitched whines. The man and woman seemed aware of nothing but each other.

Diana rushed ahead with what clawed at her throat and begged to be told. "Who asked you to come charging into our lives? Nobody needed you or wanted you. We were doing fine before you came. I'll go to jail willingly as a poacher, but don't you dare try punishing the slaves who knew about me and my house or I'll report you to the law for cruelty. Have me locked up in jail. What could be different from being locked up in your house where I'm treated—"

Luke cut her words off with some equally as angry. "How can you mouth such ridiculous nonsense? You've never been mistreated at Fairfield." He stepped forward and grabbed her hand before she could snatch it out of reach. "You've done nothing but tell me lies since the first. I've been waiting so long for you to show up"—he gestured toward the darkened house with his head—"that I went inside before it got dark and looked around." When she glared up at him in the pale light and still struggled to free herself, he went on in a cutting tone. "Yes, I know a hell of a lot about you and your folks now. I discovered the cemetery on my way here."

"So?" Diana wanted to slap his face but feared what he might do in retaliation. She had never seen him as upset.

"Your parents were close friends of the Fairfield couple, weren't they?"

"Yes."

"Everybody on the place knew where you came from and went along with this farce. I want to know why."

Diana sliced him a look designed to wound—silvery, cold. When he tightened his grip on her wrist, she winced. "Because they thought you were a devil."

"I suppose you fed them that lie."

"No. When the news first came over the slave grapevine from New Orleans, it said your name was Lucifer and—"

"My God! Do you believe in such nonsense, too?"

Diana gulped. "I didn't know what to believe." Should she tell him how she had stopped the rumors the night she had ministered to Florina over at Fernwood? No, she dared not mention her dealings with the slaves on other plantations. He might decide to punish them, too. His piercing black eyes demanded more answers. How could she make him understand? "You were awfully bad-tempered and mean about not letting me go that night after I returned your dumb old watch."

Luke considered the surprising news he was hearing, not liking the picture Diana was painting. After finding her missing from Wingate and discovering that nobody knew where she was, he had already berated himself mercilessly for meddling in her life. Anger at having been hoodwinked by the young woman before him stepped to the forefront again. "How could you pretend you were a poor neglected illiterate? Inside I found where you've written your name in books. The bit about your being ignorant was a lie, wasn't it?"

Diana nodded hesitantly. "Yes."

"God! You've made fools of us all. I can't believe I've been thinking lately that we might be becoming friends or that you were already friends with Lallage and Salathiel."

Diana twisted her head away, but Luke grabbed her chin with his free hand and forced her face back up near his, his thumb and fingers sinking into her tender jaws. Her eyes appeared mysterious and stretched open too wide. "You have no inkling of what the word *friend* means. No friend would have deceived another by slipping away as you've done. You scared the hell out of Lallage and Salathiel, not to mention Odille and the others at Fairfield. Are you no different from other beautiful young women, living only for yourself and manipulating others to satisfy your whims? How gullible I was to think there was something good and decent about you, that there was more to you than outward beauty!"

Words of denial and sorrow for what she had done tried to form but Diana found they lodged behind the monstrous lump in her throat. Her pulse had been building into a wild storm and was now threatening to explode momentarily in her ears. Her heart was forming a painful knot in her chest, even as his hand dropped from her face.

Diana shook her head, feeling her unbound hair shift around on her back and shoulders as if it were a long fall of moss disturbed by a night wind. She had not realized those who cared for her might suffer genuine concern and be upset, she wanted to say. It was just that she was so scared and—

Then Luke grabbed both of Diana's upper arms in his arms and stared into her widely spaced eyes, plundering those pales depths for answers. His mind was reeling from her open confession that she had lied from the beginning about her background. He was still remembering how she had spilled out the words as if glad to get them said. He was trying to ignore the obvious facts that she was trembling, near to crying, and looking up at him with unadulterated fear.

His voice deep and thick with anguish, Luke made a confession of his own in a kinder tone. "I nearly went out of my mind trying to figure out what had happened to you when nobody could find you at Wingate. I got there a little late and I started looking for you right away." His voice thickened as he remembered. "Then I became afraid you might be ill or might have been harmed . . . until I conferred with Lallage and Salathiel and Odille. All of us realized then that you never intended to go to the party."

Contrition crippled Diana's reply. "I'm sorry, truly sorry that I caused concern. I never meant to hurt anyone, not today or at any time. I meant to get back before dark." The question that she wanted answered most formed and burst out in jerks. "How did you find me? Did you threaten Tabitha—"

"Damn, but you make me even madder by insinuating that I'm some kind of beast!"

Diana slid a cautious look down to where his hands were gripping her arms painfully. "Hasn't it occurred to you that you give me reasons?"

Luke loosened his hold but he did not release her. His pulse pounded and he blamed it on his relief at finding her unharmed. The ever-increasing din of the night callers penetrated his ears for a moment and he felt as if the two of them were lost in some primeval spot removed from reality. A mosquito whined and darted close, winging off into the partial darkness when Luke shook his head impatiently. "Tabitha conveniently was out of sight when I raced back home with Salem and Odille tearing up the road behind in the carriage. It was King that made me follow the slight path through the weeds in the pasture. As soon as we got back, he barked and headed this way, then kept returning to me until I followed him."

Diana glanced around, glad of an excuse to escape Luke's piercing black gaze. "Where is King now?"

"Salem and Odille came down soon after we got here. Salem pointed out the pirogue was gone and that you likely would be out in it till dark. I told them I wanted to wait for you. King must have been hungry, for he followed them to the house.''

''What about Lallage and Salathiel?'' Diana had not believed her heart could squeeze itself into a tighter knot, but it was doing so with each new revelation Luke threw at her with apparent relish. How foolish she had been! Why hadn't she realized that nobody was going to dismiss her absence with the same nonchalance she had employed when giving in to her little private fears? She confessed that her need to challenge Luke's authority over her had played its part, too.

''Salem was going to ride over to Wingate and tell them we knew where you were.'' Luke paused for a moment, then went on in a voice laden with the same thickness that Diana had heard earlier when he related what had happened. ''After it began to get dark, I was afraid you weren't ever coming back. And in a crazy way, I couldn't have blamed you if you had not. Salem assured me that you could take care of yourself in the swamp, but. . . .'' He sucked in a ragged breath. ''You played us all for fools. What were you hoping to gain by your trickery? How you must have laughed, must still be laughing.''

She whispered, for no stronger sound would come, ''I never laughed, Luke. Never.'' From only inches away in the near darkness, the imprisoned Diana watched Luke's eyes blaze with something akin to pain. Why was she gaining a kind of pleasure from his confession of fear for her well-being? If eyes were a pathway to one's soul as she had always believed, then she was gazing into a man's soul that appeared troubled and puzzled about whatever stirred its depths.

Then Luke's mouth claimed her attention. His lips seemed on the verge of trembling and they bore an almost tangible look of suffering. The grip of his hands on her arms loosened more as they stared into each other's eyes, struggling for control.

Without warning, Diana felt oddly at peace with some of the protesting emotions still whirling around inside, searching for landing places. Did she truly fear and despise Luke Greenwood? Or was she, perhaps, falling in love with him?

Her heartbeat speeding up even further, Diana thought of how her father had told her that when she met the right man for her, she would know it. He never warned her that she might be unaware of such a remarkable discovery right off, that it might take awhile for it to happen and for her to recognize it. A smile tried to lift the corners of her trembling mouth. The thought that she might be falling in love with Luke, the one she had deemed her jailer for nearly four months, seemed ludicrous—and exciting.

Just then Luke pulled Diana close within his arms and kissed her. Something about the way her pale eyes were washing marveling looks over his face seemed to suggest kissing.

As soon as Luke's lips touched Diana's, he confessed that he had been eager to kiss her again ever since that first time earlier in the week. Any soul-searching beyond that mark, he was unwilling to do. He counted it blessing enough that he had found her safe and unharmed and that she was again returning his kisses with sweet ardor.

His mouth moved against hers more insistently when the punishing thought of how he would have suffered had he not found her rose and taunted him. While Luke's senses reeled from the heady feel of the barely clothed Diana clinging to him and welcoming his kisses, the miniscule part of his brain furnishing thought sent forth no mention of his earlier anger or his absurd bet with his brother.

"Luke," Diana murmured when he lifted his head and gazed down at her. "I've been such a fool." Stepping back only a few inches and delighting that his arms still rested across the portion of her back left uncovered by her skimpy top, she savored the feel of his neck and shoulders beneath her gently caressing fingertips. How much better would they feel without his shirt covering them?

If she told Luke right then that she suspected she was falling in love with him, Diana wondered, would he tell her how he felt about her? Maybe he did not love her yet, but she entertained the wondrous notion that they were meant to be together. Why else had he discovered her in the moonlight on Midsummer's Eve? The entire scene had seemed eerie, but now that she had labeled what drew her to the often baffling Luke Greenwood, even when she fought against being attracted, she felt certain she understood it all.

On one level Diana thought about her belief that what will be, will be. She thought about matters she viewed as natural and predestined, like the moon and the tides and the Almighty's plan for the universe . . . and one man, one woman, bound by eternal love. Luke and Diana.

Deciding she might have to wait for Luke to begin falling in love with her before she confessed her feelings about him, Diana let her thoughts fly to a baser level and focus on the moment. Luke smelled warm and manly, familiar. Being with him felt right. "Hold me close again. I love the way you hug."

Luke returned her mesmerizing smile and pulled her closer. "I think you've become something of a flirt." Luke loved the way Diana had been peeking up at him from behind partially lowered lashes ever since their kisses ended. What could be bringing such a delightful curve to her lips?

"Have I?" She heard the admiration in his voice.

"Yes, and I approve as long as I'm the one being favored." He leaned to kiss her again, surprised when she twisted her head sideways. When had he ever been able to figure out Diana? She was unlike any other young woman he had known. The way her pale hair brushed across his arms and caught a reflection of the moonbeams filtering through the overhead trees stole his attention for a charmed moment. He reached with one hand to stroke her hair, then mold it gently to her well-shaped head. "Have you become a coquette as well?"

"No, but I'd like to know what you're thinking before you kiss me again." She leaned against the hand resting at the back of her head and sending delicious tremors racing up and down her spine. "Are you still angry with me?"

"I'm thinking you're the most beautiful armful of woman in the world."

Her lips forming a little *moue*, Diana asked, "Have you held many like this?"

Luke chuckled. The feel of her partially clad body against

him was prodding at fires banked low in his groin. Her skin was like warm satin. Her full breasts spilled against his chest in a way that screamed of delectable woman. "Don't tell me you might be jealous."

"Would you be jealous if a lot of men had held me"— she glanced down at the way she rested within the circle of his arms, their bodies touching intimately all the way down to their knees, then looked back up at him candidly—"like this?"

Surprised at her question and at his instant hatred of the idea that anyone but him might ever hold her as he was doing, Luke replied in a husky bass, "Let's just say I wouldn't like it worth a damn."

Diana heard what she wanted to hear in Luke's deep voice and felt her heartbeat speed up again. Surely, his remark and his voiced concern for her well-being meant that he was feeling something strong for her, something bordering on love, something that could evolve into love. She took the initiative and pulled his head down to hers.

With her lips almost touching his, Diana whispered with an innocence and expectancy that reached out and curled itself around Luke's unsuspecting heart like the tendril of a newly greening vine, "Kiss me as if I'm the only woman in the world."

Luke obliged. He kissed Diana with warmth and depth. He kissed her as if she were something rare, precious, fleeting. Yes, the only woman in the world.

Then, with fires igniting throughout his racing blood, he kissed her with a young man's moist passion that proclaimed it was too vaulting to be pacified with mere kissing. His tongue, rough and hot, rediscovered the soft inner sides of her full lips, then plunged with raw hunger into the virginal recesses of her mouth. Diana was setting his senses ablaze.

Nigh breathless, her heartbeat deafening, Diana stood on tiptoes and clung to Luke, offering him ecstatic kiss for ecstatic kiss. Her tongue teased his with equal fervor. Gone was the green girl. Her aroused woman's body reigned. What had hovered about as a promise back when he had kissed her the first time now rose as certainty. Was she not nature's child?

The young woman who once had denied she believed in magic felt she was ripening into someone new there in Luke's arms in the silvery rays from the full moon aborning on the horizon. Her skin tingled delightfully where his hands caressed—on her back, underneath her loose blouse up to her shoulders, at last around to her rib cage where her throbbing breasts overflowed.

As the full moon rose and beamed its ethereal rays on the embracing couple—one so dark, the other so fair—both felt a kind of illumination taking place within, a kind of private moon glow. His senses inflamed, Luke tore his mouth from Diana's and masterfully lifted her into his arms.

Diana's eyes sent luminous messages of consent as she smiled up at him. Their shimmering gazes met, intertwined intimately, and created an infinite longing, rather like the emotion that remembered strains of love songs can call up in lovers long after they have heard them played.

With moonlight showing him the path, Luke carried Diana into the little house and lay her on what he had figured out earlier was her bed. Their wondering smiles helped illuminate the room. Later he might puzzle over what possessed him. In his attempts to evade truth, he might label it moon madness. Right then he had no wish to question the magic settling over them since their first kiss out on the porch.

Fourteen

Convinced that destiny had brought them together, Diana slipped out of her scanty costume in her shadowy bedroom, then lay watching as Luke finished shedding his clothing. Why should she care about spoken commitments when her heart was singing joyfully about what was meant to be?

The silence stretching between Diana and Luke seemed to her almost palpable with something too private to be voiced. Her father had been wrong in one instance, she decided with new-found womanly wisdom: Magic did exist. It was all around her, like moonlight. When a mockingbird warbled from a nearby tree, she heard the piercingly sweet notes as echoes of what was plumping her into a maelstrom of throbbing emotion.

As Luke sat on the edge of her bed, Diana smiled up at him and held out her hand. Never had she felt more like nature's child. She felt in harmony with everything around her, with her inner self, with the handsome man smiling down at her and covering her hand with his. "Luke, I wonder if I might not have been waiting for you all my life."

Diana's beauty and candor almost overwhelmed Luke. His senses were still whirling from their earlier kisses and caresses. His pulse was downright chaotic, now that their clothing lay discarded. He brought her hand up to his lips and kissed it with tenderness. When he felt it tremble and heard her indrawn breath, he turned it over and kissed its soft underside. Fixing her with a questioning look, he asked, "Could you be mistaken that—"

"Never," Diana broke in to say while drawing him down to lie beside her. She melted into his arms, loving the way her head fit naturally in the hollow between his chin and neck. She heard his pulse racing in rhythm with hers. His warm skin smelled as she remembered. Slightly salty, very manly.

From close against his neck Luke heard her whisper, "Hold me, Luke . . . and love me." Savoring the shivery sensation that her invitation and the touch of her soft breath fanning against his skin created, he groaned and tightened his arms around her silken nakedness.

The delights Luke tasted that night in the Hathaway cabin fed both his soul and his alerted senses. He kissed Diana in all the places he had secretly longed to savor since first seeing her that night in the moonlight and wondering if she might not be the mythical goddess of the moon. The Diana he held was no myth. Her sweet lips were moist, warm, molding themselves to his. Offering. Begging.

As if he had all of the time in the world, he claimed her treasures. First, the hollows of her lovely throat—she arched her neck, the better to accommodate his kisses—then the dark tips of her pale breasts—her sighs of pleasure thrilled him almost as much as the sensation of his lips gliding over her satiny skin—and the delightful curves of her slender hips. His lips lingered overly long on the barely curving planes of her belly with its tiny indentation that denied she was truly a goddess.

He lifted a strand of her pale hair, fascinated by its texture and the way it curled around his fingers as if it, too, responded to his worshipful touch. Silvery light angled through the solitary window of the small bedroom and with mysterious benevolence bathed the couple lost in each other's arms, lost to all but their glorious feast of senses. Luke could not remember ever feeling as entranced as at that moment. Was Diana real? "You are as divine as the moonlight," he told her, awe and desire furring his voice.

"I feel a bit like moonlight," Diana confessed with a shiver of expectancy. Sending him a radiant smile, she reached to rest the underside of her hand on one lean side of his handsome face. Her fingers transmitted what she already knew about his features. Perfection. Was this moment real? "And no wonder, with such a handsome man making love to me."

Luke recognized the fire roiling throughout his body and centering in his groin. There was something different about the flame, but he could not imagine what. Did it have to do with his suspicion that the woman in his arms had mesmerized him? "I want you, Diana. You're so beautiful, so sweet."

"You're making this a perfect night."

Diana learned from Luke that tender lovers can spread warm, bone-tingling pleasure with kisses, with caresses, with whispered phrases of adoration. Her turgid breasts ached under the wet magic of his tongue and mouth, ached more when deserted for thrillingly new patches of skin. Once she heard the sough of a nearby tree and wondered if it might not be trying to give voice to the ancient mystery of what compels one particular man and one particular woman to seek each other out and become one.

An apt pupil, Diana was soon following Luke's lead and giving in to her desire to make love to him. Her fingers roved through his thick black hair, memorizing the shape of his head. While his sometimes gentle, sometimes frenzied caresses on her hips and thighs added to the delicious flame licking inside her womanhood and threatening to melt her, she slid her hands down through the tight curls on his chest. She felt his nipples spring into nubs before she moved her hands around to his back to trace the smooth contours of his unbelievably hard muscles.

Adoring the way she could sense his latent strength beneath her fingertips, Diana sighed and snuggled closer for more of his titillating caresses. How was it that no matter how close she pressed against him, how entangled their limbs became, she could not be contented to lie still? On impulse she leaned to kiss his biceps, then the V-shaped hollow at the base of his throat where his pulse leapt in a dance as wild as her own.

She gloried in the fragrance of his skin, in its familiar, barely salty taste. She gloried in Luke.

When both of their bodies burned too intensely to remain separate flames, Luke rose above Diana and eased his pulsating shaft into her moist gateway. She writhed with eagerness and unbridled passion, restless until he penetrated past the sign of her maidenhood and wrought a tearing pain throughout her being. Flinching, yet hugging him closer in her frenzy, she unwittingly provided a quicker pathway to her begging center. Overcome by the magnificent sense of being one with Luke, she cried out and rained kisses on his face, his mouth.

Once her virgin, velvety warmth embraced his throbbing length, Luke felt a multitude of sensations claim him. He burned with more than desire but he did not seek a label. Never before had he made love to a woman who emanated rapturous passion back to him as sweetly as Diana was doing in her natural innocence and spontaneity.

Luke moved within her. She thrilled him anew when she moaned in delirium deep in her throat. Then she was curling one leg over his buttocks with abandon. His entire being seemed to expand from Diana's obvious delight.

Then the ancient rhythm compelled both lovers. Their frenetic joining evolved into a scintillating rush of resplendent light that encased them for a brief moment before firing them into one straining mass and melding their souls. Together, the lovers created their own private sparkle of ecstasy and basked in its loveliness, even as it burst back upon them, exalting them with its searing brilliance.

When all vestiges of the incredible beauty of their joining had faded into fleeting intangibles, a bit like stars paling and receding at the first signs of the rising sun, he sank against her, satiated as never before. Diana slid her arms from Luke's neck to his back, hardly daring believe the wondrous feeling of heavenly lassitude seeping throughout her body and threatening to float her into another world.

Diana smiled to herself while entertaining the fanciful notion that Luke had taken her to another world. Maybe he had taken her on a dizzying journey to the full moon still rising over her beloved Gator Swamp. One day, she exulted silently as she watched the moonbeams dance overhead, he would take her on an even more spectacular journey of the senses: He would tell her that he loved her and wanted her to become his wife.

"Oh, Luke," Diana said when he lay beside her with an arm pulling her close. She loved saying his name in the stillness broken only by night callers out in the swamp. Both had mastered normal breathing again. Moonlight and contentment merged and hovered over them like an airbrone blanket.

Almost shyly, for she had no idea what Luke might think of her talking about such things, Diana went on. "I know now why what goes on between a man and a woman is called making love."

Luke had no wish to face up to reality yet, even had he possessed the strength to do so. During his twenty-eight years, he had had too little magic transport him out of himself to let go of it more quickly than necessary. Something kept trying to remind him that never before had he experienced anything at all like what he had shared with Diana moments ago. Thoughts about what their lovemaking was going to do to their relationship kept trying to surface but he batted them down. He was in no state to think about anything of consequence. "Let's not try to understand it."

Diana shrugged blithely, then leaned up enough to prop on her elbow and gain a better view. If she had not known better, she would have suspected he was asleep. Her forefinger caressed the bridge of his nose, then traced the curve of his dark eyebrows. They belonged to her now. "Doesn't tonight change things between us?"

"In what way?"

"For one thing," she replied, withdrawing her hand from his face and attempting to disguise her disappointment at his seeming lack of interest in conversation, "I don't think you should hold me to our pact."

Diana thought of how surprised—and maybe pleased?—

Luke was going to be when he released her from their agreement and she then told him that she wanted to go with him to New Orleans because she would love having him escort her around. She sent the silent man a sidewise look of adoration, glad to see that he had opened his eyes and was looking at her—how? Pensively? Moonlight, with its intriguing shadows, *was* deceptive. His heavily muscled body no longer seemed threatening.

Suddenly, Diana realized that because of the handsome man watching her, she was feeling lightheaded, beautiful, womanly, and, for the first time since having heard that a new master was coming to Fairfield, in control of her life again. Just as suddenly a chill rode the November breeze whispering through the fronds of moss outside the window and drifting into the room, setting off a tingling down her spine. "Luke, we can forget all that business about the pact now, can't we?"

Luke sat up and slung his long legs over the side of the bed. Despite his attempts to foist it off, reality had returned. He threw Diana an assessing look over his shoulder as he retorted, "Is that why you were willing to make love with me? Now you think it's time for me to pay up."

Luke did not know what he expected Diana's reaction to be now that he had taken her virginity—not that she had protested, he reminded himself sanctimoniously—but he had not expected her to try striking a bargain with him as if he might be indebted. His temper reared its devious head and took command. She had duped him again and he had helped her do it! "God! You really aren't that different from women reared in a normal way, are you?"

"What's normal to you might not be normal to me," Diana shot back. "You really aren't the judge of what's normal for the world, Luke Greenwood!" Drat him! And here she had thought Luke might already be feeling tenderness toward her, might be mulling over some way to tell her he was falling in love with her. How could he not realize that their relationship had taken on special meaning? He had not changed at all! He was still domineering and concerned only with his own interests. "Why would you think I'd be willing to go to New Orleans with you now that you no longer have anything to threaten me with?"

Angrily, Luke reached for his clothing and began covering his nakedness. He had not wanted to think about the bet with Frederick. He had not wanted to think about anything for awhile, but, no, Diana was unwilling to let their moments of afterglow die naturally. She had to bring up the damned pact before he had matters sorted out in his mind. "You'll go though. I know all about you now and I'm not going to let you back down on your word, not after you've bamboozled everyone around here."

Even as Luke stalked out of the bedroom, Diana was hurrying to where the clothing she had worn from the mansion hung on the back of the bedroom door and was snatching it in place. How could she help but despise him for refusing to release her from their pact? she fumed as she tied her sash with force enough to strangle him had it been around his neck. The thought flashed to mind that she wished it *had* been around his neck.

While brushing her tangled hair and listening to Luke clomp around outside on the porch, Diana despised herself for having believed that he would abolish their agreement. How foolish of her to think earlier of offering to go to New Orleans with him because she wanted to. *Bloody balls of fire!* She aimed the hairbrush across to the very spot Luke's naked bottom had last rested on her bed, pleased when it landed where she intended. What a dolt she had been to mistake her increasing fascination with him as the first steps of falling in love!

Not that it made one iota of sense, but Diana found herself recalling half-forgotten stories told long ago by the blacks about a hoodoo woman who had sealed her fate by sleeping with the devil. Diana reminded herself that she did not believe in hoodoo. Neither did she believe that Luke Greenwood was associated with the devil. Still, the tenuous association with mythical evil fed her exalted sense of being caught up in something mystifying. She would have to remember to ask

Tabitha what happened to the woman. Nothing good, she was certain.

"Let's go," Luke ordered when Diana appeared in the doorway wearing her gown and shoes. He glanced at the moon now floating in full splendor above the tops of the ghostly trees deep in the swamp. "It's getting late."

It had occurred to Diana as she dressed that maybe it would be best for her to remain in her home and end the farce once and for all. Later, though her heart slashed her at the thought of facing her dear friends, she would visit Salathiel and Lallage and explain everything. She sent Luke a haughty look and angled her chin higher, ignoring the breeze that was mussing her hair and flinging strands forward around her face. "What if I refuse to go?"

"Then I'll throw you over my shoulder and take you." Luke knew that he would do just that, though he still did not understand what kind of dark mood had ruled him ever since they had made love. All he knew for certain was that, no matter what it took, he had no intention of leaving Diana there or of going to New Orleans without her.

Not even the breathtaking sight of Diana's silvery hair clouding around her beautiful face softened Luke's resolve. He determined that no longer was he going to allow moonlight or the one he had so fancifully associated with the mythical goddess of the moon charm him. *His* Diana was of an earthly bent.

Had the overwrought young man noted his use of the possessive before Diana's name, he would have hooted with far more emotion than a distant owl was doing at the moment. He took a step toward her, demanding, "Well?"

"You wouldn't dare!" How could she have suspected what she felt for him earlier might be love? She must have been out of her mind! He was arrogant and unworthy of a second thought. She almost backed up a step, but changed her mind. No longer was she going to kowtow to him.

Scowling, Luke took another step toward her. "Try me."

Diana huffed and brought her fists to her hips. "What can you do to me now?" She stared at his impassive face in the moonlight, awareness of his strength bringing a *frisson* of doubt. His eyes looked like black agates, cold and unfeeling. "Are you implying that you might punish the blacks who knew about me and kept quiet?"

"Do you want to take a chance and find out?"

Haughtily, Diana cloaked self-control around her sagging spirits and started off at a dignified pace down the familiar walkway. She barely noticed the beauty of the moonbeams drenching her beloved swamp. She heard none of the songs from the nocturnal creatures. All she could hear were Luke's footsteps echoing from behind her on the rough board walkway.

Much as Odille had responded the night before when Diana pleaded her case and begged forgiveness, the next morning Salathiel accepted the distraught young woman's lengthy, sometimes tearful recital of her wrongdoings. Immediately, he forgave her for what she termed her horrid lies and behavior.

"We shall put these unpleasant matters behind us and consider the unfortunate circumstances leading you to hold back truths," Salathiel remarked after all was said and a small silence linked the two of them in the library. His fingers had hovered around his mustache throughout much of the telling and his dark eyes had seemed overly bright at times. He admired her for accepting full blame and not shifting at least part of it to Luke, where, to Salathiel's way of thinking, the total burden rightly belonged. "I realize that you acted out of fear for the well-being of your friends."

On the preceding evening, long after Diana had gone upstairs, Luke had confided to Salathiel about Diana's background. Afterward, Salathiel had given full vent to his initial disapproval of forcing Diana to remain at Fairfield. From the abject misery he had seen on Luke's face, Salathiel suspected his former pupil had learned a painful lesson. At breakfast Luke had appeared no more cheerful.

Snatching Salathiel's thoughts back to the moment, Diana lifted her head proudly and said, "I promise not to let you down when we go to New Orleans. I meant it when I said

I'm grateful for the many things you've taught me that I would have had no way of learning on my own. Lallage, too. I'd like to keep studying with you. I hope you'll still be my friend.''

"Thank you, my dear. I assure you that we shall always be friends.''

"I hope Lallage will be half as kind about my deceptions.'' Diana's hands twisted together on her lap. Tears were threatening to return at the mention of Lallage's name.

"Have no fears about that. After Salem brought the news that you were all right, she sent word that she cannot get away to visit until after her house guests depart. She asked me to invite you to accompany me this afternoon in the carriage and take tea at Wingate.''

"I'd like to go with you, Salathiel. I'll try to cause no more problems. I feel dreadful about telling so many lies.''

"Give the matter no more thought now that you seem to have learned deceptions lead nowhere but to more deceptions and, eventually, great harm. Luke was waiting up for me last evening to explain all about what happened. I was so relieved to learn you were truly unharmed that I shan't spend another moment thinking about the matter.''

Diana shifted around on her chair, the tenderness between her legs reminding her about last evening's happenings more vividly than she cared to be. She did not truly believe Luke would tell about their making love, yet the thought that he might had occurred to her.

A sidewise look at Salathiel's composed features and benign mien convinced Diana that he was not making references to lovemaking between Luke and her. She had been around Lallage and the Englishman often when Lallage was flirting with him and she knew that anything having to do with what went on between man and woman always brought a flush to his face.

From where he had gone to stand and look out toward Selene Bayou, Salathiel continued. ''When Salem rode over to Wingate before dark and informed Lallage and me that all was well here, we went ahead and enjoyed the festivities. Both of us regretted that you missed out on dancing to real music, but there will be time enough for that in New Orleans.'' He turned and peered toward Diana's downturned face. ''Luke tells me there's been no change in plans for you to accompany us to New Orleans.''

''That's right,'' Diana said in a resigned manner.

Shortly, Diana pled fatigue and hurried to her bedroom where she lay face down on her bed and drifted into a somewhat hazy sleep.

A raised masculine voice drifted upstairs and pulled Diana from her restful state. She left her bedroom, pausing near the top of the staircase to listen while remaining out of sight to those below in the foyer.

The man continued. ''As I've been telling my mother, you left the party at Wingate yesterday afternoon shortly after arriving. You may think my stepfather never told me about the quarrel you two had over that poker game in New Orleans where you grabbed title to Fairfield, but he did.'' His voice, breathy but loud, took on a grievous tone then. ''Julius Waskom and I had become very close recently.''

Diana heard Luke say, ''I repeat my condolences to you, Mrs. Waskom, and to your family on the death of Mr. Waskom. I also repeat my denial of having any reason to quarrel or fight with him. He and I worked out our grievances back in the summer when we met by chance near the fence between our plantations.''

A feminine voice replied and Diana had to move closer to the head of the stairs to hear. ''My husband told me of the talk you two had,'' Frances Waskom replied. ''The only reason we're here is that my son insisted any foul play that might have caused my husband's heart failure could have come only from you.'' Tears threaded the woman's cultured voice. ''When we arrived home last evening from Wingate and discovered Julius hadn't returned from fishing, the slaves found him lying in his pirogue near the bank of Gator Swamp. If I hadn't found his fishing gear on the back veranda and figured out he hadn't gone into the swamp to fish, I never would have become suspicious. Please forgive us for bringing our family troubles here.''

Diana's eyes widened. Someone apparently had accused Luke of harming Julius Waskom. Was it Maynard Oates she had heard speaking? She peeked over the handrailing to see who was gathered below, recognizing only Luke and Salathiel. Her hand flew to her mouth when she saw the pinkish-gold hair on the man standing with his back to her. Obviously he was Maynard Oates. She had seen those twin swirls at the top of his head yesterday afternoon from her secret bower, both when he had come from down the swamp pulling a pirogue holding a tarp-covered object and when he had returned a while later without the second pirogue in tow.

The crux of what Diana had seen in the swamp hit her then and she tightened her hold over her mouth. A painful knot gripped her belly and shot up to her throat. Horror sent chills racing throughout her blood. The tarp-covered bundle in the pirogue towed by Maynard must have been his stepfather's dead body. Tears of compassion for Julius Waskom's family stung her eyelids. And then she was wondering indignantly how anyone could believe that Luke could have had anything to do with the man's death.

Small exchanges went on between Frances Waskom and Luke for a few moments. Then Diana, recovered enough to creep down the stairway one step at a time, heard the woman address a younger woman standing beside Salathiel.

Frances Waskom said, "Doreen, we may as well go into Calion and see the sheriff."

"Why do you insist on going to the sheriff, Mama?" Maynard Oates asked. "Until I find out where Luke Greenwood went after he left Wingate, I won't be satisfied he had nothing to do with Julius's death." He turned to Luke. "Be good enough to explain where you were after leaving the party."

Ever since Mrs. Waskom and her son and daughter by her first husband had burst into the foyer a few minutes earlier, Luke and Salathiel had been in shock. First, the news of Julius's sudden death while his family attended Lallage's party; then, Maynard's outburst of accusations toward Luke.

Luke was aware from Mrs. Waskom's impassioned declarations upon arrival that she did not accept her husband's death as natural and that she intended to report her suspicions of evil doings to the sheriff. He was also aware from the widow's words that Maynard was his mother's prime suspect and that Maynard was seeking to place blame on Luke. He had heard of people who could never accept the death of a loved one as the result of illness or pure accident. Was Mrs. Waskom such a person? She appeared to be levelheaded and intelligent, but—

The thought of revealing that he had been at the Hathaway house repulsed Luke. He had no wish to involve Diana. Something about the loyal way the blacks had remained silent about her and her family over the years impressed him. He found himself adopting an even fiercer protective attitude toward Diana. "I returned home when I left the party."

"Can anyone but your slaves support your claim?" Maynard asked.

"No," Luke answered with icy calm.

Diana caught her breath. Why didn't Luke report that she could verify his statement? Up until then she had wondered if she should go down and tell everyone that she had seen Maynard in the swamp or if she should wait until the visitors left and tell only Luke and Salathiel.

"I can vouch for Luke's whereabouts," Diana said as she descended the remaining stair steps and joined the group. "I was at Fairfield with Luke after he left the party." Surprised and encouraged that the presence of three staring strangers brought no more than a patter of heartbeats, she went on. "Before he and I met up, though, I was out in Gator Swamp."

"Who are you?" Maynard asked, his small eyes bugging. He seemed aware that the beautiful blonde was staring at him as if she knew him.

Quickly, Luke and Salathiel introduced Diana as Salathiel's niece from Alabama. Though Diana pointedly ignored Luke, he fixed her with a baffled stare. Why had she spoken up for him when she must despise him after their encounter last evening? He still had not come up with a way to resolve matters between them, but he determined that no one would throw taint upon her name. She should have remained quiet.

But had he not already learned that Diana Hathaway had a mind of her own?

Then Diana was explaining, "While I was near the main channel, I saw a man in a pirogue towing another with something heavy and covered with tarpaulin in its bottom." She shivered before adding in an emotion-choked voice, "I realize now that it could have been a body."

Maynard Oates, taking a step backward from where all stood together in the foyer, glared at the beautiful blonde. His mouth opened and closed once before he pushed words past his thin lips. "She's lying, Mama! No decent young woman goes into the swamp alone. She's lying!"

Luke scowled and pointed threateningly toward Maynard with a forefinger suggesting the barrel of a loaded pistol. "Sir, I suggest you hush until Miss Hathaway finishes her story. Afterward, you may offer her a proper apology."

Surprised and pleased at Luke's defense of her, Diana thought that Luke deserved an apology more than she. Doggedly she continued. "The man had twin crowns of pinkish-red hair and he was wearing a white shirt and dark suit." She was aware that Luke and Salathiel were watching her with consternation.

Heartbreak further saddened Frances Waskom's eyes as she stared at her eldest son. "Then it was you! I knew you were weak and capable of cruelty, but I never dreamed you would—"

Maynard pleaded in a whining tone. "Mama, don't talk like that. You know I rode in the carriage to and from the party. This young woman never saw anybody"—his eyes darted toward the still-scowling Luke who, with fists clenched menacingly, had stepped nearer—"er, she must have made a mistake. I apologize, Miss Hathaway. But I was at the party."

Speaking up for the first time, Maynard's sister, Doreen, said, "You weren't there every minute. I looked for you a couple of times and nobody could remember seeing you since our arrival. Then all of a sudden, at dark, you showed up near the orchestra. Where did you go?"

Diana recognized that what was happening was bizarre and frightening. Fighting down her absurd wish to seek shelter in Luke's powerful arms—for a moment she had almost forgotten she detested him—she concentrated on the pretty young woman's poise and calm voice. She sensed that under less strained circumstances she would like knowing Doreen Oates.

"Since you've brought us here and falsely accused our neighbor of being involved, then insulted his guest," Frances Waskom said to Maynard, "I think he and his guests have the right to hear this out. Or you can tell it to the sheriff."

In a placating tone Maynard related his version of how his stepfather had robbed him of his birthright and how he had thought to scare the man into loosening his hold on his mother's purse strings. All he had wanted, he insisted with increasing self-pity, was to get away from St. Christopher Parish and live the way he chose.

"So," Maynard went on to the five stunned people listening, "I planned for Julius to meet me in the swamp behind Wingate during the party. He went along with it for he didn't want Mama to learn that we were still arguing about money."

Glancing at his mother, who had lowered her gaze, Maynard continued. "I had learned Julius feared snakes, so I got one of our blacks to catch a water moccasin and hide him in a sack and put it in a pirogue at Wingate. I told him I wanted to play a joke on somebody. I slipped away from the party to the fishing pier. I took the pirogue with the tarp lying in it and hurried to meet Julius in the main channel."

Frances Waskom let out a keening sound. "You knew that he had a weak heart on top of fearing snakes, didn't you? How could you be so cruel, so unfeeling?" When Doreen put her arms around her mother, Frances went on in a sorrowful tone, "That's enough, Maynard. Let's leave." She lifted her grief-lined face toward Luke. "Please forgive us for intruding and involving you and your friends in our family problems."

Diana admired the kind but masterful way that Luke took Frances's arm and walked with Doreen and her toward the front door. His bearing denied that Maynard had ever made the ugly accusations against him. She heard him say to the distraught widow, "We forgive you. How can we help?"

"Will you report what you've learned to the sheriff?" Frances replied. "I fear I can't bear any more pain today."

Maynard rushed to follow his mother, babbling hysterically. "But I didn't kill Julius! All I did was let the snake loose in his pirogue when he told me he wasn't going to ask you to increase my allowance. I meant only to scare him. The blamed snake wiggled out of his pirogue without touching him. I swear! His heart just stopped. I didn't kill him! I even towed him back near our place so somebody could find him easily. There's nothing to report to the sheriff."

Frances and Doreen exchanged doleful looks, then Frances said, "Let's return home and discuss this later." She seemed unable to meet the desperate eyes of her son. "By now the servants should be through laying out Julius. I want to be there in time to make sure he looks nice for his wake."

Diana, her stomach in knots, remained on the porch while Luke and Salathiel accompanied the women to their carriage and helped them climb inside. Maynard stalked behind, paying no heed to anyone. Even after he settled on the seat opposite where his mother and sister were sitting and exchanging subdued farewells with Luke and Salathiel, he appeared to be looking at something fearful within that only he could see.

"Yes," Luke assured Frances just before he gave the signal to the driver that all was in readiness for returning to Fernwood, "I will spread word about your husband's death and the funeral tomorrow afternoon. Please let me know if there's anything else I can do for you or your family."

After the last crunch of the carriage wheels had faded, the men joined the sad-eyed Diana on the porch. The three went inside, silent.

Fifteen

Later in the day Luke declined Salathiel's invitation to join Diana and him for tea at Wingate, saying, "I'm leaving now for Calion to spread the word about Julius Waskom's death."

Though Luke's reason for not accepting was valid, tragically so, he feared that he was not up to being around Diana for any length of time without, maybe, revealing the chaotic state of his mind. Last night he had slept scarcely at all. He had no wish for her or anyone else to suspect that he might be any different than he was before she returned last evening to her house in the swamp.

Luke was different deep inside, though. He knew it in the tenuous way that he knew when he had slipped on a stocking wrong side outward in the dark. How much of the change should he attribute to Diana's jarringly negative observations about him? How much to their damnably unforgettable lovemaking?

As for Diana, the grave news about Julius Waskom's death and Maynard Oates's cruelty had troubled her already burdened heart. She convinced herself during the carriage ride to Wingate that she was glad Luke, with his brooding face and absent-minded remarks, had not come along. She was finding it impossible to forget their lovemaking and the memory of their heated words before and after.

Despite her attempts to place the blame on Luke, Diana failed. Perhaps her having to accept responsibility for all that had taken place in her home last evening was what kept her mind fluttery. Her thoughts about Luke and his role in her life had plagued her most of the night, then had come rushing back in the light of day. Drat the man, anyway!

Heedful of dark clouds looming in the south, Diana wore a velvet cape of sapphire blue over her rose silk gown. In sad voices Salathiel and she talked about the death of Julius, then chose to forget it when the carriage reached Wingate. Neither wanted to wear gloomy faces while having tea with Lallage and her house guests.

Afterward, while Lallage was bidding the couple private farewells on her front veranda, Diana listened to the assurances from Salathiel and her that their pupil had handled herself exceedingly well around the dozen visitors still at Wingate. Though Diana welcomed their words, she was far happier to hear Lallage's whispered forgiveness for her heartfelt confessions of subterfuge.

"My house guests will be leaving in the morning," Lallage said in parting. "Please come by tomorrow on your way to the church for the Waskom funeral so that we can travel together. I'll have my gardener gather everything in bloom and send flowers ahead to the church."

Salathiel smiled adoringly at the red-haired woman. "You are always so thoughtful, Lallage."

"We'll stop by," Diana said, wondering if she were going to have to nudge Salathiel to remind him to let go of Lallage's hand, not that the pretty widow seemed to be objecting to his lingering touch. "We'd better hurry. Salem is waiting."

Rain, introduced by claps of lightning and rolls of thunder, had begun falling soon after their arrival at Wingate. By the time the carriage returned to Fairfield, it was pouring down in sheets and turning the primitive road into sticky black mud. Reminding Salem to change into dry clothing as soon as possible, Diana pulled her cape closer and, with Salathiel not far behind, raced up the steps to the front veranda. Darkness and a bite to the moist autumn air made the glow of candlelight coming from within the large house seem especially cozy.

Diana sniffed at the welcoming smell of wood smoke being forced downward by the wind and rain and shivered in anticipation of the warmth awaiting them in front of the massive fireplaces. She would have been shocked had she realized that for those few moments she was associating the endearing qualities of home with the mansion and not with the small, deteriorating house in the swamp.

Odille met them in the foyer, her usually calm face looking troubled. At once Diana remembered the vicious looks Maynard had sent Luke when her story led all to see he had been falsely accusing an innocent man of his own wrongdoing. Her heartbeat faltered. "Has something happened to Luke?"

"No. He's waiting in the library," Odille told the suddenly white-faced Diana.

When Diana and Salathiel hurried into the room, Luke rose from the sofa in front of the fireplace with its blazing fire. His eyes searched Diana's strained face. She seemed to be holding her breath and he felt a strange urge to put his arms around her and comfort her. He had been thinking about her and how the events of the past twenty-four hours must have jolted her. "I can think of no gentle way to report more tragedy. A boy just brought the news that Maynard went to the barn during the rainstorm and hanged himself from a rafter."

"How dreadful! I can't imagine anyone choosing to die," Diana exclaimed, one hand settling above her unsteady heart and tears rushing to her eyes. Why had she been concerned about Luke's well-being? Only a brief time ago she had been dratting him right and left. Immediately, she shifted her thoughts to the morbid realization that now two men lay dead at the neighboring plantation. "Poor Maynard. He must have been suffering unbearable pain. My heart goes out to Mrs. Waskom and her children."

"This is frightful news," Salathiel remarked. "Whatever got into the man?"

His features grim, Luke replied, "Doreen sent a note telling that Maynard had left behind a letter confessing that he no longer cared to live and that he could not atone for hurrying Julius's death. Mrs. Waskom wishes to have a double funeral tomorrow afternoon after the customary wake tonight. She asked me to notify the proper authorities in Calion.''

Salathiel spoke then, ''They are fortunate to have you as a neighbor on whom they can lean, Luke. I shall go on over to Fernwood to be with the family while you ride into Calion.'' He turned to Diana. ''Would you care to come along, my dear? Learning about the sad aspects of life in a community is just as important as learning about the lighter ones.''

Remembering her grief at her father's death only last year, Diana replied, ''I was thinking that I'd like to let Doreen and her mother know of my sympathy.'' She was already pulling her cloak closer and did not see the soft approving look on Luke's face at her request. ''Maybe I can be of help.''

While Diana watched Luke leave for the stables, she scolded herself for ever having believed he was a man without a heart. Plainly he felt compassion for his neighbors.

Within a short time the three had gone out into the stormy night, Luke riding Jasper toward Calion, and Diana and Salathiel climbing into the carriage for the brief journey in the opposite direction to Fernwood.

The night of the wake at Fernwood was one Diana doubted she would ever forget. The pale, strained faces of the boys, Clayton and Alexander who, along with Doreen, had been genuinely fond of their stepfather, showed their grief. Alexander, at sixteen, seemed protective of his younger brother and went with him upstairs soon after neighbors and friends began arriving.

As Diana sat with the teary-eyed Frances, Doreen, and Salathiel in the morning room running across the back of the mansion, she tried to forget that in the living room near the front door, the bodies of Julius and Maynard lay on hastily constructed, sheet-draped tables surrounded by flickering candles. She reasoned that Julius Waskom had gained the love and respect of all of his new family except that of his wife's eldest son. Perhaps Salathiel's ruminations on the way over about how Maynard at thirty-one likely resented being displaced as the man of the family were true.

For Maynard, or anyone else, to have harbored such jealousy and hatred seemed odious to Diana. Had he perhaps been seared with a kind of madness? Already she had thought about how gruesome it was that she had seen a dead man's body from her secret bower. And the man who had contributed to his death paddling through the dark water.

Diana sighed and accepted the cup of coffee that a kind servant brought her. She realized that despite the grimness and sorrow of the occasion, she was no longer on the fringes of the white world in St. Christopher Parish.

News that death had visited Fernwood brought silent male visitors throughout the night to sit with the bodies, as was the custom in the region. Occasionally, the sounds of the men tiptoeing from the front door into the living room, where others already sat in the shadows formed by the flickering candlelight, drifted down the foyer to the morning room where Diana sat with the family. Salathiel wandered between the living room where the solemn wake was being observed and the morning room where the women sat.

Diana noticed that after the visitors expressed their sympathy to the family, they spoke then about happier topics. Left to themselves for brief periods after Frances departed at midnight to rest in her bedroom, Diana and Doreen found much to talk about and divert their thoughts from the bodies lying only two rooms away.

"You must be pleased to be a graduate of an academy," Diana said after learning that Doreen had returned only recently from a summer of visiting school friends. "I know I would be."

Diana had heard over the years that Doreen was away most of the time at a boarding school in Natchez. Somehow, the fact that Doreen was growing up at Fernwood at the same time she was growing up in Gator Swamp never had seemed real to Diana until they had met. "Studying with other girls sounds like fun."

"It was," Doreen confessed. "I liked school but now I'm ready to get on with my life as an adult, if nineteen years qualify me as one. Have you always studied with a tutor?"

"Yes," Diana replied, wanting to change the subject so

as not to pile lie upon lie. Her father could be classed as a tutor, what with his having graduated from Harvard. She liked the way Doreen's friendliness made her feel accepted and not a lot different from her. New appreciation for all that Lallage and Salathiel had taught her welled up. Just as Diana had discovered while having tea at Wingate with Lallage and her guests several hours ago, she was not having to grope for ways to communicate. "Would it be rude or improper for me to ask what your plans are now?"

A small smile relieved some of the tension on Doreen's pretty face. "Not at all. I can't imagine you being rude, Diana. Your manners and diction are exquisite. My teachers would be envious of yours. They never quite rid me of my drawl." When Diana murmured her thanks and looked flustered, Doreen went on. "You don't act as if you even know how unique your looks are. I've never seen hair so blonde and pretty as yours. It must have come from your parents."

"Thank you. My mother had hair this color."

Having already learned from their previous conversations that Diana's parents were dead, Doreen returned to the subject broached earlier. "As for my future plans, I intend to put the sorrow of this weekend behind me as soon as possible and look for the perfect man to marry. All of us at school talked of little else. I'm counting on my heart telling me when he comes along." When Diana lowered her eyes and appeared doubtful, Doreen asked, "Isn't that what most young women believe?"

"I suppose so." Would Doreen find, as she had, that one's heart could be as deceiving as men's actions? Suddenly, instead of feeling like a child when Doreen talked about the world outside St. Christopher Parish, Diana felt older and wiser than her eighteen years. Thanks to Luke Greenwood and her throwing herself into his arms.

"Tell me about Luke Greenwood. He's so devilishly handsome that I figure he must have broken a million hearts already."

Diana swallowed hard. He was not going to break hers, not if she could ever stop thinking about being in his arms.

The thought of the numerous women he must have held and kissed ripped a gash in her composure. "Luke doesn't discuss his women friends around me."

"Mama says she suspects he might be one of those men who don't marry until they're old and gray because they like having a different pretty face to look at every few months."

"I don't know anything about his social life," Diana admitted. Why had Doreen brought up his name? Was she enamored of him already? "I've known him only since I started living at Fairfield in June. He's gone a lot."

"It's unfair you were feeling bad and missed the party at Wingate. When Luke showed up for a brief spell, all of the women started making eyes at him. Miss Linda Lee, the wife of Mr. Bergerone who owns the huge general store in town, grabbed her two daughters and the three literally surrounded the poor man."

Diana studied her hands. Had Luke been searching for her then?

Doreen continued. "On the way home Mama said she'd heard Miss Linda Lee had already invited Luke for dinner before he had time to think up an excuse. Have you ever heard of such gall? I never got more than a chance to meet our richest, most eligible bachelor before he bolted and left."

Shifting her position on the sofa the two were sharing, Diana stared into the fire flickering in the fireplace. She could not imagine why hearing how some women had fawned over Luke was making her feel flushed and annoyed. After all, Lallage had related a similar tale recently. Had she not discovered for herself that when it came to dealing with women, Luke apparently cared for little but that which brought him happiness? Not only was there the business of their ridiculous pact, but also that of their lovemaking. Once it ended, he seemed to go out of his way to make it clear that making love to her had meant next to nothing.

Facing up to the fact once more that she had been a fool to have believed she might be falling in love with Luke, and a greater fool for having surrendered to her passion, Diana called up what Lallage would have termed a "ladylike mien of polite interest designed to conceal inner turmoil." She replied to Doreen in a tone as devoid of emotion as she could manage, "I guess a man like Luke would just naturally receive a lot of attention from women."

"And why not? He is reportedly wealthy, and he's too handsome and charming for words. Everybody has been dying for him to get Fairfield fixed up the way he wants it and throw a party." Cocking her head and looking keenly at her companion, Doreen leaned closer and added, "Are you smitten with him? I vow I would be if I'd been around him as much as you must have these past months. He seems so masterful."

Masterful? Diana reflected with irony. Luke fit that description, as well as most of the others. She was searching desperately for an acceptable answer when Salathiel ambled back into the morning room. She welcomed the Englishman's quiet comments for she did not like the direction of her thoughts, leading as they did to Luke and what had gone on between them in her house last evening.

In hushed voices the three talked about the weather and how the rain had stopped. Before Luke arrived in the still hour before dawn with a group of men from Calion, Diana Hathaway and Doreen Oates had become friends.

Diana sensed Luke's presence even before he entered the morning room. If she had not known better, she would have assumed that he already knew where she sat. As soon as he appeared in the doorway, his gaze flew across the room and settled on her features. For an inane moment Diana felt that he had touched her in greeting. She was almost certain that he sent her a slight nod. Then she was hoping he had, for she was sending one to him.

Luke spoke with his voice to the others in the room, but his dark eyes, scarcely leaving Diana's face, sent a host of indecipherable messages. Diana blamed her faulty heartbeat on fatigue and sorrow for her new friends.

"Hello again to our parish's newest planter," a feminine voice said, breaking into Diana's musings and drawing Luke's full attention. "Cousin Frances tells me that you've been a godsend to everyone at Fernwood, Luke Greenwood. I want to add my appreciation to hers."

Soon after arriving, Diana had met Marilyn Quinette, a pretty, black-haired widow who claimed kinship with Frances Waskom. Apparently up from her period of rest, she now had come into the room and was addressing Luke. Diana had noted earlier that Marilyn's large green eyes flashed knowing looks with the same frequency and suggestiveness that her hips swayed when she walked. Whenever the curvaceous widow entered or left a room, every male therein seemed alerted. To Diana's way of thinking, the suddenly attentive Luke proved no exception.

Perturbed, and unable to understand why she was so utterly discomposed, Diana became deaf to the exchange between Marilyn and Luke. She promised silently that in the future, she would avoid all private encounters with Luke Greenwood and bury the memories of their lovemaking. With deliberation she could prevent allowing her gaze to become locked with his again. She must. After chiding herself for even noticing Luke's arrival, she leaned toward Doreen and attempted to strike up a new conversation.

Diana's lovely face would have flushed to a more noticeable pink had she permitted herself to glance toward where Luke stood with the fawning widow. He appeared to be listening and responding to her chatter, but his searching gaze kept lingering on Diana.

Sixteen

The harrowing ordeal at Fernwood would never fade completely from the minds and hearts of those involved, but each day offered much needed solace and varying degrees of acceptance.

During the third week after the double funeral, Salathiel asked Diana to stay in the library after her recitations ended. "Could you please look over this list?"

Diana, after perusing the neatly lettered calendar of events planned for their visit in New Orleans, replied, "Odille is already packing and she knows better than I what I'll be needing. I told her this morning that I didn't know what I'd do without her." She gave a silent thanks for the many kindnesses that the warm-voiced, efficient quadroon had shown her, a thanks not as effusive as the one she had bestowed upon Odille earlier that day. "Has Mrs. Waskom made up her mind yet whether or not she'll permit Doreen to go with us tomorrow?"

Salathiel stroked his mustache lightly with two fingers. "I feel sorry for the poor woman. She wants to do what is proper but she does not want to prevent Doreen from getting on with her young life."

"Yes, I know. Doreen told me some of her friends from

school are expecting her to be in New Orleans for the winter season. I'd dearly love to have her go along.''

''Mourning the deaths of one's family is considered a private matter, my dear,'' Salathiel explained. Sometimes, as now, his heart squeezed when he thought of all that Diana had missed out on learning during her secluded upbringing. ''In England and in Mobile as well, Doreen and her mother would be expected to refrain from social appearances for at least a year. I expect the same is true in Louisiana. As you know, Lallage has spent the past two years in mourning for her husband. Each has to do what seems right on the inside.''

Diana said, ''Doreen wants to get away from the sadness at Fernwood for a brief spell before Christmas. She has no wish to go ahead with the original plans for the entire family to go stay in their townhouse until after Mardi Gras.''

Odille, after tapping on the door facing, stuck her head in the library. ''Miss Doreen is here.''

Diana and Doreen rushed to embrace and exchange greetings while the quadroon and the Englishman swapped looks of fond compassion for the pretty young women. Whereas Diana's blonde loveliness and regal bearing were stunning, Doreen's brunette prettiness was less arresting. Not as tall and slender as Diana, Doreen possessed lusher curves and a darker complexion. They served as delightful contrasts to each other.

''Mama says I can go with y'all if you can get me back home in time for Christmas,'' Doreen announced with a wide smile. Her hair, the same rich brown as her eyes, fell halfway down her back in clusters of shining curls. ''I'll have to stay with my aunt and cousins who are also in mourning for Maynard and Julius. She said I can go to the Charity Ball with them if they decide to attend and watch from a balcony. Mama's other sister from up the bayou will arrive tonight to stay until Christmas, so she won't be alone with the boys.''

''That's marvelous news.'' Smiling, Diana reached to squeeze her friend's hand. ''No wonder you're looking so pretty this morning.'' It would have been nicer if they could have stayed at the same place, but just the thought of having Doreen along on the trip pleased her.

Doreen explained, "Mama can't stand the thought of me having to miss out on happiness because of Maynard and what she calls his madness. She blames herself for not keeping a tighter rein on Maynard after our father died eight years ago. She thinks Julius would have wanted me to go."

While Salathiel added his approval of having Doreen accompany them and explained their schedule of travel, Diana thought about how, in addition to the companionship of her older friends, she also enjoyed that of others nearer her age. She had not realized what she was missing until she had experienced it with Doreen . . . and, during a few times in the past couple of months, with Luke.

Seemingly caught up in setting his plantation on its feet and transacting business in Calion—or was it social life? Diana often wondered—Luke no longer rode with Diana. Hoping to restore a semblance of their former, friendly relationship while they rode together, Diana wrestled with her trembling pulse one evening before he rode off on Jasper and asked, "Since you always seem to be busy or absent, is it all right if I ride Duchess alone? Salathiel said the decision should be yours."

"You may ride in the pasture alone or you may invite Doreen to join you," Luke had replied.

Gruffly, Diana thought, recalling his exact tone of voice while Doreen and Salathiel discussed the upcoming journey to New Orleans. The few remarks Luke addressed to her nowadays were always delivered gruffly. As had become his custom since their lovemaking, his dark eyes showered her with unfathomable looks. How she wished that she could read his mind!

Though Salathiel had about given up trying to coax praise from Luke for her many accomplishments, Diana reflected, he still broached the topic too often to please her. Why was Salathiel blind to the fact that Luke had no personal interest in her, that he merely tolerated her because he had need of her presence in New Orleans?

Diana recognized that her mind and heart were jumbled puzzles that she could not solve. At times she longed to ask Luke if he was making headway with his plans for putting a steamboat on the bayou, but she refrained. With enthusiasm, she shared with Salathiel what she and Doreen saw and did while riding horseback together. Luke, if present, appeared deaf. Whenever she was in his company, he vacillated between being cold and aloof and being politely attentive yet distant. She detested both sides. She consoled herself with the thought that the Luke Greenwood with whom she had *mistakenly*—she always accented that word—believed she was falling in love was a figment of her imagination. She wanted nothing so much as to get behind her the fulfillment of the pact he had coerced her into making.

Though Diana had confided to no one about the brass key left her by her father, she was already trying to figure out how she might slip away to visit the bank in New Orleans where Philip's box was located and find out what it held. She had counted on Odille's assistance until she realized she might be putting the slave in jeopardy with her master and should not get her involved. Diana slid an appraising look toward her new young friend. Could she depend on Doreen to help her find her way about the city?

As at those few times when she had slipped away in the night to tend the sick, Diana felt her heart lift at the knowledge that Luke only thought he knew all about her and controlled every aspect of her life. She would forget all about him and find happiness. Perhaps after she lived up to her part of their bargain in New Orleans she might be able to escape with her few hoarded coins and seek a new life, maybe visit her kinfolks in Boston. Such thoughts buoyed the confused young woman, gave her hope.

Diana was uncertain as to what she might find in Philip's deposit box, but she hoped there would be money enough to take care of her until she could find somewhere she belonged. Despite her private admission that she would miss her friends, both black and white, and her beloved swamp, she had decided there could be no future left for her in St. Christopher Parish, not with Luke Greenwood living at Fairfield.

After Doreen and Salathiel seemed to be through discussing the details of their departure tomorrow and their return a few days before Christmas, Diana shut down her private musings and said, "At least we can enjoy traveling together, Doreen. You're going to love getting to know Lallage Winston better. Her daughters are adorable."

On Luke's last evening at Fairfield before the journey to New Orleans, he went over final plans with Jed Latour for handling matters during his absence. Each realized the accomplishments of the past five months were many and that the future of the sugar plantation seemed bright. The list of purchases for Luke to make in the port city of New Orleans seemed complete. By the end of the evening both Luke and his overseer were feeling mellow.

Jed rose as if ready to leave the library where for almost two hours the two had discussed plantation business and sipped French brandy. "Fonza really liked you when she met you last month. We appreciate the two horses you gave us for a wedding gift. For you to let them feed and stable with yours seems mighty generous. You've not forgotten that we'll be getting married before you return, have you?"

"No, and I repeat my regrets that I won't be here for the happy occasion. Fonza seems like a fine young woman, and I'm pleased you both like the horses. I'll look forward upon my return to welcoming your bride to Fairfield." Luke noted that his words came out abnormally slow and thick in the large room. Was he close to being intoxicated?

"Maybe it won't be too long before I can be counting on meeting the woman who'll become mistress here. Now that you've found your spot on earth and settled down, you're going to be wanting that wife and children you used to talk about."

Luke rubbed his chin briefly, recalling that before they came to Fairfield, Jed had served him as valet and as listener on a few occasions when Luke had voiced his plans for the future. "I have too much on my mind right now to be giving thought to marriage."

"Shoot!" Jed said with a broad grin splitting his dark features. "A man's mind doesn't seem to play much of a role when it comes to taking a wife, not when she's that special somebody.'' He elaborated a bit on how his meeting with Fonza had brightened his life and given it new meaning.

Luke's countenance showed that he was listening with interest to Jed's enthusiastic talk about his plans to wed his beloved Fonza and bring her to the newly completed overseer's house. On the inside, though, Luke was experiencing a twinge of jealousy that Jed had captured a happiness canceled for him ever since he lost to another the only woman he could ever love. Sylvia Lindstrom. He amended *Greenwood* to her name and reminded himself that she had chosen his brother over him. It was done. Over. He knew himself as a man capable of loving only once.

It was nearly midnight by the time Jed left the silent mansion. Luke was relaxing on the sofa in the library and savoring a final few moments before the fire dying in the fireplace when thoughts of Diana filtered to mind and took it over. Damn! he thought with annoyance. Such intrusions had become almost commonplace, especially since that night they had made love. Were those haunting memories of Diana in his arms merely slashes on his conscience?

Such must be the case, Luke reassured himself. He did not like recalling how he had succumbed, like a man crazed, to towering emotions and made love to an innocent virgin. He had given up trying to understand why and how matters had happened as they had.

Instead, the ruminating master of Fairfield chose to relegate his helplessness in curbing his emotions that evening to something indefinable, like suffering from moon madness or some other kind of spell. Just remembering the feel, the taste, the fragrance of Diana in his arms set his blood afire. Diana. Almost three weeks had dragged by since he had held her. Yet, just thinking her name rearranged his heartbeat. Were such absurdities signs of being under a spell?

Now that he was allowing himself to think about it, Luke realized that ever since that night, he had fled from Diana's presence because he felt tongue-tied and inept around her. Because he yearned to hold her, kiss her pretty mouth, and once more feel in harmony with the universe. Could a spell have seized him, one akin to the hoodoo that some of his slaves embraced despite his voiced disapproval? Each time he reeled from that tenuous theory, Luke's practical self hooted. Since when did he believe in any kind of magic?

Luke watched the desultory flames in the fireplace hissing and wavering, diminishing themselves a bit more with each sound and movement. From outside he heard an occasional eerie moan of wind as it chased through the bare trees.

Then Luke was ignoring his already sluggish state and pouring himself another splash of brandy, thinking that when he downed it, he would go up to bed. Tomorrow promised to be a long, taxing day, as Salathiel had reminded him before Diana and he had gone upstairs hours earlier. Now that he suspected he had overimbibed, he would not be surprised if he suffered a headache when he awoke.

Luke recognized that for him to drink more than usual was a sign that he had far more on his mind than he could think about clearly. Was he that on edge about his relationship with Diana? How much of his agony came from thoughts about taking her to New Orleans and escorting her to the Charity Ball to dangle in front of Frederick? He fingered his chin, then ran his palm over his face, as if to wash away unwelcome thoughts.

When Luke turned back to gaze again at the languishing fire, he almost gasped. A flash of blue in a sputtering flame was the exact hue of Diana's eyes. It seemed to be watching him. Watching him and accusing him, too, as though daring him to doubt hoodoo or magic of any kind.

Then, in spite of his trying to channel his mind into other paths, Luke could think of nothing but Diana's beautiful wide-spaced eyes and the way they had looked at him with adoration in the moonlight while they made love. He guessed it was the sight of a brilliant orange flare writhing amidst a licking tongue of yellow flame that reminded him of the searing passion transporting him while he poured his hot seed into the sweetly surrendering blonde. A throbbing in his loins fed his memory in a manner he found salacious, alien. He promptly blamed his wayward mood and thoughts on too much brandy and too much talk with Jed about his upcoming wedding.

Diana, the tormented young man pleaded silently in his ordinary inner voice, *can you ever forgive me for losing my head and robbing you of a treasure meant for your bridegroom?*

Maybe you should marry her, then, and ease your conscience, a surprising second inner voice replied.

Why, I can't marry Diana! She deserves a husband who can love her and make her happy and one whom she loves. Luke frowned for a moment. What the hell was he doing defending himself to an imaginary voice? Just to test his sanity and find out just how drunk he was, he added, *She probably hates me. She seldom even smiles around me.*

Are you certain you aren't the man meant for her? the voice shot back smugly. *Maybe she should hate you, and maybe she does, but have you ever asked her what she thinks of you? It seems to me you've worked damned hard to avoid talking with her about anything ever since she came here. You told her that night you played dominoes you wanted to be friends. Didn't you mean it? What are you afraid of—that you might be in love?*

This is absurd! Luke drained his glass, then set it down. Cautiously, he glanced around the library, lighted now only by a few candles burning low and dripping wax on their brass holders. He blinked and realized when he opened his eyes again that some of the candle flames he had judged to be double ones were actually single. *In the first place I don't know who you are to be speaking to me this way. In the second, I can never love another woman. I've already been in love.*

Is there a limit to how many times a man can love?

Of course!

It seemed to Luke that the despised second voice sniggered but he ignored it and decided he really should snuff out the candles and go up to his bedroom. He knew the way even though it was dark.

Luke's first footstep on the stairs sounded too loud and,

admitting that hearing the second voice had seemed somewhat spooky, he looked around in the darkness. Yes, he was alone. Wavering then from stair step to stair step, he held on to the handrailing and made his way upward.

"What the—?" Luke demanded in a quarrelsome tone when someone or something ran into him from behind, causing him to trip and sprawl forward up the stairs. "Damn! I had 'bout reached the top step," he complained with the self-centeredness of a man in his cups. At first he suspected King might have sneaked inside. When no whines or friendly licks from the dog's tongue came, he muttered with what seemed to him his last bit of energy, "Who the hell is't?"

Stopping in her tracks, Diana shivered but she doubted the chill of the night air she had just left outside triggered it. She had only that moment returned from overseeing Chloe's ministrations to a feverish little boy in the slave quarters behind the stables. As always when dashing around on her missions, she had discarded her regular clothing for her old brief skirt and top. Covering it was a jacket that Tabitha had draped around her at the last moment. Though she did not feel cold, she found it difficult to stop trembling.

Diana had been pleased when Chloe had asked her a while ago to teach her what she had learned about healing, for she had fretted about leaving the blacks without someone to take her place. During the past several weeks the young black woman had accompanied Diana on her secret night missions.

Until she bumped into Luke on the stairway, Diana had been feeling good about how skilled Chloe was becoming at using her methods and concoctions. Of all the rotten luck to have run into Luke!

For a moment, Diana reflected that had she paid attention to her nose, she would have smelled him. He reeked of spirits and was now mumbling incoherently. She remained frozen there behind him, urging her tremors to cease. What should she do?

Diana had no desire for Luke to learn of her missions at night to assist those needing her help. With indignation she thought of how the man had no right to know every blessed thing about her. Drat him, anyway, for ever having come to

Fairfield! The slurs in his words reminded her of the way her father and Uncle Owen had sounded sometimes when they emptied too many wine bottles. Was Luke drunk?

From where he still lay on the steps near the landing to the second floor, Luke reached low behind him and felt a slender leg, capturing it in his hand. The leg was smooth and cool but maddeningly alive. He labeled it Diana's.

Luke was not sober enough to put together the facts that if his suspicions were true, Diana was in an unexpected place at an unusual time and that she had nothing covering her legs. His hand eased up the satiny limb past her knee, then slid back down to her shapely calf and slender ankle, not once loosening its hold. Why was she so still . . . and so silent?

"Diana, oh, Diana, lovely moon goddess," Luke murmured. Too much brandy and his earlier eerie conversation with a traitorous inner voice had tangled his thoughts. "You don't hate me, do you?"

Diana's second surprise came then, quieting the inner storm that Luke's hand on her leg was creating. She heard a door whispering open and Odille's soft voice coming from the landing. "Master Luke, do you need me to help you to your bed? You must have tripped on the stairs."

Her head jerking like a shot, Diana looked up and saw a soft light spilling from her open bedroom door. Had Odille heard the commotion on the steps? The quadroon's familiar shape was kneeling close to where Luke's head rested on the top step.

"Come on now," Odille crooned, never looking anywhere but at Luke who was peering up at her, "take my hands and see if you can manage to stand."

Diana stood like a statue until Luke's hand released her ankle and reached out for Odille. She heard him mumble, "Tell Diana not to hate me. I wanted us to be friends."

Even after Odille had led Luke to his room and helped him sit on his bed, he was still trying to figure out what had happened to make him think somebody—why had he thought it was Diana?—had bumped into him and sent him sprawling. No doubt he had imbibed more heavily than he had thought.

He fell back against his pillow, letting sleep snuff out all reasoning.

Silently, Odille pulled off Luke's shoes and dragged his feet and legs onto the bed. After his breath became slow and rhythmic, she tiptoed from the room.

Uppermost in Diana's mind loomed a startling compassion for the man she had frequently labeled arrogant, unfeeling, a jailer. The compassion had emerged when he first mentioned her name and the possibility that she hated him. Where had he gotten the romantic phrase *moon goddess*? Diana confessed that she had acted unwisely in mistaking her fascination with him as love. Despite the way his kisses had made her feel, she should not have given herself to him. She had acted like a colossal fool. Even so, she did not hate him.

Was it possible, Diana reflected while discarding her scanty costume, that Luke Greenwood cared what she, or anyone else, thought of him? She never had viewed him as being vulnerable in the way of ordinary people. Had he, perhaps, been hurt in the past and erected a shield around his heart to avoid a second mutilation? She had read about such things, had also heard her father expound on the theory.

Diana, thoughtful and still unnerved from her encounter with Luke, had slipped into her nightgown and was getting into bed by the time Odille came into the bedroom. Though Diana had no fear that the quadroon would bring harm to her intentionally by reporting to Luke, she wondered what the older woman would say if she told her all. Her thoughts were all aflutter.

"I couldn't sleep and came up to see if you needed anything," Odille said, her dark eyes meeting Diana's pale ones in the light coming from the single candle on the table beside the bed. "I decided to wait until you returned."

"No, thank you. I don't need anything but some sleep." Diana smothered a yawn. "I slipped off with Chloe to nurse a sick child in the quarters. I hope you weren't concerned."

"No. I've learned about your kindness to the sick people and I admire you for it." When Diana could no longer hide her yawns, Odille added, "We have a long journey ahead tomorrow and the next day. Good night."

The next morning when the carriages from Fairfield and Wingate set out for New Orleans with trunks tied on their backs and women, children, and hand luggage filling their spacious interiors, several men on horseback escorted them. Luke and Salathiel led the way while two blacks from each plantation brought up the rear.

Despite the bumpy, single-track road of black gumbo soil, much laughter and excited talk spilled through the uncovered windows of the carriages that cool morning in late November. Diana became swept up in the general mood of her light-hearted companions. She wanted to believe their declarations that what awaited them in the capital of Louisiana in 1831 would prove to be exciting and memorable.

Once during a lull in the feminine chatter, Diana recalled how back in her little house on the day Tabitha had told of Fairfield having a new owner, she had entertained the disturbing thought that things seemed to be changing too fast. Since that unforgettable Midsummer's Eve when Luke Greenwood had captured her, Diana had learned how accurate her observation had been. What would she have done had she known that ahead lay greater changes and revelations?

Seventeen

"I can't believe all I've seen," Diana exclaimed to Odille on the evening of their arrival in New Orleans.

"It's nice to see you so happy." The quadroon had waited in the guest bedroom on the third floor of Luke's Royal Street townhouse until Diana returned from supping with Salathiel and him on the ground level. While helping her abnormally talkative young mistress undress, she appeared to be enjoying what had evolved into their nightly ritual.

First Odille removed the simple but lovely jewelry Luke had provided Diana and put it away. Tonight the animated young woman wore a gold lavalier studded with small sapphires and a delicately wrought matching bracelet. Her gown, the next item her attendant removed, was of embossed blue satin with an embroidered bertha collar of creamy silk. Usually by the time Diana was free of her gown, she was pulling impatiently at her undergarments and freeing her feet and legs. Tonight was no exception.

After discarding her slippers and stockings on the plush rug amidst the pile of beruffled petticoats, Diana took her long nightgown and pulled it over her head. The first touch of the creamy white silk falling over her nakedness felt cool and brought a momentary shiver of delight. She then returned to her observations, unaware that ever since she had reached

New Orleans, a remarkable ebullience had seized her and that words had tumbled forth as never before. "New Orleans has so many buildings and such a hodgepodge of people. Luke and Salathiel said there must be nearly seventy-five thousand living here."

"Yes. It's famous as an exciting port city," Odille replied, her dark gaze washing over the beautiful young woman with open fondness and compassion. "You must find it overwhelming, since you've never even visited Calion with its eight hundred citizens . . . in the daytime."

"I'm glad you keep secrets well." Diana smiled conspiratorially at the friendly *café-au-lait*-colored face reflected alongside her fair one in the mirror over her dressing table. "Isn't it wonderful that Lallage's townhouse is only a few blocks away and that Doreen's aunt also lives in the Vieux Carré?" She laid down her hairbrush and turned to face Odille. "I like your term for this oldest part of the city better than the one Luke uses, French Quarter. When you were with Mrs. Frontage, did you live nearby?"

"No, the Frontage home is across Canal Street."

"Luke has a lovely place here, what little I saw of it before it was time to get ready for dinner." She rose then and stretched, first trying to disguise the yawn seizing her, then giving in to it with gusto.

Odille said, "You've had a great deal of excitement over the past couple of days. Shouldn't you get to bed?"

Diana agreed and promptly stepped up the foot piece beside the tall bed. She sank upon the white, lavender-scented sheets and leaned back against a pillow, one hand pulling up the sheet and lightweight eiderdown comforter to her waist. A back at home, she mused, the November night air was heavy with moisture and apt to make one feel chilly even when the temperature was moderate. She liked having the two windows open and glanced across to admire the pleasing fan shape forming their tops.

When Odille went to close the green-painted shutters with their jalousies, Diana protested, "No, please leave them open. I want to watch the sun rise tomorrow over those beautiful tile roofs."

"I've never seen you so excited," the quadroon said turning back with a permissive shrug.

From where she lay looking up at the pink satin underside of the mauve damask tester stretching across the four mahogany posters, Diana asked, "Did you notice the tester has tiny pleats running from its center out to each corner? I can hardly see the mosquito netting tucked up underneath the outer flounce. Whoever did the decorating did a fantastic job everywhere." Remembering Luke's involved talks with Salathiel and Jed about the changes to be made at Fairfield and how he had gone around the mansion with paper in hand for notations and sketches, she smiled and mused aloud, "Do you suppose Luke had a hand in it himself?"

As soon as Luke's name fell from her lips, Diana could not seem to stop talking about him. While listening, Odille was moving around the bedroom putting up discarded garments, hanging some in the handsome armoire standing tall against one wall, laying others in Diana's new, camel-backed trunk.

"Actually," Diana continued after relating Luke's kindness when Minerva died, "he isn't at all what I imagined he was when I first met him. Until I bumped into him and knocked him down on the stairs the other night, I had figured he didn't care if I liked him or not—or if anyone else did either. He often calls up an air of brooding, a kind of aloofness. Maybe Tabitha was right when she said I mistook it for arrogance."

"He seemed mighty concerned that night with your opinion of him."

"That's what got me to thinking about maybe I've been wrong. Father always talked about how judging people should be objective or else should be shoved aside until one could be objective. I wasn't doing that at all."

Diana lay her head back and closed her eyes for a moment, liking the way Odille's slippers made little whispering noises against the soft carpet with its subtle patterns of roses and leaves in shades of mauve, pink, and muted green. It seemed to her that the sounds blended nicely with the sputtering of the candles as they leaned every once in a while in the rushes of damp wind coming from the Mississippi River only a few blocks away. No mosquitos braved the crisp night air.

No, Diana confessed, she had been far from objective. She had allowed her emotions to color every judgment she had made of Luke Greenwood since that first night he had captured her. First, fear; then what she had foolishly believed was the forerunner of love, and now—Her eyes popped open. What could she call what she now felt for Luke? Compassion, maybe, because she had learned he might not be as serene on the inside as he led others to believe? Did fascination still rank as a contender?

Whatever she felt for the man, the musing young woman decided, it seemed to feed her pulse and contribute to what Odille had labeled excitement. Now that she was being truthful with herself—or as truthful as she in her naiveté about men knew how to be—Diana realized that ever since she had met Luke, she had spent an inordinate amount of time thinking about the handsome, raven-haired man. "I got the impression the other night that Luke is sad and maybe a little lonely, but works to hide it. Does that make any sense?"

"It could, yes."

A contemplative expression claimed Diana's features. "I remember how kind and helpful he was to the neighbors when Mr. Waskom died, and afterward, too. He was most considerate on the trip here. He seemed more concerned about how everyone else was faring than himself. Yet there he was, riding a horse all the way while we were riding in carriages." One hand half covered her mouth as she giggled at a memory. "Did I tell you that when I first heard Fairfield had a new owner I heard his name was Lucifer and I imagined that he might be in cahoots with the devil?"

"No, you didn't. You must have been terrified."

"I was." Diana's eyes rounded at the memory of how helpless she had felt when Luke had captured her. When she noted that Odille had the room tidied and had no reason to stay any longer, Diana realized she was not ready for her friend to go down to her own room on the ground floor. "Would you stay and talk with me a little longer?"

Odille did, her expression indicating that even if Diana did not realize that she was doing all of the talking and that nearly all of it centered on Luke Greenwood, she did. Not until the past few weeks had Diana become as frank with her attendant; not until tonight had she expanded on her thoughts about Luke.

Diana confided, "I've changed my mind about thinking Luke is mean."

"That's good."

Several emotions warred behind Diana's blue eyes and brought a trace of a frown to her pale forehead. "I think of him as someone who is basically kind. Why, just look at the wardrobe he has given me. He says I'm to keep it even after he's through escorting me around New Orleans. I don't plan to, but. . . I think he has shown me more kindness than I've shown him. Once he told me that he wanted us to start over and try being friends."

"Did you refuse?"

"Well, not exactly." Diana watched her fingers as they traced and retraced the heavily embroidered monogram on the top sheet, *LAG*. Lucien A. Greenwood. She would have to ask him what the *A* stood for.

Some things connected with Luke, Diana forbade herself to remember, such as the ecstasy she had felt while in his arms. Others she preferred not to recall.

What Diana wished not to recall was that right after Luke had made the suggestion they become friends, she had mistaken her feelings for him as the first steps of love and had invited him to make love to her. Since then, they had had no kind of relationship at all. To her way of thinking, she was the culprit who had botched things; it was up to her to rectify them. "I intend to start tomorrow letting Luke know I want us to be friends. He said back then that our time together in New Orleans would be much more fun for both of us if we agreed to bury our differences."

"That makes sense."

"You're one of the best things to happen to me, Odille. I even owe having you as my friend to Luke."

Odille smiled her appreciation and adjusted her blue tignon, the movement setting her gold earrings swaying in the candlelight. "Before I met Master Luke, I had heard through our grapevine that he was a kind man who was looking for a ladies' maid."

Her curiosity about the underground news system sparking her eyes, Diana asked, "How does the grapevine work?"

"Since the blacks have so diligently kept secret the fact that you and your parents lived in Gator Swamp, I believe I can trust you to keep one of our secrets."

"You can."

"You'll recall how Tabitha and Chloe are always singing as they go about their tasks." When Diana agreed, Odille went on. "You'll hear the blacks singing around town, may have already. Whites might think they're hearing no more than a simple song coming from a kitchen or courtyard or the streets. Actually, there'll be words stuck in here and there that don't belong. Those words spread news. A black hearing will adopt the tidbit and add it to his song as he moves around town doing chores. The first thing you know, blacks across the river are picking up the news and singing it for others even farther away."

"How clever!" Diana exclaimed admiringly. "I've often wondered how Tabitha could get news from New Orleans. I'm glad that you came to Fairfield."

"So am I. You're looking sleepy now." She snuffed all the shortening candles save for the one in the small brass holder with a handle that she used to light her way around the house. "Good night."

After Odille closed the door and left, Diana watched the stars peeping through the open windows. She could not explain it but she felt a new tingle of excitement in her heartbeat. Could it be New Orleans stealing into her bloodstream? Or could it be her new determination to patch things up with Luke? She stretched languidly, reveling in the luxury of being young and healthy with her whole life starting over at each new dawn.

The eerie staccato of a dog barking in the distance reminded Diana first of King left behind at Fairfield and induced a pang of homesickness for her beloved pet. Then the barks, faint and echoing, called up the haunting mystery of the city outside

Luke's townhouse, and she permitted herself to look forward to the next day. Luke had told her that soon after breakfast, he would be taking her out to show her the French Quarter. Luke. A smile tucked up the corners of her lips as she curled on her side and fell asleep.

The next morning while Diana tried to see and hear everything at once, she clutched Luke's arm tighter at each new sight as he escorted her down the banquettes in the section of New Orleans that dated back over one hundred years. Awed, she did not bother examining the reason for delighting in having an excuse to hold on to him, for she delighted even further in having him all to herself.

"I never imagined so much activity," she told him after they had seen endless lines of drays and other clattering vehicles pulled by mules through the mucky, narrow streets. A predawn shower had left the boardwalks wet and diluted the stench of the water and refuse standing in the shallow ditches on both sides of the streets. The never-ceasing din of rumbling wheels and chattering drivers gave her a reason to lean closer as she added, "Or so much noise."

Other sounds came from the countless street vendors, and odors as well. With wide-eyed wonder that beguiled Luke anew, Diana cocked her head and listened to the vendors' varied, singsong chants offering their wares. Her straight little nose wrinkled as she openly sniffed at the curious blending of damp smells, both sublime and earthy. Though she understood little of the Creole jargon, she recognized some of the goods offered as fresh-cut flowers, coffee, fried crullers, fish, charcoal, fruit, baskets.

"Everything is so colorful," she confided to the ever-attentive Luke. She had not realized that becoming acquainted with her first city could be such marvelous fun. When she slid an appreciative look toward Luke, she felt her cheeks flush and her already rapid pulse speed up. The way he kept looking at her reminded her of kissing and—

"Yes, it is." Why had he never before noticed? If Diana had withheld her laughter and talk around him before, she did so no longer. Luke could barely keep his eyes off her animated face or answer her questions before another surfaced. He loved the pressure of her arm linked with his, the occasional brush of her skirts against his legs. The desire to kiss her pretty mouth kept fueling his elevated pulse and sometimes overrode his stern order to forget having made love to her.

The chimney sweeps, knife grinders, tinkers, candle makers, and gardeners fascinated Diana as they wandered among the pedestrians and offered their services in individual, melodic phrases. Luke paused to let Diana watch a swarthy-skinned man prying open oyster shells for those waiting in line for his pale, juicy wares.

Then a blind man sawing on his fiddle while his agile monkey jigged around on the banquette and held out a tin cup to passerby captured Diana's attention. Unprepared for the humanlike wisdom showing in the monkey's eyes, she sent Luke a radiant smile when he rained coins into the cup. Not until the little brown monkey bowed and doffed its perky red hat did she realize that a small chain tied the animal to its master. Her tender heart expanded crazily when she looked at Luke and read on his handsome face a compassion equal to her own.

"Do you like it?" Luke asked Diana after she had dutifully sampled the *café au lait* at one of his favorite coffee houses in the French Quarter. Watching her was feeding his soul. It was smashing right and left his preconceived notions about what she meant to him.

"Oh, yes." She smiled across the small marble-topped table at Luke. He evidently had been as ready as she for them to start acting like friends, Diana reflected. Even without her having said a word about their earlier agreement, he had been playing his part admirably ever since they stepped onto the banquette outside his townhouse. What a perfect day for second chances! "This coffee is even better than what Francy served at breakfast." She sent him an impish smile that created a new sparkle in his black eyes. "If you tell her, I'll sneak your razor and use it for shaving off strips of walnut to make baskets, or maybe for whittling."

Luke grimaced playfully at the thought of his honed, straight-edged razor being subjected to such treatment. In mock interrogation, he asked, "Have you had experience ruining a man's razor that way?"

"Well," Diana confessed while sending him mischievous looks from behind her half-lowered lashes, "I did sneak my father's once with something like that in mind. I discovered it was sharp but harder than my knife to maneuver against a block of wood and turn out a smooth strip." Her gaze dropped to her hands and she lifted one toward him. "The scar is still on my thumb but it's almost gone."

Luke felt a pang inside when he leaned over and saw the tiny white line on the pad of her dainty thumb. A curious urge to touch it seized him and he found his forefinger tracing the old wound. What ensued then, a kind of electricity arcing between them, caused him to jerk back his hand in search of his spoon, or of anything to bring him back to his senses. "I didn't know you make baskets."

"I do, but mine are far from the works of art we saw the peddlers hawking this morning."

"You mentioned whittling."

Flipping one hand jauntily and sending him a smug look, she replied, "I have some wildflowers that I whittled last winter during the rainy season."

"Will you show them to me someday?" The thought of Diana being alone in the small house in the swamp since her father's death last year smote his heart, not, he realized, that she would have wanted or accepted his sympathy. A major aspect of her upbringing that still amazed him was her inordinately optimistic outlook.

"I might, if we can remain friends." Diana met Luke's gaze head-on. Was that a softening back in those dark depths? It must be because he was the most handsome man she had ever seen that she was wishing his arms were once more around her pressing her close and. . . After having noted some passersby staring at them earlier as they strolled arm in arm, she had figured out it was because Luke looked so fetching in his green coat and cream-colored trousers.

"I see no reason why we can't," Luke assured her, squelching a dozen reasons threatening to surface and punish. "We've gotten off to a great start today."

"Yes, and I like that.." All morning, Diana had felt the same unreasoning elation she had first acknowledged last evening. How else to explain it, but to confess that she was in love with life in a way never before experienced? The tall, dark-haired man exchanging smiles with her across the small table was not the only reason for her exalted mood. Or was he? Her tongue wet her suddenly dry lips. "I don't know when I've had such a good time. New Orleans is fascinating."

"And somewhat dirty, crowded, noisy—"

"Are you criticizing the place where you used to live?"

"I'm comparing it to where I now live and finding it has some shortcomings—a little to my surprise, incidentally." He admired the charming way her hair fell in shining masses of near-white waves and curls across the top of her dark-blue velvet cape.

Then Luke was recalling how his first sight earlier that morning of Diana wearing a blue-and-white striped gown and the fashionable blue velvet bonnet he had chosen to match the cape had sparked his blood. Even now he could detect no lessening in the pace of his pulse. He had not needed the blatant looks that all on the streets directed toward Diana to remind him that he was escorting a rare beauty. His memories of making love to her three weeks ago were reminders aplenty of her charms. Too damned many. And increasing with each passing moment. A restlessness seized him. "Shall we go see more of the city?"

After they left the coffee house, Luke offered Diana his arm again. He was glad the weather was cool and that the sometimes offensive odors from the open sewers running alongside the narrow streets did not dominate the morning air. Nice, too, was the blue sky overhead, for frequent rains were common occurrences in the city that lay a few feet lower than the Mississippi River curving around its docks.

Glancing up at the red-and-white striped pole standing outside one of the shops ahead, Diana recalled having read about trade signs. "That must be a barber shop."

Still forgetting every once in a while that Diana was not only new to New Orleans but also to any town, Luke said, "You get a 'very good' for your astuteness."

"Coming from you, that's an easy 'perfect.' " She paused to look through the window where a man sat on a tall chair wearing a voluminous white cloth over his clothing while another snipped at his hair with scissors. Though she did not have to look at Luke to know that his thick black hair was shining and that it lay brushed back across his ears, then fell neatly across the back of his neck, she did anyway.

It came to Diana as a bit of a shock that she adored looking at Luke Greenwood's lineaments. She did not know what had happened to change his disposition since they had left Fairfield, but she was delighted to be rediscovering the disarming man who had taught her to waltz and to ride Duchess. Deliberately, she had erected a brick wall around the memory of the other pleasures he had taught her. Or so she had believed. All morning bricks had seemed to be dislodging. Scary. "Did you ever come here to get your hair cut, Luke?"

"Sometimes. Why did you say that about the 'perfect'?"

"Because you've always been so stingy with praise for anything I do." Diana tossed her head, impatient at his failure to catch her meaning right away. Their images in the window of a dress shop signaled for her attention. My, but Doreen was right! Any woman would look good on Luke's arm. Preening, she tucked in a curl she could see was straggling from underneath her bonnet, then straightened the front edges of her cape. Some pedestrians passed them and she wondered why they were looking back and smiling.

"I can't believe that I never praised you." Luke was almost certain it was unladylike for Diana to be primping in front of a shop window, but he had no wish to play the role of tutor and dampen her carefree mood. God! but she was utterly delightful in her enthusiasm for all she was discovering. No wonder Lallage and Salathiel had come to adore their protégée. With difficulty he put aside for the moment all thoughts of their lovemaking and realized that he had missed out on something precious during the past five months by denying himself more of Diana's company. Had he been out of his mind?

"Not once, no matter that I was always tripping over myself to please you." A doubting look chased across his face and she added hastily, "And Salathiel, as well."

"I apologize. I had no idea I had been lax." With his teeth flashing white in the sunlight, he smiled down at her. "Let's go inside the shop down the way and I'll try to make up for my neglect and beastly manners."

Within moments after they went inside, Luke had asked the proprietor to bring some trays of his goods to where a somewhat dazed Diana and he stood at the counter. "Yes," Luke said, "that's what I'm looking for. Something with diamonds and sapphires together."

Diana gazed in awe at the gems displayed against the black velvet of the jeweler's trays. Their brilliance in the sunlight streaming through the window was nigh blinding. Too dumbfounded to utter a syllable, she allowed Luke to remove her cape and toss it on a nearby chair. When he lifted a necklace grander than anything she could have ever imagined and fastened it around her neck, she gasped. "This is too much penance."

Luke grinned, aware that Diana did not notice the bugged eyes of the clerk when he heard her innocent remark. "Look in the mirror. Don't you believe that this is the perfect piece to set off your white ballgown?"

Diana did as Luke instructed, more aware of the warmth of his fingers touching her neck than of the beauty of the elegant necklace with its numerous teardrops of alternating sapphires and diamonds. From where the oval stones began falling from a heavy platinum chain into the pattern of a bib, they increased in size down to their stopping place, an artistic curve barely above the swell of her breasts. The mirror reflected a young woman with a pink mouth opened in wonder and with widely spaced blue eyes being made bluer by the wondrous sparkle of sapphires and diamonds. "It's the most beautiful thing in the world."

"I quite agree," Luke managed a moment later in a hushed tone. He knew he was not speaking of the necklace.

In his mind's eye Luke was seeing as the background for the gems not the blue-and-white striped gown Diana was wearing, but rather that of her exposed skin when she donned the low-cut white ballgown that the seamstresses had made. Salathiel had asked Diana to show Luke and him her new clothing one evening. When Luke had seen the simple white gown fashioned along Grecian lines in the manner he had requested, he had known it was the perfect one for her to wear to the Charity Ball. Frederick would never know what attacked him and. . . . Luke frowned at his last thought.

To the alert clerk Luke nodded his acceptance of the necklace. "Now we'd like to see earrings, bracelet, and a ring of similar design and settings. I'll want delivery by the Saturday of the Charity Ball."

"Luke," Diana said a while later after they left the shop, "you really shouldn't have bought such jewelry for me. Lallage said the pearls and lavalier you've already bought will do fine. Maybe you got carried away because I was trying to make you feel guilty—"

"Not another word," Luke broke in to say, his voice heavy with emotions he lacked the courage to examine. He vowed not to think another time about Frederick and their damnable wager. "Unless you can manage a simple 'thank you, Luke.' "

Her eyes mirroring her recent decision to show Luke that she did not hate him, that she truly liked him and appreciated the many kindnesses he had shown her, Diana said softly, "Thank you, Luke, for the beautiful jewelry and for all the other things you've given me."

"Diana, I—" He stopped and so did she. He felt her puzzled gaze on his face. Misery gnawed at his heart. What could he say? That he was a reprobate, that he did not deserve her thanks? If he did, she might drop her hand from his arm and the intoxicating, approving glow on her face might fade. The perfect day would end.

"Yes, Luke?"

"I'm glad you like the jewelry."

Soon they were strolling across the former parade grounds in front of triple-spired St. Louis Cathedral. Luke explained that during the years of French rule, the large open area was called the *Place d'Armes*; under the Spanish, the *Plaza d'Armas*. Diana paid close heed, her head cocked to one side as if she were listening for the long-lost sounds of marching soldiers who had drilled there. Today the square rang with the happy sounds of children and dogs playing chase under the watchful eyes of nursemaids and parents who sat on benches underneath the palm trees.

Next the handsome couple reached the levee where the wharves stretched for miles up and down the wide Mississippi. Their ferry crossing at dusk the preceding evening had been farther upriver with no large vessels in sight.

"I've been dying to get closer to the ships ever since we saw their tops," Diana confessed when at last she gained a full view of her first seagoing vessel and of her first river steamboat as well.

Floating at anchor two and three deep because of the lack of space against the wharves, ships and boats fluttering colorful flags of at least a dozen nations stretched before Diana's disbelieving eyes. They lay so close that a person might move without a bobble from vessel to vessel. She sent a look of appreciation to Luke, surprised that instead of taking in the fabulous scene, he was watching her with an unreadable look in his dark eyes. "I'll never forget this day."

Luke replied softly, "Nor will I."

The noise and the seemingly disorganized scurry and bustle of the hundreds of seamen and dock hands fascinated Diana almost as much as the sight of the goods being loaded or unloaded. She turned to Luke. "How can you take all of this"—she gestured toward the sights so new to her—"for granted? It's a marvel!"

"Perhaps I've seen it too many times," Luke replied, suddenly feeling a bit jaded. With an interest that surprised him, he answered her rapidly fired questions about things he had long taken for granted. Her smiling face and sparkling eyes kept turning to him as if he were the source generating their animation.

In her excitement, Diana squeezed Luke's arm tighter and openly stared at all the wonders of rigging and sails, smokestacks and triple decks. Pointing to a side-wheeler tied close to the dock, she asked, "Is that the kind of boat you want to put on Bayou Selene?"

Pleased that she recalled his plans, Luke admitted it was and went to great lengths explaining how his boat would have to be much smaller and modified to suit the needs of the people in St. Christopher Parish. "Tomorrow I'll begin investigating the possibilities of getting a small shipping and passenger line launched by next spring."

"Wonderful! You're so . . . so sure of yourself. I admire that. I know you won't fail."

Luke had tried innumerable times to interpret the penetrating look Diana had given him while she thanked him for the jewelry and then later when she told him she would never forget that day. One explanation kept haunting him. Could it be that her remarkable change of attitude toward him was caused by her belief that she might be in love with him? Almost doing him in, memories of their lovemaking flooded his mind. He kept remembering the way she had told him then that she had been waiting for him all of her life. Afterward, though, when they had clashed. . . .

Before they returned to his townhouse, Luke began paying closer attention to Diana's smiles and her approving glances. Yes, he decided with anguish over his earlier blindness to such a possibility, Diana was so innocent and inexperienced at being around young men that she was mistaking her gratitude to him for his gifts as love. He cursed himself for having contributed to her apparent confusion by giving in to his passion that night in her house. About the only decision he could reach during their excursion around the city was that he had no desire to take further advantage of Diana Hathaway.

That night after dinner, though, after denying to himself for years that any woman alive could hold a special place in his life, Luke lay on his bed and at last let the problem of the beautiful blonde fan out before him. He faced some painfully jarring discoveries.

Up until that moment, Luke confessed, he had lied to himself. Lies no longer satisfied him, not after he had spent a day with Diana and drunk in her laughter, her loveliness, and her engaging spontaneity. He was in love. He was more in love with Diana Hathaway than he had ever been with Sylvia Lindstrom.

Instead of the discovery pleasing Luke, it sucked him into an abysmal, black mood. How could he speak of his love to Diana when she had never had the opportunity even to meet any other young men? He fought against accepting it, but only one conclusion rose up as worthy of Diana. To be honorable, he must keep secret his feelings and allow her to find out for herself what kind of man might bring her happiness.

Isn't it a bit late to be thinking of "honorable" in connection with Diana? inquired the deriding inner voice that had taunted him back in his library that night. Luke threw his pillow into the farthest corner of his dark bedroom and muttered a string of self-directed curses.

The pink of dawn was lightening the windows in Luke's bedroom before sleep rescued him.

Eighteen

Diana went up to her room early that evening, but only after Luke insisted that she must be exhausted from their day's excursion. Because she chose to entertain thoughts of the carefree Luke who had escorted her about the Vieux Carré and not the serious-faced Luke joining Salathiel and her for dinner afterward, she fell asleep in a state of near euphoria.

Vexed the next morning because she had slept till the sun rode high, Diana rushed through a hasty toilette. Apparently, Odille had come earlier, for fresh water filled the tall porcelain pitcher with its bouquet of hand-painted roses.

Diana was searching in the armoire for a gown to slip over her petticoats when she heard the door open. "Why didn't you wake me, Odille?"

"I thought you needed the sleep," came the quadroon's soft voice. She moved quickly to choose a gown of maroon bombazine and help Diana slip into it.

"Has everyone already gone for the day?" Diana asked as she settled on the bench in front of the dressing table. She would have denied it had she been questioned, but she knew she had used the word *everyone* for *Luke*. Salathiel had announced after dinner that he would be leaving early to shop for new clothing. Luke had volunteered nothing. Twisting her head in protest of Odille's hearty attack on her tangles with the hairbrush, she grimaced. "Ouch!"

Odille smiled. "If you relax I can style your hair more easily. What has you feeling cross? You didn't mention any plans for today outside expecting Miss Lallage and Doreen and her cousins to come for afternoon tea."

"I'm not cross." Diana heard how puerile her denial sounded and laughed. "I'm acting like a dolt, and I'm sorry." She met Odille's thoughtful gaze in the mirror. "You're right about today's schedule. I was hoping, though, that if I showed up downstairs for breakfast, Luke might invite me to go with him around town again."

"He's already gone. Francy's daughter, Little Bit, heard him tell Mr. Salathiel that he had business to attend to and likely wouldn't return until time to get ready for the party at Governor Roman's home tonight. A messenger brought around the invitation last evening after you had retired."

"Am I to attend?" Diana's heart fluttered and threatened to sink lower. She had expected to endure a trial appearance before going to the Charity Ball next week, but not so soon.

"Yes, according to the master. Before Mr. Salathiel went out, he had already received confirmation from Miss Lallage that she will attend with him."

Diana's trepidations increased, despite the welcome news that both Lallage and Salathiel would be along. An appearance at the home of the governor of Louisiana loomed as ominously as a storm cloud on the horizon of a formerly fair day.

Left to herself after her breakfast of *café au lait* and beignet dusted with fine sugar, Diana pulled a pale shawl around her shoulders and explored the courtyard stretching in front of the three-story house. Masonry walls, broken only by wrought-iron gate to the street, hemmed in the spacious area on three sides, while the front of the house served as the back wall. The flowers, greenery, and music of the fountain with its graceful statuary fascinated her, soothed her fears.

Diana wandered to a corner of the large open area, admiring the slender stalks of bamboo rising in leafed spikes among group of broad-leafed banana trees. She peeked at the small clusters of bright-green fruit pointing upward at the blue sky, imagining them as they would be when they ripened into the succulent yellow fruit she had seen at the markets yesterday with Luke. Then it seemed she viewed everything in a softer light, as if the tall darkly handsome man might again be beside her awaiting her observations about all that was new.

Diana knew she would have told Luke, had he been there, that she liked the way the blue-gray flagstones fitted together without grouting. Earlier she had asked Sonny, Francy's son who was tending the plants growing in tall clay pots, the name of the stones. Right off she had decided they complemented the apricot color of the brick townhouse and its protecting tall walls. Was it unique to everyone or only to her, the way most of the buildings in the Vieux Carré were painted in soft shades of cream, green, blue, and pink and had angled roofs of rippling, orangish-red tiles?

Hearing the muffled cries of the street vendors outside on the streets and imagining that she could again smell the odors of ripe fruit, fried crullers, and fresh fish wafting on the chilly morning air, Diana sent her gaze wandering to the intricately wrought ironwork on the narrow balconies that extended across the front of the second and third floors. Then she noticed the slender flight of stairs of matching ironwork at one outer edge of the house, leading to a small landing on each floor.

Diana wished Luke was present. She would like to ask if the outer stairways served as a safety precaution against a repetition of the destructive fire of 1794 when, according to what Luke had told her yesterday, some people had become trapped within the upper floors of their homes. When she had told Luke how much she liked his townhouse yesterday, he had explained that he had bought the elegant home from an elderly Spaniard who had built it long before Louisiana became a state in 1812.

Feeling drawn to the sunny center of the sweet-smelling courtyard where the graceful fountain burbled, Diana sat on the low brick edge of the circular pool of water. Her eyes wide with delight at yet another unexpected sight, she discovered fish of varied sizes and hues of orange swimming indolently among fronds of water ferns. The lovely creatures seemed undaunted by the steady splashes of water falling from the upended vase held high by the smiling young woman carved of marble.

Diana chose not to let her gaze linger on the statue's eyes. They were glaringly white and blind to all the beauty captured within the courtyard off Royal Street.

Soon after Salathiel returned from his outing and joined Diana in the living room, Francy announced Doreen Oates and her cousins. Overjoyed that Doreen's aunt had permitted the young people to call, Diana ignored the fact that her visitors wore mourning for Julius Waskom and Maynard Oates.

"Charmed," Doreen's cousin, George Armand, said upon being introduced to Diana. His nice smile seconded his words. "My pleasure, sir," he murmured to Salathiel. George's stocky build and dark coat with a wide black band of mourning on one sleeve gave him an air of being older than his twenty-five years, but his twinkling gray eyes belied any suggestion that he was stodgy.

"You're every bit as lovely as Doreen has told my brother and me," Amy Armand said after introductions were made all around and the guests seated themselves in the spacious room. Near Doreen's age and almost as pretty, she eyed Salathiel with a dimpled smile. "And you, sir, are even more an exemplar English gentleman than our cousin has hinted."

Doreen, plainly delighted that her cousins and her new friends from St. Christopher Parish were getting along well, looked wistfully around the living room and said to Diana, "I was hoping Lallage and Luke would be joining us for tea. I wanted my cousins to meet them."

Just then a decidedly feminine commotion from the court-yard announced the arrival of Lallage Winston and her four daughters, with their attendant, Lily, fluttering along behind. By the time another round of introductions and small talk stirred the air in the high-ceilinged room, Francy and Little Bit were bringing in trays with tea, little sandwiches, and fruit tarts. Lily shepherded Lallage's daughters to the court-yard for their refreshments.

After Diana served tea to all from the low table in front of her chair, Salathiel sat beside Lallage on one of the sofas set at right angles to the fireplace, wherein a small charcoal fire burned. The fond, effusive greetings that Japonica, Ca-melia, Daisy, and Hyacinth bestowed upon him had brought a becoming flush to his face. Creating an inner glow was the affectionate greeting from their pretty mother. In a private voice he said, "Lallage, I am grateful that you chose not to bring Pooch along to New Orleans. He undermines my self-image in an abominable way."

Lallage sipped from her cup, then sent the man with whom she was madly in love a flirtatious smile. She was still floating from having received his note that morning inviting her to go with him to the governor's party. "Pooch is trying only to protect me from bounders."

Though at one time Salathiel would have been shocked at her words, now that he knew the pert widow and suspected he had fallen in love with her, he merely chuckled and smoothed his mustache. "How the dog could sniff me out is amazing."

"Well, darling," Lallage said in *sotto voce* with a saucy look that sent Salathiel's rising blood pressure up a new notch, "I wouldn't have him around if he couldn't. After all, boun-ders are all that appeal to me."

The four young people, eager to expound on the bounty offered by New Orleans as each saw it, sat on the other sofa and on chairs pulled up to face the fireplace. Soon they had drawn the older couple into their enthusiastic conversation.

Comfortable in her role as hostess, Diana was grateful for all the times Lallage had supervised her during teatime back at Fairfield. Approving smiles at intervals from Lallage and Salathiel fed her confidence. If only Luke could be there! She longed for him to see how far she had advanced toward being the cultured young woman he wanted her to become.

"Did you enjoy having people over for tea this afternoon?" Odille asked Diana that evening. She was toweling the last of the moisture from Diana's hair after her leisurely bath and shampoo behind a mahogany-paneled screen in the corner of the bedroom.

"Yes, but I wished Luke had been present. We had such fun yesterday. He seemed to take to the notion of our being friends as much as I did." Diana's lips formed a *moue*. Maybe she had only imagined Luke had warmed up toward her.

"He's home now getting dressed. He brought a valet with him from his visit to his cousins out near Lake Pontchartrain. Such a busy and important businessman as Master Luke needs someone to keep his wardrobe in order and help him dress."

Important? Diana never had thought about Luke being an important businessman. Was that why Governor Roman had sent invitations to his party? Somehow, she had thought Luke no more than a lucky gambler who had ended up with a sugar plantation and a pile of money. Of course there were the monumental changes he had wrought at Fairfield, plus his plans for putting in an enormous crop. Too, there was his talk about running steamboats on Bayou Selene.

Diana tried to remember if she had ever heard Luke mention having family in New Orleans. All she could recall was that he had a brother, Frederick, and married sister, Maurine, living in Mobile. Evidently, Luke had gone that day to visit some cousins living near Lake Pontchartrain. If the two of them were truly friends, why had he not asked her to go along?

At least, Diana consoled herself while Odille went about helping her into her clothing and then styling her hair, she would be with him all evening at the governor's party. Suddenly, her earlier fear about attending such a small function sailed out the open windows on the damp breath of the late November evening. The big ordeal—December and its Charity Ball—still waited around the corner.

"You look lovely," Odille said. She stepped back to admire her charge, her hands lost inside the pockets of her habitual white apron. "Blue is a good color for you." She leaned to fluff the long silk skirt of the simply styled gown. "I like the lace medallions marking the empire line underneath the bustline."

"Are you sure there's not too much bosom showing?" Diana leaned closer to the mirror, a frown marring her smooth forehead when she saw the expanse of exposed cleavage. The three-stranded pearl choker around her neck seemed miles above the deeply scooped neckline.

"You know I wouldn't mislead you."

Diana touched the pearl earrings visible amidst a few small curls Odille had managed to dangle in front of her ears before sweeping most of her hair into an elaborate nest of curls high at the back of her head. Though Diana had protested that Odille's plans to intertwine a long strand of small pearls among the curls atop her head might make her look like a hen pretending to be a peacock, she confessed now, "You were right about the little pearls in my hair. They do seem to fit in with its color and add a glow."

Then it was time to put on the white leather gloves, loop the drawstrings of her dainty black reticule over one arm, and let Odille drape her shoulders with a black silk cape lined with ermine and edged all around by narrow bands of the pale fur. "Wonder why Luke had this sent today?" Diana asked for the second time since having opened the long box found in her bedroom after tea. Inside she had discovered the luxurious garment and a note saying, "Wear this tonight for me. Please? Luke." She mused aloud, "I already have capes that would do. It isn't cold enough to need fur for keeping warm."

Running her fingers over the soft fur lining, its pale color competing successfully with that of Diana's hair, Odille replied, "I doubt many women could truly say they can't enjoy wearing something so beautiful."

"I have to agree," Diana conceded when she surveyed her image in the mirror. The woman therein appeared worldly. Only her widely spaced eyes seemed familiar.

All the way down to the living room on the ground floor where Odille said Luke was to meet her, Diana thought about the new her who had been created to please the handsome owner of Fairfield. She remembered numerous bits of feminine wisdom Lallage had shared with her. Had Lallage not said that men liked being flirted with, even though they might not have initiated a flirtation? Diana pursed her lips. Had Lallage not won Salathiel's attention, and likely his heart as well, by letting him know she found him attractive long before he showed reciprocal feelings?

Though Diana could hear men's voices coming from within the library at the foot of the stairs, she swept into the living room to wait. She was putting together her thoughts about Luke and recalling some of Lallage's ploys for gaining a man's undivided attention.

Maybe, Diana mused with what she believed was cool logic, she had been wrong to mistake an infatuation for love, but she was certain now that Luke was important in her life. It seemed that she must be somewhat special to him, else why was he distressed about her opinion of him that night she bumped into him on the staircase?

Being with Luke all day yesterday and getting to know him better had convinced Diana that until she knew for certain what he thought about her, she entertained no desire to accept attentions from any bachelors she might meet. Instead of fading as she had once believed they would, memories of their lovemaking permeated her every thought. She could not forget that she had become as close as possible to what Luke apparently deemed an ideal young woman. Maybe in time—

Luke stepped from the library, still in conversation with the trim black man walking beside him. They paused, as if aware that someone from the living room across the foyer was watching.

"Come, Isaac," Luke said, the sight of blonde hair from across the way filching his attention and flipping his heart upside down. "I want you to meet my house guest."

Luke managed what he assumed was an acceptable introduction and polite comments, for within a short while, only Diana and he remained in the living room. His pulse was still bucking like a colt turned loose in a pasture after being confined in close quarters. Never had he expected to find the Diana who stood before him with such poise, such perfection. He drank in the feminine sights of white gloves on dainty hands, blue silk clinging to luscious curves, pink lips, blue eyes. He wondered if the key to all her beauty lay in her pale luminous skin. It shamed the cultured pearls around her graceful neck, on her partially hidden ears, even the tiny ones looping through her near-white curls amassed at the top of her pretty head. When she moved, he admired the three long curls spiraling in the back from the elaborate cluster.

Yes, Luke reminded himself, he had known from his first sight of Diana that she was beautiful. He had seen her in many of her lovely gowns—had seen her clothed only in moonlight, too, his tortured heart reminded him—but something about her seemed different tonight. It was more than the stylish coiffure, though he admitted the fashionable way her blonde curls framed her exquisite features was breathtaking. Was it because he now knew he had fallen in love with her that he could not seem to get enough of looking at her? The possibility seemed as ludicrous as his runaway pulse.

"Do I pass inspection?" Diana asked, slowly turning around before Luke, her cape with the ermine side out whispering against the carpet as it trailed from where she had tossed it carelessly over one arm. Her smile grew more radiant when she completed a half turn and looked up at him over her shoulder, hoping that her gaze from behind partially lowered lashes was half as flirtatious as some she had seen Lallage aim toward Salathiel. She saw the desired soft look deep within his dark eyes. Then the remembered slow smile creased his lean features and rewarded her with a view of his beautiful teeth. "I adore the cape, Luke. You're far too generous. Is it time for you to put it around me?"

Luke swallowed. His mouth had gone dry. What had she asked earlier? He licked his lips. "Yes, you pass inspection." He forced his gaze from the swell of her breasts to her lips, then to her eyes. "I call it an easy 'perfect.' "

"How generous of you." Diana grinned, so pleased that she almost hugged herself and giggled and spoiled her plan to dazzle Luke with her sophistication. Lallage had been right! Luke was liking it that she was flirting with him. What else had Lallage said? Something about making the man feel that the woman cared for nothing but to pleasure him. She fluttered her eyelashes again before looking up at him. "I hope I've not kept you waiting and that you'll be glad you invited me."

"No," Luke said, almost stammering before he could get control of his speech. Where had she learned to flirt like that? "Yes. I mean you haven't kept me waiting and I'm already glad I invited you. Salathiel took the carriage over to get Lallage. He'll send Homer in for us when they return."

"I'm looking forward to going to the governor's party with you." With her free hand Diana touched her pearl choker. It seemed too tight, what with the pulse in her throat beating as fast as the wings of a hummingbird hovering over a blossom.

"You aren't afraid of being around a group of strangers?"

"Why, no. I'll be with you," Diana assured him. She realized she was not having to fake her answer. Neither was she having to fake interest in Luke. Excitement was heating up her blood. He was devastatingly handsome in his black coat and trousers and white brocaded waistcoat. The dark-red neckcloth seemed to make his faintly olive skin glow. He must have shaved recently, for she could detect a faint masculine fragrance. Spicy soap, maybe? "Why would I be afraid when I have you to look after me?"

Homer entered the foyer then, his tall-crowned black hat in his hand. When Luke stepped to the open door of the living room, the black man said, "The carriage is out front when you's ready to go, Master Luke." He sent a polite nod toward Diana who had followed Luke to the door.

"We'll be along shortly," Luke said.

Still somewhat in awe of the elegant beauty beside him and what she was doing to his emotions, Luke took the cape from her and held it out by its black silk shoulders. His hands were trembling. The tiny rustling sounds of silken garments tickled his ears as Diana sent him a doting look and moved gracefully to stand close enough for him to settle the garment on her shoulders and bring the front edges together below her chin. A whiff of the French fragrance he had given her, which had already pleased his nostrils when she pirouetted before him earlier, became more seductive from such close proximity. He fought the desire to twirl her around for a kiss. More. He wanted more than a kiss. He wanted to crush her against. . .

His jaw set firmly in victory over the temptations threatening to seduce him, Luke drew Diana's white-gloved hand through his bent arm and escorted her across the lantern-lit courtyard to the waiting carriage. He was achingly aware that thoughout the brief walk, Diana kept her gaze on his face.

Luke felt his heart sinking into the same black abyss housing it last night when he first realized he was madly in love with the beautiful blonde. Her openly adoring ways reiterated that he had been right. Diana *did* think she was in love with him. What a pile of miserable muck his compulsive actions that night beside Selene Bayou had created! Had there been a touch of madness radiating from that cypress moon?

By the time the foursome arrived at the party amidst laughter at Salathiel's latest witty story, Diana's heart was overflowing. Her vision seemed limited to scenes involving Luke Greenwood.

In the lavishly decorated home of Governor and Mrs. Andre Roman, Diana admired tall plaster ceilings with carved mouldings and medallions, marble floors, arched doorways. Gilt-framed mirrors reflected the gleaming beauty of sparkling crystal-and-silver chandeliers, their supporting chains draped in pale damask. She detected exotic fragrances from fresh flowers and perfume floating on the air and mingling with the homey smell of beeswax. There were massive paintings, a curving staircase, tapers everywhere, along with smiling faces and cultured talk. The most impressive sight was Luke, who seemed to know almost everyone present. He was always at her side, gallant, beaming as he introduced her.

Later at the banquet table where twenty-two guests sat down its grand length and Lousiana's governor and first lady presided at either end, Diana succumbed to the charms of the host and hostess, the congenial guests, and the appeal of sumptuous courses served by white-gloved blacks. Luke, in her eyes the most handsome man present, rarely removed his gaze from her face. Her head was no more than an airborne feather.

"Oh," Diana whispered to Luke, her eyes widening when her ears convinced her she was not dreaming, "real music!" She touched his arm in her enthusiasm and glanced in the direction of the sound. Where were the musicians?

"There'll be dancing across the foyer in the ballroom after dinner," he whispered back with one of the warmest smiles he had given her all evening. He found Diana's spontaneity enchanting and was aware that others sitting around them apparently did also. In fact, Luke already had sent blunt stares of forbiddance toward two unmarried men known to be rakes about town. "That's where the orchestra is playing."

Diana's excitement piled atop excitement when at last dinner ended and Luke led her onto the dance floor. As if she might never have struggled back at Fairfield to master dancing, Diana went into his arms and waltzed with style and grace. What with Luke being so dark and handsome and Diana so fair and beautiful, the other formally dressed guests in the spacious ballroom kept sending them admiring glances.

Upon seeing that Diana's smile of delight lent a special piquancy to her lovely face, Luke felt his heart expand. Surely, he told himself, his meddling in her life could not be construed as all wrong when she was plainly enjoying the evening. If the signs he had read on the faces of the bachelors in attendance were any measure, a host of suitors would be calling on Diana at his townhouse. His last reflection sobered him.

"Is something wrong?" Diana asked.

"No," he denied, chiding himself for letting his thoughts show. "What could possibly be wrong? I'm dancing with the most beautiful young woman in New Orleans." *In the world!*

"Really, Luke? Do you think I'm beautiful?" When he nodded and swept her around so that she was the one moving forward, Diana said, "I'm glad you're pleased. Did I act all right during dinner?"

"Perfect. You get another 'perfect.' "

Diana flashed him a smile of appreciation. "Isn't the music grand?"

"It is."

"I think I spotted the violas." Her gaze shifted to the

several musicians performing across the room beside a mass of potted ferns. "Would it be proper for you take me over and let me get a closer look?"

Luke smiled. "Proper or not, I'll do it when they pause for intermission." How could she look so devastatingly seductive and retain her delightful awe for everything new? His hand tightened its pressure on the back of her waist, the movement bringing her closer as they glided in three-four time across the parquet floor.

"You're so good to me, Luke. Thank you."

Remembering his earlier vow to keep Diana at a distance since she, in her innocence, apparently thought she was smitten with him, Luke loosened his hold on her back. How could he have taken advantage of her that night at her house? His increasing feelings of guilt for having turned her life upside down for something as asinine as a bet with his brother bore down on him unmercifully. "You've already expressed your gratitude, when actually I'm the one who's indebted to you for living up to our pact. Let's not talk about such matters anymore. Will you do that for me?"

Diana sent him a speculative look from behind half-lowered lashes. Something other than admiration for her as his partner for the evening was glinting in his eyes and making him look pensive, almost sorrowful. Aware that she spoke with candor, she replied, "I would do anything you asked."

Luke made no comment. His burdened heart was stealing away his breath.

Some young officers from the nearby army post had appeared by the time the first dance ended. Looking resplendent in their uniforms, they smiled as Governor Roman introduced them to his guests. Soon the young officers began bowing over the hands of the comelier ladies and leading them onto the floor.

In a way, Diana was disappointed that Luke relinquished her to the arms of a young officer, Lieutenant Grayson. When she saw during their dance that Luke watched them whirling around the ballroom with his brooding expression, she forced herself to remember what Lallage, and even Luke, had told her that young women were expected to do while dancing.

Perhaps a bit of flirtation with her partner would bring back Luke's earlier smiles and looks of approval for her numerous accomplishments.

Diana lifted her face to the young officer and smiled. The lieutenant, who was blond, tall, handsome, and plainly enchanted by his dancing partner, returned her smile with a hearty one that crinkled his blue eyes in an endearing way. She felt his hand tighten at her back and gave herself up to the marvelous music and the exhilaration she had enjoyed all evening. Lallage was right, Diana thought as she had earlier that evening. Flirting was devilishly exciting . . . but far more so when the man was Luke Greenwood.

"Have you noticed Luke?" Salathiel asked Lallage when he was able to dance again with her later that evening. To his growing dismay he had discovered she was almost as popular with the men as Diana. A compulsive need to lay public claim to the lovely red-haired widow jabbed Salathiel into making up his mind once and for all that he definitely was in love. By Jove, he decided while his blood yet boiled from having watched Lallage dance with others, he intended to ask her to marry him. Soon. Tonight. "He looks positively livid with jealousy."

"He does, doesn't he?" Lallage countered. She frowned prettily. "What do you think is going on? I adore seeing our Diana so vivacious. She appears downright flirty."

Salathiel smiled and led Lallage through the required forward and back steps of the minuet. If Lallage had shared even half of her knowledge about how to beguile a man, their beautiful protégée could not help but be successful. "I wonder where she gets her ideas."

Lallage batted her eyelashes, forgetting for a moment to make the required quarter turn. Once she recovered and made the gliding steps of the next pattern, she said, "You rogue. How would I know?"

"Perhaps because you're a queen of enchantment yourself."

Hand in hand, they were into the approaching and retreating steps then and Lallage thought of how the minuet was sometimes called the dance of courtship. The dancers moved without progressing a single step and ended up at the spot from which they began. When Salathiel pulled her close with his face turned toward hers, she asked, "Am I truly enchanting?"

"You have me totally captivated."

"Well," Lallage remarked as Salathiel glided past her with his gaze fastened to hers, "it took long enough."

"I think I am going to have to spend the rest of my life with you to keep the spell intact."

"Salathiel Morgan, if this is a proposal, I demand that you come right out with it."

"Will you marry me, dear Lallage?"

"I'll give it serious consideration."

Salathiel sputtered. He was the one to miss a step that time. "That is no civilized answer."

"But then I'm no civilized woman . . . all of the time."

"I have no desire to change you in any way."

"Good, for I have no desire to change . . . unless it's my name." She squeezed his hand and sent him an arch smile. "I have a penchant for having men propose on their knees."

"You have a genius for cruelty." He added dryly, "I like that in a woman." Salathiel recalled how Luke had told Frederick that night in Mobile that when the right woman came along, she could bring any man to his knees. How right Luke had been! "Later, when we reach your place, I will prove my honorable intentions by bending before you on one knee."

"Perhaps I'll have my answer by then." Lallage's brown eyes twinkled at the man she loved, signaling her answer without the need for words. She glimpsed Diana across the ballroom and noted that her eyes seemed to be more on Luke than on her dancing partner. "Do you suppose Diana and Luke are finally recognizing that they're in love?"

"Come to think of it, neither has had eyes for any but the other all evening."

"They haven't seemed as testy with each other ever since we left Fairfield." Lallage narrowed her eyes and pursed her lips, aware that Salathiel watched her with adoration even as he led her expertly through the final pattern of the stately minuet. "I doubt either wants to be the first to admit it."

"Facing up to such matters of the heart is harder for some than others."

Lallage laughed low in her throat and tendered Salathiel a seductively teasing look. The minuet was over. "I'm quite sure you are one who would know, darling."

"You were the belle of the evening," Lallage told Diana after the four of them settled onto the soft leather seats of Luke's carriage and Homer was driving from the governor's house. "I hope you had fun. I was achingly proud of you!"

"I'm glad," Diana replied. "I never dreamed I would have such a wonderful time at my very first party."

"I was pleased also, my dear," Salathiel chimed in with unmistakable happiness plumping up his English accent. He glanced at Luke, who was fingering his chin while sitting beside Diana and gazing out into the night. Had Lallage been right in suspecting that Diana and Luke had been in love for some time and were beginning to realize it? Not that he knew much about such affairs, but Salathiel well remembered how at first he had hoped the two would come to care for each other, then discarded his wish as impossible after they frequently and openly clashed. "Were you not proud of our young lady, Luke?"

Luke brought his fingers down from his chin. "Yes, but I thought she rather overdid the bit about charming each of her dancing partners. Ye gods! The governor must have imported an entire battalion to dance with his guests when it wasn't necessary at all."

Diana preened in the darkness broken only by the occasional gleams from the gas lanterns hanging from the corners of buildings in the French Quarter. Had Luke, perhaps, become jealous of the several young officers fawning over her? She said, "I thought Governor Roman did the gentlemen a favor by providing alternative dancing partners for the ladies. That way you didn't have to dance every dance."

"Who said the gentlemen don't care to dance every dance?" Luke shot back in an aggrieved tone. "If one escorts a young lady to a party, it's quite probable that he has no wish to stand in line for the privilege of dancing with her."

"Really, Luke," Salathiel remarked when nobody answered Luke's peevish comments, "I think you are missing the major point. Lallage and I are delighted that Diana was able to make such a notable impression on the upper circles of New Orleans society and have a good time while doing it. You might not realize how hard she worked to accomplish this feat. For a young woman who never before danced until a couple of months ago and learned with nothing but our clumsy attempts to—"

"I realize as well as you two that Diana is to be complimented, and her teachers as well," Luke broke in to say in a tone closer to normal. He had not meant to let his jealousy form, much less show. What was he going to do if one of the eager-eyed bachelors showed up at his townhouse to call on the "niece **of S**alathiel Morgan"? There had been no other way to explain the presence of the young woman in his townhouse or to indicate that there was no attachment between Diana and him. No attachment, when he was blindly in love with her? What a farce! "I don't need a recital of how this came about. You may recall that it was all my idea in the first place."

Salathiel did recall, in fact seldom let the realization settle very far back in his mind. If Diana and Luke *were* falling in love, perhaps the tedious matter of Luke's having meddled in Diana's life could result in a happy ending. How was Luke going to explain to her what had set him on such an errant course?

With a fond look at the pretty red-haired woman sitting beside him, Salathiel shoved aside the weighty problems facing the younger couple. He had a vital question to ask soon and an equally vital answer to hear.

Diana stared out the window into the night, shutting out Lallage's animated talk about the party. What had made Luke upset? She discarded her earlier thought that he might have been jealous. He sounded only slightly annoyed about her dancing often with others. If he were as bothered over that as he seemed about some other matter, it would mean he cared for her as more than a friend. Somehow the mental image of Luke falling in love with her would not form.

After all, Diana's thoughts rolled on along with the wheels of the carriage, Luke's stated purpose in transforming her into whatever she had become was to present an unknown young woman of apparent culture to his friends at the upcoming Charity Ball. From the beginning he had known far better than she how such social affairs were conducted and that she would be expected to dance with many men.

No, Diana decided with a pang of what felt like disappointment, jealousy was not what was making him irritable. Maybe some business matters were not working out to suit him. For certain his earlier jovial mood had vanished.

"Would anyone care to come inside for a cordial?" Lallage asked when the carriage stopped outside her townhouse.

"I should be delighted," Salathiel answered in a rush.

"No, thank you, Lallage," Luke replied, not giving Diana the courtesy of being consulted. He sensed that if he did not remove himself from his beloved's company soon, he would give in to his punishing desire to kiss her, confess his love. "It's late and I have an early appointment tomorrow."

Diana let out a silent sigh that echoed the immeasurable pain in her heart. There was the crux. Luke had his mind on business, not on her. Suddenly, she felt deflated and dangerously close to tears. She had been an idiot to pin false hopes on imaginary fond looks and gestures from a man who held no special regard for her feelings.

"Do not wait up for me, Luke. I shall walk the few blocks after our cordials," Salathiel said just before leaving the carriage. "Good night to both of you."

After bidding Diana and Luke good night, Lallage stepped down from the carriage with a perfumed rustle of silk and satin. Salathiel's hand on hers felt strong, warm, and deliciously masculine.

Nineteen

"I can imagine how you feel, Diana," Doreen said a few afternoons later as the two young women hurried through the Vieux Carré toward Canal Street. Though Doreen's cousin, George Armand, was officially their escort, scurrying pedestrians on the narrow banquette sometimes, as now, forced him to walk behind. "I should have come over sooner."

All day, gray skies had scudded low overhead. Sporadic gusts of wind careened around corners and seemed to speed up the normally lackadaisical pace of people on the banquettes and streets.

Doreen went on, her pretty face revealing concern. "I'm sure nobody is leaving you on your own by design. Probably Lallage and Mr. Salathiel are too carried away with their plans to marry in the spring to realize you're feeling left out."

"That's not it. I'm happy for them. They've already given me much of themselves. I see Salathiel at least once a day and hear about how they're dashing about town shopping and seeing the sights. Lallage has joined Salathiel and me twice for dinner. He gave her the most exquisite ruby ring you can imagine." Diana smiled from her thoughts about the newly engaged couple. "I'm dining with them at Lallage's this evening. It's Luke's absences that I don't understand."

Doreen flipped a hand in dismissal. "As for him being gone almost day and night, well. . . ."

"Well, what?"

"Well, you know how men are."

"Maybe I don't. Tell me."

Doreen glanced over her shoulder to make sure George was still a couple of yards to their rear. From behind a guarding hand, she went on in a lower voice. "Lots of men take mistresses. Cousin Amy told me Luke has been known to keep one here in New Orleans. I gather people here think of him as quite a dashing gambler and man about town. It's my guess he's spending time with a woman."

"Lallage said a 'man about town' is something of a rake, a man whom proper young women avoid." Diana knew what *mistress* meant. Her face flamed at the knowledge that she had given herself with abandonment to such a man. Drat him! How could she have thought that she might be falling in love with him?

"That's true," Doreen replied knowingly. "Even so, Amy says that Luke is popular in the best social circles. Are you still going with him to the Charity Ball tomorrow night?"

"I have no choice but to go."

"Don't worry," Doreen consoled When she noted her friend's flushed face. "Luke will have to treat you like a lady, what with everyone who's anybody in New Orleans society there. Not that you've indicated he treats you any other way, still—"

Diana's head jerked upward. She fixed her wounded gaze on a fat pigeon fluttering overhead from one eave of the adjoining buildings along Royal Street to another. Luke was not away from his townhouse because of taxing business affairs. Neither was he away for the reason Lallage had suggested—to thwart the bachelors she had met at the governor's party who recently had been leaving their cards and requesting Luke's permission to call on his house guest. No, Luke was basking in the charms of some woman. She felt as if a giant fist had squeezed her stomach.

George caught up with them then and walked alongside. "The Planters Bank is just around the corner, Diana." H plainly adoring smile went unanswered. "I'm glad you're doing business with the bank where my uncle works."

"And I'm glad—no, grateful—that you and Doreen came calling this afternoon and were willing to accompany me on my errand," Diana replied, sending one hand to feel again the brass key lying at the bottom of her cloth reticule.

Diana thought of how since the night of the governor's party, Luke had become so secretive and evasive about his comings and goings that she had seen him only a few times at the dinner table. She always became rattled in his forbidding presence and kept forgetting to ask his thoughts on allowing Odille to escort her in the city. Where had she found the courage to flirt with him so brazenly the night of the party? She had been wrong to think they had become friends. Thoughts of having to accompany him to the Charity Ball tomorrow night loomed as threateningly as the overhead clouds.

Shortly after the three young people entered the bank, they were sitting in the office of Samuel Armard, executive vice president, explaining the purpose of their visit. To Diana's immense relief the kindly man seemed familiar with Philip Hathaway's deposit box and summoned a clerk to escort her to a small private room nearby.

As soon as the clerk left Diana alone, she sent shaking fingers to fit her key into the lock of the metal box. First she read the letters found in an envelope addressed to "Beloved Child of Our Blessed Union." One was from her mother, dated nineteen years ago.

Through tears Diana read Drusila's account of her life on Jamaica and how her gift of healing had earned her the unwelcome title of Silver Hoodoo Woman. Drusila must have known that one day the child she carried might need to know the truth about the unfounded talk connecting her with black magic, Diana reflected with sadness on her mother's brief life.

Seeing the names of her grandfather, Herman Dusendorf, and her uncle, Karl, lifted Diana's heart. She could write and let them know of her existence. Or she could book passage on one of the ships moored only blocks away on the Mississippi and appear unannounced in Kingston at her grandfather's trading company. A shiver of apprehension shook her. Would she be welcomed?

Philip's nineteen-year-old letter to his unborn child also held a wealth of information about family. Eagerly, Diana read the names of the Hathaways in Boston, shocked to learn that her grandfather, Soames Hathaway, was a shipping scion. A paper covered with fine print revealed that Philip and his heirs owned a percentage of the elder Hathaway's company. Were some of the ships tied up at the wharves down the street part of Massachusetts Shipping? Even back in 1812 Philip had reported that twelve ships from the firm plied the seas with goods.

Diana's blood raced with hope as she read about the four Hathaway sons and two daughters. Why, Diana thought with surging emotions as she blinked away her tears, she had a wealth of kinfolk. Her parents may have severed ties with their families, but both apparently believed their offspring would be received. She was far from being alone in the world. She did not have to depend on the generosity of Luke Greenwood or anyone else. Doggedly, she swept aside thoughts of the enigmatic, handsome man who had seized a grip on her life one moonlit night in June.

For her parents to have kept secret what they told in their letters seemed strange to Diana. Maybe it was just as well that she never knew what led them to seek seclusion in Gator Swamp. They evidently had acted in what they believed were the best interests of their unborn child and themselves. And life in the swamp had been one of happiness. Until Luke Greenwood stepped in and rent her world apart.

Diana trembled and her stomach knotted tighter when she recognized that telling choices faced her. She could contact her mother's father and brother in Jamaica and her paternal grandparents or her aunts and uncles in Boston. Surely, some were still alive and at least one kinsman would issue her an invitation. Again the haunting question assailed her: Would she be welcomed? Could she find a place where she belonged?

Even while lifting the envelope containing the letters from her parents, Diana had noted gold and silver coins almos filled the rectangular metal box. Now that she had appeased her vaulting curiosity about the contents of the letters, she stilled her fears and fingered the coins. Viewing them as gifts of love, she dropped a handful into her reticule and left the others with the envelope.

That evening the sultriness of the afternoon increased, along with damp gusts of wind, but the atmosphere inside Lallage Winston's townhouse reflected only happiness. After a tasty meal of redfish cooked inside a clay pot and a host of colorful steamed vegetables tossed with butter, followed by custard topped with bananas swimming in a flaming sauce of rum and brown sugar, Diana sat in Lallage's parlor with the engaged couple. She had waited until the girls went up to bed before revealing what she had discovered that afternoon at the bank.

"I am delighted that you know how to get in touch with your family and are planning to write them," Salathiel said afterward. He smoothed his mustache with two fingers before going on. "Have you told Luke about your findings?"

"No. I've seen him only at dinner a few times since the governor's party. I can't imagine him caring, anyway. His only interest in me is my performance tomorrow evening at the Charity Ball."

Lallage and Salathiel exchanged troubled looks, then Lallage said, "Luke may seem distracted because he has much business to attend to while he's in town. I'm quite sure he would want you to tell him your good news."

Salathiel spoke up, plainly perturbed. "I can hardly fault Luke for neglecting you when perhaps Lallage and I have also been guilty. I truly thought he was still showing you about the city."

Diana shrugged and flipped her hand in casual dismissal, determined not to mar the couple's happiness. "Please don't say anymore. I'm capable of taking care of myself—thanks chiefly to the two of you."

A knock on the door came then. Homer had come to announce that Luke had sent him to deliver Diana and Salathiel back to his place. It was apparent by then that the winds were increasing and that a storm from the Gulf of Mexico threatened to strike before dawn.

Having been born and reared in a freshwater swamp less than fifty miles from the treacherous Gulf, Diana well knew what kinds of storms could roll inland. She said to Salathiel, "It was so warm I didn't bring a wrap. I'm ready to return."

Salathiel looked from Diana to his intended. "You look frightened, Lallage. Would you prefer that I not leave yet?"

"Yes. The storms are much worse here than at home." The pretty widow's face revealed her genuine fear. "I've never stayed alone here during a storm." She blushed and looked more discomfited than either Salathiel or Diana had ever before seen her. "I mean without a man under the roof."

"Perhaps I should stay on an hour or two." Salathiel harrumphed. After all, they *were* engaged. Too, there was the safety and well-being of four youngsters to consider as well as that of their mother. It pleased the nurturing part of him to think that before Easter, the pretty girls would become his daughters.

"Please spend the night. I have a guest room that can be readied in moments," Lallage pleaded when Salathiel seemed hesitant. "Luke will look after Diana. I need you."

Unable to resist his beloved's soulful plea and the wave of paternalism pairing with his deep love for her, Salathiel agreed he should stay. With Lallage at his side, he escorted Diana outside to the carriage.

Odille, dressed as always in her neat blue dress, spotless white apron, and blue tignon, was waiting in the courtyard. Once inside, Diana could hear men's voices coming from the library at the foot of the stairway. Homer volunteered to inform Luke that she had returned safely and that Salathiel would be staying overnight at the Winston townhouse. Diana agreed, telling herself that she had no desire to see the "man about town."

After Diana and Odille went through their nightly ritual, Diana slipped between the lavender-scented sheets of her bed. While the winds outside sped up and sometimes set the closed shutters to rattling, she confided to Odille much of what she had found in Philip's deposit box at the bank.

"Do you know what you'll do after your pact with Master Luke ends?" Odille asked when Diana's voice grew still.

"No, but I have better options now," Diana replied. "I'll find where I belong." Upon glimpsing a sorrowful look in Odille's dark eyes, she leaned forward enough to pat her arm. "Don't worry about me. I'll manage."

"What about the associations and friendships you've made? If you seek a new life elsewhere, can you walk away from them completely?"

"I promise to stay in touch. With Luke around, King won't miss me long. As for Tabitha and the others back in swamp country,"—her involuntary sigh revealed her anguish—"I'll miss them, but I believe Chloe can take my place with the sick. She seems to have a talent." Diana's heart pained her, but she continued relating what she had made herself accept about her inevitable desertion of the needy black people. "I overheard Luke telling Salathiel not long ago that he's going to try persuading a doctor to take up residence in Calion so that everyone in the parish can get better medical treatment."

"I think everyone will miss you dreadfully, especially the master."

Diana looked down at her hands, for a moment seeing not them, but Luke's lean face. The expressions on it were as fleeting and erratic as the winds outside—sardonic, smiling, aloof, laughing, brooding, teasing. From underneath those imagined black eyebrows his dark eyes watched her. "No, he won't. I was wrong about him needing or wanting me to be his friend. He's quite self-sufficient."

With relief, Luke heard Diana and Odille come into the house. Homer's report broke up Luke's discussion with his new valet, Isaac. After sending both men off with instructions about how to combat the approaching storm, he poured a measure of brandy and thought about the day's happenings. Things could not have gone better, if any dealings with his brother could rate such a banal term.

Frederick had sent a message earlier in the week from Mobile for Luke to meet the *Falcon* when it docked in New

Orleans. That afternoon both Frederick and Nathaniel Dace had whacked Luke on the back the minute they disembarked.

"We've come to attend the theater and opera as well as some parties," Frederick announced. He hooked a sly glance toward Luke. "I'm scared to death you might have discovered a rare beauty who might ensure your winning our wager and perhaps end my single days." Though his smile appeared facetious, Luke suspected something vulnerable lurked within his dark eyes.

Then Luke was wondering if perhaps the wisest thing might not be to present Frederick with the blooded horse of his choice right then and concede defeat. No, an inner voice warned. Frederick was clever. Once he met Diana, he would learn she was new to the city, put the facts together, and gloat. He might try charming her away from Luke immediately, as he had ably done years ago with another young woman.

Luke, who knew himself to be a coward only in matters of the heart, brushed aside questions about how anyone could charm Diana away from him when he had no hold on her heart. In fact, he had avoided her ever since the governor's party so as not to feed her imagined infatuation with him.

Alone now in his library, Luke puzzled over the way Frederick had not acted suspicious or offended about Homer driving Nathaniel and him to Ashwood, their kinsman's plantation near Lake Pontchartrain. Could it be that since his brother and Nathaniel apparently were spending most of their free time together that some of Nathaniel's innate decency had rubbed off on Frederick? Maybe now that their sister was married and Frederick was the only family member left on the huge plantation, he was becoming mature at last. He grimaced and, as welcome as they were, discarded both possibilities.

Luke was glad that on his earlier visit at Ashwood with Alexander Ashley, first cousin to Frederick and him, he had carefully prepared the way for Frederick and Nathaniel to stay in the mansion with Alexander and his family. Luke's parting words to the visitors from Mobile had said it all succinctly: "Salathiel and I will be tied up until time for the

Charity Ball. Alexander said you can ride in with Viola and him. We'll see you there.''

After Luke put away thoughts about his reunion that afternoon with Frederick and their longtime friend, Nathaniel, he crawled into bed. The velocity of the wind increased and set shutters banging, sending him to his feet.

Diana never knew what awakened her. The wind whining outside and vague dreams drifting through her mind kept riddling her already fitful sleep. Perhaps a new complaint from the shutters? The rattling of the wood slats protecting the windows did seem to be sounding a different note. When she heard the door to her bedroom open, she figured it was Odille coming to check on her. Despite her restless slumber she had no real wish to open her eyes and release her dream world.

The dim glow of candlelight crept behind her closed eyelids. ''Odille?'' Diana called.

When no answer came, Diana opened her eyes. Was she truly awake? ''How strange. I was just dreaming about you and you were wearing that very maroon-colored robe. I thought it would be Odille standing there.''

''She was on her way up, but I told her to go back to bed, that I would come to see if your shutters are still closed. Mine flew open. I'm sorry I awakened you,'' Luke replied over his shoulder while setting his candleholder on the mantel. He felt her gaze on him as he went to the windows, opened them, and tightened the latches of the shutters.

''You didn't wake me. I've not slept very soundly.''

''Are you afraid of the storm?''

''No, I've never been afraid of storms.'' She combed her fingers through her tousled hair, too drowsy to wonder at her calmness upon finding Luke in her bedroom and too drowsy to recall what Doreen had told her about him being a rake with a mistress. ''I don't wish for them, but I've always loved watching the wind dance in the trees.''

''You're a very unique young woman, Diana Hathaway.''

''Because storms don't frighten me?''

''That's one thing.''

"What's another?"

"I need to leave now so you can go back to sleep."

"I don't feel the least bit sleepy now, Luke."

"Neither do I."

Luke's thoughts lingered over his last words. No, he did not feel sleepy when he was around the beautiful young woman who had stolen away his heart. In truth, he seemed to feel more alive in her presence.

When? Luke wondered. When had Diana captured his heart? Not that it mattered. The job was done so thoroughly that he had been like a madman ever since having been forced to share her with the men on the dance floor at Governor Roman's home. How could he bear to present her tomorrow night to society, to Frederick? No, tonight, he corrected when he thought about the lateness of the hour.

A higher-pitched gust of wind whistled around the third-floor windows, testing the shutters anew and jerking Luke back to the moment. "The rain has arrived," he said when Diana's eyes widened and her gaze raced from the windows to his face. "Likely there'll be a downpour now that will pelt the tiles so hard, it might take a while to get used to the noise."

"I like the tiled roofs." She cocked her head and tucked her hair behind her ears. "Listen to the wind."

Back in swamp country in such a storm, Diana reflected, she would be hearing the wind attacking the giant trees and perhaps watching them nod and bow to each other as if preparing for some stately, primeval dance. Thunderclaps would rumble and boom almost continuously. Fiery jags of lightning would leap and split the roiling black clouds overhead, leaving behind the damp, acrid smell of sulphur.

Since no giant forest served as buffer for the tempest, Diana found little familiar about the near-deafening winds outside. The flame of the candle flickered eerily. Standing as he was with his back to the candlelight, Luke could have been no more than a dark apparition with ghostly eyes and teeth. But never a devil, she reminded herself with a twinge of guilt for her former dramatic musings. "The raindrops sound like miniature carriages rolling over the roof."

Luke chuckled softly. "I'd not care to be out there."

"Oh," Diana said, her expression mischievous, "you'd not get wet, for you'd be one of us fairies riding inside."

Luke smiled at her childish fantasy, thinking that the candlelight was transforming her pale hair into a frothy cloud touched with gold. Was she really as unafraid of the storm as she claimed? Or was she deliberately calling up pretty images to divert her fears? For a moment he let himself imagine being beside her in a secluded carriage and—"I doubt it."

"With an attitude like yours," she chided mockingly with widened eyes, "you probably deserve to get wet."

Suddenly, a fierce gust of wind blew one of the shutters open and slammed its halves against the outside wall. *Bang!* Luke dashed over to open the window and pull the shutter in again, finding the task of closing it tedious while the gale winds opposed him. Rain angled through the open window and peppered his face and robe without mercy. Behind him on the mantel the candle flame sputtered, leaned with the wind, then vanished.

"Let me help," came Diana's voice from right beside Luke's ear. Heedless of the blowing rain, she leaned out and grabbed the shutter half he had pulled almost closed and held it. "Now get the other. The wind will help me pull this one to."

Within a few drenching moments, they managed to get the shutter secured again. This time Luke fumbled in the dark until he found the safety lock near the top and slid it into place. Quickly, he repeated the action on the second shutter before it could flap open, then lowered both windows. He realized that he had meant to set the safety catches earlier, before the suddenly awakening Diana had distracted him.

She was one hell of a distraction now, Luke reflected when he turned in the darkness and collided with her damp, shivering body. How could he not put his arms around her? He trembled, afire all over. "I'll find the candle and light it. Then you can see your way back to bed before you get chilled."

"I can find the mantel easier than you," Diana said in a

late-night voice blending with the rain and the wind and not sounding at all like hers. Luke still held her lightly within his arms. She was trembling. He smelled warm and masculine and . . . dear. Blindly, breathlessly, she took a step toward freedom, but her bare feet stumbled over his and she had to clutch his arms to keep from falling.

To Luke, lost and seeking, Diana's hold on his arms served as an invitation to a haven believed gone forever. Against his will he was pulling her closer and murmuring her name hoarsely. Why was he entertaining the absurd idea that the two of them were alone in a world gone dark and that no amount of buffeting from a storm was going to shake them? Their mouths, yearning and warm, met and clung with an explosive fury akin to that roaring outside. His heartbeat pumped his dizzying emotions ever faster.

"God! How I've tried to forget how you feel in my arms," Luke whispered against her lips when their kiss lessened in ferocity and eased into one of tender hunger. The taste of her was sweetly potent, almost drugging. She smelled like woman aroused from sleep, tempting, vulnerable. She smelled like Diana, beloved Diana. Something tried to warn him to release her before he once more lost control.

Diana voiced no reply. She experienced an echo of his unspoken sentiments before she curled her hands around his ears and neck, surrendering more fully to his kisses. His mouth kept slanting across hers, back and forth with tantalizing moistness, and calling up fierce responses. When a furred note came from deep within his throat, she heard one trilling an answer in her own.

Diana knew she should step away, muster her pride, and ask him to leave. How could she make any logical moves, though, when the realization that she had lied to herself for weeks, maybe months, was storming her senses? As incredible as it seemed, she recognized that in spite of her weeks of agonizing about the matter, she had already fallen in love with Luke Greenwood. Her knees went weak.

The twin forces of Diana's discovery of her love for Luke and of their rekindled passion combined to serve as master. She did none of the things her logic would have exacted.

Instead, she ordered her knees to stiffen while she leaned closer against him, rejoicing in the tightening of his arms around her and in the feeling of his arousal against her silk-clad body.

"You kiss exactly the way I remembered," Diana whispered with what little breath she could muster. As soon as their lips parted, she had dropped her head to nestle underneath his chin. While quivering on the inside from joy, she rubbed her flushing face against his robe until it slipped askew and rewarded her with a resting place against his bare skin.

Through the mat of chest curls pressing against her face, Diana could hear Luke's heart thundering against her own. For the first time she became aware that he, too, was trembling. Her bare feet still nestled half on top of his. Both were damp from the raindrops blown on them earlier, but the air was not cold. In fact, it seemed laden with the heat repressed within two yearning bodies.

As if designed to whip up deliberately concealed thoughts of how Diana likely was enamored of him because she never had known any other young men, her words about remembering his kisses quelled Luke's leaping passion. They brought him up short. He dropped his arms and moved toward the fireplace, feeling as gawky as an untried boy.

Luke agonized that in the first place, he had been wrong to feed Diana's imaginings that she might be in love with him by kissing her. Worse, he had played the deuce with his long-curbed desire to make love to her again, for now his groin was aching and he was finding it hellish to think of much else but his fiery blood. With his voice failing to come out gruff and sensible as he intended, Luke said, "I really should light the candle and let you go back to sleep."

While Luke groped around for the candle and the flint and steel lying on the mantel, then lighted the wick, Diana stood in quandary. Her father had told her that a man's actions often tell more about him than his words. Could Luke have kissed her as he had, made love to her that night, and not felt anything at all? His declaration that he had tried to forget how she felt in his arms—was that something an uncaring man would say? Would he have come into her bedroom to ensure her safety if she was nothing to him but a responsibility?

Diana surmised that Luke could have allowed Odille to carry out that task rather than have sent the slave back to her room as he said he had done. Then she was recalling his refusal to tell that she could verify his whereabouts when Maynard Oates had made his wild accusations. She could not forget his anguished plea that night on the stairs for Odille to tell her not to hate him. Hate him? Why, she loved that man more than she loved herself! Tears for her past asinine misconceptions about Luke stung behind her eyelids.

Across the room he stood in the circle of candlelight watching her with the exact unfathomable expression she had observed countless times on his handsome face. Why had she fallen so madly in love with such a complex man?

Luke kept his gaze averted from the bed where he longed to be with the beautiful young woman who was sending him puzzled looks. How was it that Diana's proud stance seemed even more an intrinsic part of her as she stood with her little bare feet peeping from underneath her clinging nightgown? Flickering candlelight danced in her gloriously tousled hair. He drank in the way it framed her lovely features and strayed forward in pale wisps over her full breasts. "I'm sorry I disturbed you. The storm seems to be moving off now. Good night."

Diana fought the impulse to run to Luke, barefooted and begging for answers. She wanted to throw her arms around him, confess she loved him. She wanted to tell him why she did not believe he was as indifferent to her as he tried to appear. Would a man's eyes and mouth appear as soft and vulnerable if he was not looking at a woman holding a space in his heart? Not once since he had come into the room had his voice sounded normal. If there was one thing Diana had become an expert on, she mused as her heart filled with promise at each thought, it was the way Luke Greenwood talked.

Suddenly Diana felt wise. Back in her cabin when she was flirting with the idea that she might be falling in love with Luke, she had entertained the thought that she could win his ove. She embraced the intriguing idea again. In time, he would see as plainly as she did that they were destined for each other. Would the telling moment come at the Charity Ball?

Diana mustered a shaky smile. "Thank you, Luke, for making sure I was safe. Good night."

Twenty

On the evening of the Charity Ball, Diana jiggled impa
tiently on the stool before her dressing table, feeling the brush
of curls on her single bare shoulder. "Odille, my hair looks
fine. Isn't it almost time to go downstairs to meet Luke?"

"It's early yet," Odille replied. "I want to trail a few more
wispy curls on your temples and the nape of your neck."

Soon the quadroon eyed the upswept section of silvery
blonde hair with approval. She smiled when she saw how the
tiny jewels sparkled amidst the shining curls fastened at the
back of Diana's head before their ends spiraled down in
seemingly aimless, airy profusion. "When all that jewelry
came this afternoon, I wasn't expecting to find the long string
of little diamonds and sapphires for your hair. I heard you
telling Miss Lallage about the other pieces that came."

"It was a surprise to me, too." Diana gazed into the mirror
at the ornate necklace of diamonds and sapphires, amazed at
how its addition turned her gown of white silk into a festive
costume.

Back when the seamstresses were making the gown with
its single shoulder drape, Diana had commented on its rather
austere, draped styling. Lallage had told her the style was
Grecian and that Luke had suggested it. Luke. Her pulse
drummed faster. Only a man caring deeply for a woman

· 308 ·

would have taken such interest in her appearance. She felt dizzy just thinking about seeing him soon, about having him see her in the gown and jewelry he had chosen.

Diana said, "Wasn't Luke thoughtful to provide me with such elegant things to wear tonight? The ring keeps stealing my attention." The candlelight loosed a prism of rainbow colors as she looked down at the twinkling diamonds edging the large rectangular sapphire. She waggled her right hand and smiled at the new display of brilliance. What a lovely day they had spent together! She knew well that the purchase of jewelry had nothing to do with the excitement she had shared with Luke.

Even when Diana had waked that morning to clear skies, she knew she had been right in acknowledging to herself in the stormy night that she was deliriously in love with the man she had once reviled as her captor. Her words came out as a kind of litany. "Luke really is a kind and generous man."

"Yes, and he's going to like the way you look."

"I hope so." Diana leaned close to the mirror, biting her lips lightly, as Lallage had taught her, so as to enhance their natural pinkness. "Odille, I feel very special."

Diana fought the urge to giggle and hug Odille and skip around the bedroom. Surely, Luke would approve of her this evening. The heartbreak and upheaval in her life during the past several months would be worth the pain if she could live up to his expectations and pass as a young lady of culture and good breeding. Though she still could not imagine why for her to do so obviously meant much to Luke, it had become her primary goal. "I want Luke to be so proud of the way I look and act that he'll wonder if I'm not somebody brand new."

While Odille rested a fond gaze on the lovely young blonde, she said, "Are you positive that you won't need me to help you get ready for bed? I can wait till later to go spend the night with Mrs. Frontage's grandchildren."

"No, I like the idea that you'll be visiting with the children you've known since their birth. When their mothers brought them over this week, I fell in love with all five. They seemed excited that December is here and you're going to spend the night and tell them stories while their parents go to the Charity Ball. I could tell they've missed you terribly.''

Odille straightened her tignon, adjusted one of her swinging earrings, and glanced at Diana's small reticule and ermine-lined cape lying on the bed. "I'll wait and leave after you do. Charles Street is only a few blocks away. It's still a while before time for you to go downstairs.''

"Botheration! I can manage nicely. Run along.'' Diana rushed to throw her arms around the tall quadroon. "Thanks for helping me look the way Luke wants. Have fun.''

After Odille left, Diana paced in front of the fireplace once, twice. Ignoring her cape and purse, she hurried to the stair-way. It might be too early to leave for the ball, but maybe Luke was already dressed and downstairs. He had been gone all day again. Her desire to rest her eyes on the man she loved had her keyed up as tightly as the strings on the viola that he had shown her at the governor's party. Wasn't it uncanny, how nearly all of her thoughts since that June night in some way included Luke Greenwood?

While Diana, her head airy from love and expectation, was descending the last flight of stairs, she heard men's voices drifting from the library. She noted the double doors were not quite closed and almost turned back. Luke and Salathiel were engaged in what sounded like a heated conversation. She paused, their words freezing her motionless.

"Now that you have broached the subject of Diana and asked my advice, at least have the decency to admit I warned you about meddling in her life,'' Salathiel was saying in a harsh tone. "Why you have persisted in this absurd wager with Frederick is beyond my understanding.''

Luke said something Diana could not make out, but the Englishman's answer floated out to where she stood frozen on the third step with her mouth open and her pulse thundering.

Salathiel said, "For God's sake, Luke, it has been ages since Frederick stole Sylvia Lindstrom from you and married her. Granted, his actions were despicable, both toward her and you, but what good is served by your holding a grudge all this time? Ever since she died over five years ago, you have kept your head in the clouds. The woman was no saint"—Diana heard dissent from Luke, but only for a moment—"and she obviously knew what she was doing when she chose to marry Frederick over you. What were you then but a schoolboy? Worshiping a memory, and an imperfect one at that, and seeking revenge against your brother has warped your thinking far too long. It's time for you to face up to the truth."

"I gather you have no trouble recognizing truth," Luke retorted loud enough for Diana to hear easily. She guessed he might have turned toward the door. "I tried all day while with Frederick and Nathaniel to back out of our bet, but he was adamant about the time extending to the first of the year. If I didn't know better, I would think he's truly hoping to meet a woman like Diana. He seems different somehow. I don't like this unexpected turn. When he sees Diana, he's going to be enchanted. Every man there will be."

"That should make you elated. You managed to find a beautiful young woman and turn her into what you figured would bring Frederick to his knees, all for the sake of winning a fine horse. Do not expect me to congratulate you. Today my conscience demanded I tell Lallage the entire sordid reason for your cold transformation of Diana Hathaway into live bait. She was as appalled as I that you could be so unfeeling about manipulating such an innocent."

Devastated at what she was hearing, Diana gripped the handrailing tighter. Her world was crashing! Once she had fallen from a tree and felt the same jarring loss of breath and orientation. A searing knot climbed from her chest to her throat and threatened to choke her. Her suddenly boneless knees prevented her from dashing back upstairs and giving in to the scalding tears prickling behind her eyelids. How could she have been misled into thinking Luke was kind? She felt a kinship with the unseeing statue in the courtyard.

"Damn it, man!" Luke exclaimed. "I'm not looking for congratulations. You did right to tell Lallage. I'll offer her my apologies in private. I intend to make Diana understand. You should have forced me to let her go."

"Spare me, please. I tried more than once."

Diana recalled the night she had overheard the men talking at Fairfield about Luke's plans to settle a sum on her after their pact ended. Had she begun listening earlier or later that night, she might could have learned then what was going on and confronted Luke. She felt sick all over. Luke's voice lured her back to the awful present.

"Salathiel, you worked with Diana more than anyone else."

"You bloody well know why," Salathiel shot back. "You were threatening to take over her lessons yourself and you, my boy, had the poor girl frightened to death. I could not bear standing by and watching you bully her further."

"I wasn't bullying her. It was just that I suspected she was deceiving us—which, of course, we found out was true."

"Can you blame her? I admire Diana for trying to put a stop to the ridiculous business of transforming her into what you wanted her to be just so you could parade her around at the ball tonight in front of Frederick. You never once intended to punish any of the slaves on the place or to send her to jail either. Perhaps I was at fault by not telling her right off what you were up to and then calling your hand."

After a silence Salathiel continued. "However, I admit she charmed me and I found myself drawn into wanting to help her become literate and socially acceptable. Later, when the truth about her background came out, all of us were too caught up in the farce to back away. By then she seemed to want nothing so much as to please you—not that you appeared to notice. I accept a share of blame, but the bulk is yours."

"I'm suffering enough without your lecture. God! Can you know what it's been like to be around her lately and see the trust in her eyes, hear her thank me for. . . . You were right in saying I would be punished. I'm punished every time she looks at me as if she thinks I'm wonderful."

"I have suspected since the governor's party the other night that Diana is in love with you."

Diana's head lifted from where it had drooped lower at each overheard word. She clapped her hand over her trembling mouth to keep from crying out. *No!* she wanted to yell as her stomach knotted up in protest at what Salathiel wa saying, *don't tell the arrogant man that. I'll forget him and never give him another thought.* She felt naked and achingly alone.

"The same thought has crossed my mind," Luke was saying, "but I know that's impossible. She's never known any other man and she doesn't know what kind of man might make her happy. I don't deserve her love."

"That may very well be true," Salathiel agreed.

Diana felt hot tears stinging her cheeks. Drat the sanctimonious Luke Greenwood! Her knees seemed to be regaining some starch and she turned toward her bedroom.

Even as the tear-blinded Diana inched back up the stairs, she heard Salathiel's clipped voice going on. "You have not helped matters by ignoring the messages from the young men leaving their cards here."

"None of them are worthy of Diana."

Her vision blurred by tears and unable to listen to another word, Diana crept on up the stairs after Luke's last comment. Worthy? Bloody balls of fire! She pounded the handrailing with her fist so hard it smarted. *What did he know about being worthy?*

Mental images of her safe, beloved swamp barraged Diana with each step she took. A near-crippling homesickness swept over her. How was it possible that every one of Luke's actions apparently had been carried out with no consideration of the fact that she was human, with feelings and dreams of her own? All that gambling rake cared about was winning some stupid bet. How degrading that she had fallen in love with such a monster—no, devil, a wayward part of her insisted—and had given herself to him.

The old tale circulating among the blacks about the hoodoo woman who had slept with the devil rose up and taunted her. That woman, or so Tabitha had said when Diana questioned her, had ended up living in hell. A strangled sob escaped when she at last reached her bedroom.

Back in the library Salathiel took his time before replying to Luke's added remarks about the unworthiness of the bachelors who had left cards. "Is Frederick worthy of Diana?"

"God, no!"

"Your dilemma seems to be growing as time runs out."

Though Salathiel's heart had pained him since the beginning of their conversation about Diana, he had disguised his abiding love for his troubled younger friend and allowed his intense feelings to flavor his remarks. Reckoning time had been late in catching up to Luke.

Salathiel thought about how since he had fallen in love with Lallage, he no longer shied away from emotional confrontations. Lallage made such explosions seem acceptable, even desirable. Perhaps, he reflected guiltily, if he had not clung so tenaciously to his old belief that more harm than good resulted from such bursts of intense thoughts and feeling, he could have faced up to Luke that very first day after he brought Diana to Fairfield and confided his dastardly plan.

Smoothing his mustache and glancing at the clock on the mantel, Salathiel harrumphed and said in a kinder tone, "It's almost time for Homer to bring the carriage around. Lallage will be expecting us, and Diana will be coming down soon."

Luke broke the ensuing silence with a deep-voiced plea. "Help me, Salathiel. What am I to do?"

"What do you want to do?"

"I want to tell her I love her and ask her to marry me right away. I want to apologize for wronging her."

"At last! I detect a trace of the Luke Greenwood I feared had disappeared forever. What in the bloody deuce are you waiting for? She will be down shortly."

"Don't you agree that I owe it to Diana to let her meet the unmarried men at the ball and encourage her to let them call? I would be piling wrong atop wrong to make my feelings known to her until I'm sure she has other choices. The though of others around her tears me apart, but the knowledge tha I've abused her pains me even worse."

"For a young man of considerable intelligence about mos matters, you sound like a blithering idiot when it comes t dealing with this woman you say you love. When she come down, grab her and tell her the whole sordid mess."

Upstairs in her bedroom Diana prowled from one side t the other, fuming. Anger had helped her chase away her tears She would leave, go as far away as her money would tak her. No, she must stay. Never would she give Luke an excuse to harass her black friends. Before she left his roof for good, she would live up to their pact in such grand fashion that he might someday feel regret over her disappearance. Oh, how she latched on to the idea that in some way she could inflict a degree of hurt on Luke Greenwood!

Thoughts of leaving behind forever all that was dear and familiar in St. Christopher Parish tore at Diana's slowly returning composure. Her pretty mouth pursed in renewed pique as she brushed away the last trace of tears. Luke had invaded her life and turned it inside out. *Unfair!*

Everything was unfair, Diana's thoughts ran on as she snatched up the small reticule and the luxurious black silk cape with its ermine lining and trim. It was unfair that Luke had managed to impose his will on Salathiel and her. Too, it was unfair that until this evening, Salathiel apparently had lacked courage enough to face up to Luke. Drat all men!

Diana caught sight of her image in the mirror then and paused. Was this grim-faced stranger the butterfly that had been forced from its unadorned carapace? She abhorred the cold, blue eyes. They reminded her of a pair of near-black ones that often had borne a similar, detached look.

Well, Diana conceded when she marshaled her thoughts and watched the alien, brooding look fade from her face, the botched affair had produced a few known positives. Lallage and Salathiel had come to know each other in a short time and had fallen in love. Barring those first weeks, her time with her tutors had been marvelous fun. She felt a glow of affection for the older couple who had devoted so much of their time and talents to turning her into the kind of woman who apparently was supposed to bring Frederick Greenwood to his knees.

Thanks to Lallage and Salathiel, Diana reflected, she now felt comfortable in society and more knowledgeable about the world outside Gator Swamp. She did not feel a speck of guilt for excluding Luke as one who had contributed greatly to her metamorphosis. In fact, she refused to let his name surface.

Not to be overlooked as positive results were her friendships with Odille and Doreen Oates. Since she had been planning yet dreading a trip to New Orleans before the year was out to examine the contents of her father's deposit box, Diana acknowledged her gratitude for her new friends' preparing her well for visiting the city. She now knew about her family and the money making it possible for her to strike out on her own.

Diana swallowed hard and gave one last look in the mirror before marching downstairs. No outward trace of her tears remained. She vowed to make the last evening spent with Luke Greenwood one that neither would ever forget.

Luke stood at the bottom of the staircase looking up when Diana rounded the last landing. "Hello, Diana. I've been waiting for this moment."

"Yes," Diana replied, sending him a crippled smile, "I can imagine you have." Her first sight of Luke since he left her bedroom after the storm knocked her nigh breathless. For a moment she could not move. She never before had seen him, or any other man, dressed entirely in white. The sight dazzled her. How could he appear so handsome on the outside?

Luke's breath lodged back in his throat. No matter that candlelight from a wall sconce danced in and out of the myriad diamonds and sapphires in Diana's pale hair, around her neck, on her arm and right finger, all that Luke's gaze could center on was her beautiful face. Was that fright darkening her widely spaced eyes and slowing her descent?

Luke decided that Diana had overcome her fright because she moved on down the staircase, her every step sending his heartbeat scudding. His brave, beautiful Diana. Her one-shouldered gown of heavy white silk, pristine in its Grecian draping held close underneath her full breasts and across her lower rib cage with diametrically crossed silver braid, flowed like liquid along with her long-limbed, slender body. Never had she appeared more like a goddess. His love for her emanated throughout his being and struck him dumb.

With the haughty air of the goddess Luke was imagining, Diana, her head high, moved regally down the stairs, dragging behind her with one careless hand her ermine-lined cape of black silk. The elegant garment whispered against the stairs as if it were no more than a trifling rag trailing along.

"Where's Salathiel?" Diana asked sweetly when she stepped onto the waxed brick floor of the foyer and faced Luke. Amidst a susurrus flurry of silken garments spiced with alluring perfume, she gathered her cape over one arm. "I want to try out my flirting for him and see what he thinks. You were most kind to let me practice on you the night of the governor's party. I've meant to ask ever since if I was convincing, but"—her dark eyelashes fanned downward, then opened enough to reveal disquieting blue pools—"you always seem to be out."

When Luke continued to stare at her as if he were seeing her for the first time, Diana wondered if her quaking innards would ever again be the same. Had she shocked him speechless? Good! She babbled on. "I want to learn more about the ways of bachelors so that when I meet possible suitors tonight, I'll know better how to please them. Do you have suggestions?"

Luke's countenance revealed inner agitation and his hand moved up to rest momentarily on his chin.

With her eyes opened wide and her mien contrite, Diana continued. "Have I said something wrong?" She watched his long fingers caress his chin, almost getting lost in the close-up sight of his well-shaped lips. He smelled like new clothing and fresh-shaven, virile male all dressed up for an exciting evening. "I hope not. You're the only young man I know. I had hoped some of the men I met at Governor Roman's would call on me and teach me more about what men like."

The thought that Luke's brother, Frederick, had once hurt him by stealing his beloved rose up and almost made Diana feel sorry for the black-haired man staring at her with a pained expression. Hard behind that thought came the memory of how cruelly Luke had used her to try getting even with Frederick.

With her chin lifted a degree higher, Diana hugged her cape close against her churning middle and pushed ahead with her plan to erase any notions Luke might entertain that she was in love with him. "Didn't you indicate you wanted everyone at the ball tonight to find me attractive?"

In a fuzzy quandary over his reaction to seeing Diana and hearing her inexplicably inane chatter, Luke searched for an answer, unsure he had found one when he replied, "Yes. Something like that."

What did Diana mean about "practicing" on him? Luke reflected irritably. Had he misread her attempts to play the role of a fashionable coquette according to Lallage's standards as signs that she might be thinking she was in love with him? His face burned at the possibility and he rammed his hands deep into the pockets of his white trousers. He should not have confided his suspicion to Salathiel. Certainly, Diana was not sending him any looks at the moment but those of a beautiful, insouciant young woman conversing with her escort.

Where in hell, Luke wondered, had Diana gotten the monstrous idea that she was supposed to court the attentions of eligible bachelors? True, he had decided she needed to know some other young men before he declared his love for her. He had even agreed with Salathiel back at Fairfield that New Orleans was a likely spot for her to find a husband. But for Diana to plunge into the ticklish matter of encouraging suitors was not what he had in mind. No, indeed!

"My dear," Salathiel said then as he came hurrying inside from the courtyard, "you look divine." He bent over Diana's hand and, in the way they had practiced, she lifted it for his polite kiss. She was achingly aware that Luke still watched her with his brooding expression. Was he afraid she might not charm Frederick and ensure his winning the wager?

Diana's head was spinning. It never settled down during the carriage ride to Lallage's townhouse, or afterward on the short drive to the Orleans Ballroom on Orleans between Royal and Bourbon. An apparent addition to the Théâtre d'Orléans, the ballroom presented a dull facade lacking any adorning graces of architecture.

Once the foursome went inside, however, Diana could see why, according to the radiant Lallage, the Orleans Ballroom had been the center of numerous elegant dances since its erection some dozen years earlier. "Oh, Luke," she whispered, forgetting for the moment that she was angry with him, "look at the crystal chandeliers and the marvelous paintings."

"I like the statuary, too," Luke replied. Diana's sudden reversion to her natural enthusiastic self was soothing his ruffled feelings. "Your beauty outshines that of the lovely ladies in marble."

Diana, conceding that in matters pertaining to him she had been as blind as the statues, felt her face flush. "Thank you. I'm glad that you're not disappointed in me on this last evening of our agreement." When Luke appeared about to say something weighty, she burst out with more praise for the long ballroom with its lofty carved ceiling, its inlays and paneling of fine woods, ending lamely with, "The balcony is nice."

"It looks out over the gardens behind the St. Louis Cathedral," Luke explained. "Sometimes those in mourning gather there to watch the dancing and listen to the music."

Diana saw dark-clad groups sitting at tables on the balcony, disappointed not to gain a glimpse of Doreen and her relatives. Maybe they were not coming.

Then it was time for the two couples to move ahead in the line, allow attendants to relieve the women of their wraps, and be announced to those already gathered on the ballroom floor in talking clusters. The orchestra was tuning up from across the long room while a white-coated, white-gloved man standing on the raised entry read from the invitations handed him and called out the names of each couple.

"Miss Diana Hathaway, escorted by Mr. Lucius Greenwood," the man announced in resonant tones.

Standing with her arm looped through Luke's, Diana felt the force of innumerable eyes washing over her. For a moment she leaned against Luke and felt faint. What was she doing in such a grand place?

Smoothly, Luke's hand closed over hers where it clutched his arm. Even through their white gloves, she felt his touch transmit both reassurance and a surge of excitement. Her eyes met his and for an instant she glimpsed within those dark depths that velvety look she favored, the one that made him look vulnerable and caring. "Don't worry," she whispered in a stricken tone, "I'll live up to my part of our pact."

By the time Lallage, resplendent in a purple gown with a daring décolletage, and Salathiel followed Diana and Luke down to the dance floor, two tall men were wending toward them through the gathering crowd. Diana almost gasped when she saw the dark features and athletic build of one of the handsome men. She knew she was looking at Luke's brother, Frederick.

Soon the six of them were talking amiably while the orchestra completed its final tuning. Both Frederick and Nathaniel Dace seemed overjoyed upon meeting Lallage and learning that their former tutor was to be married in the spring to the vivacious redheaded widow. Other fashionably dressed people drifted over to join the lively group and meet the newcomers.

Diana was aware that Luke became edgy, almost terse during his exchanges with his brother. Though Frederick seemed at ease with the others, to her surprise he became shy and somewhat tongue-tied each time that she attempted to talk with him. Could his apparent reticence around women have caused him to challenge Luke to find him an attractive mate far from Mobile? Remembering her own discomfort when she first began conversing with large numbers of people, Diana listened to her tender heart and sent the ever-watchful Frederick a compassionate smile.

Diana discovered she liked talking with Nathaniel of the easy smile and soft drawl. Once when she glanced toward the balcony and at last saw Doreen with her cousins and exchanged smiles with her friend, she noted Nathaniel's gaze following hers. She explained about Doreen and the period of mourning for her brother and stepfather.

"Your friend is beautiful, even from this distance," Nathaniel replied. "Will you please introduce us?"

After a brief consultation with Luke, Nathaniel was leading Diana up the stairway to the balconied area where Doreen sat with her aunt and uncle and her cousins. Once greetings and introductions were over and the others carried on a quiet conversation with Diana, Nathaniel asked Doreen, "Could you perhaps dance with me at least once?"

"Thank you, but no," Doreen said, the flush of pink on her cheeks revealing her pleasure from the handsome young man's invitation. "I promised my mother I'd do nothing but sit on the balcony and listen to the music."

"If it pleases your uncle, I beg leave to join your party and do likewise," Nathaniel said, his admiring gaze never leaving Doreen's pretty features.

After Nathaniel gained the permission sought, he escorted Diana back to Luke and his group and returned to the balcony. Diana realized then that Frederick was studying her somewhat secretly. Though his exchanges with her still seemed shackled, he was responding more easily to her talk about the newest waltzes from Vienna. From up close she could see that despite the similarity of color, his dark eyes differed from Luke's in the way they were set in his head. His mouth lacked the sensuousness of Luke's.

From out of nowhere the idea struck Diana that while both Greenwood brothers were strikingly handsome, Luke's presence was far more dynamic. Had such always been the case? If so, had the older brother sensed it and perhaps felt intimidated?

"May I claim the honor of the first dance, Miss Hathaway?" Frederick asked when the orchestra ceased its discordant tuning. He smiled down at her with open admiration.

"You may not," Luke said, reaching for Diana's hand and gripping it firmly. "Find your own partner. I escorted the most beautiful woman here and I shall dance with her." With Diana in tow he followed Lallage and Salathiel out onto the floor of quarter-sawed oak, the one that Lallage had told the group was known as the finest dance floor in the United States.

Diana caught up the bottom of her full, flowing skirt in her right hand and went into Luke's arms, a perplexed look on her countenance. His nearness, his unexpected claim on her, and the suddenly singing violins fogged her mind. She had no wish to let him know she was aware of his bet with Frederick, but she was dying to ask why he was dancing with her when she was supposed to be charming his brother.

Before Diana could untangle her thoughts, the combined magic of the candlelit ballroom, the Strauss waltz, and her handsome dancing partner swept her up. She smiled up at Luke. He outdid her hesitant smile with one of dazzling brilliance. She meant to drop her gaze. His held hers so steadily that she forgot her intentions, forgot everything but being in his arms.

After Luke tightened his hold on Diana's back, he whirled her around in perfect waltz step until she felt a dizziness that she doubted came totally from their movements. His smile mesmerized her; his eyes sent messages that intrigued.

Diana found herself wishing that she had only that moment met the tall, dark-haired man. Wouldn't it be wonderful if all they knew about each other was that they liked to dance together? What fun it would be to get to know him without the hindrances suffered because he had held her prisoner. How marvelous if he could like her for herself and not because she might bedazzle his brother and lead him to win a bet.

"You don't seem as happy as you did at the governor's party," Luke said when the music stopped.

"You're imagining things." She felt her cheeks warm up.

"I hope so. I can't think of anything I want more than for you to be happy." His smile was slow and devastating.

Diana cocked her head and said pertly, "I'm beginning to think women aren't the only ones who know how to flirt on the dance floor."

Luke had been noting throughout the waltz that at each movement of her head, candlelight from the overhead chandeliers set the tiny diamonds in her elaborate coiffure to sparkling and winking. "Are you objecting?"

Was she? Diana thought of how heady it had been to have him appear fascinated with her while they danced. "No, just curious as to why you're wasting your talents on me."

"Have you ever considered it's because I think you're the most beautiful, desirable woman I've ever seen?" Luke's gaze wandered lazily to her bare shoulder, then downward.

"Never." She felt as if he had touched her with more than a look. Every inch of her felt keyed up. Tingly.

"Then you're not as clever as I had believed." Didn't she realize that since their entrance she had captured almost everyone's attention, especially Frederick's? Obviously, she had not noticed that he himself had been unable to look anywhere but at her. He felt his pulse still dancing.

His smile strained, Frederick came then to where they stood. "Now may I dance with Miss Hathaway?"

"Call me Diana, please," Diana said. What was bringing that speculative look to Frederick's features as he studied first her face and then Luke's?

"I was hoping you'd find another partner," Luke said in a belligerent tone.

"I want to dance with the lovely Diana." Frederick drank in the sight of the gorgeous blonde whose presence had filled him with awe since his first glimpse of her. Like many of the others full of questions about the stunning stranger, he wanted to know all about Diana. He wanted to call on her.

Frederick judged from Diana's unique gown, splendid jewels, and regal bearing that she must be of genteel, wealthy parentage. At first he had suspected Luke of bringing Diana to the ball to dangle before him as proof that a young woman existed who could charm him. But after her company had so surprisingly rattled his composure and curbed his customary glib tongue, he was wondering if Luke's words about certain women being able to bring men to their knees might not be true—and prophetic. Diana Hathaway was that kind of woman.

"Perhaps later, dear brother," Luke called over his shoulder as another waltz began and he whirled Diana away.

"You're acting like a lunatic," she said when she managed to catch her breath.

"I very well may be one. After all, we did meet in the moonlight." He winked at her. "Are you afraid of lunatics?"

Diana's eyes stretched open wider. She was not imagining it. Luke *was* flirting with her. But why? "Lallage might have apoplexy if we don't dance with other people soon." Her gaze flitted across the crowded room until it rested on the smiling faces of Lallage and Salathiel. "She told me only engaged or married couples dance more than one number in succession."

"Are you saying you prefer dancing with Frederick?"

Diana faltered, relieved that Luke was a master at leading and helped her recapture the waltz rhythm. Why should she allow his sudden flirting with her to gloss over the grievances she had against him? She wanted the evening to end so that she could get on with forgetting what Luke Greenwood even looked like. Being held in his arms and recalling all the other times he had held her was creating chaos inside. The sooner she tried to charm Frederick, the sooner the evening would end. "You said once that when we came to New Orleans, you'd like for me to find suitors. Frederick is unmarried, isn't he?"

"Yes. His wife died several years ago." Luke wondered if the blow to his heart and his pride showed. Again, he had been wrong in thinking Diana entertained any kind of special feelings for him. Why, he had no better chance of winning her love than anyone else falling under her spell. Maybe less.

Realizing that his earlier thoughts about giving Diana the opportunity to meet other men were honorable and that few of his deeds concerning her had even a nodding acquaintance with honor, Luke swallowed his pride. The moment they had entered the ballroom, the need for Diana to respond to his overtures this evening had consumed him. Then he could have confessed all, his love included. He would permit her to have this evening, but tomorrow. . . .

Luke cleared his throat. "Diana, I apologize for being dense. After this dance I'll release you to Frederick and all the other bachelors." He tendered her a lopsided smile before pulling her close enough to whisper, "I don't have to like it though, and I bloody well won't."

Luke's decision evidently pleased all of the unmarried men at the Charity Ball, as well as some of the married ones. He made himself dance with former acquaintances and pretend he was not watching every move the beauteous Diana made as she went from the arms of one man to those of another. Did she have to bestow so many smiles? Luke's misery drove him to seek out some of his older friends who stood smoking cigars and talking business in the courtyard opening off the ballroom.

Frederick hovered on the edges of the ballroom floor, coming alive only when gaining another dance with Diana.

"Please tell me I may call on you tomorrow evening," Frederick said while leading Diana through a minuet. When she made no reply, he added, "You did say you're not promised."

"That's true, but you know nothing about me."

"I know and like what I see. Tell me where you live."

"What if I'm not what I appear?" She glanced toward the open doors leading to the courtyard. What was keeping Luke out there so long? Once he had relinquished her to dance with others more than an hour ago, he seemed to have forgotten she was present. Likely he was relieved to have seen Frederick was paying her attention and was already celebrating his victory.

"I wouldn't care."

"Deception wouldn't bother you?"

"What kind of woman are you, Diana Hathaway? Here I've been throwing myself at your feet all evening and you do nothing but discourage me and hint that you have a mysterious past. I assure you that mine will cancel yours. Don't you like me?"

"I like you well enough."

"But you like another better. Is that why you won't permit me to call?"

Diana shook her head in denial.

"Have pity on a widower. I may have waited until late to face up to it, but I want to find love and companionship." The minuet ended and he guided Diana toward the privacy offered by huge pots of ferns decorating one corner of the ballroom.

Diana had noted that throughout the evening, Frederick had become as easy around her as he appeared to be with others. Did that mean he trusted her now? She detested the thought of half-truths and recalled how from the beginning, they had complicated her relationship with Luke. "I won't agree for you to call because I know about the wager between you and Luke. I feel terrible about having any part in it.''

When Frederick showed his surprise, Diana hurried on. She did not hush until she had told a brief version of how she happened to be attending the Charity Ball that December night.

''I'm flattered that you confided in me, Diana. You seem to have restored my faith in beautiful young women.'' Frederick cleared his throat, shocked that her story explained many things about Luke that he had not understood, perhaps had not wanted to understand. He had learned something about himself, too, and he did not like it. ''To be perfectly honest, a rarity for me, I've been prepared to concede defeat since we first met. I can think of nothing I'd like more than to stay in New Orleans until I might win your affection.''

''Don't say that, please. I can't think of such matters now. I've a purse full of cards from nice young men whom I have no plans ever to see. The evening has distressed me.''

Frederick saw the inner turmoil in Diana's blue eyes and felt strangely moved to be considering the feelings of someone other than himself. Maybe there was hope for him yet. ''Tell me how I may help.''

''Will you take me to Luke's townhouse? I must get away.''

After Frederick agreed, he and Diana paused beside Lallage and Salathiel, who were holding hands and sipping champagne near the main entry.

''Yes,'' Salathiel assured Diana when she made her plea. ''I will tell Luke you were feeling tired and that you asked Frederick to escort you to the townhouse.'' He tried catching Luke's attention out in the courtyard but when he recognized one of the men in conversation with him as the owner of a fleet of riverboats, he gave up. ''Are you sure you will be all right? Let me fetch Luke—''

''No, please,'' Diana insisted. ''Frederick can return to the ball before Luke is even aware I've gone.''

Lallage leaned her head close to Diana's, asking in a private voice, ''Is something wrong, darling?''

''No,'' Diana replied. ''I'm ready to leave, that's all.''

Lallage sent her a compassionate look, then gave her a quick hug. "Salathiel and I are ecstatic over your smashing success this evening. We adored seeing the line forming to dance with our belle. The young men are going to be devastated that you're slipping away before the dancing is over. All of my friends have asked me to bring you calling."

"I'm glad I pleased you," Diana said. The strain of the evening weighed more heavily on her with each passing moment. She included both Lallage and Salathiel in her parting words, "Thank you for being my friends. Good night."

Relieved that the engaged couple were too besotted with each other to pursue further their apparent concern for her, Diana avoided their baffled, penetrating gazes and turned away. A discreet wave at Doreen and her party on the balcony—Nathaniel Dace was still there—and the beautiful blonde who had dazzled everyone during the first part of the Charity Ball swept away on Frederick's arm.

Twenty-One

Diana refused to grant Frederick's repeated requests to call on her. After thanking him for his courtesy and urging him to return to the Charity Ball, she left him at the entry to Luke's townhouse.

A hazy plan came together in Diana's troubled mind. Dare she awaken Francy and ask her help?

"Odille," Diana exclaimed when she entered her bedroom and saw the quadroon. "I thought you were spending the night with the Frontage grandchildren."

"I figured you might need my help and I returned after they went to sleep." Already she was helping Diana remove her necklace. "You're home early. It's only midnight."

While Odille helped her shed the beautiful jewelry and gown, Diana explained how she now had lived up to her pact with Luke. In a voice heavy with pain, she added, "I hate admitting that I'm in love with Luke. I must get away."

"Running won't solve anything. I can't believe he meant to harm you. Perhaps if you wait and talk—"

"He would only feel sorry for me after making such a jumble of my life." Diana reached for her purse holding the coins brought from the box at the bank, her thoughts racing ahead with her plans. "Father often quoted a speech from Shakespeare as one of his favorite philosophies. 'To thine own self be true,' it goes, then ends with 'Thou canst not then be false to any man.' I've not been true to myself. Until I am, I'm not ready to deal with my feelings for Luke. Right now I despise his behavior. Will you please help me get away?''

Odille demurred at first, but by the time Diana had finished her plea for help in escaping Luke and putting in order her thoughts about him and her future, she agreed.

"I don't like maybe putting you in jeopardy for helping me," Diana said when it was time to go. She blinked away her tears and hugged the older woman.

Odille returned her embrace, then said, "Don't fret. Nobody saw me come back here, and we'll make sure nobody sees us leave."

Luke Greenwood carried on like a lunatic when he returned to his townhouse within the hour and found Diana's bedroom empty except for the collection of jewelry and clothing he had given her . . . and a sheet of paper lying on the mantel.

Dear Salathiel: I beg you and the others not to search for me. I'll contact you when I get my life in order. Forgive me for any pain I may have caused.

Diana.

Cursing under his breath that Diana had not addressed her terse farewell to him, Luke summoned Homer, Isaac, and Francy. When all declared they were unaware that Diana had returned earlier, much less that she had gone out again, their irate master found no reason to doubt their honesty.

Luke raved. He ranted. After deciding against going to the police until he had explored every realistic avenue, he sent Isaac to inquire discreetly at the hotels and all places still open. Surely, if some misfortune had befallen Diana, there would be at least one pair of eyes that had seen.

Soon he was racing on his horse to his cousin's plantation near Lake Pontchartrain. But Frederick, who with Nathaniel had left the Charity Ball soon after Luke, had no news of Diana.

"As I told you when I returned to the ball, Diana seemed weary. She mentioned nothing about going anywhere," Frederick said as the grim-faced Luke turned to leave the guest bedroom at Ashwood. "If there really are some women who can bring men to their knees, Diana Hathaway is one. I've never before met a young woman with her candor and charm." He noted that Luke had paused to listen. "Diana told me about her life in the swamp when she didn't have to. She also told me she had overheard a conversation between Salathiel and you before the ball that revealed our wager and the role for which she was groomed. Where is the horse you would have me give you? You've won."

"Winning no longer means anything to me. I ought to smash your face for ever having brought up such a crazy bet." Luke's hand raked across his face as if washing away something distasteful. God, for Diana to have learned of his deception in such a cruel way! How agonizing the evening must have been for her. His heart turned over. His beautiful, brave Diana. Could she ever forgive him? "On the other hand, you or somebody should smash mine for taking part in the bet and then treating Diana like a toy. I had no right to use her as I did. I was a complete ass!"

"I couldn't agree more. Unless I've been reading the signs wrong all evening, you're madly in love with the woman." Frederick glanced out the window at the skies lightening in the East. "Diana is in love with you, too."

"Did she say so?" Luke felt his heart lift. Once he had believed that nothing had to be done all at once. No longer. All he could think of was finding her right away, holding her, begging her to forgive him, marry him.

"No, but I could tell. I never thought I'd be saying anything like this, but I guess if I can't have Diana—and she assured me I could not—then you deserve to win her."

Luke studied his brother's face. The slight change that he had suspected since meeting him at the dock that day seemed more noticeable. Was that truly compassion in Frederick's eyes? Warily he replied, "Thanks."

After leaving Ashwood, Luke rode to the Frontage home to query Odille. The quadroon, her face impassive as always, assured him that she had slept in the room with the children of the house. The black housekeeper standing nearby nodded her agreement. Odille's troubled eyes and voiced concern for Diana's welfare convinced Luke that she was telling the truth.

Luke stopped next at Lallage's townhouse, where Salathiel and his beloved were finishing up a festive breakfast. Sorrow and self-loathing tinged Luke's report that Diana had overheard Salathiel's and his conversation. Admittedly shocked at Luke's news, his untoward appearance, and Diana's letter to Salathiel, the couple had no answers either.

"Have you checked to see if she's with Doreen?" Salathiel asked after perusing the letter again.

"Francy did," Luke responded. "Doreen knew nothing."

Lallage spoke up, a tiny frown marring her forehead. "I feel terrible that I became so involved with my own life"— she sent a doting look at Salathiel, another at her daughters out in the courtyard—"that I haven't seen Diana alone much lately. Poor darling, she must feel desolate after learning. . . ."

"I apologized to Salathiel and you last night for getting you involved in my shabby business," Luke said. "If only I had done the same to Diana. Until Frederick told me, I had no idea she had heard me talking with Salathiel. I've been a fool."

Her expression pensive, Lallage went on. "Maybe she sailed for Jamaica or Boston, now that she has learned she probably has family in both places. During dinner here that evening after she went to the bank, she told us she's eager to meet all of her kin."

"What's this about relatives and a bank?" Luke asked. How was it that he thought he had known Diana well? "I hadn't even thought about checking the ships and riverboats."

After filling the agitated Luke in on all that Diana had discovered in her father's deposit box, Salathiel added, "She could very well be on her way to family this minute."

"That's the only answer," Luke replied in a ragged voice, "unless something dreadful has happened to her." He rubbed his chin and wished such a simple action could soothe his heavy heart. Luke had tended his fragile vanity by escaping

Diana's company whenever it pleased him and pretending until recently that she held no important place in his life. He had been blind to her needs. Blind, and an idiot caught up in a senseless wager. He could have told her a million times that he loved her. The "if only's" scorched his soul.

Luke felt ill. There was no need to ask why Diana had told him nothing about the deposit box and her discoveries. "I kept hoping I'd learn she was with somebody we know and I could talk with her. I've not been to the police yet or heard from Isaac, but I'll tell the authorities she's missing before I go check the passenger lists of any vessels headed for Jamaica or Boston."

"It's as if Diana Hathaway never existed in this whole damned town!" Luke raged to Salathiel, Frederick, and Nathaniel Dace late that afternoon in his library. "She must have paid off every dock hand as well as the captain of the ship she's bound to be on. Why didn't I go to the docks first?"

While the others exchanged concerned looks, Luke stalked to the window and rammed his hands in the pockets of his soiled white evening trousers. "A ship left at dawn for Jamaica. No other is slated to go there until after Christmas. Nor is one available for hire. No matter what rewards I offered, I could learn nothing. Two ships sailed for Boston earlier this week but no others will be going until after the holidays. Damn!"

"Salathiel must be right in his supposition that Diana is on her way to her grandfather's in Kingston," Frederick said. By then Salathiel had shared all known information with Frederick and Nathaniel. "The police are certain they have no altercations reported last evening involving a blonde woman. Anyone ever seeing Diana Hathaway could not forget her."

Nathaniel spoke up. "Frederick is right. When we checked with the night watchmen who were on duty at the wharves last evening, they said they saw nobody who fit her description."

Salathiel harrumphed and worried his mustache with his

forefinger. "Luke, I suggest we accept that Diana has chosen to visit her mother's people in Kingston. By the time you can book passage there, she likely will have sorted out this unpleasant business in her mind. She might be willing to listen to your side of it after she gains some time alone. I believe she cares deeply for you, but now she is in pain."

Luke winced. "I see no other choice but to wait." He fingered his chin and realized upon finding stubble there that he had not slept or shaved since the preceding evening. "I'll return to Fairfield right away and get everything in order so that I can leave on the first ship for Kingston after Christmas. If Diana isn't there, I'll go to Boston and search. The blacks here say they'll keep their ears close to the slave grapevine. I told Odille she could spend the holidays with the Frontages."

Frederick and Nathaniel accepted Luke's halfhearted invitation and stayed for dinner with Salathiel and him. Afterward they announced that they would be returning to Mobile within a few days. Their party moods had sagged noticeably.

"Lallage and I will expect both of you to come to our wedding the Sunday before Easter," Salathiel reminded the two men before they departed. "We in St. Christopher Parish can claim spectacular scenery and friendly people."

Salathiel heard the way he was including himself as a citizen of the remote parish and smiled at his previous blindness to its attractions. How his love for the vivacious Lallage had expanded his view of life! His heartbeat sped up from the fleeting thought of her. How could he have imagined himself old at forty-five? "You might wish to stay for a long visit at Wingate and help keep the girls company while my bride and I honeymoon here in New Orleans. You could get in some hunting and fishing."

"Also," Luke said, lacking enthusiasm for anything not having to do with locating Diana, "you could spend some time at Fairfield even if I'm not back from my search."

"Count on me," Frederick said. "The weeks can stretch mighty long now that both Maurine and Salathiel are gone." His troubled gaze centered on his brother's haggard face.

"And me," Nathaniel added. He glanced fondly at Frederick. "Since I agreed back in the summer to spend time with Frederick and keep him honest, I can't afford to have him meet more pretty women than I do. He might need my advice, or I might need his. Besides, I'm planning on getting to know the charming Miss Doreen Oates much better."

Luke studied the faces of his brother and their childhood friend while the men joked back and forth about their single states. Had the fact that they had been spending a great deal of time together contributed to Frederick's more amicable manner? It seemed incongruous that anything remotely good could have resulted from the wager between Frederick and him, but perhaps it had . . . for someone other than Diana and him.

Fairfield's restored beauty did not comfort Luke and Salathiel when they returned from their stay in New Orleans. King bounded out to meet them with his usual aplomb; Luke felt a twinge of guilt that he was unable to explain to the big dog what had become of its mistress.

With apology and sadness thickening his voice, Luke asked the solemn-faced Tabitha, Chloe, and Salem to share his bad news with the other slaves, then told how Diana had disappeared in New Orleans and likely gone to visit her kin in Jamaica. The only good news were Jed's reports as overseer, combined with his glowing comments about his life as a married man.

The December days dragged by. Luke made his usual rounds on Jasper, frequently in the company of the enthusiastic Jed Latour, but his former zest for the activities of the plantation had diminished. Not even thoughts of the considerable progress he had made in New Orleans to get his fledgling shipping line on Selene Bayou in operation by summer cheered him. Small wonder. With Diana in mind, he had ordered his first steamboat bear the name *Bayou Goddess*.

Neither Luke nor Salathiel spoke of the emptiness tha Diana's absence created, but both harbored memories of he voice, her laughter, and her indomitable spirit. When Doreen and her mother drove over from Fernwood one afternoon and learned that Diana's whereabouts were still uncertain, Doreen failed to hide the tears forming.

Salathiel's propensity for Lallage's company, plus his agreement to serve as tutor for the Winston children until a new one arrived, led the smitten Englishman to spend almost every afternoon and evening at Wingate. Luke waved away Salathiel's frequent apologies for leaving him alone, even invited Lallage and her four daughters to dine at Fairfield a time or two. The occasions were not the same without Diana, though, and Luke gave up seeking the company of the engaged couple as a way of brightening his dark mood. Salathiel's droll declaration that his beloved's little dog, Pooch, no longer growled at him brought no more than a half smile to Luke's unhappy face.

Christmas was only two days away when Salathiel cornered Luke about the holiday. "Lallage and the girls insist that you join us at Wingate. Some of her family from Baton Rouge will be there and the occasion will be quite festive. I am on my way there now so as to tutor the girls before time for dinner. May I tell Lallage that you will come on Christmas?"

Luke gazed out the windows of the library toward Selene Bayou where he had caught Diana that night in the moonlight. A full moon had risen the preceding evening and Luke's midnight wanderings around the house in search of peace had led him repeatedly to that same view.

The thought had come to Luke then, as now, that Diana had done far more than become his temporary prisoner that fateful evening. She had become the mistress of his heart. He marked how the trees in front of the mansion had no leaves now and the once vibrant flowers, grass, and weeds bore a dirty brown look. What beauty once had reigned lived only in memory. The implied promise of spring did not register in his troubled mind.

"Yes," Luke replied. "Thank Lallage for me and please tell her that I promise I'll not be a gloomy bugger." He turned to face his old friend, summoning a cheerful mien. "Next week it'll be time for me to go to New Orleans and take the ship to Jamaica. I'm feeling more optimistic each day."

After dining alone that unseasonably warm December evening, Luke wandered coatless to the backyard. He heard the familiar sounds coming from the kitchen as Tabitha and Chloe cleaned and set it to rights—the rich drawls of the women as they talked in the patois the blacks preferred when they talked among themselves, the scrape of a wooden chair against the uneven brick floor, the tintinnabulation of something light and metallic falling to a hard surface and bouncing, the good-natured laughter when somebody retrieved it.

Luke cocked his head to hear better a nearby tree frog screeching its plaintive call for rain. Then from somewhere far away a dog howled, wolflike. The lonesome, mournful notes seemed to be calling to that mysterious, universal sadness harbored down deep in the breastbone of souls familiar with suffering. Like his.

Cursing himself for inflicting more self-punishment, Luke watched the full moon rising over Gator Swamp and thought about Diana. Always Diana. Was she somewhere watching it, too? King came trotting from the shadows, whining and wagging his tail as he rubbed against Luke's legs.

Luke recalled that it was while he was wandering in a half-awakened state on the night before Midsummer's Eve when he had first seen Diana and the big dog cavorting in the moonlight and had imagined he might be watching the mythological goddess of the moon and a frisky deer. He closed his eyes and saw again the beauty of her silvery hair floating behind her as she skipped around on bare feet in her scanty skirt and top. Diana, a permanent part of him now.

"Where would you have me go?" Luke asked King playfully when the dun-colored dog raced ahead, then turned back as if to check the long-legged man's progress. He realized that King was following the barely discernible path leading to the Hathaway cabin in Gator Swamp, the one the dog had led him down that day Diana had not shown up at Lallage's party and he was frantically searching for her. Memories waiting there might finish him off. He had purposely stayed away. "Come back, King. I've no wish to go to the swamp."

When King paid no heed and kept bounding ahead, Luke shrugged. Why not humor the big dog? The evening was warm. The light from the rising moon was turning drab wintry landscape into silvery works of art, touched here and there with intriguing shadows.

While ambling behind King, Luke wondered at his gall in having snatched Diana up and turned her into a "lady." *Lady?* he hooted with self-derision. Diana was a lady long before he ever inveigled Salathiel into tutoring her.

A self-mocking smile creased Luke's face as he recalled how cleverly Diana had hoodwinked both Salathiel and him into believing she was illiterate, with the manners of a backwoods hoyden. As painful and vexing as the clashes with the feisty Diana had been, Luke found himself wishing he could hurt that way once more. He had felt only half alive since Diana had vanished.

"No, King," Luke told the dog when he realized that while lost in reverie, he had followed him to the porch of the dilapidated Hathaway house. From where they cascaded over the low limbs of the surrounding trees, long fronds of airy moss swayed in a gentle breeze, turning from dark gray to ghostly silver where the moonlight bathed them. "I can't bear to go farther. It's my fault Diana left us. I love her more than life itself, but I can stand only so much punishment. I won't rest easy until I find her and make her my wife. Diana belongs at Fairfield with me, you know."

King, his ears lifted eagerly, looked up at his companion and whined as if in agreement. A click from inside the shadowed house transcended the chorus from night callers. Disbelieving his eyes and ears, Luke heard the door creak open and watched a moonbeam bounce off a gun barrel poking through.

"Leave before my gun goes off," came the voice Luke had feared he might never hear again. "This is *my* house!"

His mind reeling and his pulse thudding, he ignored the threats and stepped forward. King dashed to his mistress, looking first at her, then back at Luke. "Diana!" His voice sounded hoarse. "Thank God I've found you and you're safe!"

"Go away, you arrogant, blundering, lying—"

"Didn't you hear what I just told King?" Luke broke in

to say. Did she intend to shoot him? He recognized that he probably deserved punishment, but he could think of nothing as vital as holding her in his arms or telling her of his love and his wish to marry her. His heart kept shouting, *Diana is here!* even as an inner voice warned, *But she's as mad as the devil!*

"I heard." *Luke came looking for you, just as you hoped!*

"Then why are you threatening me with a gun?"

"Maybe I want to hear you say the words to me, not to my dog, you numbskull. How thickheaded can you be?"

Like a poisoned dart Diana's words pierced Luke's heart and reminded him that he had called her unflattering terms during their first stormy weeks. "Diana," Luke said as he dropped to one knee, his pulse pounding, but not from fear of being shot, "I love you and want to marry you right away."

"If I say yes, will I have to leave swamp country?"

"Only when it pleases you to—like, maybe, when we honeymoon in Jamaica and Boston."

First Luke heard the solid clank of metal on wood as she lay down her gun. Then came the squeak of the door and the whispering sounds of her bare feet on the planks. His breath got trapped back in his throat at the sight of her standing before him in the moonlight, her silvery hair framing her face and her legs spread slightly apart. The young woman studying him was the real Diana, Luke reflected, the Diana with whom he must have fallen in love soon after he first saw her. He secreted away a vision of her appearance right now, for he sensed that he never wanted to forget it.

With awe for her grace and imposing presence, Luke realized that Diana wore the same scanty costume of homespun that she had worn when he first saw her streaking around in the moonlight. Her scanty skirt revealed shapely thighs and long slender legs, thighs and legs that he once had adored with his hands and lips. Her brief top exposed a wealth of pale, satiny skin above her waist and below her breasts. His tongue wet his lips at the memory of how her naked, pliant silkiness had felt underneath his fingertips. Underneath his pulsating body.

Then Luke jerked his attention back to Diana's beautif

face and her marvelously sensuous mouth. When his gaze feasted on her hair cascading unfettered around her face and shoulders, a shimmering curtain of silvery white, he could no longer stay away. It was as if Diana were the moon and he an ocean, Luke reflected as he walked closer, amazed at the direction of his thoughts. A bit like an ocean, he was a powerful entity in his own right, yet he was subject to the mystical pull of the celestial being. Diana.

"Have you worked some kind of spell on me?" he asked, smiling into her lucent eyes and bringing her hand to his lips. Touching her once more should have served as an anodyne, but it did the opposite and set his pulse ablaze, weakened his knees. He was unaware that King flopped down on the porch nearby, yawned noisily, and rested his head on his front paws.

Diana shivered from the touch of Luke's warm kiss on the back of her hand. The huskiness of his deep voice slid into secret chambers and fed her soul. After glancing out into the moon-kissed swamp as if seeking answers, she looked up at him and smiled the smile of a young woman certain of her charm. "What if I have worked a spell on you?"

"Then I want it to go on forever." His arms went around her then, gathering her loveliness to him with reverence. "Will you marry me? Can you learn to love me as I love you?"

She waited until his anxious face hovered within kissing distance before she said in a voice both sultry and laden with promise, "Yes, I will marry you. I love you more with every breath—though at times you're something of a tyrant."

Luke winced, even as he hugged her closer and felt his heart rejoicing at her answer. "Forgive me, please. Let me tell you how it all happened and how sorry I am for treating you as I have. I was a fool, a lunatic."

So close that her hair grazed his face, that her breath mated with his, Diana nodded. "And a numbskull."

"That, too." Only whispers now; they called up goose flesh on her spine. "And a blind idiot."

"The worst I ever heard about." Her widely spaced eyes sparkled with provocative messages unrelated to her words.

"Never again will I forget you're nobody's pawn, least of

all, mine.'' How was it that a beam of moonlight was high-lighting her hair and eyes and bedazzling him anew?

Curling her arms around his neck and pulling his head down to hers, Diana smiled up at her man. Love (how glorious to learn it was returned!), thanksgiving (she was with him again!), and longing (she could almost feel his lips on hers) became entangled, stole her breath for a moon-drenched moment, and made her bold. "Can you wait to tell me all that after you've kissed me?"

Luke groaned back in his throat as his mouth touched hers, the sensual notes nourishing Diana's hungry heart like raindrops restoring life to a parched garden. How was it that the honey of her lips tasted even finer than he recalled?

He kissed his Diana with tenderness, then with awe. He kissed her with reverence, his lips slanting across hers first one way and then the other. Would he ever get enough of her sweetness? A brush fire could not have burned more quickly or more out of control than his senses did when he felt his beloved standing on her tiptoes and pressing her slender body against him, returning each tantalizing kiss with equal ardor.

Maybe Luke's title of moon goddess fit Diana at times, but vibrant, loving woman was what she became as she opened her hungry mouth to his searching tongue and let her own meet each impassioned thrust with mounting fervor. She pressed her suddenly tender breasts closer to his manly chest, elated that her heartbeat raced in rhythm with his.

The touch of his hands on her back, then on the bare patches of skin between her brief top and skirt scattered the last of Diana's previous thoughts of telling Luke off if she ever saw him again. When his hand slipped under her top and found the soft fullness of her breast, all thoughts of telling Luke anything negative sailed off into the swamp. Her blood was singing. Her womanhood was throbbing with that remembered warm, moist wanting. Ah, yes, Luke Greenwood was her man. And at last he was treating her right.

"How in the deuce did you get here without anyone knowing it?" Luke asked a good while later when their initial hunger seemed momentarily appeased. When he realized that his legs felt as wobbly as his heartbeat, he led her to the swing on the porch, loving the way she moved in rhythm with him and, after sitting within the circle of his arms, leaned away only enough to gaze into his face. Before she could reply he noticed again how beautiful she looked in the moonlight and murmured, "You'll always be my moon goddess."

"Um-m, I like that." She licked her lips, savoring the taste of his words, his recent kisses. "Will Silver Hoodoo Woman serve as a title, too?" Her musical laughter bubbled out, feminine, bewitching.

Luke tilted his head so as to have a better view of her lovely face. "What are you talking about? If I'm a victim of a Diana brand of hoodoo, I surrender. Willingly."

She laughed again and sent her forefinger to trace the bridge of his noble nose. "You asked how I returned here without anyone knowing. The blacks managed it, the same way they kept secret my family's presence here in the swamp."

"And that was no small feat."

"When I returned, I begged Tabitha for the truth. I had heard the term *Silver Hoodoo Woman* used a few times but never could learn what it meant. Tabitha told me that because my mother learned to heal with herbs and potions while growing up in Jamaica, many of the blacks there believed that she possessed a white magic and referred to her as the Silver Hoodoo Woman. They let the myth die when she came with my father to Louisiana, where practicing any kind of hoodoo, or voodoo, is outlawed. Tabitha said that the slaves still adored her and felt protective of her and her family. Perhaps because I also have what the blacks call silver hair and try to help heal their illnesses, they pay me similar homage."

Luke continued to hold Diana within his arms on the swing and give her looks of amazement as she explained more about Drusila and Philip Hathaway. In between searing kisses and murmured endearments, she garnered a special delight when Luke confessed he had never suspected she slipped away in the night on her missions.

His features revealing his surprise at Diana's revelations, Luke summed it all up. "That night after the Charity Ball you and Odille slipped over to the Frontage home. She handed you over to the slaves there and went upstairs to sleep with the children.'' Diana nodded throughout. ''Because the blacks revere you for tending the sick, they sheltered you until they could sneak you back to St. Christopher Parish.''

''I didn't like having to use deception but I had to return here to my roots and sort out my feelings. I was hoping you might find you cared for me and would look for me here.''

''King deserves the credit,'' Luke admitted. Both angled fond looks at the sleeping dog. ''I nearly went mad when none of us could find a trace of you. Odille and the Frontages's housekeeper took pains not to lie out-and-out, but they didn't tell the whole truth.'' Luke shook his head in a quandary. ''No doubt by the time I returned, Tabitha and Salem and all the others knew you were safe here in your little house.''

''You're not angry with any of them, I hope.'' She planted a kiss on his cheek, then sent him a pleading look.

''No. I'm too happy to have you in my arms to be angry at anyone. Now I understand much more about the woman I love.'' He looked her over wonderingly, then with the knuckles of his fist he gently tipped up her chin. ''How did I manage to overlook the fact that you're beautiful on the inside, too?''

Diana drank in Luke's deep-voiced question. Before closing the small space between their lips and kissing him, she wondered if she might not have fallen in love with him all over again. She sensed that the two of them fit into the natural pulse of the swamp surrounding them, that their coming together was what nature had intended. The secretive whisperings of night birds and small creatures as they answered their primeval yearnings in the night meshed with those churning her love for her man into rising ripples of desire. ''Make love to me, Luke.''

''We'll be married by this time next week, won't we?''

''Yes, but I can't wait so long to get lost in your arms.'' She stood, smiling when he rose with her and swung her up into his arms as he had done that first time.

After they reached Diana's moonlit bedroom and shed their clothing, Luke gazed at the one who would forever be to him a moon goddess of delightful flesh and blood. The sight of her pale slenderness created a maelstrom of emotion. "Diana, I love you! I promise to make you happy."

He held out his hand, humbled when she walked to him and took it trustingly. Her eyes, silvery blue and appearing almost translucent in the moonlight angling through the window, radiated wondrous messages he was eager to decipher. Desire streaked throughout his being like lightning. The storm brewing earlier in his groin took on a fierce fury when he gathered Diana's nakedness close to his and kissed her soft, parted lips.

Waves of glorious feeling washed over the reunited lovers as they sank upon the bed amidst a delicious tangle of seeking arms and legs and clinging lips. Whispering "I love you," and hearing Diana's faint echo with more than his ears, Luke stretched out full length on the smooth sheet and fitted her body to his. Fueling the mounting rapture of the moon-drenched lovers were the close-up, sensuous sounds and movements of full breasts spilling against muscled chest, soft belly meeting hard belly, curved hips matching up with lean hips, triangular patches of hair seeking to curl into one as legs entwined. Woman was blending with man.

Diana sighed and arched with undisguised ecstasy when Luke leaned away enough to move his lips, heated inch by heated inch, down her neck to her breasts. Flinging back her long hair to lie like a pale shawl of silk on the bed, she cried out in wonder when he laved a nipple with his tongue and sucked the hard tip into his mouth. While he continued working his magic on her breasts, her fingertips tingled as they caressed his cheeks, his ears, his neck, then his powerfully muscled back.

"I love everything about you, Luke." It came to Diana's passion-drugged mind that if she could soak his dear essence into hers through her fingertips and hold it within forever, she would. She closed her eyes and savored the taste, the smell, and the feel of his skin, wondering if her mind might not be floating like the moonbeams joining them there on the sheets warmed and perfumed by their yearning bodies.

"I feel the same love for you," Luke murmured huskily.

Titillated to new heights by the tender, bold caresses from Diana, Luke sought with his mouth and hands to transport her to a similar state of ecstasy. He loved the way she sighed and tightened her hold in his hair when he made a warm, moist track down her smooth belly with his mouth. Fingers of licking flame plumped his already swollen shaft when she opened her silken thighs for a new pleasure, feeding their tempest of raw frenzy. Then the moment came when their breaths and caresses turned into a kind of painful mockery. He found he could no longer refrain from accepting the invitation from the velvety, pulsating gate to her womanhood.

Glorying in her love for the man turning her into a warm, wet vessel of desire, Diana welcomed Luke as he gave her his firm, hot length. She curled her legs around his hips, pulling him closer, savoring the storm of throbbing sensations deep inside. She felt as if she were wrapped in splendor, but changed her mind when he moved within her and caused her to cry out. Then she wondered if she had surrounded *him* with splendor.

When the lovers began moving in the age-old rhythm, Diana decided, with what little rationale she could muster, that the two of them were creating the mysterious splendor claiming them, that the splendor had no existence until they joined and called it into being. The half-formed thought awed her. She felt all powerful, in touch with something magical. She felt a bit like a goddess.

Gigantic waves of passion lifted the straining lovers and flung them as one into that star-filled space of perfect union. Their voices joined in loving celebration. They gasped for breath, clutched each other blindly.

After Luke sank down beside Diana, she hugged him close then opened her eyes and listened to their breathing returning to normal. The moonbeams had stolen out the window, were no more now than shadowed reflections from the moon climbing higher overhead. There *were* sounds and movements beyond the small bedroom, she mused languidly, though they were the familiar late-night ones of the freshwater swam and its creatures. Her lips curved into a tremulous smile of satiation and of joy at being a woman wrapped in her man's loving arms. She knew with certainty now where she belonged. It had nothing to do with walls or a roof or a geographic location.

"I'm going to love you forever, Diana, and I'll never again deceive you." Luke lifted his head to gaze at her lovely face. His thumb settled underneath her chin; his fingers, on her finely sculpted cheek that pulsed with life and promise in a way that the cheek of a mythical goddess never could.

Reaching to brush back a straying lock of his black hair from his forehead, Diana sent Luke a worshipful smile. Not once since he had arrived earlier had his eyes borne that cold, harboring expression, or his face, that brooding mien. Whatever had haunted him previously seemed laid to rest and she sent up a private prayer of thanksgiving. "I'll always love you, too, Luke Greenwood. Will you truly be honest with me from now on?"

"Always." When she slid him a pensive look from behind half-closed eyelashes, he pulled her to rest face down atop him, smiling at the surprise in her eyes when she felt the warm bulge of his growing arousal. "Is there a problem?"

"Well," she said, savoring the provocative way his puissant body felt underneath her and sensing that they soon would be creating their private splendor again, "there's something I've been dying to know."

"Ask it." Luke loved it when her eyes appeared silvery and mysterious as they did then. He ran his hands lovingly through her hair, down her back, and over her satiny buttocks, not surprised that the caresses stoked the blaze in his groin. He sent her a devilish grin. "I feel I'm a man who knows the answers to everything tonight."

Diana shivered from the delicious sensations bestirring within her again and almost forgot her question. "Was there really a wildcat jumping from a tree that afternoon we were racing our horses?"

The bursts of laughter coming from inside the small house resting on stilts startled King awake from where he slept outside on the porch. He popped open one eye, half lifted an ear. Then, when the laughter faded and no further sounds reached his ears, the big dog thumped his tail, sniffed once, and again lowered his head. Harmony reigned once more in the moonlit world of Gator Swamp in St. Christopher Parish.